UNDERGROWTH

GIBSON HOUSE PRESS
Flossmoor, Illinois 60422
GibsonHousePress.com

ISBNs: 978-0-9861541-6-4 (paperback); 978-0-9861541-7-1 (Mobipocket);
978-0-9861541-8-8 (epub); 978-0-9861541-9-5 (PDF)

LCCN: 2017940163

Cover design by Christian Fuenfhausen. Text design and
composition by Karen Sheets de Gracia in the Malaga typeface.

Printed in the United States of America
21 20 19 18 17   1 2 3 4 5

∞ This paper meets the requirements of ANSI/NISO Z39.48-1992
(Permanence of Paper)

UNDERGROWTH

A NOVEL

NANCY BURKE

GIBSON
HOUSE
PRESS

CHICAGO

For Steve

PART

ONE

I

THERE WAS A stand of short, craggy trees with leaves like cupped hands that filled with water in the rain and held it, forming pools that were already teeming with life by the time the rain subsided. All the rest of the afternoon, as if the trees had burst forth into blossom, a thousand civilizations, each different from the rest, grew in those small ponds, depending upon which insect had landed where, or which spore had fallen. They flourished until the sun dried them up, and left their residues in the leaves' thick palms, to be dissolved by rain the next day.

In the forest, there are plants that grow with such speed and force that they might be mistaken for animals, and others that grow so slowly they might as well be stones. Each has a heart with an audible beat—a single strand in an infinite density of sound—as well as its own form of silence. The pulse of their vibrations pushes up through the human stem, moving us toward and away from what we love.

To say that Larry was unsure as he boarded the plane for Rio would have been inaccurate. Rather, he was compelled to follow a certain course, and yet had sufficient self-awareness to understand that although compulsion seems, on the surface, the embodiment of purpose, it is also always blind. He was being thrown, or carried, or held, and thus was freed from the necessity of looking forward, as a child in its mother's arms can allow its eyes to wander. His uncle, James, who was already engrossed in a magazine, sat to his right, and beyond him sat a row of strangers with their heads bowed, each of whom struck him as distasteful. Their stillness seemed to him to convey passivity and compliance, in stark contrast to the stillness of their reflections in the window, which seemed almost holy as they spread out, translucent, over the dark carpet of the earth. His freshman roommate had jokingly called him a misanthrope, which had upset him; far from being incapable of human love, he was so deeply sensitive to it that he could be swept away by a scent, or a reflection in a window, and true human contact could easily overwhelm him. James, however, had no such sensitivities, and threw himself into the thick of one scene after another. The nephew and uncle complemented each other; they understood each other with a sort of sharp intuition, and would have looked forward to planning many future adventures together, except that the uncle was dying.

"Do what you have to do," said James, looking up from his magazine with resigned amusement as Larry started to unbuckle his knapsack. "When you're ready, I have something to show you."

"In a minute," said Larry. He began to arrange his possessions on the floor by his shoes, on his tray table, and between his leg and the arm of his seat. He lined up his books, then pulled them into his lap and started again. When you are headed south, as they were, you cannot afford the illusion of a magical relationship to time that travelers to Europe have, in which the duration of night seems miraculously tied to the length of the trip. Rather, time is resolute, particularly when you know that the first flight will be the prelude to a series of longer and longer ones that cover progressively less ground. Larry remembered this, even though he had last made the trip to Pahquel eight years ago, when he was just eleven. He remembered endless plane rides, endless waits for planes, waits in hot, shabby offices for tickets, or visas, or permits, or directions; rides on buses, sandwiched between people and packs and goats, interminable rides in carts, on leaky boats in the pouring rain; rides in cars that broke down more often than they ran. That he had a clear sense of interminability made it all the more urgent that he arrange the space around him with deliberate economy. When he was a boy, he would fantasize about how he might set up his belongings in a smaller and smaller space, in a space the size of his bedroom, or a bathroom, or a shower stall. He would build a shelf at the very top of the stall for his guitar, which would just fit diagonally, a shelf for his clothes, a shelf for food, and two shelves for books. Were he ever to end up in a concentration camp, he knew exactly how he would arrange his things along the side of his tiny corner of sleeping space, or underneath the planks in the floor. Fluency in the language of space, invincibility in regard to it, allowed him respite from whatever impending sense of helplessness he felt in the face of time.

"Just let me know when you're ready," said James again, more eager for his attention now, but also still amused. James tended to fill the space available to him with his own body, which seemed to inflate until it pushed against the confines of whatever held him. Larry had always thought, growing up, that his uncle's capacity to fill a void was simply the result of his bulky, haphazardly proportioned, six-foot-three-inch frame, but now here he was, so much diminished and yet still so physically voluble, hanging over the armrest that divided their two countries, unaware of the borders he was crossing. In fact, James possessed little that wasn't a part of his own body; his shaving kit, his bedroll, his few articles of clothing, all had become melded to him after years of use. They even came to smell like him, so that as Larry began to turn the pages of the handwritten notebook James laid out in front of him, he had the sense of being saturated by it as he read.

"There it is!" James said in Pahqua, nodding towards the book.

"There it is!" Larry repeated.

"When you have that in your hands, it's like you're holding the one bird," said James, using a Pahqua figure of speech. On the first page, over pencil lines drawn with a clearly dented ruler, he had written: "Pahqua: A Dictionary of Grammar and Definitions by James Lawrence Ardmore." James searched Larry's face for a sign of awe and found it, though an onlooker would have only seen the nephew wince.

"Amazing to see it all together, isn't it? An entire civilization! An entire life's work!"

"Amazing," said Larry in English.

Larry couldn't tell his uncle that it wasn't the notebook but the sound of the words that had amazed him. When had Pahqua ceased to have a sound? Before their first trip, and during the year after it, before Larry had started junior high, and before James had left, they spoke all the time. They would sit at the dinner table at Larry's house and ask each other to pass the meat in Pahqua; they would reminisce in Pahqua. His parents never showed the slightest curiosity, or even irritation, at their exclusion. They spoke a few words to each other while Larry and James were talking, and it seemed to Larry in retrospect that their conversation was equally impenetrable and foreign.

Then James disappeared—to Alaska, as far from the Amazon as he could get—and there was no one left to talk to, and the memory of Pahqua eroded until the language itself seemed to have less and less to do with sound and more to do with a sensation, in his stomach or his head, a pure intention which he knew before he spoke it. That he would never again, he could only assume, meet another living soul who even knew of Pahqua, let alone could understand it, rendered it even more intimately suited to him. Because he was as desperate for solitude as for communion, it was enough that it made possible an internal dialogue, a sort of instantaneous translation or reinterpretation of his thoughts, and thus a sense of confirmation, simultaneously from deep inside himself and from a great distance away. To hear James's voice confused all that, and yet also stirred in him something else, an onrush of gratitude or relief, over what he couldn't say.

The notebook was divided into three sections separated by sheets of heavy red cardboard, and each section was filled with pages written in awkward capital letters on hand-ruled lines. There was something desperate, Larry knew, in the makeup of someone who would spend eight years, off and on, in a freezing cabin in Alaska, trapping squirrels to fend off starvation and painstakingly transcribing the contents of an entire duffel bag filled with scraps of paper—corners ripped from government documents and pages ripped from books, their margins filled to the edges with tiny lettering—into a cardboard binder. That it was the product of such a powerful irrational force commanded the sort of reverence one felt for nature, and that the force originated in James made the reverence personal.

"It's yours now," said James in Pahqua. "It's all I have."

Larry closed the notebook. He crossed his arms over it, holding it against his chest, and felt it pull him forward, as though it were a hook that held him, and the reel was hidden somewhere in Pahquel.

Up and down the aisles, lights were being switched off, like the lights in the houses on a street. By midnight, only Larry and James and a few scattered others were awake, their isolated beacons suggesting watchfulness or sleepless yearning. But Larry and James harbored reasons not to think about phantoms such as yearning, and avoided confusion by rationalizing their decision to fly together halfway around the world, at an expense neither could afford, James having pleaded to his sister that he needed Larry to help him finish documenting the language before he died, and Larry implying that he needed to gather data for his thesis. No one can afford not to give reasons, particularly at those times when they have the least bearing. But despite all reasons, it would have been hard for an outsider not to see the two of them as ridiculous, as dreamers, engaged in a desperate search for something they were each destined to find and lose again and again. By the time James reached up at last and turned off their overhead lights, all pretense to reason had long fallen away, and they each felt brush against their skin, for a moment before they slept, the rough weave of disappointment and fulfillment from which the cloak of fate is sewn.

II

IN PAHQUEL, THERE were certain gods who could take a joke and others who were so easily offended that their names couldn't even be spoken without some small or terrible consequence, and everyone knew which ones were which. Only James, who in three hands of appearances still confused Saptir and Saratir, called out the older god's name and yet still came and went, rain after rain, with the blessings of the living and the dead. In fact, by the way they traded insults—James sang his name into the wrong places in songs and Saptir sent a ripe Pura fruit down on him, so that his hair dripped green with the reeking pulp—they had to have been of common blood. At least that's what Asator said, and he had more reason than anyone to know.

III

LOOKING LIKE A modern-day Quichotte and Panza, wearing rumpled clothing and contrasting expressions, arrayed in a comically heroic pose (the taller one pointing out toward the street in front of them with an improbably long arm), James and his nephew stood at the curb of a busy intersection in Rio amid an island of packs and duffel bags.

"Why not just take a taxi?" Larry asked quietly, for the third time, in the same tone he had used before, to emphasize his conviction that he was doomed to ask the same question endlessly.

"Do you remember where Rua Caldwell crosses Valadones?" asked James, without turning to look at him. "I thought it was up this way," he said, scratching his head with his hand, and pointing now with his elbow.

"Why not just take a taxi?" asked Larry.

"Maybe we'll have to ask someone," said James, slowly lowering his arm as he turned around. "You're looking dismal," he said, suddenly noticing Larry.

"I'm tired," said Larry.

"All right. Let's hit the road," said James, reaching for his pack. "I'm sure I know where I'm going."

"Why not just take a taxi?" said Larry.

"Yes," said James, and hailed one.

The inside of the cab didn't so much offer protection from the noise and chaos of the streets as it provided an alternative chaos of its own. James leaned forward and embraced the empty seat in front of him, gesturing first with one hand and then the other, talking to the driver in a

Portuguese that, Larry had no doubt, made up for its inaccuracy by virtue of its volume and speed. Larry leaned back and looked at the vinyl ceiling, which was oozing tufts of once white padding through its cracks. Every so often, James turned and pointed out some landmark to Larry in English, and Larry commented on it weakly, without raising his head. James was full of emotion, overcome by relief that the city remembered him after all, as he concluded by virtue of the fact that he remembered it. "My youth! My youth!" he said mockingly to Larry over his shoulder.

Were it Larry's reunion rather than James's, he would have been horrified to see how much was changed, or missing, and to resent everything new as a blot on some part of his past. Even now, he felt overwhelmed by the number and intrusive power of the new smells that swirled inside the cab despite the windows being open so that anything that wasn't glued down seemed to be gesturing frantically, and scraps of paper were pulled loose from the rubber bands on the visors and sucked out the windows with a snap. In the thick whirlpool of body odors and the smells of metal fittings rubbing together, of hair grease, of old cigarettes, Larry searched for something comforting, and was disappointed. James, meanwhile, found in the sight of the cathedral, encroached upon on all sides by novelty and disintegration, only further proof of the solidity of things. To James, the more improbable the survival of the familiar, the more significant, and thus incontrovertible. It was for this reason that when they at last reached their destination, the home of one Silvio Amanza, longtime friend of James Ardmore, former *sertanista*, fellow agent of the Indian Protection Service and himself survivor of many life-threatening situations, James expected Silvio to register only delight in the discovery, after all this time, of their mutual capacity to endure.

"Why, it's half my dearest friend!" Silvio shouted in Portuguese, jumping up as they came in, staring hard at James.

"I'll trim an inch off your mustache!" bellowed James, embracing Silvio while Larry stood outside their circle holding a bag in each hand.

"Oh, my God! It's Larry!" Silvio shouted, breaking away. Larry felt his body grow rigid at the sound of the old name. "It's *Larry!*" Silvio moved forward to embrace him, but Larry held up his bags, blocking his access.

"Sorry! So sorry!" shouted Silvio, taking the bags and placing them at Larry's feet. He grasped Larry by the shoulders and planted a kiss on each cheek. "Look at you! A grown man! Are you thirsty? Are you hungry? What can I get you?" he blurted at Larry in heavily accented English. But before Larry could answer, Silvio had turned back to James, leaving him alone.

Larry lowered himself into a wooden lounge chair. A small rotating fan sat in one corner on a low wooden stool, and when its stream of air brushed over them, the leaves that reached out from the walls like hands moved as one in a wave. Had it been absent of people and chairs, the space might have been intimate, but only artificially so, for the lights that peered through the canopy of leaves were not stars, but from surrounding sky-scrapers, and the sounds that intruded, so that voices had to be raised, were urban sounds, tangled rather than layered.

"Where have you been? Where have you been?" Silvio was shouting at James despite standing within a foot of him and shaking him by the arms. "Until Claudio called to tell us you were coming, we thought you were dead!" He stopped suddenly, as though struck by the irony, but didn't back away.

"You know how I am—I go and I come. I come and I go," said James, striking a match, holding it so close to Silvio that it looked like he was lighting the end of Silvio's nose rather than his own cigarette.

"Okay, so out with it—what's your crazy plan?" said Silvio, leaning in and blowing out the match. "I think I know, but I want to hear it from the horse's mouth." From across the courtyard, Larry watched Silvio and James each pull against one end of their conversation as though it were a rope they were drawing taut between them, so that each assertion on the part of one was felt in the shoulder, in the spine, of the other.

"We get to Santarem on Sunday, and we'll call Jorge when we get there. By then, I'm sure you'll have been able to dig up one last assignment for me," said James. "I just want the chance to go on one last assignment. And I'm taking Larry with me on it, as I'm sure you've figured out by now."

"I've beat you to it there," said Silvio. "I spoke to Jorge yesterday. I have something all set up for you."

"Now, I still remember how to make my own calls," said James. "I can talk to Jorge myself. Don't you forget what a resourceful guy I am."

Larry followed their conversation with his body, leaning first toward the one and then the other. Only when James ran off suddenly to the bathroom with Silvio behind him did Larry lean back in his chair. He inhaled slowly, scanning the patio to be sure he was alone, but as he watched, the face of Silvio reemerged and loomed from the darkness beyond the doorway like a genie forming out of clouds in the sky. It floated forward, extending its over-muscled Popeye arms outward like an overblown parade balloon.

"So my man!" Silvio said, grasping Larry's shoulders. With a dramatic nod, he reached into his shirt pocket and drew out a piece of paper. He leaned forward and transferred the paper to Larry's front pocket, patting it closed.

"Call me if you need me," he whispered in English, with the approximate volume of another man's speech. "And keep this with you." He moved away, and then even closer. "And don't forget!" he said in full voice, gesturing with his head toward James, who was reentering the porch from the same black doorway. "We love each other, he and I, you know?"

Larry had no choice but to nod in agreement. He could feel the paper snag against the inside fabric of his shirt as he breathed. Whatever was on it, it was, at the least, an obscure but irrefutable reminder that the tense intimacy between James and Silvio somehow included him as well.

As James and Silvio resumed their shouted conversation, Larry sat forward again, fixing the entire scene in a heroic tableau—two men, each holding the other by the shoulders, suddenly silent as their eyes met. For a moment, in the night sky, the clouds parted to reveal the infinite darkness beyond the city lights. The leaves stilled, the street noise blurred and slowed, and the air became strangely heavy. Then, just as quickly, the sky snapped shut again and everything flew back into its place. The momentary silence was absorbed into the walls, and the music of distant radios, eager as the tide, rushed in to fill the space. The leaves reassembled themselves in their proper positions, and were graceful on the vines. Silvio and James, who seemed to have been frozen in mid-sentence, as though under a spell, suddenly came alive and began shouting again, alternately chastising and punching each other.

Larry jumped to his feet, standing awkwardly. At last, James noticed him and came up, drawing him into the house and up the stairs. As Larry looked back over his shoulder, he saw Silvio turn to follow them with a tense, barely suppressed smile.

IV

JORGE WAS SHAVING when the phone rang. That was the joke between them, that Silvio always knew from two thousand kilometers away to catch him when his face was covered with foam. He picked up the receiver in one hand and held it away from his face while he continued with the razor with the other.

"So guess who's been found?" Silvio's voice boomed through the space between the receiver and Jorge's ear.

Jorge dropped the razor, which nicked his cheek as it fell. He looked down at the two rivulets, of clear and bloody water, which merged as they approached the drain.

"You there?"

"I'm here," said Jorge, steadying his voice and reaching for a towel. "What's the story?"

"Do you think he'd tell me the story? Does James L. Ardmore ever tell me the story?" Jorge knew Silvio well enough to visualize his gestures, and Silvio knew Jorge well enough to know what his silences meant. "He's with Larry; you should see the kid! Tall, with the sideburns and everything."

"Should I fly down?"

"No, no, that's the thing; I'm going to put them on a plane tomorrow. I told him when I saw him that I'd already talked to you and worked it all out. I'm sending them commercial until they get to you."

"And then what?" asked Jorge, walking to the window as though to scan the sky for their arrival.

"And then it's up to you, to refuse to take them where they want to go!"

"Me? How's that my job?" Jorge turned from the window and walked back to the bathroom, laying the receiver down in the sink so the cord couldn't pull it away. He could hear Silvio swearing at him as he finished shaving and wiped his face on a towel. He could imagine him pacing, waving his free hand wildly, like a conductor at the climax of a symphony.

At last, he picked up the receiver again.

Silvio stopped swearing and was silent for a minute. "We both know he has no intention whatever of following through with any assignment I give him, and we both know where he's going to ask you to take him. So I'm saying, don't do it." A crackling sound competed with his voice, but Silvio simply turned up the volume. "I'm not saying don't do it for me because you love me," he shouted. "I'm saying don't do it for James because you love James. You'll see," Silvio went on, "he's much changed."

"*Ate. Ciao,*" said Jorge, and replaced the receiver on the cradle with a sigh, but gently, as though it were as fragile as he knew himself to be.

V

LARRY'S SURROUNDINGS WERE gradually becoming more manageable, as though drawn to an increasingly commensurate scale. Each plane, airport, and city had been smaller than the last, giving him the sense of looking at a map being magnified again and again, on which the small red dot marking "You are here" was slowly becoming visible. In the airport in Rio, everything had been in motion—people, planes, luggage, seemingly the walls themselves. On the plane, he and James were barely settled in their seats before James slid a manila folder out of the side pocket of his travel bag and began ripping its contents into pieces smaller than words.

"Bogus. It's bogus," he said, keeping to the task. When he finished, he took the airsickness bag out of his seat pocket and held it open. Larry thought for a minute that James meant it to be for him, but then saw that he was to pour the scraps into it. When the stewardess came by with the drinks, James tossed the bag on top of her cart.

"What was that all about?" asked Larry.

"That," said James, "was our alleged assignment from Silvio. He's trying to distract us, hoping we'll give up on Pahquel. But I called Maria in Rio yesterday, just to be sure. Like I thought, she said there's no reason at all to follow through on that old chestnut. It's something Silvio dug out of the back of a drawer just for us."

"Silvio's taking care of you," said Larry.

"We can take care of ourselves," said James.

Larry was always secretly relieved to hear how automatically James included him. Like most people who recede from conversations, he was unusually sensitive to signs of having been forgotten, and was more dependent than he knew, or could admit, upon reassurances that his place on the sidelines was secure. At the airport in Belem, while they waited for their plane to Santarem, he was content to retrieve their bags and watch over them for what turned out to be hours, his passivity thereby imbued with purpose, while James held court with various old friends he had called to meet him at the airport bar. The sun was setting by the time Larry looked up from his book to see James walking towards him with a dark-skinned older man.

"This is Joaquim, my friend for thirty-five years. Thirty-five years!" James said, shaking his head and putting his hand on the old man's shoulder. "You met him last time, but maybe you don't remember him. You know, my *chefe* in the Indian Protection Service, Rondon's right-hand. He made all the contacts. He was *Silvio's* boss! And most important for you, he's the one who gave you your compass."

Larry reached into his pocket and held out the compass, which he had treasured for reasons that had lost none of their power for his having forgotten them.

"A grown man!" said Joaquim, embracing him and then pulling on his sideburn, rubbing his cheek with the back of his hand, admiring the stubble.

"You may not owe it to Silvio to change your plans, but you do to me," Joaquim said to James over his shoulder with his hand still on Larry's face, "and to him. And, you need to talk to him." He nodded in Larry's direction.

"I owe you? Okay, okay! What'll it cost me?" asked James in a mocking voice, reaching for his wallet in a last, doomed attempt at humor.

Larry imagined for a minute that Joaquim was James's father, before he remembered that James's father would have been his grandfather, dead long before he was born, and of course, light-skinned.

"You know," said Joaquim.

"What do you want me to tell him?" asked James after a long silence, in a soft, compliant voice that was unfamiliar to Larry.

"About your dying," said Joachim.

"Not yet," said James, turning to Larry without looking at him. "There's still plenty of time."

"No, now," said Joaquim, placing a hand on Larry's shoulder to lower him into a seat and keep him there. He and James sat down on either side of him.

"How long do you expect to live?"

"Plenty of time. More than a month. Long enough."

"Are you in pain?"

"I take an extra one of these when I need one," said James, pointing towards his stomach and administering an imaginary injection. "I have enough to last three months at least."

"Does Larry know how to give a shot?"

James hesitated and then took a breath. "Do you?" he asked in his expressionless new voice.

Larry sat silently, with tears rolling down his cheeks, crying not from sadness, he told himself, since sadness was an emotion that could only be felt from a great distance, but rather from a fear he would explode.

"Show him," said Joaquim, and James obeyed, reaching into his bag and pulling out a small bottle of alcohol and another vial and a syringe with shaking hands while strangers stopped to watch. To see James taking orders was, to Larry, to bear witness to an event more painful than his death. His hatred of Joaquim sparked into flame, and the flame, at that instant, illuminated his memory of a story in which Joaquim, guided by the compass, had once saved James's life. All the more unjust for him to take it now.

"And how will I find you?" asked Joaquim when James had put away his bandages and needles.

"Now, you know better than to ask me that!" said James, in a voice more like his familiar one.

"But what will we do if Larry's stranded without you? How will we know how to reach him?"

James looked at Larry, into his face this time, and said quietly, "It's up to you."

The voice with which Larry answered was as unfamiliar as James's had been, louder and coarser than his old one. "We'll leave the coordinates sealed up somewhere. But not with Silvio. With Jorge. James told me about Jorge. He trusts him."

Joaquim shook his head and gave James a pat on the knee. "He's your man," he said, leaning his head towards Larry. "Now what do you need us to do for you? Anything you want us to take care of?"

"The rest of Larry's papers; his visas and permits and things," said James. "I can give you some money if you need it, since it's all going to be off assignment."

"For how long?"

James paused and looked again at Larry.

"A year," said Larry.

"Anything else?" said Joaquim, turning now to Larry. "Say what you have to say—don't leave any ghosts."

Larry looked up from his haunted, unspoken world and thought for a minute that he might, despite himself, pour something out. He might cling to James's ankle, or even express a sentiment like love. At the very least, he might have said that in this dense network of people whose lives had been saved by one another, he was certainly one. But he couldn't push aside the sense that words only ruined thoughts like those, rather than lend them dignity. As though to protect them all from witnessing such ruin, the words he did choke out sounded almost reproachful.

"I thought you said they'd be able to cure you in Pahquel," he finally said, as quietly as he could.

"Maybe they will," said James.

VI

IN PAHQUEL, IT was called *Xenge tunge,* grabbing the mosquito, the act of catching an insult in flight, holding it tightly by the stinger and watching it flail like a fish on a spear. When Anok overheard Sunap refer to her as *rajora,* as the end of a line, and called back, "Your line will end when you eat your children, old boar!" that was *Xenge tunge,* and when PaXaj called Asator "*Jitana tarara,*" one who shirks his duty to a child, and Asator retorted, "You always think I'm the reason you can't get in!" that was *Xenge tunge* too. But when Irini said to James, "*Pora Amat pi namama,*" that boy hunts fish in the garden, and James replied quietly, "*Namama ni,*" he hunts dreams, that was not *Xenge tunge,* but *Xenge hetera,* grasping in vain at the air.

VII

THERE WERE ENTIRE weeks when the telephone clinging to the wall in the kitchen like a lizard, its black tail dangling, was as sinister, in Jorge's view, as the lizards that scurried across the walls of every hangar he ever flew from. Jorge had always hated lizards, an odd preoccupation for someone who was nearly native-born and almost always in the field besides. Even now, he could summon up memories clear as photographs, of an anole on a Kapok, the flash of a gecko, a mottled skink, rustling the leaves as it fled, which he had observed as a child with his father on their forest walks. Most disturbing, and hence fascinating, had been the ability of those creatures—which in their strangeness blurred the boundary between what was inert and what was living—to disappear completely into their surroundings, an ability which, in humans, always proved tragic in the end.

But during the weeks when he was on assignment, Jorge couldn't afford not to answer the phone.

"I have news!" Joaquim began when Jorge picked up, preempting the formality of a greeting.

"I already know."

"Silvio told you?"

"Yep."

"And I suppose he told you not to take him."

"Yep," said Jorge.

"He's with Larry," Joaquim added tentatively, as though he were sounding Jorge out. Jorge pushed the hair from his forehead and began to pace from one end of his tether to the other. "I can see why you wouldn't want to," Joaquim went on, "even aside from the issue of using an IPS plane off orders."

"Yeah, and why not?" Jorge asked suspiciously. Joaquim had the ability to get under his skin in a way that, otherwise, only James could.

"I can't imagine you've forgiven him yet for disappearing on you," Joaquim said softly, anticipating the click of the phone as though the space between them, extending as it did five hundred kilometers from west to east, were as thin and clear as glass. In the kitchen, Jorge's pacing slowed like a pendulum resigned to gravity. At last, he picked up the phone again and dialed.

"*Alo alo!*" said Joaquim on the other end.

"They're going to be staying for a while with Marco, since for some reason, James doesn't want Larry to know about my mother, but they're all coming to dinner here tomorrow night," Jorge offered by way of reconciliation.

"Enjoy," said Joaquim. "*Ate. Ciao.*"

"Joa?" said Jorge, tentatively, catching Joaquim before he hung up.

"Eh?"

"You know you still owe me that stop in Lamurii?"

"I'll let my good credit speak for itself," said Joaquim. "How about if we talk about it when I get there?"

Jorge placed the receiver back on the cradle and walked to the door, turning briefly, before he went out, to the now lifeless black form on the wall, which betrayed itself as he regarded it, only by its twitching tail.

VIII

IN THE FOREST, there are trees whose trunks are made of wood so soft they crumble like dirt, and others that, once fallen, slowly break apart over two hands of cycles of heat and rain, their crowns combing the rivers, sheltering the beavers and the moles. Then there are the narrow *tiXaja*, which take a hand of men a hand of days to fell, and that never dissolve into the earth. These stand forever where they are placed, at the thresholds of huts and of Pahquel itself, marking the edges of the world. Stripped of their bark, they are not referred to as wood like the trunks of the other trees. Everyone, alive or dead, only calls them bone.

IX

JORGE LEANED BACK in his chair, laced his fingers behind his head, and studied Martina in profile. That was how he knew her best, never head-on. She was sipping an acerola juice, and he could see the muscles working under her chin as she swallowed.

"You're much too quiet today," she said in her heavy accent between sips. "Even for you. It's making me nervous." That was her mark, that pervasive accent, and the fact that, constant foreigner that she was, there was no language in which she spoke without it.

"You? Nervous?" said Jorge, smoothing her hair. He knew that he was like a spider that ventured out when he felt movement on his web, but otherwise drew back behind the eaves of the house. "I do have something to tell you though, that you're not going to like," he added, studying her reaction. "I think I'm going to have to ask you to wait a little longer for the Marajo weekend."

"Why?" she said, trying to give him the benefit of the doubt. "Silvio's throwing you another job on top of everything else?"

"Nope," said Jorge, pulling his hand away. "This one's mine, a personal jaunt."

"Oh," she said, and fell into silence.

"How long?" she said finally.

"I don't know," said Jorge. "But maybe longer than shorter." She turned away, revealing to Jorge the curve of her hairline, which ran like the path of a new river from the obscurity behind her ear.

"I do want to tell you about it," he said, removing his glasses and wiping them on his shirt. "I mean, the part I can."

Martina turned back until she was almost facing him and began to jab at her glass with the straw.

"It's to Lamurii," he said, waiting for her to land the first blow.

The paper straw against the bottom of the empty glass made a sound like the muffled ticking of a clock.

"I guess I can't really explain it after all," Jorge went on, pausing between words. "All I can say is, I don't have a choice. I know that doesn't make sense. But you have to believe me."

They both looked off in the same direction, as though they were watching a play. In it, Jorge would be standing in an opulent parlor, wearing a satin smoking jacket and explaining with exaggerated mock stoicism to the woman in the bobbed wig that he need only avenge his father's death to be free at last to propose. Or else the woman would be screaming at him, chasing him around and around the upholstered settee, throwing her high heels at his head. Either way, the audience would laugh at the absurd caricature of domesticity, at how hard the two lead characters had to work just to misunderstand each other.

The worst of it was, he didn't disagree with what he imagined her to think. He knew that trying to sit down with a group of people who still believed that his father had betrayed them, who still hated his father even after they had killed him, must seem like an act of the most indulgent self-destructiveness, a pitiful betrayal of a father by a son. But in his mind, the difference between the absurdly puffed-up heroism of the buffoon in the *serie* he imagined Martina to be absorbed in and himself was dependent upon the intervention of Joaquim, to whom he was indebted and hated being so.

"I think Joaquim's going to owe me one hell of a favor by the time this week is out," he interrupted her, as though walking between her and the drama she was watching. Unlike the other women he had known, her attitude towards him was less of deference than of pity, and to bring up Joaquim's name was in itself a risk; whenever he did, he hated the way she admonished him to remember that Joaquim wasn't his father.

But then at other times, she surprised him. "Do you want me to come with you?" she asked, leaning towards him, looking straight into his eyes. She had pulled the straw out of the glass, and a drop of juice fell from the tip of it onto the table. Jorge watched it fall, relieved to pull his eyes from hers.

"You can't, you know that," he said quickly, as though to give himself no time for hesitation. Of course she knew that. She always knew that sort of thing, or knew what was true about it and what wasn't. She sat silent for a few minutes, and resumed her tapping of the straw against the glass, as though a clock that had stopped had once more begun to tick. When she leaned in towards him, her voice was almost a whisper.

"Neither one of us has a choice," she said.

X

LARRY SPENT A long afternoon sitting in the shade of the palms and the *chichas*, drinking fruit juice and looking around, distracted rather than curious, at the circumscribed world of the *Museo de Santarem's* inner courtyard. He passed an hour watching a pair of lizards dart back and forth over the lip of a small fountain, and another watching a spider weave the stem of a lily into the stucco flank of a wall. When the rain came, he walked slowly through the exhibits, past cases of pottery shards, past his own reflection, repeated again and again like a film over each display, and when it stopped, he walked at the same slow pace towards the *Avenida Tapajos*, to the place where the vast bodies of two rivers lay side by side.

The harbor in Santarem was peaceful from a distance, but grew noisier as Larry approached. He chose a cafe outside the ring of restaurants that lined the waterfront and sat down to wait for James, growing impatient when the waiter, noticing his book on the table, spoke to him in English, the language he had hoped to leave behind. The capacity to leave things behind seemed to Larry, over the past week, to be a gift of almost limitless beneficence, allowing him to fill the spaces where thoughts had been erased with images of rock and water, with the sharp sound of his footsteps on gravel, with the shadows of birds moving over the uneven surface of the river, with the taste of orchids in the air. In the late 1800s, the town of Santarem had swelled with an influx of American refugee slaves and confederate soldiers, each escaping to the same bluffs and forests, living together in exile, the sort of peace whose precondition is forgetfulness. Larry wouldn't have hesitated, had he thought about it, to credit the town itself with the capacity to absorb human resentments and fears into its thick, humid air and release them in its downpours into the massive rivers, for which memory was no match. This freedom from his own thoughts and worries had allowed him to join the conversations at meals, surprising everyone at dinner at Jorge's on Friday night by answering a question, for the first time, in Portuguese. Most surprising of all was that their compliments on his accent didn't seem to bring with them the same sense of humiliation that, in his experience, compliments tended to elicit. Jorge hadn't leaned in too closely, and James had tapped the back of his hand in an unconcerned, distracted way.

From the very beginning, Larry had been intrigued by the way Jorge's small round glasses drew his features into a tense knot at the center of his face, and by the way he was constantly brushing the hair from his wide forehead, pulling at his shirt, adjusting his posture, as though to demonstrate that the parts of his own body had never managed to coalesce. He was younger than the others, and deferential to James, a fact which James seemed to find alternately endearing and irritating. Larry imagined that, like himself, Jorge's place at the table was secured not so much by virtue of the strength of his personality as by where he came from, and by what he had to offer them. James rarely mentioned anyone to Larry before he introduced them, perhaps assuming that Larry knew them because he did, or else that it was unimportant whether Larry knew them at all. Jorge was the only one he talked about beforehand, as the best of the SPI pilots, as someone Larry would come to consider a friend. The Lamurii had killed Jorge's father when he was still young, James had told him, a fact that accounted for the troubled look he always wore even when he laughed. Thus, Larry wasn't immediately alarmed by the air of worry Jorge conveyed even at a distance as he came towards him from the direction of the *Museo* to tell him that James was at a house at 11 *Rua Galdino Valoso*, appearing to be ill.

XI

BOOKSHELVES LINED THE longest wall of the room in which they stood, and an overstuffed sofa covered with dark red pillows pushed its back against the wall opposite. The house, Jorge mentioned quickly to Larry as they entered, belonged to Sara, a woman with whom Larry wasn't familiar. That the room was of a sort that appealed to Larry made him all the more resentful suddenly, of James's connection to her, whatever it was. In all the time that he had been aware of James's life outside the family, he had never so much as heard his uncle refer to any close association with a woman. The idea that James might have had such an involvement of any kind made him feel fearful and alone, his dread of James's death amplified by the intrusion of the unfamiliar into life.

"He's in the bedroom," said Jorge from behind him. He walked around Larry and led him down a hallway to the semi-darkened room in which James was lying, his head propped up by pillows, alive and quite awake.

"I got the hammocks and the netting," James began before Larry had fully entered, "but we're going to have to wait until tomorrow for the rope and the tarps."

Ashamed of having been fearful, Larry came over and sat down in a chair by the head of the bed. "I would have done the shopping," he said, realizing as soon as he spoke that James had probably insisted on going alone because he had planned to stop at Sara's also.

As though sensing his thoughts, James said, awkwardly, "I'm not sure you've met Sara."

"No, you've never mentioned her," said Larry, not intending to be harsh.

27

"Well, you'll get your chance. She's out at the market, but she should be back."

"Are you resting?" asked Larry, aware that something should have been mentioned by now about his supposed infirmity.

"I think I'll take a few more minutes," said James, addressing Jorge for the first time. "The bags are on the counter by the sink. Why don't you unpack them and see what's there?"

As they stood in the kitchen, rolling mosquito nets and hammocks and tying them with string, Jorge said in a low voice, "she's gone to the *Fundacao Esperanca* to talk to the doctor. James won't see him." He looked at Larry as though expecting a reply.

Larry was grateful for the texture of the netting on his hands, for the roughness of the string and the subtle sea smell of the rope from which the hammocks were woven.

When he saw that Jorge was still watching him, in place of a response, he offered to hold a roll of netting so that Jorge could use both hands to tie it with. He was just about to reach for another when he heard James call out in a soft, raspy voice and took off down the hall.

His first glimpse of the inside of James's room was of an empty indentation at the center of the pillow at the headboard. Despite himself, he addressed that place guided by the fact that it's easier to face a ghost than a living man. It took another sound from the foot of the bed to make him turn towards James, who was sitting crumpled up, holding his knees to his forehead.

"Shot," James hissed.

Larry looked around for James's bag and prepared the syringe, unaware of his hands as he worked. He tried to pry open James's grip but couldn't, so he sat down behind him and circled him with his arms, threading his hands through the open triangles made by James's elbows. With his chin on his uncle's shoulder, his cheek pressed against hair and sweat, Larry slid the needle into a fold of flesh and pushed the plunger down. The smell of James's suffering, the press of his spine against his chest, the barely audible, piercing scream of the ceiling fan in its socket, the distant sound of a key in a lock; no one could be expected to bear such things. When James began to loosen his fingers, Larry pulled him up toward the top of the bed and lowered him until his uncle's head rested on the inside of Larry's thigh. Breathing heavily, James looked up at him and cleared his throat to speak.

"Larry, this is Sara," he whispered, turning his eyes to the door.

"You need to leave now," said Larry in desperation, unable to look up.

"I'll be in the other room," said a woman's voice from the doorway.

"And I'll be in my room, if you need me," said Jorge, who had been standing next to him all along without his noticing. Larry looked up in time to see Jorge's back disappearing into the hallway. He pulled a pillow from behind him and put it under James's head, slowly sliding his leg away. Then he sat up next to James and rested his head on the headboard. Outside the window, the sun was setting. Larry got up to open the curtains and then sat down again, looking out.

"I wonder if I've done right by you," said James, his voice once again his own.

"Of course you have," said Larry, with the same panic as before. It wasn't, at that moment, that he didn't wonder too.

"Are you in pain?" he asked, looking at James's body, which now covered every corner of the bed except the one he was sitting on. He thought of ancient graves, in which the bones had become detached and spread over an area as large as that.

"Better," said James. "I think I didn't give myself enough. In the heat of the moment, I don't always pay attention."

"How long has it been like this?" Larry asked, his voice a bit calmer for his having found, at least, a direction for his thoughts.

"I don't know," said James. "A month or two?"

"Why didn't you tell me?" Larry asked. James was silent for a long time, until Larry began to wonder whether he was asleep. He watched James's stomach move up and down. Finally, James opened his eyes and stared ahead.

"Now you know," he said.

An hour passed. Larry had always wanted to spend a week watching a plant sprout, to witness imperceptible changes, so as at last to be able to believe in continuity. The shadows on the walls crept smoothly and then faded, but when he suddenly noticed that the room was dark, he felt cheated, as though he had missed some steps along the way. It was unsettling to think that the process into darkness was jagged and lurching, that there were holes in his perception of the flow of time. Perhaps his own lack of vigilance had prevented him from noticing James's decline except in a few jarring, disconnected moments, from creating in his mind a path smooth enough to pull James back across it into what he used to be.

"Why did Jorge say he'd be in *his* room?" Larry said at last into the darkness. "Does he live here?"

"Not any more," said James's voice from beside him.

"He used to?"

"He grew up here. Sara's his mother."

"And you're his father?" Larry was gripped suddenly by outrage at James's betrayal.

"No," James laughed. "I've told you who his father was."

"His step-father then?"

"No," said his uncle with another laugh. "The only 'son' I have is you."

Larry felt a swell of relief and shame, a gratitude so deep as to allow him, for just a fraction of a second, to forgive James even for dying. "Are you hungry?" he asked his uncle, to distract him from his gift so he couldn't take it back.

"I'm not so interested in food right now."

"I think I'd better eat."

"Sara will feed you well."

"I snapped at her," said Larry, hoping despite his guilt that James would smooth the way between them. He knew though, that to ask reassurance from a dying man must be an unforgivable sin, especially since he had been given more than his share already. He got up quietly, as though James were asleep, and headed for the door.

"I'll get up in a bit," said James after him.

Larry walked alone down the dark hall toward the sound of voices. He could see the room up ahead, its soft yellow light swirling out to meet him, and felt, simultaneously, hunger and dread. He could hear the sharp rhythm of a knife against a wooden board, and the sound of water being turned on and off. Jorge ran to him as he stepped in from the hallway.

"There you are!" he said, reaching out for Larry's arm. "Come and talk to us."

Larry followed Jorge into the room. Sara looked up from the kitchen sink as they came in and stood, knife in hand, without saying a word. What Larry saw at that moment was Jorge's face surrounded by a garland of white hair, the same density of features counterbalanced, this time, by a thick white braid that extended down to the small of her back. His relief at finding something in her that he knew allowed him to go on.

"We're almost done," said Jorge. His voice seemed to re-animate his mother, who began again to move and talk.

"Would you mind dicing tomatoes?" she said, handing Larry her knife. The three of them stood with their backs to each other, each engaged in a separate task, growing more familiar in light of the familiarity of each with the work. After a long silence, filled by the sound of knives against wood, Sara asked with her back still turned, "Is he in pain?"

"I don't think so now," said Larry. "He says he didn't have enough medication. Did you talk to the doctor?"

"I did, and we can give him all the morphine he needs. If he revives enough, he should still be able to go."

Larry somehow hadn't realized that the fluid in the vial was morphine.

When the chopping was done, Sara called them all to the stove where they placed their offerings of onion and tomato and garlic and chiero verde, into a pan and watched them intermingle in the oil. Last of all came the shredded pirarucu, king of the river, which sat in a regal mound in the midst of the crackling mixture until Jorge stirred it in with a spoon.

That night, they ate in James's bedroom, one chair on either side of the bed and another at the foot. James told a story of once making *Desfiado de Pirarucu* without first soaking the salt from the fish, and after some quantity of wine, Jorge began to call him Master Pirarucu. They were in high spirits, aware that James had eaten his entire portion and Sara's leftovers as well. A sense of excitement and anticipation had replaced the fear and sadness of the day, due equally, in Larry's mind, to their having

triumphed over some still mysterious threat to James's life, and their having vanquished the awkwardness between them.

It was well after midnight by the time they went to bed. Jorge had
offered to make up the back bedroom, but Larry unrolled his sleeping mat
on the floor in James's room instead. He gave James a shot before they
went to sleep, and another at 3 A.M. when he heard him whimper. James
didn't speak, but reached out in the darkness and patted the hand that
held the needle, holding onto Larry's finger as he snapped the cap into
place. The night was full of sound, and the sound seemed to hold James's
breathing securely within it. Larry leaned back on his pillow and listened,
encouraged to hear it so slow and deep. At last, he drifted off, and didn't
wake up until the sun was high in the sky, the smell of fried plantain had
drifted in through the window between the curtains, and James, having
pulled his knees up to his chest in the night, was dead.

XII

HOW DO YOU mourn something that never existed? In Pahquel, if a baby died before a hand and two of moons, it couldn't be inscribed into a *cha-jan*, couldn't be danced for or wailed for or sung about, couldn't be claimed for a line. Without a name, how could you call out to it, in a night sky already crowded with insects and ancestors and stars? A mother who had lost a child before its name-ceremony—and there were many—was said to be *rat rititi*, out of the world. She too lost her name for the eternity of a moon cycle, and didn't venture past her *chajan* even to haul water or tend the garden or cook. She took in gourds of food and drink and returned them full of urine and excrement, and waited for the moon to turn its face to her again, to call her name and lead her back into the world so she could speak.

XIII

LARRY COULD TELL by mid-day that the sun had in mind to burn the water away. A thin strip of off-white sand revealed itself at the edge of the river and intimated more. Larry turned his back on the water and walked up the *Travessa dos Martires*, pushing step by step against the sun's weight, which he felt too weak to carry. By the time he managed to find the Telepar, his dread had gathered itself in the pit of his stomach, so that it was all he could do to keep himself from crouching down in the booth after he dialed.

The sounds of the dial tone and the ring were unfamiliar to him, and for a minute they soothed him and held his interest, so that when his mother's voice came on the line, he was startled by it.

"Hi mom. It's me," he said.

"Larry! Where are you? When are you coming home?" Larry was often struck by the capacity of her voice to convey urgency and indifference simultaneously.

"I don't know," he said, emotionlessly. "James died last night."

There was a long silence on the line. At last, his mother said, bitterly, "He never should have gone back to that country." In the silence that closed in again behind her words, Larry was horrified to hear what sounded like gasping noises through the receiver, which at first he couldn't make sense of. It was unimaginable to him that his mother would cry—he had never seen it—and the thought of her wearing human emotions openly struck him as grotesque, against nature and utterly confusing. More grotesque and frightening still was his own sudden wish to hold her, to offer her comfort, or even forgiveness. As he stood paralyzed in his little glass booth four thousand miles away, listening to his mother as he had never heard her, weep, he felt the booth fill up, starting at his feet, with his own misery. The thought that things might have been different between them was far more unbearable to Larry than the fact that they never were.

"Will they at least send him home to be buried?" his mother said finally, her voice still not recovered.

"No, he left instructions in a notebook by his bed. He wants to be cremated here and"—and Larry's voice began to waver also—"I'll scatter his ashes in the forest. He wanted you to do something at St. Thomas."

"I want to bury him myself. Here. I've owed it to him, since he buried Maggie," she blurted out, as though she needed to tell him, or had forgotten he was there.

"Who's Maggie?" asked Larry, the knot in his stomach growing tighter.

"Your sister," she said.

The level had risen higher in the booth. Larry could feel it lapping at his neck, and longed for it to overtake him. It penetrated into whatever small opening was made inside him by his momentary sympathy, and washed out that crevice, and filled it with rage.

"When are you coming home?" she said.

"I'm not," said Larry sharply, and then more softly, trying to keep an even tone. "There are things I need to do here, to wrap everything up. I'll call you when I know more."

"I think you should come home," said his mother.

"Okay," said Larry.

"Did he suffer?"

"Not so much, I think. Some."

"Do you have enough money to get home?"

"My tickets are already paid for."

"Then come home," she said.

"I will," said Larry. "Say hi to dad."

On the street, the people seemed to be walking in slow motion, and in silence, as though the humid air were water. Larry looked into courtyards and windows as he walked; he wandered up and down the aisles of shops, looking for clues. He tried to keep his body moving, pushing hard into the thick, warm air. To Larry, moving felt like an answer in itself, the only possible answer to an endless stream of deprivations and uncertainties. He walked against the flow of traffic, leaving in his wake a string of cars and bicycles and cow carts. His sweaty shirt slapped back and forth across his back, following the rhythm of his arms.

Between the buildings in front of him, he could see the glare of the sun on the river. He turned off to the right, heading without thinking toward the *Museu de Santarem*. His eyes didn't stop moving even when his body sat down on a stone bench in the courtyard, and his thoughts didn't stop when, at last, he settled his gaze on the paving stones at his feet. A small, gray bird landed nearby and pecked at the dirt between the stones. He imagined himself through the bird's eye, a hunched, despondent creature.

As he sat immersed, he felt someone sit down beside him, a body that mimicked his own pose, its shoulder at his shoulder, knee touching his knee. He slowly moved his gaze to the left and saw the tip of Jorge's shoe, and the fringe of his leg hair hanging over the top of his sock.

"James told me yesterday to look for you here if I didn't find you at the cafes," he said.

They sat for a long time, watching first one beetle and then another struggle over the rocky ground. Drops fell on the paving stones leaving wet circles that quickly shrank and dried, and fleeting trails of water where the beetles waded through them onto shore.

"Do you want to be alone?" Jorge asked, shifting towards the end of the bench.

"You can stay," said Larry.

Overhead, birds were reeling in the sky, their wings flashing in the spaces between the trees. Their calls grazed the walls of the courtyard and mingled with the sounds of the fountain.

"I've lost someone too," said Jorge, brushing his hair from his forehead and looking back down at the ground.

"You still have someone," said Larry, the bitterness in his voice reminding him, for a minute, of his mother's.

"That's true," said Jorge.

Larry began to feel irritable again, angry at Jorge's kindness and his own relentless subtle cruelty, angry at the hardness of the bench, and at his mother, and at James, and at all the useless beggars who wandered the streets of Santarem, one of whom he could easily become. He imagined crushing the beetles with his shoe. Over time, the anger passed.

"How old were you?" he said.

"Ten," said Jorge. "The day after my tenth birthday." He took off his glasses and cleaned them on his shirt, squinting up into the tops of the trees. "I can't really say it goes away."

A lizard darted across the pavement, scattering the tiny oceans at their feet. Jorge jumped up but forced himself to stay, clenching his fists at his sides.

Without looking at him, Larry straightened and took his place beside him. They walked together out onto the street, where a line of old men fed cornstalks to their cows while cars and motorbikes sped by. They tried to walk side by side down the *Rua Bittencourt*, but boys on bikes filled the sidewalk, forcing them into single file with Jorge in the lead. When the town center was behind them, Jorge slowed his pace until Larry caught up with him again.

"Did they come for him yet?" Larry asked when they neared Sara's house.

"A while ago," said Jorge. "Not long after you left." He took the key out of his pocket and put it into the lock.

"You'll stay with us?" he said, his hand on the key, without turning around.

"I don't know," said Larry as they went in.

The living room was as appealing as it had been before, generous in its appointments, and empty of people. Larry walked through it by himself to James's room, and stood for a time just inside the doorway. The bed had been made, and the pillows were plumped up and neatly arranged along the headboard. His sleeping pad was rolled up and tied, and the rest of their bags had been brought over from Marco's and piled up in a corner. His pack and James's leaned against each other, as though both were very tired. Larry watched the two of them for a minute and then turned and headed down the hall to Jorge's room, taking a seat at the end of the bed when Jorge looked up from his desk.

"What are you doing on Saturday?" he asked without looking at him.

"What are *you* doing?"

"I was thinking I'd go ahead on my own," said Larry.

"Bad idea," said Jorge. He shook his head, scattering his hair across his forehead and then herding it back with his hand. "I can't do it."

"You're kidding!" said Larry, turning to look at him. "I thought that was the plan." In light of Jorge's obsequiousness towards James, and his air of sad fragility, and the indulgent kindness he had shown, it had never occurred to Larry that he could be anything other than compliant.

"You're not prepared," said Jorge, his voice almost angry. "What do you think, I'm going to drop you out in the middle of nowhere, where you don't speak the language, and you won't know how to find food, and you'll end up as lunch meat, if you don't die first of malaria?"

"I do speak the language, and I've done this trip before," said Larry, desperate.

"With James. And do you know how long James had been at it by then? Twenty years, with a few narrow escapes and a lot of luck. And do you know how upset everybody was when he went off assignment? Silvio was livid when he found out James had brought you in with him. I only took you because, for some reason known only to him, Joaquim stepped in."

Jorge was leaning forward in his seat, his head thrust out into the space between them. Larry could see the veins standing up on the sides of his neck. He found intolerable the idea that Jorge might know more than he did about the circumstances of what he thought of as his personal sojourn with James. When he thought back, all he could remember of that day was a seemingly endless wait in a small, hot, run-down airplane hangar in the middle of nowhere. James and a few other people he didn't know were huddled together arguing in one corner while he sat in another, reading a book. He remembered the book clearly, though; it was *The Hobbit*.

"Besides," said Jorge, "now there's nobody with you who's even remotely connected with IPS. Even if we found a way of getting around Silvio, I'd never get authorization to take you."

"James didn't work for IPS this time either."

"Officially, he was on leave, with at least the pretense of taking a real assignment." Jorge said with an exasperated sigh. "Why do you even want this?"

"I don't have a choice," said Larry, despondent, understanding clearly now that life was going to defeat him.

"Let it sit," said Jorge, wiping his glasses with his shirt as he stood and walked to the door.

XIV

MARTINA SAT AT the wheel and started to kick while she rolled the clay between her palms. If people asked her about the work, she would tell them, "It's no different from breathing." It was also like eating; every batch of clay had a different flavor, which she tasted through her pores, and through the cracks in her palms. Despite the wheel's own rhythmic, raspy breath, it was, above all, silent work; when Jorge came, as he often did, to take her to dinner, they were sometimes halfway to the cafe before she felt ready to speak a word. Jorge was the only man she knew who didn't mind her silences, unlike the others who seemed to need her to be chatty; he told her she was the only woman he knew who didn't seem determined to disturb his thoughts with endless talk. That was their starting point, a small, superficial quirk of character that meant nothing and yet portended well for them.

The other important thing about working in clay was the fact that it depended on memory of body rather than memory of mind. Throwing demanded attunement, sensitivity to degrees of pressure and angle, but of an almost unconscious sort, so that her thoughts were free to wander. "I'm still dreaming," she would say to Jorge as they sat together at the *Boutu Vermelho* waiting for their dinner. Then she would start slowly, telling him about whatever she had been reading the night before, Chaucer or Santayana or Jung. Sometimes she would read him passages in English or Italian or German or Portuguese, always *sotto voce*, in her heavy accent, so that he would have to listen hard to hear her.

When Jorge showed up at a quarter after two, she was in the midst of thought, bent over the wheel, but when she saw him, she rinsed her hands and followed him into the front room where the finished pieces were displayed. She watched him move from one shelf to the next, picking up vases and bowls and looking at their undersides, as if searching for some answer he had once known but had lost.

"What are you doing?"

"I don't know," he said.

"You're so early! Do you want to go out?"

Jorge kept on the search, as if he hadn't heard her.

"What is it?" she asked.

"Nothing," he said. Then finally, "Larry's in trouble."

"What trouble?" she said, her voice tinged with impatience.

"James is dead," said Jorge hollowly.

"Oh, you poor man!" she said, running to him and taking him in her arms. She pulled him back toward the dusty wooden church pew that sufficed for a sofa in the throwing room, wiping it off with a rag so they could sit down. Jorge stared down at his shoes, and then lifted his eyes to the far wall. He sat transfixed for half an hour, as though he had forgotten she was there. Then he stood up and smoothed out the wrinkles in his pants and shirt and brushed off the clay dust before walking slowly to the door.

"Where are you going?" she asked.

He pressed her hand for a minute and then let go abruptly, stepping out into the bustle of the street.

XV

THEY CALLED SILVIO *"O Apresentador de Marionetas,"* "The Puppeteer," because of the web of threads and thumbtacks that covered the map on his office wall, and because he allowed no doubt as to who it was who placed and pulled the strings. Like the ones who orchestrated the endearing violence of Punches and Judys for coins in the Cathedral Plaza, his greatest contribution was found not in the stories he fabricated, nor in the nuances of his characters, so much as in his willingness to embody the universal fact that control over even one's own body is approximate, mediated, tenuous, knotted, remote. As he paced the diagonal between his desk and the wall map, Silvio could feel his own threads stretch and contract, alternating between tension and slack. As a visible analog, the cord between the phone and the receiver coiled and extended as he moved from his desk to the wall along the worn path in the floor.

When he couldn't get an answer at one number, he stopped beside the desk and dialed another with a finger grown stubby from constant, insistent service. Finally, hearing a voice, he stopped and covered his other ear with his palm.

"Alo? Alo?" he barked into the receiver at the operator. *"Pois nao e urgento!"*

"Silvio?" said Sara's voice at the end of the line.

"I can't find anyone!" Silvio shouted, though it wasn't clear if he was still talking to the operator or to Sara. "Not Marco! Not James! Not Joaquim! Not yesterday! Not today! Where the hell is that good-for-nothing son of yours? If he's out there with James and Larry, he's out of a job, as far as I'm concerned. You can tell him that for me!"

"I need to talk to you," Sara started, but Silvio cut her off.

"Tell him to call me! Now!" he shouted and hung up. Sara lifted the receiver and looked at it, a strange artifact from an even stranger culture. As she placed it on the cradle, Jorge passed her without a word, stopping to take a coin from the bowl on the windowsill on his way to the door.

XVI

WHEN JORGE TURNED the key, the Beaver's engine jumped up to meet him, offering, without hesitation, its reliable droning solace. He checked to see that the radio was off and then eased the plane up and out, leaning forward, stroking the panel as though he were a jockey. He hadn't planned on taking her up today, hadn't told his mother he was going. But waking in his old bedroom with its child's airplane-patterned window shade, and reaching for his glasses in their old place at the base of his blue wooden Cessna-shaped bedside light (a childhood gift from Joaquim), and hearing his mother move around in the kitchen, and listening to Larry run the water in the bathroom, and hearing the phone ring at five-minute intervals, and knowing from the bits he could piece together from his mother's end of conversations that at least two of the calls were from Martina, he had been filled with the sort of desperation that could only be eased in the pit of a newly-washed DHC. Those were the extremes that his work offered him—entanglement on the one hand and a sense, on the other, of breaking free, as though a million strands were being stretched taut and severed in a chorus of soft pings.

The truth was that from the moment of his arrival at the hangar, while he was hosing down the plane and crawling around in the hold with his broom and flashlight, checking her over for lizards and leaks, he had all but forgotten that James was dead. He had hummed to himself while he threaded the hose in through the window of the cockpit to fill her up, and he had hummed even louder when the sound of the engine kicked in to offer him a cover. Looking down as he circled to the south, the town of

Santarem was even smaller than he imagined it to be when he was in it, a tiny bauble resting against the soft throat of the earth, suspended from the juncture of two knotted river-strands.

At first, he allowed the familiarity of routine to lead him to believe that the day was like the others, a string of IPS dropoffs and deliveries, as dictated by the clipboard he had drawn from his canvas pack. Only when he looked down and saw the dusty airstrip of Itatuba recede behind him without his having landed there for a pickup, the first item on his job list, did he acknowledge to himself that he was headed elsewhere, beyond it by a hundred kilometers and almost twenty years. The magnet that had repelled him from Lamurii for so long had suddenly been turned on end, and he felt his spine push against his seatback, the engine accelerate his pulse. He knew its coordinates exactly, as one is at some level acutely aware of the location of the object of one's fears, and he bent his path toward it, peeling off from the companionable escort of the *Rio Tapajos*. "Second star to the right!" he whispered to himself as he turned the wheel instinctively. The sensation wasn't so much of flying as of falling towards it at two hundred kilometers an hour, though to an observer, he might as well have been suspended there, between the urges to see and not to see. An hour later, it came into view, a jagged parting between the trees that harbored a tiny clump of circular thatched roofs resembling toadstools as much as human dwellings. He steered himself toward it as though to plant the nose of the plane into its heart and then suddenly jerked up again, climbing her as only a Beaver could.

XVII

WHEN THE HOLES for the *tiχaja* have been dug to the height of a boy, and the trunks have been inserted side by side like a man and a woman, and the lintels have been placed across them like a bridge, then it no longer matters whether the walls have been woven yet and tied into place. All one needs is a doorway in order to travel between worlds.

XVIII

WHEN JORGE WALKED in at a quarter after eight, his mother refused to acknowledge him. She had arranged the table with the plates and forks and glasses, and had put out guest towels in the bathroom, and had assembled, on trays in the refrigerator, an array of meats and cheeses. She had shaken out the rugs and dusted the bookshelves, at some level knowing she owed her sudden furious energy to her son, as much as to James. Larry had done his best simultaneously to serve and to avoid her, floating through the day as though it were already a memory. He watched her from the corner of his eye, envying what appeared to him to be a fierce efficiency that left him more ashamed than ever of his own foggy confusion. When Jorge came in, he stood beside the door and watched her too, but what he saw was not efficiency or self-control, but something he knew also in himself: a silent current of desperation that no channel, no matter how deep, could be trusted to contain.

XIX

THE NEXT MORNING, Jorge and Sara set off early, and separately, but Larry feigned sleep so as to be left behind. Now he found himself alone in the living room, a bowl of mango slices in one hand, flipping through a pile of photographs without interest or recognition. As he was about to put the pile back on the shelf, he looked more closely at the one on top and saw, suddenly, that the tall young man in the khaki trousers, framed by a wall of trees, dangling a large fish from the end of a line, was James. The one beneath it showed James again, standing arm-in-arm with a man who looked like Silvio and another man Larry didn't recognize until later on, when he came upon him again in a family portrait holding a child who was unmistakably Jorge on his lap, underneath which was written, *Giorgio, 8 m.* There was James at the edge of a river, preparing to dive, and James surrounded by a group of dark-skinned, nearly naked young men who barely reached his shoulders. There was James in a canoe and James in a cafe, as strange and unreachable in youth as in death. In the last picture on the pile, which was in color, James was standing in a doorway, his hands on the shoulders of a boy. Larry felt a stab of jealousy, and held the picture up in front of him to try to see what the boy looked like. He could tell right away that his hair was too light to be Jorge's, but it took several more minutes for Larry to realize that the boy was him. He had no recollection of the picture having been taken.

Back in his room, Larry reached for the strap of James's travel case and hoisted it onto the bed. Then he began to pull out folders, working his way through them with the narrowness of vision characteristic of someone looking for something in particular, but because he did not know which particular thing he sought, he barely saw anything at all. There were medical bills and check stubs, lists and ticket stubs from movie theaters and instructions for fixing a bicycle. Larry rifled through a blue folder labeled "Documents," and a brown envelope stuffed with cash register receipts. He felt as though he were running through scenery that grew more streaked and blurry the faster he went. At some point the thought crossed his mind that he might not find what he needed among the folders marked "Supplies," and "Evidence" and "Cancer." Even the "SPI" folder seemed to hold nothing of promise in its pages of contracts and instructions, all in Portuguese, some underlined sloppily in red. By the time Larry came to the bottom of the pile, he felt exhausted, like a runner at the end of a race, and fell back into the pillows, holding the last folder, labeled "Joaquim," in the air in front of him. He opened it slowly, expecting more old scraps of paper to fall on him, but he found instead drafts of James's letters, some of which looked like they'd been crumpled up and then smoothed out again.

Larry flipped through the pages impatiently. At best, writing had always been a struggle for James. Larry had felt pity, and sometimes disdain, at the discovery that someone so verbally imposing could write so poorly. He had sensed that James's clumsiness on the page had something to do with his incongruous reverence for the written word in general, and for Larry's fluency with it in particular. Only such a person, Larry had thought, would devote so much of himself to the task of transforming a spoken language into a written one, a task Larry cared about only because James did. But no matter how deep James's faith might have been that the Pahqua notebook could be a sufficient legacy, Larry understood at that moment how little it had to offer in proportion to what he needed. He went to his own pack and found it, and threw it onto the pile of folders with a rage that surprised him. Then he turned back to the letters, fighting off the urge to crumple them again.

At intervals, his mind continued to register a few of the fragments he read, "stay awhile," and "not much contact," and to move them around to arbitrary rhythms. "He's like a foundling," he repeated to himself, until he suddenly began to listen to himself and turned back to the page. "He's like a foundling," he said under his breath while his eyes sought out the words. "He's like a foundling," he read, "because despite all Judy's efforts, she's in no shape to care for him. It's all a mess. David's useless. So I'm off assignment for now—tell S. I'll call when I get back. Just say something came up." Larry stared hard at the page. He felt strange, as though something were wrong with his eyes, as though everything was closer than it should have been. He waited for a minute to see if the sensation would pass, the feeling that someone was there, in the chair, or at the door, trying to tell him that people had made efforts on his behalf, that James had been a real person after all, a man in a cafe, in a doorway, his hands on the shoulders of a boy.

Larry retrieved the picture from the living room and propped it up on the bedside table, referring to it, looking up from the folder at intervals as though he were reading its description. "You wanted me to put down roots, and so in my own way I have, though as you know I can never stand it here for long." As he turned the pages, Larry looked up at James's hands, which covered his shoulders like epaulets. "It's better when we get away. I'll bring him to meet you. I know you'll love him, not just for my sake." Larry saw that James's mouth was open, as though he were talking to whoever was taking the picture. "We'll come in June and see you, and then go about our business. That's enough for now." Larry was looking off to the right, frowning slightly, as though to avoid the camera's interest. He had never been comfortable with cameras or mirrors, and because he lacked a sense of his own image, he assumed that others did as well. The idea that James would think of him, or write about him, was as foreign as the idea that he was not automatically a part of everything James did. Larry imagined his uncle bent late at night over the desk in his parents' guest room, which had always looked to him like a girl's room, for reasons he now understood, writing the letters he had in his hands. He could see him turn slowly to look up and then back to the page, scratching his head with the end of his pen.

As Larry put the folders back in the bag and lowered it to the floor, he imagined that one side of his house had been cut away, like a dollhouse. He could see James at his desk in that room, with its pink wallpaper and bedding, and his mother in the room next door, folding back the old maroon bedspread and turning on the light by the head of the bed. His father was asleep on the sofa downstairs, washed by the flicker of the gray light from the TV, and he was upstairs, alone in a crib, or older, sitting on the floor of his room reading a book. Eventually, he knew, James would come in and sit with him until he fell asleep. James never read to him; sometimes he read to James, but most often, James would tell him stories about nature, about animal dung, and water lilies as big as their dining room table, and spiders whose webs were like bridges between the trees. He would teach him phrases of Pahqua, and occasionally, painfully, sing him Pahqua songs. Then there were the months and years when James was gone, and the people in the house froze in their places, and the only movements were the flickering of the TV light and the back-and-forth of Larry's eyes over the pages of his book. Larry had always had the impression that during those times, they had all simply ceased to exist, but now he saw it differently. He found he could imagine that James had not just disappeared, but had gone to a place somewhere, to a place where, even if he couldn't write, he could look for stories about nature to bring back to him. The thought crossed his mind that even now, James might be keeping his eyes open for something new to bring back and tell him, but as soon as it occurred to him, he knew he didn't need it; it was enough, somehow, that James had intended, during each of his absences, to return. When Larry walked out to the living room to put the picture away, the world seemed oddly populated, not by his own ghosts but by people driving cars and listening to music and talking to one another as they walked, side by side, down the hill to the *Mercado Modelo*. When he heard the key turn in the lock, he fought his instinct to run back to his room, and stood at the door, waiting until Sara tumbled in with her packages to help Joaquim with his bags.

XX

LARRY SAT AMONG a group of men, all old and most drunk, each with a story about James, whom Larry doubted that any of them knew. He looked around, desperate, for Jorge and when he didn't find him, for Joaquim, who, unsettlingly, appeared deep in conversation with an unfamiliar, much younger woman. Panicked now, he sought a path of escape, sliding out between the backs of chairs and down the hallway to his door.

His room was as crowded with sounds and shadows as Sara's living room had been with people. The walls were thick with silhouettes, and the air with night noises—the buzz of insects interrupted now and then by the hum of a car driving off, the crowing, in the distance, of an errant rooster, the nasal cries of swallows, and the ebb and flow of voices from the other room. As he lay on his back in the bed that had been James's, feeling alone and lost and exposed, he found a moment of comfort in the fleeting thought that if he could only push himself deeper into the mattress and pillows, he might yet feel the heat of James's body, and rest his thoughts in the contours of his head.

The night was full of ghosts, but James was not among them. If a ghost, by definition were someone with no resting place, then his uncle, who seemed to carry his home inside himself, would certainly never have qualified. He had made himself comfortable in the houses of strangers, pulling bottles of beer from their refrigerators before he had been invited to do so. He had spread his legs out into the aisles of movie theaters, pushed his seat back in airplanes, stretched out in chairs in waiting rooms, and slept. Larry trusted him to make his home, with equal unselfconsciousness, in death, to be easy among the ashes, to spread out in all directions along the forest floor. He couldn't bear, at that moment, to think otherwise, nor, given the depth of his own loneliness, could he rid himself of the sense that James had abandoned him in this other, restless world. He heard the gathering in the other room breaking up. He saw the lights go out, leaving the world outside the window in an even deeper darkness. He saw how the dead make ghosts of the living. He wove in and out among all the other strangers in the shadows, and looked down at himself in the bed. He stood, for a moment, and watched himself, a thin, terrified figure looking up from under quivering eyelids, and then he too wandered off, leaving himself behind to let sleep find him when, or if, it would.

XXI

ANOK WAS SMALL and hunched, but because she spent so much time struggling with the *chajans,* she was stronger than most of the men. She never became angry at the wood, at the fierce resistance it showed her, because she was like that too—unwilling to be moved or changed by anything but the most fundamental of the events around her, or at least that's what she wanted to think. But that didn't mean there was no anger in the work itself. Anyone who watched her wield the *maata* might have guessed that despite its sharpness, it took the force of all the accrued small rages and passions of a lifetime to give it power sufficient to make its mark. It was also true that once a mark was made, it could never be erased, blotted out, sanded down, dug out, painted over. "That's what it is to remember," she told Aran.

XXII

MARTINA'S AUNT JANTJE used to read to her every night before she tucked her in, from a heavy old book of nursery rhymes and stories she had managed to carry out with her in her small suitcase. That was the only request her mother had made of her spinster older sister—that she continue to read to Martina every night, to preserve her daughter's Dutch in the face of the threat of yet another strange tongue. That was the only way to assure their future contact: to preserve their ability to understand each other. Inside the front cover of the old volume was the only surviving photograph of the two parents, the handsome young strangers who themselves, in the seven years she had had with them in Munich, according to Aunt Jantje, never spoke a word of German to her, but always, only Dutch. When Auntje would close the book each night at the end of the story, a faint odor would be forced from the pages, which Martina always assumed was the odor of her mother. But during the rest of the day, Auntje never spoke to her in anything but Portuguese, even from the very first, when all she knew to say was "*ta bom*" and "*adeus*." Only later, when Martina was old enough to read by herself, far too old to be read to, and continued to allow it only with irritation, for her aunt's sake, did the question about her parents' true motives emerge. She and Auntje had come home from a late evening service at the church, eaten a quick dinner of fried fish and plantains, and retired straight away, after washing their faces in the cold water from the pitcher her aunt had filled from the spigot by the door. After the ritual closing of the book, Auntje had leaned over her, so close that her breath eclipsed the odor, by now stale and oppressive, that slipped from the pages as they fell.

"I have something to tell you," said Auntje, surprisingly, in Dutch.

"What, Aunt?" Martina had answered, also in Dutch, more alarmed by her aunt's choice of language than her tone.

"Your parents won't be joining us ever, Marti," her aunt said slowly, "nor Mina either."

"I know those were your letters, not theirs. When did they die?"

"Years ago, Marti, with the rest of the Jews."

XXIII

WHEN THEY HAD finished dinner and stood to move into the living room, Jorge slipped ahead of Larry and sat down in the wing chair, leaving Larry no other choice but to take the empty seat beside Joaquim on the couch. Larry was sure without raising his eyes that Joaquim was looking at him, but Joaquim addressed Jorge instead.

"*Perdao?*" said Joaquim into the silence, clearing his throat.

"So, what *about* Lamurii?" Jorge blurted out.

Until then, it hadn't occurred to Larry that some of the awkwardness over dinner might have come from sources other than himself.

"I promised I'd take you," said Joaquim, nodding his head. "You should trust me more."

"You're the only one I *do* trust," said Jorge. "That's why I'd feel better if we could pick a date, before you disappear again."

"Well, you're about to get your wish," said Joaquim, glancing up at Sara, who had come in from the kitchen and was standing with her hands on the back of Jorge's chair. "I can go with you this week, if you can make time in your schedule."

"Really?" asked Jorge.

"There's a catch, though," said Joaquim, smiling slightly.

"What's that?" said Jorge, returning a tenser version of Joaquim's smile for a minute and then letting his face drop. "No!" he said suddenly, shaking his head.

"Do you know what I have in mind?" asked Joaquim.

"I do. Forget it."

Larry leaned forward.

"I've been thinking about it all week. It makes no sense. There's nothing to discuss," said Jorge. He started to rise out of his chair, but Sara, who was still standing behind him, put her hands on his shoulders to keep him in his seat.

"I'm glad you've been considering it," said Joaquim.

"Larry just doesn't know what he's doing," said Jorge, not bothering to gesture toward Larry.

"Neither did any of us, at the start."

Larry listened from the sidelines, unsure as to whether he was really there, or had a right to comment on the fate of this person who bore his name but seemed otherwise unfamiliar. Only a twinge of desperation forced him to speak.

"I found all of James's maps in his travel bag. I'm going to take the boat to Itatuba on Monday, and then buy a rowboat to take to Paruqu, and hike in from there. I have the money. James has a friend there who can help me. That's where we started from last time," he said. "I'm sure I can find the way in from there."

"See? It's completely impractical. He hasn't thought about the realities at all." Jorge turned to Larry and addressed him directly. "I'm trying to look out for you. I'm *afraid* for you." They regarded each other for a moment in silence. "You're still a kid," Jorge said, changing his tack. "You still have lots of time. When I was your age, my mother didn't let me go around the block by myself, let alone fly my own missions." Sara opened her mouth to protest, but Larry cut her off.

"My parents always let me do whatever I want," Larry retorted, feeling suddenly strong and defiant and superior, capable of conquering darkness and fear. "They said I was born taking care of myself!" He leaned farther forward as though convinced that by setting off impulsively on his own, he had escaped their opinions, their reservations and their claims on him. He was relieved to have forgotten that the sense of triumph was, for him, invariably the prelude to an even greater fear.

"Larry," said Joaquim in his quiet, measured voice, "Why do you want to do this?"

"I asked him that!" said Jorge, but Joaquim raised his hand to stop him.

Larry felt paralyzed, pinned by Joaquim's gaze. His resolve had come and gone in an instant. The sounds of the night creatures, which he had for a minute, kept at bay, came crawling in under the door and through the open windows, their eyes glowing. He tried unsuccessfully to turn away from Joaquim, who was waiting for him with no sign of impatience.

"I don't know." His voice sounded weak and pleading. "I have to. I don't have a choice," he said.

Jorge opened his mouth to speak, but Sara tightened her grip on his shoulders.

"I know you don't," said Joaquim, putting his hand on Larry's arm for a minute, before turning back and gesturing to Jorge. "And he doesn't either."

Jorge suddenly looked like he was going to cry. "Why are you making me the bad guy?" he said to all of them.

"Nobody's against you," said Sara, leaving for a minute to drag a chair in from the kitchen table. She sat down beside her son and patted his hand.

Jorge pulled his hand away and got up to go.

"Are you leaving?" Sara asked.

"I'm getting the coffee."

He returned with two cups, and gave them to his mother and Joaquim. Then he brought in the other two and handed one to Larry.

"How about this?" said Joaquim, sounding suddenly amused.

"What?" said Jorge.

"We have to stop in Itatuba anyway, pretty close to Paruqu, if we're going to have anything to bring with us to Lamurii, since there's all that leftover barter there. How about if we take Larry with us, so he can get a feel for it? We can approach Paruqu by boat from the South, stop overnight, maybe bring the ashes and see if there's a place there for James." He looked at Jorge and smiled. Jorge looked away.

"Oh, and one more thing," said Joaquim, winking at Larry.

"What?" said Jorge.

"I think if you want any hope of a decent outcome in Lamurii, you should bring along that woman of yours," said Joaquim. "I had a long talk with her last night. You're going to need her."

"Oh, for Christ's sake!" said Jorge, jumping up. He looked around the room, from one side to the other, and started pacing between the kitchen and the living room. Then he walked to the front door and began twisting the handle rhythmically. At last he stopped, turning to rest his back on the doorframe. He took off his glasses and wiped them with his handkerchief. "There's more coffee," he said.

XXIV

ASATOR AK HAD waited for a hands-and-feet of moon cycles after Timir's death to approach Anok, though he had thought of it long before then. The two moon-cycles of Asator's disappearance, in which it was said that the Gods had called him back to prepare him to lead, marked the start of his new life, and thus called for a new *kartir* to be painted across both sides of his *chajan*. Of course this painting was more elaborate than the sort that would be done for a first birth, and Anok took her time mixing the deep red and the ochre, carving out the design with the sharpest *maata* she had, so that it would be the deepest of his *katira*. She could feel him watching her as she worked, and for that reason, rarely looked up from the paints. When he came near, she would whack at him with the brushes as a joke, threatening to paint his knees rather than the *chajan's*, but even then, she wouldn't look into his face. After he was chosen to lead, she was even more remote, and huddled against the pole when once he stood behind her and put his hand on her shoulder as she carved out a spot. But the next evening, when he returned from the far village, he could make out, by feel as much as by his waning sight, her small mark on the inside surface of his *chajan's* thigh, carved as deep as any.

XXV

"THIS COFFEE TASTES like silt from the river bottom," said Claudio, dipping his finger into the sludge.

"Just the way you like it!" said Joaquim, dumping their ashtray into a bucket as Claudio patted him on the back.

Of all the cafes in Belem, Joaquim's chosen one was *Le Figaru*, in the shadow of the Teatro da Paz, because it attracted the artists, the actors, the academics from the new university, and the misfits who lived on the fringes of such fringe professions. By the age of thirteen, he had managed to talk his way into a job there, washing dishes, emptying ashtrays, and waiting on the regulars, who called him Jobao and pulled the brim of his grey felt banded hat down over his thin face to his collar bones. While his school friends were out playing soccer or roaming the streets in packs, looking for girls to avoid and then whisper about, he was talking to grizzled old men about socialism, and the Constructivist movement, and Mario Quintana. (*"O destino e o acaso que enloqueceu . . ."*). And of course, treasured among all the grizzlies, as he called them, were the adventurers, marked by their darkened skin and cracked fingernails and disregard for how they smelled, who told of strange monkey-eating tribes and gunfights with loggers and enormous snakes, the girths of which bested their own. They were the early crowd, the first ones to arrive in the morning, and it was worth it to Joaquim to pull himself out of bed before dawn to open the café for them an hour early, before even the owner arrived. They never minded the day-old pastries, which was fortunate, as the delivery truck from the bakery didn't make its rounds until nearly a quarter past six.

"More sludge?" said Joaquim, looking into Claudio's cup.

Orlando laughed. Abarta, the owner, walked in past them with a nod, singing *"Bom dia! Bom dia!"* in every direction, scratching himself as he went. That was usually the cue for Orlando to start chiding Joaquim not to be late for school, which he was every morning anyway, in large part because of them. Instead, they motioned for Abarta to come over, and showed him the sludge with mock indignation.

"This one we no longer regard as qualified to make the coffee."

"Pois nao! Pois nao! Nao foi nada!" said Abarta with a good-humored frown.

"I think we're going to need to take this one away with us, for some training. Can you part with him for a month or so? I promise that by the time we return him to you, he'll be the finest brewer in Belem!"

Joaquim watched, wide-eyed, not sure what he was hearing.

"Take him away!" said Abarta, patting him on the back. "He's ruining me with his terrible reputation for sludge!"

"What do you think, boy? Want to go? We're down one assistant, and thought you might fit the bill. Can you manage it? Whose permission do you need to get?"

Joaquim's face fell. There was only his father at home, and although he barely saw him—his father was asleep when he left, and also by the time he got home—he relied on the money his son made at the café. "I guess not," he said quietly, looking at the ground.

"Of course, there'll be a stipend up front in case you don't come back."

"What's a stipend?"

"How much do you pay him here per week? About two cruzeros? That's about what he's worth, huh? Anyway, bring me the check, and write the number on it, so we can see how well you think of him."

Abarta brought over the check on a small black wooden plate, as he did each day; the *sertanistas* never ran a tab the way the artists did. When Joaquim leaned in to try to see what was written on it, Orlando pushed him away. "So you're sure you can let us have him? One month only?"

Abarto knocked the ashes from his cigarette into Orlando's cup. "I know you two. One month, and then one year, and then forever!"

Orlando shrugged and turned to count out bills into the tray. "Pay your busboy and get him out of here." Abarto took out the price of the coffee and the stale brioche and placed the rest in Joaquim's hand. Joaquim's eyes widened again when he saw that he was being given three times as much as his usual month's wages.

"Now run that over to your father, and tell them at the school that you'll be out, so they don't start to miss that snoring commotion from the back of the class. Meet us back here with your clothes by half past ten."

Joaquim stuffed the money into his pocket and headed for the door.

"I've heard from Alejandro's kid that that's what he does—he really does sleep all day, with his head on the desk!" said Orlando after Joaquim left.

XXVI

WHEN JAMES'S BELONGINGS had been laid out on the bed, Larry looked them over and found them all familiar. There were some things, khaki pants and socks and white v-neck T-shirts, which James owned in multiples. The others, the green-and-white checked shirt with snaps instead of buttons, and the blue short-sleeve shirt with the pleated pockets, and the olive canvas roll-up hat, with their spots and holes and stretched-out places, bore the marks of their specific, visceral importance; Larry was sure that he could find them, if he looked, in the pictures on the stack in the living room. He stood back and surveyed them, understanding well enough that all losses give way to other losses, that the things that were laid out in front of him belonged together, like a set of china dishes the integrity of which was lost when the smallest piece was broken. He took the green-and-white shirt and put it to one side. The socks and underwear went into a shopping bag to be left at the church, and the rest of the clothing was piled in the center of the bed. After hesitating for a minute, Larry placed the pile neatly into James's pack on the floor, as though to ready him for a journey.

Certain principles of packing were transparent to Larry; he had an intuitive feel for exactly the things he would need for comfort under the most difficult of circumstances, the right selection of books, and the pen that felt best in his hand, and the perfect metal box to hold the bottles of pills and vitamins that James had assembled and labeled. He packed in anticipation of the events that would take place inside himself, because he did not know how to prepare for the events of the world. Throughout the next two days, things were sorted out and condensed and refined. His possessions were mingled with James's and then divided up again. He lined his books against the pillows with their spines out and moved his eyes from title to title, acknowledging each one. At last, he pulled out a few of them—his old boxed copy of *The Lord of the Rings*, Henry Walter Bates, the *Aeneid*, James's battered Comte, a paperback copy of Van Gogh's letters—and put them in his pack on top of his clothes. Then he reached into James's pack and pulled out a few things that James might need were he to change his mind and join him after all, an extra hammock and *mosquitero*, his roll-up hat, the checked shirt, and laid them on top of the books. At last he turned and knocked on Jorge's open door. When Jorge looked up, he came in and put James's small gold penknife beside his elbow. Jorge turned and smiled at him reluctantly, standing to put the knife in his pocket. But instead of sitting down again, he pushed in his chair and walked with Larry towards the door.

"You and Joaquim are going to have to be ready at 5," he said.

"Where are you going?" said Larry.

"To my place. I haven't slept there in a week."

Larry followed him to the front door and stood awkwardly beside him.

"Who's Martina?" he asked.

Jorge looked at him for a minute in silence. "James was oblivious too," he said, "and I loved him like a father."

"Oh," said Larry, looking at the ground.

XXVII

OVER TWENTY YEARS, the memory of his father had eroded almost completely, but if Jorge had noticed, he never admitted it to himself. The images that bound the two of them together had become rote from overuse, as unremarkable as the thumbtacks with which he pinned his maps and memos to the bulletin board on the kitchen wall next to the phone. Thus, when Martina Barend—after knocking over his shopping bag at the market and helping him retrieve the onions that had rolled beneath the partitions between the stalls, and compensating for the bread that had slipped from his bag into the dust through the purchase of two ices from a street vendor—had leaned forward on the bench on which they sat and introduced herself by saying, "Moretti's not Brazilian. So tell me where you came from," the words he used to answer her barely claimed his attention.

"I came here with my parents from Italy when I was four," he said.

"And how old are you now?"

"I'm twenty-nine."

"And what work do you do?" she continued.

"Is this a job interview?" said Jorge, simultaneously amused and irritated. "I'm a pilot."

"And what does your father do?" she said, clearly not yet satisfied.

"Why?" he asked, suddenly angry.

"That always says a lot," she said.

"He's dead," he said.

"How?"

"That's kind of personal," said Jorge, reaching to pick up his bag and then putting it down again at his feet. "Thanks for the ice."

"I'd like to know," she said.

Jorge regarded her for a minute, her heart-shaped face and her nut-shaped eyes with their intensity of color and expression. Then, despite himself, he started, while she leaned in to hear him over the commotion of the market behind them.

"In Italy, he was a potter," he began, "but when he got here, he got a job at the *Museu*, restoring artifacts, and ended up meeting this guy who got him a job with the IPS, the Indian Protection Service." She nodded as if she knew the story already, and waved him on. "He was trying to broker a deal between this tribe and a mining company that wanted their land, and the Indians took him hostage, and these two friends of his tried to rescue him, but they couldn't, and they barely got out themselves."

"So you hate those friends of his?" said Martina, as though she were nonchalantly handing him a wasps' nest.

"No," Jorge shot back with pure anger. "I love them. They risked their lives for him. They're like fathers to me."

"I meant that too," she said.

"So why don't you tell me where *you're* from?" he said, aggressively.

"Rotterdam, Lyon, Amsterdam, Munich," she said, folding the empty paper cone that had held her ice.

"And what does *your* father do?" he asked, less with interest than out of a wish for revenge.

"Birkenau," she said, as though she had decided to take back the nest for herself. "The camp. And my mother and my sister."

When he was silent in response, she went on. "So you must know something about ceramics. Why don't you stop by my shop sometime, and give me some pointers?"

"I don't know anything about ceramics," said Jorge,

"It must be somewhere in your blood," she said. "You could give it a try. 172 *Bartolomeu de Gusmao*," she said, smiling at him as he stood up and gathered his bags.

XXVIII

AFTER YEARS OF squatting and facing the *chajans* from sunup to sunset, Anok had become used to speaking over her shoulder, without looking up into the faces of those she addressed. Meanwhile, everyone else had grown used to talking to her back, knowing that she could tell by their voices what their expressions and gestures were like. Yet while her posture had come over the years to be as unremarkable as that of the *chajans* themselves, her face had become that much less familiar, and therefore all the more startling, even when her expression and her tone of voice were kind. Even her short stature, the fact that she seemed to shrink so much as she aged that most of the men in Pahquel might easily have picked her up and moved her at will between the three interconnected villages, made her seem inhuman and therefore frightening, lending her fragility itself a fierce and threatening aspect. This was the real reason why even those who were closest to her always addressed her by her honorific, *Ak*, and watched her from the corners of their eyes while she moved with her pigments from hut to hut. And it was one of the reasons she had remained with Asator for as long as she had; because she knew that he was the only one whose regard for her was based upon something other than fear.

XXIX

SARA DIDN'T GO with them to the airport. Ever since Jorge had started to fly, she had refused to see him off. Instead, she insisted that he drive the five blocks to her house every morning before the sun was up and wait while she reached into a small ceramic pot for a one *cruzero* coin, which she would give him as a loan, after securing his commitment to repay it. The *cruzero* was always warm when he took it, even on chilly mornings; it contained the heat of her anxiety, which he could feel for a minute as it fluttered against his skin and broke through the veins in his arm, disappearing into his bloodstream. As they drove off, he looked up to see his mother in the window, ephemeral on the other side of the glass in the gray half-light, her hands empty at her sides.

In the back seat, Larry and Martina studied each other's knees in silence, sizing each other up, and then turned away to look out their windows onto opposite halves of the world. The landscape streamed by on either side of the cab like the two rivers, one black and one clear-running, that came together with a force too strong to let them mingle. The car seemed to follow a river's course, turning first one way and then another, heading toward a gray metal hangar that stood off somewhat from the main part of the airport. They pulled up at a door in the side of the corrugated metal hut and began unloading their bags onto the pavement

"Sure you're ready?" Joaquim addressed himself to Larry's back.

"Umm," said Larry, embarrassed to be asked within earshot of Martina. It was the sort of innocuous question that he hated the most, the kind that

that drew attention to the fact that the gulf between his intentions and the world's purposes was wider and deeper than he thought.

"Have you flown in one of these?" Martina asked.

"Only his old one," Larry said, still unable to look at her. "Have you?"

"It's a great plane," she said.

Joaquim looked at Jorge, who was gassing it, and smiled. "Maybe I'll turn you in after all," he said.

Martina laughed.

Jorge scowled. He put away the hose and spent a long time positioning their bags in the hold, moving them back and forth until at last, standing back to look at his arrangement, he nodded that he was satisfied. Then he motioned them in, in the same configuration as in the car, with Joaquim in front.

As the doors slammed shut on either side of Larry, a panic rose in his throat. The whole plane shook as the engine started up, and the vibrations made it impossible for him to tell how much of the tremor came from within and how much from outside himself. They taxied for what felt like several minutes and then stopped, the silence of the wheels revealing the sounds of the plane's organs working, as a runner will hear his heart beat in his ears as he stands at the starting block waiting for the gun. Just as suddenly, the plane took off with a roar and a jolt that made the bags slide backwards. Larry sat up in horror, unable to decipher from the sound they made whether they had become hopelessly unbalanced. There were windows on either side of him, but they were small and steamed over, and thus had almost nothing to tell him about their relationship to the ground. He pressed his feet into the floor and held onto the wall with one hand, nearly reaching with the other for Martina's arm.

"How are things back there?" Jorge called.

"Some of the bags slid around," Larry called back.

"Don't worry," said Jorge. "It happens. When we stop, we'll fix it."

The airport outside Itatuba was a dirt runway and an old shack. When they landed, Jorge took a ring of keys from his pocket and motioned for Martina to walk with him. Larry was struck by his having a key for the padlock on the shack's door; he imagined him walking quietly through the *Mercado Modelo* in Santarem, stopping to pick out oranges while the ring on his belt contained keys for all the secret, deserted shacks in the farthest corners of the jungle. Jorge and Martina came back carrying boxes of cooking pots and tools and medicines left over, Joaquim explained, from an aborted attempt to contact a tribe 90 miles to the south. With Larry looking on, Jorge loaded them in the back of the plane and began to move them around with the other baggage. This time, he pulled rubber cords from the sides of the cabin and fastened them in place. "Now you don't have to worry," he said as he cleaned his glasses, in a voice that mingled the smallest measure of sympathy with a larger portion of disdain.

Larry looked at the glasses in Jorge's hand and, without intending to retaliate, asked, "Do they let you fly with glasses?"

Jorge let out a laugh that was almost a smirk. "This isn't the *U*-nited States of America," he said.

Joaquim pushed Larry into the front seat and got in back with Martina. When the plane started up again, Larry felt the same sensations as before, but because now he was sitting beside Jorge and could tie specific sounds to specific movements of Jorge's hands, and because he could see out the windows, it was as if he were at last being offered an explanation for things that had frightened him with their indeterminacy before. Jorge taxied to the end of the runway and then turned around so that they could take off in the opposite direction.

When the plane lifted off, its wheels seemed to graze the uppermost tips of the branches. Then they were airborne, and more and more appeared, as though a curtain were being pulled aside in stages to reveal the breadth of the world. What had been individual trees became threads in a carpet of finer and finer weave. On this carpet lay, at rest, a translucent snake whose scales, blue and silver, flashed when they caught the sun. All was quiet, Larry sensed, in that world beyond the crackling of the radio and the grind of the propellers. The horizon turned so gracefully as they turned, and the soft green surface rose and fell, in the measured rhythm of breathing. Only once, when Larry looked down, did he see a blemish on that perfect body, a bald and ashen wound through which the dark blood oozed. It disappeared from view as the plane turned again and headed due west.

From such a great height, it was possible to see and to think. The four of them sat absorbed in private thoughts they could never say out loud. Jorge stared straight ahead, as though he had their destination already fixed in his view, but Larry continued to look down. He imagined them flying higher and higher, until it was impossible to tell which was smaller and more fragile, them or the earth. Then the plane began to slow and sink, lowering itself by inches towards the land, caressing the mottled textures with its shadow. In an instant, the pulse of time began to race, the trees became single again and flew by, and the wheels hit a hard ribbon of gravel and dirt. They bounced and rattled to a stop at the end of an overgrown runway, a stone's throw from the river, beside a few old rowboats that lay lodged in the sand like decomposing fish.

XXX

JORGE WAS THE sort of person who liked to do only one thing at a time. Martina knew better than to talk to him when he was working on his plane, or when he was thinking, and kept a book with her, not so much to read as to reassure him that he was safe from the possibility of her interrupting. She sat off to the side while he carried their packs and duffel bags from the plane to the boat, arranging and balancing them as he had in the hold. Joaquim and Larry were given the job of dumping the boxes to check them for insects and lizards and then loading them back onto the plane, a task that largely kept them out of Jorge's field of vision. Thus, when Jorge recognized the old familiar tightening of the muscles in his stomach that he associated with being interrupted and looked around to see the others silently occupied, he had to acknowledge that the disruptions he felt were only in his mind.

He had worked hard to convince himself that this particular mission was routine, and had given no conscious thought at all to Lamurii. His blindness might have been predictable, given the tendency of things one wishes for or dreads over long periods of time to recede in importance compared to the wishing or dreading itself. But Jorge had not only minimized the trip's importance but forgotten about it altogether. He found himself listing the errands he needed to do when he got home from Paruqu, envisioning his own front door, his kitchen, rather than the straw huts and stubble of the open field at Lamurii he had seen from the air. But like all floundering swimmers, things that are forgotten in that way tend to grasp out for other things, pulling them beneath the surface in an effort to save themselves. Thus, Jorge realized, a half an hour down river, that he had left the second of his two small canvas travel bags on the floor beside his seat on the plane, and despite the fact that there was nothing in them that he needed, felt compelled to ask them to turn back to retrieve it.

XXXI

MEMORY RETURNED TO Larry, along with the tingling sensation of circulation returning to a limb, as they stepped out of the boat at Paruqu. There was the rickety old dock, still balancing uncertainly on its thin, wayward legs, and the open shack that served as a bar, and the tiny houses crouching together on streets that barely got started before they contracted to a trickle like drying rivers. The same slat-walled shop marked the center of the town, and the hotel, which was not a hotel at all, but the Prefect's house, still wore its drooping jacaranda robe askew, not having bothered, in all those years, to straighten it. Larry left the others with the boat and made the climb from the riverbank alone. To be the one to lead the approach was a role for which he was completely unsuited, but he knew he needed to prove himself, especially to Jorge. Pushing against his nature, he forced himself up to the threshold of Sr. Catalpa's door, where he hesitated for a minute with his hand on the knocker, listening to his heartbeat in his ears.

The door was opened by the Prefect himself, whom he immediately recognized by his bald head and his cartoonishly ingratiating manner. Sr. Catalpa looked over Larry's shoulder to each side, and only after finding no one else behind him, welcomed him in with exaggerated warmth.

"Could you be Larry?" he said in what sounded like mock disbelief.

Larry nodded and stepped past him into the large foyer with its faded flocked wallpaper and its worn Persian rugs. He remembered how on his previous visit he had found the interior of the house to be not just welcoming but almost magical, in that it contained all the elements, save a working bathroom, which at the age of eleven he had assumed a proper mansion would have, a chandelier and paintings in gilt frames and floors of marble rather than wood. Now, looking around, it was precisely the house's European pretension that unsettled him, as though its owner had been one of the many madmen consumed by the need to erect, in the heart of the jungle, an Alpine village, a grand theater, an American suburb, against the humbling press of the forest. He stopped short of associating such colonial delusions with his own efforts, which bore no obvious trace of the sort of bravado that would lead to the erection of an ornately paneled library and the hanging of damask curtains in a place in which mildew would inevitably gain the upper hand.

"Come in, come in! You're late!" said Sr. Catalpa, gesturing toward a clutch of overstuffed chairs. "I was beginning to wonder whether you were coming. Is James down with the boat?"

Larry's palms began to sweat. He suddenly felt woozy and overheated. "No, he isn't. He died on the 23rd, and I'm here with a few of his friends."

Sr. Catalpa sat heavily into the nearest of the chairs, and Larry, in reflexive sympathy, sat down heavily across from him. "It couldn't be! I have a letter dated less than a month ago! He said he was feeling better!" He started to rise from his chair as though to find the letter and prove Larry wrong, but seemed to realize the futility of the effort and sank back into the chair again, lowering his face into his hands. The top of his bald head floated like the moon in the room's semi-darkness, glowing and silent and inert. Then, with resolve, the moon shot up as the Senor straightened suddenly and strode over to Larry's chair. "Will you all stay a while?"

"We'd like to stay overnight, and hike in a bit to spread some of James's ashes. Then we're going to head out to Lamurii. And then, if it's okay, I was planning to come back soon to work on James's research."

"Ah, the elusive research. Are you going to be as secretive as James was?"

"I guess so," said Larry.

"Of course you remember our little altercation last time? I didn't like it then, and I like it even less now, in view of your current situation."

Larry couldn't afford to know to which current situation the Prefect was referring, and had no recollection of an argument. He did remember, if indistinctly, the odd wallpaper in the foyer, and the patterns in the mosaic on the floor, and a smell that he could now identify as mold. He stood up and followed Sr. Catalpa out the door, into the bright sunlight and down the gravel path to the river.

As they approached, Larry could see Joaquim and Jorge sitting side-by-side on the dock, looking down into the water as Martina, to Jorge's right, surveyed the far shore. The two men were clearly engrossed in a conversation to which Martina was indifferent; Larry wondered the extent to which he was the subject of it. He strained to listen as he and Sr. Catalpa came up from behind, but the thick air absorbed sound like a sponge so that even their footsteps made only muted, indefinite thuds.

"Ah!" said Sr. Catalpa, forcefully enough to penetrate the air, when he caught sight of Joaquim. Joaquim and Jorge stood up and turned to face him, but neither stepped forward.

"Welcome," Sr. Catalpa said pointedly to Joaquim, walking towards him with his hand outstretched.

"Yes," Joaquim said, with a nod of his head. He shook Sr. Catalpa's hand and turned to survey the river. "I've been looking forward to seeing you again."

"I'm Jorge Moretti," said Jorge loudly. "And this is Martina Berand."

"Welcome, welcome," said Sr. Catalpa, also loudly, extending his hand to Martina and bowing slightly. "What can I carry?" he said nervously, looking over at Joaquim. "Should I send Gabriel?"

"Is that too heavy?" said Jorge, jumping down into the boat and handing up a pack. He sounded irritated, and threw Larry's pack up to him with more force than was needed.

Sr. Catalpa caught the pack with a grunt and shouldered it with difficulty. "Shall we?" he said, again addressing himself to Joaquim.

They turned and walked silently up the bluff with Larry, who was to have led them, bringing up the rear. He could tell from the way Sr. Catalpa raised his eyes now and again to look at Joaquim that however sincere his grief at the loss of James might have been, it was also fickle, its intensity rechanneled now into an anxious wish to win Joaquim's favor. And he could tell, from the easy way he swung his arms as he balanced the weight of his pack, that Joaquim was enjoying immensely, with a kind of understated bravado, the prospect that their encounter would play itself out like an extended practical joke. Larry couldn't afford the thought that the person he had no choice but to trust more than any other might act cruelly, even in jest, so he held back, allowing a buffer to emerge between himself and the two older men. Instead, he tried to move closer to Jorge and Martina, to highlight their kinship as outsiders to this unexpected drama, consoling himself with the thought that he would soon be on his own, in the company of creatures who were more akin to his nature.

When they reached the Prefect's house, they set their packs in a pile on the verandah and went inside. They were too coarse and sweaty for their surroundings, trampling with their big unwieldy boots across the inlaid floor. Sr. Catalpa motioned for them to sit. He pulled in a chair from the dining room for himself and stood behind it, surveying his guests, wearing a nervous smile that made it difficult to tell whether he was intentionally allowing them to get their bearings or had rather forgotten his lines. In the awkward silence before he spoke, the roar of a generator swelled in for a minute as it started up and then receded while the electric lights, made necessary by the overgrowth and the dark curtains that partially covered the windows, flickered like the candle flames they were molded to resemble.

"What can I get you all to drink?" said Sr. Catalpa, as though the generator had suddenly started him up too.

Larry leaned forward, trying not to get his sweat on the back of his chair.

"Is Lucia with you here?" Joaquim asked, looking around.

"I guess James hadn't mentioned it. She's been gone almost three years now."

"He hadn't," said Joaquim. "I'm sorry. So who is still living with you?"

"They're all gone," said Sr. Catalpa. "My three moved out in April. They're living with Marta and Carlos in Brasilia; Jose, my youngest, is starting high school in the fall. I'm actually going to follow him there in December, as soon as I get things squared away here."

"Very good," said Joaquim, nodding, and Sr. Catalpa's shoulders seemed to ease at the neck, as though he had taken Joaquim's comment as a general assessment of his competence.

"Let me get you a drink," said the Senor, pulling on his fingers, backing out through the far doorway.

An old woman entered and placed a tray on the table in front of them. With hands covered in dark freckles, she rearranged the bottles and the glasses several times over, as though playing a slow but complicated shell game. Then she receded and Sr. Catalpa entered again.

"Help yourselves to whatever you like," he said.

"I see you're still not hurting for the finer things," said Joaquim, raising a bottle of whiskey to the thin strip of light between the curtains.

"Not in that sense, no," said Sr. Catalpa, pouring himself a drink from the bottle when Joaquim put it down. "So what are your plans?" he said, looking back and forth between them.

"We're just here for the night, getting Larry's feet wet in that river out there," said Joaquim between sips of his drink. "We'll go in the morning."

After dinner, Sr. Catalpa led them through the empty rooms upstairs, but Jorge and Joaquim slipped away to string up their hammocks between the columns on the porch. Jorge motioned to Martina for hers, and tied it next to his with the same precision he had used for parcels in the hold of his plane. Larry watched them for a minute and then pulled out his own hammock, stringing it between the wall and the column closest to his pack.

The verandah was somehow more reassuring than the rooms inside had been. A wisp of a breeze caressed the overhanging vines and brushed the moisture from the air, infusing them with the jungle's nocturnal perfume. All around them, the atmosphere brimmed with obscure activity; insect noises, and the calls of mysterious creatures rousing themselves for the night, and the violent thrashing sounds of the branches those creatures released as they sprang from their beds. The world Larry saw as he looked back in through the window, a room overflowing with yellow light and heavy furniture, from which he was separated by that rarest of forest phenomena, a metal window screen, and in which Sr. Catalpa and the old woman darted back and forth like fish in an aquarium, bore no relation at all to the dark, raucous, forbidding world on the threshold of which he stood. As he hung his hammock from the metal hooks on the wall and on the column across from it, he nearly displaced an elegantly painted, thin-legged spider the size of his hand, who had intended to string her own hammock from the same rampart. He avoided her web as he followed Joaquim and Jorge out to the edge of the trees to relieve himself, but his face was brushed several times by other webs he couldn't see.

Finally, as the four of them lay cocooned in their netting, the lights that spilled over them from inside the house went out and they were left together in darkness. Joaquim and Jorge talked in low voices, their silences filled by the forest, and Larry remembered clearly how happy he had been on those nights in the forest with James, when they had strung the feet of their hammocks together from the same sturdy bough, and had talked until at some point, often in mid-sentence, James let out a snort to mark the boundary between waking and sleep. Even his secret fear of jaguars would diminish then, drowned out by the magically reassuring protective force of James's noisy presence. Larry felt the same contentment as he lay in the dark between Jorge and Joaquim, but his calm was disrupted, at intervals, by a flash of terror at the realization of what it meant to be alone.

"He hasn't changed a bit," said Joaquim, not so much interrupting the swell of Larry's fear as creating another track in his awareness alongside it.

"How do you know him?" asked a tiny corner of Larry, shaking itself free of the grip of his thoughts.

"I fired him," said Joaquim with a laugh. "We used to call him The Chihuahua." The obvious contempt Joaquim seemed to have for Sr. Catalpa's histrionic temperament made Larry feel even more isolated in his fear.

"You don't seem to like him," he said.

"Never trust anyone who can be swayed by a nice pat."

Larry felt his shame swell like mercury in a bulb. "But James trusted him."

"James had an unparalleled capacity for trust."

"You fired him because you couldn't trust him?"

"I fired him out of pity. He wasn't cut out for it. He's been much better off where he is, pushing papers and hobnobbing at meetings and hiring his English governesses for his children."

Larry didn't respond, but turned his thoughts away from Joaquim's talk to Jorge's silence, in order to determine whether Jorge was still angry, or had fallen asleep. Against the background of the forest's hum, he couldn't even make out the sound of breathing.

"Is Jorge asleep?" he finally asked Joaquim, rather than speak to Jorge directly.

"No, I'm not," said Jorge, sounding irritated but awake.

Martina laughed. "You'll know it, when he's asleep," she said.

"What's wrong?" said Larry at last.

"I figured out why I can't stand you sometimes," said Jorge, under the cover of darkness.

"Why is that?"

"Because you remind me of me."

They were all quiet for a long time, and the forest's skein of sound wrapped itself around them, around the porch and around the house and around the village. Under so many layers, Larry's voice sounded muffled when he spoke. "Thanks," he said. "That's an honor." He felt his hammock jerk to the side, and then Jorge's hand on his arm on top of his *mosquitero*. He reached for it and held it through the mesh for a minute, and when he released it, their two hammocks swung back and forth to the same rhythm, both moving, by increments, toward rest.

XXXII

THE WORK OF painting a *chajan* is not a process of applying pigments to a background, of envisioning an image and imposing it upon the smooth, cool surface of a feet-and-legs. Rather, one must have the gift of seeing what is inevitable, already there beneath the surface, and of spiriting it outward through the application of certain substances so that it can be seen by all. That was Anok's task. Nearly every day, someone would approach her saying, "Anok-Ak, my baby was named a hand of days ago, and still it is not on my *chajan!*" or, "Ak Anok, Pinini's spirit will be lost if you don't mark my *chajan* today!" So many of them thought she could just rush over with her *maata* and her pigments and her brushes of stacked leaves and sheathe their *chajans* as quickly as she could move the dyes. In their eyes, she was the obstacle between them and the ancestors as surely as she was the medium through which access could be achieved. Only she understood that when an image rose to the surface to merge with the one she painted, it was always stronger than she was, pulling life and death into it, severing their ties to time.

XXXIII

BY SIX O'CLOCK, Martina and Joaquim had already finished their breakfast of imported cakes and jams, had pushed aside their bone china teacups, which had been filled relentlessly by the Senor, and were stretching and yawning as they rose from the table. Jorge, who could not sit still long enough to eat with them, had already hauled his own bags down to the dock, and barely looked their way as he appeared at the top of the rise to reemphasize his obvious anxious readiness to set off.

"Larry's not up yet?" he said with quiet irritation, as though to suggest without saying so that his companions were to blame. He strode through the parlor and out through the front door with the three of them behind him to the place where Larry's hammock still hung at the far end of the verandah. But he didn't need to pull at the rolled-up bedding inside it to know in an instant the futility of the dramatic gesture he had suddenly longed to make, a satisfying flourish of the bedclothes the intensity of which might have offered him a split second of relief.

"Jesus Christ!" he hissed, kicking the hammock from the bottom in a move that brought him none of the satisfaction the other might have offered. "This is your fault!" he yelled towards Joaquim. "You must think I'm stupid! You put him up to it! You planned this!" He turned on his heel and took off down toward the water.

When the others caught up, they found him crouching sideways on the pier, his eyes fixed on the place where the clutch of battered rowboats encircled a small plot of disrupted sand.

"Well, what do you know?" said Joaquim to himself as he approached, with a tone like admiration in his voice. "I'm really surprised he did it! I really didn't think he would."

"You put him up to it!" yelled Jorge, "It was your idea! No wonder you dragged us all this way out here for half a day! No wonder you didn't let me get him up with the rest of us!"

"Actually, I wouldn't have given him that much credit, when push came to shove. I'm really quite amazed."

"Why are you yelling at Joaquim?" Martina shot back, stepping forward and putting her hand on his arm as though sensing the need to restrain him. "He's not the one who made up Larry's mind!"

"The whole thing was so obvious! The only reason I didn't stop it was that I trusted you! I should have known better than to trust you!" Jorge shouted, breaking free of her grasp. "Aren't you going to do anything about it?" he yelled as he headed for their boat.

"You're not going to find him," said Joachim soberly. "You have no idea which way he went."

"He said he was going to leave his coordinates," said Jorge, moving towards the house.

"For emergencies only," said Joachim, bowing his head in acknowledgement of Jorge's ironic smirk. "And I doubt that any information he left would help you very much. Either he's three hours downriver or he's stowed the boat somewhere. You can go after him, or we can go to Lamurii. Your choice."

"So you'd leave him, just like that?" said Jorge, betrayed by the waver in his voice. Joachim turned and reached out for Martina's arm, motioning to Sr. Catalpa to lead the way. "We'll be in the house," he said behind his shoulder.

Martina waved them on. "Do you want me to go too?" she said, after regarding him in silence for a minute, watching his shoulders shake noiselessly.

"Yes," snapped Jorge.

She turned and took a few steps up the path before she stopped again.

"Be where I can find you," he said.

XXXIV

"HE'S SO YOUNG!" said Sr. Catalpa, worrying his fingers and sucking on his teeth.

"What would you suggest?" said Joachim. A soft breeze blew through the verandah, as though to demonstrate how benign nature could be. "I imagine he'll be back within the week. You'll take care of him?"

"Of course," said Sr. Catalpa, indignant at the question.

"How often is the mail boat coming through these days? Still once a month?"

"Yes, but in an emergency I can have Joao run something over to the mission; they'll get it out within three days."

"Good then. Best for you to write to Sara Moretti—I'll leave the address—and she can send Jorge to pick him up." Joachim looked at him. "Don't send him home alone."

"There's something else," said Sr. Catalpa, as Martina approached them from the head of the path.

"He needs you," she said to Joachim, nodding her head in the direction of the pier. "Are you sure this is the right thing?"

Joachim stood up and walked toward the path. "I'll be back," he said.

XXXV

JORGE HAD MOVED to the edge of the pier, where he sat hunched up, looking down into the water.

"Ahoy, cap'n!" said Joaquim quietly as he sat down beside him.

Jorge shifted and turned his face away.

"I didn't know," said Joaquim. "It wasn't planned."

"I don't believe you."

Joaquim considered him in silence and then looked down. A seamless collage of shadow and reflection lay breathing at their feet.

"Maybe I did and I didn't, both," said Joaquim. "Maybe I was testing him. But what I know for sure is that if he was determined to go, we couldn't have stopped him. The toughest part would have been between Itatuba and here. At least we got him this far."

"He's too young," said Jorge, crumpled over, his head suspended between his knees. "He's alone!" Behind his reflection, fat grey fish were gliding slowly; sluggish, bloated thoughts, distorted by the ripples from his tears. When he caught sight of Joaquim's reflection beside his, he sat up and wiped his eyes with the sleeve of his shirt. "You don't have to say anything to Martina about this," he said, gesturing towards his tear-streaked face.

"You know what it's like to be lost, to be stuck," said Joaquim. "I know James didn't want that for him."

"Easy for you to say!" said Jorge, retrieving his handkerchief from his pocket with difficulty, grateful for the distraction of the struggle.

"And your father didn't want it for you either," Joaquim added as he stood up and straightened his trousers. "There was no one he loved more than you."

XXXVI

TO LIVE IN the forest, one must learn to see. The kind of vision demanded there is unlike the sort one relies on when crossing the street, or watching a movie, or reading a magazine. Most important of all is the ability to sense minute contrasts of movement, as though through the eyes of a cat; the odd sway of a liana that exposes its true identity as an anaconda, the quick jerking leap of a monkey high in the treetops, or the strange stillness of the parakeet among the quivering leaves. Upon first entering the forest, one is invariably disappointed at what appears to be a monotonously uniform terrain, strangely empty, devoid of the exotica promised in the brochures of travel agencies and therefore felt, after all the effort of the trip, to be one's due. Those who come to the forest to stay however, soon learn to appreciate the effort required to tease apart the separate strands of motion from the mass of endlessly interwoven skeins. The beginner can only undertake such a task while standing still, pausing in mid-step along the trail.

There is the obscure, and the obvious. Walking beneath the crown of the pejibaye, one can be deluged by a thick white rain as all its blossoms fall at once in synchrony. One can watch the white liquid pour from a wound in the torso of a tree, or come face to face with a dozen white orchids, each the size of a human hand, arrayed in a cascade along a limb.

There are extremes of temperament and sound. One can look high into the treetops where two monkeys are fighting over a single crying infant, each pulling on an arm, or low to the ground, where a fallen baby sloth cries out for its mother, who will never make the effort to retrieve it.

There are things that are invisible and others too apparent to be seen.

Amid this cacophony of intention and activity, Larry noticed very little, and more than he could fathom. Most of all, he understood he had arrived in a place in which the weave of motion was so thick and tight that he would never—and always—be alone.

XXXVII

THERE WERE TENSIONS between Anok and Asator, which preceded their connection. Most prominent among these was Asator's refusal to act as *gitana* to Aran, as her protector in the community and in the world. When Asator said "she has all the *gitana* she needs," he meant to reassure her, but instead, his certainty incensed her, as though he had refused to offer her, when they lay together, a skin with which to cover herself, when she knew that he had many. It was true that Aron had had a *gitana*, but what good is the protection of something without presence or force, in the face of the living and the dead? It was this, more than anything else, that led Anok to keep their vow a secret, as though the need, the refusal, had also never existed.

XXVIII

MARTINA WASN'T THE sort of woman to shop, and the one store in Paruqu wasn't the sort of venue in which shopping occurred. The few shelves that lined its cane-slat walls held mostly canned goods, and the clothing that hung from a ceiling beam was of a purely functional sort, T-shirts and shorts and a few wilted belts drooping from a long metal hook. She scanned the makeshift counter, lifting and replacing a bottle of aspirin, a rusty box of Band-Aids, a similarly rusty fingernail scissors, when a dark-skinned woman appeared with a coffee cup in one hand and a cash box in the other. The woman stood in the doorway regarding her.

"How much for this?" Martina asked in Portuguese, holding up the nail scissors, not out of interest, but to engage her.

"Nao." said the woman, gesturing her lack of understanding.

Martina replaced the scissors and approached her, pointing to her coffee cup and then to herself.

"Café?" asked the woman.

"Nao," said Martina. "Chavena. Copo."

"Café!" said the woman.

"Nao," said Martina, suddenly furious at Jorge without knowing why. It was hard for her to remember that it was Larry rather than Jorge who had left them and was now wandering in the wilderness alone. She pointed to the woman's cup, and rolled an imaginary ball of clay between her hands, pinching and shaping the air. Then she held one hand up to drink from its edge.

"*Sim!*" said the woman, brightening. She pointed to a shelf on which a large assortment of rough cups and bowls were stacked. Underneath the shelf were wooden crates, filled with pots and cups of all sizes, all marked with the same pattern, which suggested to Martina that they were locally made.

Martina regarded them for several minutes, weighing them, smelling them, turning them slowly in her fingers, setting them down again. At last, she turned back to the woman, returning her hands to the air, moving them over imaginary clay, and pointing in the direction of the clutch of huts whose thatched roofs she had seen from the rear window of the Prefect's house.

"*Sim!*" said the woman after a long pause, motioning for Martina to follow her. The woman led her along the path that climbed the incline behind the store and then sloped down to a clearing nested in a crook in the riverbank. Beneath the slanting roof of a straw lean-to, a clutch of women squatted in a circle working lumps of clay as they sang. Martina stepped forward and squatted beside them in the marshy dirt. She motioned to the mound of clay between them and the oldest of the women pulled off a handful and passed it to her. As Martina started to work it, the women stopped talking for a minute to watch and then turned back to their conversation. They rolled the clay, forming it into coils, and laid the coils to dry slightly, pausing to take bites of acai, which they dipped into a bag of what looked like sugar before they ate. Then they fashioned the clay into rough bowls, pinching and turning it in the palms of their hands.

Everything about the clay was foreign to Martina—its smell, its texture, its consistency and color. The women grimaced when she held the lump to her lips and took a nibble from one corner, but when she started to roll, quickly and evenly, they nodded in approval and began to include her in their conversation, disregarding the fact that she didn't understand. When Martina broke off a small ball and covered it in leaves, pushing it into her pocket, they smiled their assent, and when their faces dropped suddenly, Martina responded in an instant, standing and turning to face Jorge's tense gaze.

"Where the hell have you been?" he spat at her.

"Waiting for you," she retorted. Behind her, the women twittered and pointed.

"I thought you were going to be at the house! It's ten o'clock! I don't even know if we have enough time now!"

"Don't you try that," said Martina sharply, turning back to the women. The oldest held out her hand and Martina placed her coil of clay in it, but the woman grasped her instead by the forearm, placing the coil on the ground. Martina grasped the forearms of each of them and then turned to follow Jorge up the path. At her back, the women whispered, breaking into soft whooping sounds when, at the top of the ridge, Martina pulled him toward her, forcing her arm across his shoulders between his sweaty shirt and the weight of his pack.

XXXIX

SOME DAYS, ANOK had to wonder whether Aran would grow up at all, let alone grow up well. She was by far the strongest and tallest of the hand-and-one-rains children, and seemed to take naturally to the spear, but when she wasn't out on a hunt, she was at her mother's side, trying to help, but too headstrong to take direction. While the other girls spent their time giggling together over Karata, Bata's son, while hoeing their rows halfheartedly, Aran did a hand of rows to each of theirs, bringing an extra measure of *kakana* to Anok's portion every day, but with it, an extra several measures of concern. And then there was the fact that Bata's son seemed determined to repay her indifference with interest enough for them both, a fact of which her mother couldn't help but be aware.

"What do you say?" she asked Aran one evening while they sat together on their *kaawa*, watching the trees become shadows. "Karata's got as much promise with the spear as you have."

"I'm not going to talk about it," said Aran with irritation, turning her back on her mother.

"But when will you?" said Anok sharply, twisting Aran's long braid and then dropping it onto her back. "What are you waiting for?"

"I'm doing things as they should be done," said Aran sharply.

The problem, Anok knew, was to be able to tell the difference between something that had been lost and something that had never existed.

"*ParaXa ki jitana,*" said Anok in a resigned voice.

"*ParaXa ki jitana,*" said Aran.

It wasn't that Anok was against the idea of doing things right, though she herself had never reaped the rewards of it; she knew the *jitana* should always have first chance as a suitor. But Karata seemed as fitting as any she could imagine. More fundamentally, she suspected, the ancestors shared her confusion as to whether, in truth, it would have been more right never to have had a child at all, or whether her life depended upon Aran, just as the lives of the ancestors depended with equal desperation and ambivalence upon her own.

XL

IT WASN'T UNTIL she began to sweep the floor that the old woman found the blue canvas bag wedged behind a column on the verandah. She called out to Sr. Catalpa who was just appearing at the head of the path from the river, back from seeing them off. He took the bag and ran with it under his arm, pushing aside his temptation to stop and look inside. When he reached the dock, he held it above his head, dangling it with both hands together by the handles, calling out to their retreating boat against the grind of the motor that fanned out behind them like a wake in the thick, moist air. "Joaquim! Jorge!" he cried, waving the bag above his head, barely able to make out Jorge's reluctant wave as their boat disappeared behind the thick stand of walnut that marked the first riverbend.

XLI

THERE WAS A stirring in the scrub as a dozen people, mostly women, appeared at the edge of the forest, carrying babies, talking among themselves, and paying their visitors no attention whatsoever. When Martina emerged from the plane and tested the ground after their rough landing in Lamurii, she felt reassured by the odd juxtaposition the group presented of the foreign and the familiar, the mingling of clothed and naked bodies: An old man stood on one leg among a circle of women, wearing only a loincloth and a black, silver-studded belt. A young girl wearing only a T-shirt cradled a monkey in her arms. There was the flash of a watch on a dark, bare wrist, the snap of plastic rifles in the hands of naked children. This was still the world Martina knew, in which at least some of the pieces were familiar, but the questionable thing was their capacity to fit together.

Jorge seemed oblivious to all of them; he went about his business, emotionlessly checking the tires and the wings, walking around, absurdly, as though to make sure his craft was solid, placing his hand here and there against its side. He opened the hold and began to unload the boxes, laying them at his feet and then stumbling on them as he pulled the next ones out. He caught his finger on the edge of one and swore quietly.

Joaquim stepped out slowly, stretched and walked forward, leaving them behind, until he had joined one of the circles under the trees, seamlessly, without any sign of a greeting.

"Should you go with him?" Martina asked Jorge, who squinted at her fiercely through his glasses as though he were having trouble remembering who she was.

"Not yet," he said, sounding not so much harsh, as she had expected, as weak, or confused. "We still don't know if they'll talk to me." He looked at the ground and turned his back to her as though to walk away, but stayed. At last, she took a few steps forward and stood beside him.

"You've never been here?" she asked.

"No." He pushed at the stubble of grass with his foot, sounding ashamed of the answer. "Joaquim has, of course."

Martina stood beside him silently for a while and then turned to look out from behind the plane's wing. There were perhaps thirty people now, standing in closed circles. Clearly, the principals were going to take a while to get into position. This was a state that she knew well, in which time stopped just short of a precipice.

A white man dressed in field pants and a blue shirt appeared and took his place among the others, like an actor who had not yet noticed that he had wandered onto the wrong set. Even from across the field, she could make out the flash of his eyes, which had more in common with the sky than with the slowly congealing human scene before them. At last, a man who was clearly the chief appeared at the opening, distinguished not by his stature or the nature of his adornment—he was wearing only a pair of faded navy swimming trunks—but by his capacity to perforate the invisible membrane that had confined his people to the far end of the clearing, allowing them to stream in after him as he walked with Joaquim towards the plane. As the chief approached, a silent ring formed around them; even the dogs seemed to sense the sudden solemnity of the gathering and took their places around the circle, looking out at nothing in particular as though they too, were using most of their energy to listen. The chief took Jorge by the elbow and started to pull him along. Then the whole group turned and began to flow behind them toward the gap in the trees. Joaquim hung back to walk beside Martina, speaking in a low voice.

"So Jorge told you why we're here?"

"Who's that guy?" said Martina, lowering her voice, gesturing behind them toward the blue-eyed figure at the end of the line.

Joaquim turned back just enough to survey the heads behind him before he began, in English. That's Kamar Sodeis. You might open a mental file on him."

"What should I put in it?"

"You know the context?"

"I don't know anything."

"When Marietto brokered the deal between the Lamurii and the Clarante Mining Company, it included a commitment to allow the CMC limited mining rights in the area, in exchange for a school and a clinic and a number of other things, including a share in the profits and the right to demarcate their land."

"So who's that guy?"

"The school was never built, and the stream was poisoned with mercury. There were six stillbirths in the village in the first two years alone. Marietto didn't know any of that when he came down. He never bothered to follow up; he'd just relied on the CMC's own internal reports. He never talked to us about coming here. I imagine he expected a hero's welcome. I didn't find out until two days after he left, and by then, it was too late."

"But what do I put in the file?" she said.

"So old blue-eyes was the field administrator for the CMC," he said, gesturing back over his shoulder. "I'll be interested to know who he's working for now."

"I hope Jorge resolves what he needs to resolve," Martina said loudly in Portuguese, catching a patch of blue moving toward her out of the corner of her eye when she turned to look behind her. She focused her eyes straight ahead, straining to make out the outline of Jorge's head among the dark heads that bobbed like floats on a rope in the water.

"To make his peace with it all would be good for him," said Joaquim, also loudly, in Portuguese. "He's been stuck for years now." They walked on in silence with Joaquim in front now that the path had narrowed, and, Martina assumed, Sodeis behind her. She looked at the folds of skin layering like poured batter on Joaquim's neck and tried to push aside the sensation of eyes teasing the place on the back of her own neck where her hair met her collar.

Within five minutes, the path broadened again. The sun streamed in towards them as though the clearing in front of them were a reservoir of light already swollen by the summer. Their chain wound around between two huts made of palm fronds and branches and out into the midst of the circular courtyard they had seen from the plane. The air was heavy with human smells—of skin, of tension, of manioc boiling in clay pots. What she hadn't noticed looking down on Lamurii was that most of the houses were open to the courtyard, lacking a fourth wall in whole or in part. Only one small hut stood outside the circle, its formal doorway fitted with a door, which was padlocked. The group shifted toward a small oasis of trees on the other side of the men's house, under which logs had been arranged like benches to take advantage of the shade.

"How about if you stand over there?" Joaquim whispered to Martina, gesturing toward the space between the open huts and the shack. "This is the men's area." He left her before she could reply and walked toward the circle, motioning for Jorge to sit beside him.

Both sides started speaking at once, in pointed, clipped bursts. She heard Jorge's voice rise and crack and stop. His hands were shaking, and a red glow gathered at the tips of his ears. He stood and the chief stood, and for a minute she thought they were going to fight. They walked off together, leaving the others in the dense pool of tension they left behind.

Joaquim stood up and came over to her.

"How are you holding up?"

"Fine," she said.

"Do you want to hear about it?" Joaquim said, looking away for a minute and nodding as some of the others who had been milling around the logs came over in the chief's absence and sat down.

"Is he okay?"

"He's suffering," said Joaquim, "as only Jorge can suffer. They've gone to find the man who killed Marietto, so that Jorge can lift the curse from him, and absolve him like the Pope." He made a cross in the air and grimaced.

As her eyes followed his hand, they caught the eye of the blue-eyed man, who had been standing at a distance from their circle. She took a few steps back, putting the shack between them. While the others milled around, whispering and spitting into the dirt, she stood on tiptoe to peer into the space between two haphazardly placed boards that were hammered on to form one of the shack's walls. Inside, she could make out plank shelves in the hazy darkness, and a desk on which papers and books were strewn. She leaned in, pushing her forehead against the boards, straining to look at one shelf in particular, which was piled with clay pots of various sizes.

"They're back," said Joaquim loudly. First Jorge's head and then the chief's, moved past the sun as the two men stepped into the tent of shadows underneath the tree. No sooner had Jorge settled himself on the bench than he got up again and walked out in the opposite direction, off into the trees behind the padlocked house. Instinctively, Martina followed, stopping when he stopped. The air was thick and still, muddying the birds' cries. As she turned to look back, the colors of the trees and the sky and the clay deepened, taking on the garish intensity of velvet. The man's blue eyes were shards of sky, and his blue shirt, as he stooped down next to the chief, was as penetrating as the blue at the center of a flame. On a perch in front of a house across the clearing, a parrot, preening under its wing, saturated the air with more varied color. From behind her, she heard the sound of retching. When Jorge came up, she reached for his arm and they turned back together toward the tent of trees, while the sky's blue eyes watched them go.

"What is it?" she asked.

"Careful what you wish for," said Jorge.

The debate had grown louder while they were gone, and no one looked up as they approached.

"Go and sit with them, and I'll go back with the dogs," Martina said.

"The discussion is over," said a voice in harsh, over-articulated Portuguese. Martina turned to face Sodeis, who was standing directly behind her.

"Is that for you to decide?" she said.

"Next time, find a better pretense," he said to Jorge.

"Sit down," Jorge hissed to Martina.

When the others registered that Martina was sitting in the men's circle, a roar of squawking and clucking and pointing suddenly erupted, a wave of attention formidable enough to push Sodeis to the background. Jorge pretended to shoo Martina away. She got up and went back to her place.

Joaquim stood up with his hand raised, and a silence fell.

"Why are you here?" said Sodeis coldly to Joaquim. "You know that everything was settled. You're ruining your own handiwork, is all."

"You haven't met Jorge Moretti, have you?" said Joaquim.

Jorge stood and extended his hand. "Moretti," he said.

"I've heard so much about you."

"Jorge, this is Kamar Sodeis. I didn't realize that you hadn't yet crossed paths."

"A pleasure," said Jorge.

"I wasn't informed of your plan to visit," said Sodeis.

"I wasn't informed that you were here to inform," said Joaquim, repeating his statement in Tupi. Laughter broke out.

"Why are you here?" Sodeis said again in Portuguese.

Joaquim replied in Tupi, gesturing towards Jorge.

"Should I repeat the question?"

"There's no need. We'll be on our way in another half an hour," said Joaquim, turning back to the chief. As an afterthought, he looked up and added, "This is a purely personal visit."

"To a restricted area in an agency plane, I assume without authorization?" said Sodeis. "In this place and at this time, there's no such thing as a personal visit."

"He's right," said Jorge under his breath.

"He's not always as right as he thinks he is," said the chief. Martina jerked forward at the sound of Portuguese coming from an Indian. The chief returned to his conversation with Joaquim in Tupi, and the others returned to shouting out their asides, and the blue shirt became smaller and smaller, but lost none of its intensity of color, as it moved off toward the padlocked hut and disappeared behind the door.

All at once, the group stood as a single body. The parts dispersed, patting each other and talking as they went. Almost everyone seemed to share in a sense of relief, to move less stiffly, and to interact even with affection, as though a layer of denser air had been pushed aside, making it easier to move and breathe.

"Let's unload," said Jorge, pulling Martina in after Joaquim, who had already started on up the path.

It took eight men to carry in the boxes. This time, Joaquim walked next to Jorge, with Martina behind them.

"Are you satisfied?" Joaquim asked Jorge.

A bird was going "chit chit" in a tree.

Jorge's voice sounded oddly high-pitched and birdlike as he answered. "I'm not the sort, am I? But thanks." As though to punctuate his statement, the bird gave one last, loud "chit" and was gone. "So is he going to report me?"

"No chance," said Joaquim over his shoulder now, as they fell into single file. "I've been keeping an eye on him, which, as you notice, he suspects." As the path widened, the two walked side-by-side again, with Martina behind them. "I wasn't expecting him and he wasn't expecting me, so we surprised each other. If you don't mind waiting for another quarter of an hour, I think I'll make the most of it."

The chief's house looked like all the others, but was cluttered with pots and children and toys and a few faded three-ring binders lined up on a makeshift table. In the corner, a pile of boxes bore the Coca Cola label, and turned out actually to contain bottles of Coke, one of which their host offered to his guests, presumably to share. He seemed relieved when they turned him down, and put the bottle back in the box, closing the lid emphatically. As they began to unpack, Joaquim excused himself and disappeared into the courtyard. Martina and Jorge pulled items from the boxes while the chief looked on, holding them up for his consideration. Each was carefully examined and evaluated, not only by the chief himself and by the surrounding chorus, but by a few of the women, two of whom the chief introduced as wives, who wandered in and out carrying children and baskets and rough wooden bowls. When they had finished, while they were repacking the boxes, the chief sat down and studied them.

"So, this is your wife?" he asked Jorge in Portuguese, nodding his head toward Martina.

"*Nao!*" she said quickly.

"So what's she doing here?" the chief turned to Jorge.

"I'm a potter," said Martina. "Can I look at those bowls over there?" she said, gesturing toward a jute bag hanging from a hook over the desk. She got up without waiting for an answer.

"Joaquim said he would speak to Barbosa in Brasilia for me," the chief continued. "Do you believe he will?"

"If he said so, he will."

"I think so too," said the chief. "He's a good man."

He got up and started to walk out. Then he turned around and addressed Jorge again.

"Are you in business? Who do you work for?"

"I'm SPI. I want you to give us another chance."

The chief turned and walked out, and Jorge followed. As they stepped out into the sun, Joaquim came up from around the other side of the men's house. The chief walked around to Joaquim's other side. He pulled him down by the shoulder for a minute and whispered. Then Joaquim straightened again.

"All set!" he said, clapping the chief on the back. "Off we go!"

At the mouth of the forest, the chief left them, clasping Joaquim and then standing back to survey Martina and Jorge.

"You should get married," he said. He laughed a loud belly-laugh. "I've done it plenty of times. It's not so bad." He reached for Jorge's hand as though to shake it, but instead put something into it, and then turned and disappeared into the midst of a small group of men who were milling around watching them. As they walked toward the plane, Martina saw Jorge wipe his eyes with the back of his hand. Jorge saw that she saw, and a steel door slammed shut inside of him. A feeling far deeper than sadness washed over him: humiliation. He saw in an instant that all his talk of closure had been just that—a fantasy, an illusion that made it possible to feel that he was something other than a child. He waited until she had walked on to take off his watch, put it in his pocket, and replace it with the one in his hand.

At the plane, Jorge tried to lead Joaquim into the seat beside him, but Joaquim pulled Martina in front of him and pushed her in instead. While they were belting themselves into place, Jorge sat frozen with his hand on the throttle as though he had forgotten what to do next. Martina reached for his arm, but he pulled sharply away, snapping his head to the side. They sat in silence, each looking straight ahead into their private visions of the future. The vibrations of the plane rendered the tremor of Jorge's hands invisible, but the tears that streamed down his cheeks made strangely loud spattering sounds as they fell onto the clipboard on his lap. He moved the clipboard away, but it slipped from his grasp, and clattered as it fell onto the floor under his feet.

"What?" Martina said quietly, turning to face his nearly eclipsed profile.

He averted his eyes as he turned slowly and choked out the words. "In this time and place, there's no room for anything personal."

XLII

BETWEEN FOREST AND forest lay a wide expanse of grass and scrub, like prairie, but rockier; an old lake bed, filled up with granite and sand. It was tempting for Larry to read his journey so far as a succession of chapters in a book: The first set the stage along a well-worn path peopled by nut-trappers calling to each other, heading home to the village with their overflowing bags on their backs. There was a chapter in which his route diverged from the established paths and he followed the needle of his compass as though he were a dog following its twitching nose; another that unfolded against a backdrop of fallen tree limbs thick with vines; and then, at last, the one that contained this denouement, in which the sun streamed in through the thick cover of leaves to announce his arrival in a dazzling, gleaming city of wind and empty space. Larry stood at the gate of this Oz, blinking in the sunlight, filled with a sense of dread at its vastness and limitless height. He knew in his head that this expanse, no matter how great it seemed, was merely an island in an endless sea of forest; as he remembered it, they had traversed its width the last time in less than a day, or at least he had no recollection of sleeping on the open ground, or under one of the solitary stunted trees no taller than himself. He knew the goal: to get across it before the water ran out. He pulled up his hat by its string, retrieved his sunglasses from his pocket, and launched himself with a determined push, vowing to reach shore again by sundown.

In the three days he had been traveling, he had yet to find the heat oppressive, despite the thickness and stickiness of the forest air, but now the heat descended, as though it had been waiting to pounce when he emerged. He felt lightheaded, and began to hear the rhythm of his pulse in his temples. He made accommodations; he put on the zinc ointment he had until then refused to wear; he took gulps from a water bottle while he walked; he sat, for a quarter of an hour, beneath the uneven shade of a small stand of stunted trees and ate an extra piece of salted jerky with his dried fruit and crackers. He looked again and again at the maps he had sketched for himself, trying to judge by their scale and their contours whether he was already hopelessly adrift. The terror of what is in this world, he saw, was nothing compared to the terror of what is not, as he surveyed the emptiness around him and wondered if the grass would soon dry out completely and catch fire. And then the rain came, as though out of nowhere, announced by a crack of thunder and a band of swift-moving clouds that seemed to take the sun unawares.

The downpour was as thick and relentless as the sun had been, stinging his skin as sharply, and the few small trees were as inadequate to protect him from the one as from the other. Larry pulled out tarps and wrapped his two bags in them, throwing his poncho over his pack and himself. As he stood, paralyzed, squinting out from under the visor of his poncho, all he could think to do was to fill up his water bottles, collecting the rain in his tin bowl and pouring it into the bottles using his hands to guide him, since he could barely see. It made him feel stronger to have taken any action at all, to have been able to replenish himself in the midst of seeming hopelessness. Holding his compass nearly to his eye, he leaned into the force of the downpour with his jaw clenched, clinging tight to his bags lest the rain rip them away. Only when he grew too tired to move forward did he allow his gaze to drift up, to the feet of an enormous rainbow that towered over him and his struggles and his storm and his sloshing bowl of prairie and pushed the clouds away off to the east, leaving him exhausted and bedraggled, lying where he had allowed himself to fall, across the belly of a smooth, round rock.

XLIII

WHAT HAPPENS TO a person who's *rajora,* to a person with neither *jitana* nor brother nor *kaag* to rely on in this life? That person would end up no doubt either as beloved by the ancestors or, more likely, as a sort of necessary outcast, someone authorized to sing of the dark times precisely because of her status as pariah. In Aran's village there were already three, one of whom, Tilata, caught the eye of ItaXa from the far village, a man who two rains prior had lost the only wife he had. Now they only had to wait for the arrival of a child, which everyone knew was impossible, given that ItaXa was already a hands-and-feet of rains. But even the status of awaiting the impossible conferred enormous benefits in the worlds of the living and the dead. Although the honor to Tilata simply for pressing a claim was obvious, and was rewarded by an extra measure of the forest's bounty, the honor to ItaXa for accepting him was no less obvious, as it offered proof for all to see that her will had remained untainted by shadows, by curses, by doubt.

XLIV

THE SCALE OF the *campo* is defined by such minute events as these: the vibration of one grass blade against another, the flick of a lizard's tail, the slight bow of the stem to the butterfly. The world to which Larry awoke, looking straight out at eye level, was a world in miniature, where bridges were made of reeds, and towers were of sand, and sound was nearly inaudible and yet endlessly complex. He struggled out from under his tarps, aware now that he was standing amid a cascade of tiny yellow flowers half the size of his fingernail, and fruit fit for the tables of a metropolis of ants. He pulled his clothes, now nearly dry, away from his skin, and in doing so, created a breeze that ruffled the leaves of trees no taller than his ankles. As he hoisted his pack and moved on, he caught sight of himself in his mind's eye, towering over the cities of bugs and scrub just as he himself was towered over by the now-evaporated rainbow, by the clouds that had drifted like swirls of dust past the ankles of the sky. In his determination to move forward, he held onto the illusion of enormous height, stalking the bustling cities of leaf and stem the way Goya's monster, in the painting on the wall in his fourth grade classroom, about which he had felt the child's fascination with anomalies of scale, had stalked the cities of Spain, until he caught sight, at dusk, of the dark shore of the forest, and felt himself shrinking again as he approached it.

Still shaken, he decided not to push on farther into the forest that evening, but to make camp between a trinity of *chicles*. The trunks of the trees defined a small, inviting room by the side of a chain of marshy indentations that had nearly swelled into a continuous river as a result of the rain.

He still had plenty of camper's meals jammed into the bottom of his pack, a whole smorgasbord of main dishes and side dishes and even desserts, all tasteless in the same way despite the pictures on the packages, but he didn't have the energy to dig through to get to them. Instead, he finished the box of crackers with his fruit and jerky and a handful of nuts and went about setting up his hammock and netting as quickly as he could, thinking of nothing but sleep.

XLV

IT WENT WITH having attained a certain age, this involvement with the effects of the dead. Of James's makeshift family in Brazil, no one knew better than Sara the capacity of a person's surviving possessions to assume the force of their owner's personality, and to continue the push forward, at least for a time, along their owner's original path. Thus, the wing chair in the living room, imported at great expense from the parlor of Sara's Genoan grandmother, conveyed for many decades through the dejected sag of its cushions its original owner's disapproval of Sara's choice of a husband, and the clock on the bookshelf, by running perpetually behind, continued to manifest her mother-in-law's preoccupation with the tragic effects of time. No one knew this better than Joaquim, whose office in the back room of his house in Belem overflowed with odd seed pods, thick files, well-marked books, cross-sections of tree trunks, clay pots, photographs, and other artifacts once owned by fellow *sertanistas* who had been lost to the forest and its inhabitants. Thus, as Sara sat in the back bedroom of her house in Santarem watching Joaquim pull folder after folder from James's traveling case, she shared with him an understanding that whatever information he found would necessarily follow the arc of James's trajectory, rather than their own.

"Here's something," said Joaquim, moving his reading glasses to his nose and leaning over the folder marked "Cancer." "I guess this wasn't his first bout with it. I wasn't aware of that. Were you?"

"I'm sure no one was," said Sara, suddenly overcome by James's loneliness, which, at that moment, was indistinguishable from Larry's and from her own.

"I know you probably hate me now," Joaquim said. His voice was distracted, matter-of-fact. Joaquim was the only one other than Jorge who could generally ascertain the emotion contained in the diffuse, flat warmth she tended to convey.

"I've caught myself calling you Wendy again," he said gently. "All your lost boys."

"On second thought, maybe I do," she said tightly.

Joaquim put down a green folder of expense receipts and picked up a red three-ring binder, the thickest of the notebooks that were now spread out on the bed. He opened the cover and read out loud: "Pahqua: A Dictionary of Grammar and Definitions by James Lawrence Ardmore."

Sara came and sat beside him on the bed. "Is that his research? He never told me. Maybe I should put that one aside for Larry."

"How about if I just look through it quickly, to see if he left any information in here we can use in fishing Larry out?" He began to flip through the first section, which was labeled "Pahqua Glossary" in clumsy capital letters but was otherwise empty, its pages obviously having been removed. He turned quickly to the second section, titled "Grammato-genetics." "Well, this is interesting!" he said, leaning in now over the notebook, and reading more slowly. "Look at this! 'Holophrastic and polysynthetic innovation markers: Tzotzil/Ge/Pahqua.' Why didn't he talk about this stuff? When I hired him, I thought he'd be doing this, but he didn't want any part of it!"

"Maybe Larry can tell us," Sara said quietly.

"So you do hate me," said Joaquim, putting down the notebook and looking at her.

"If anything happens to him I will. I think you misjudged, and I don't know why I didn't step in."

"Between me and Silvio," said Joaquim, moving his reading glasses back to the top of his head, "we have two hundred and sixty-two men out there right now. If I stop listening to myself, we're all in bad shape."

They sat in silence for a long time.

"I suppose if I hate someone at this point, it's his mother," Sara said at last.

"It's always the mothers who get the blame," said Joaquim. He turned back to the last section, which contained a title-page announcing 'Genetic diffusion of novelty effects: A semiotic model,' underneath which was written, in the same awkward scrawl, 'Private: Keep out.'

"If I had known the guy could actually read and write, I would have bought him a typewriter," said Joaquim, bending his head over the page.

XLVI

ALTHOUGH LARRY CONTINUED to wear his watch, he relied on it less and less to help him estimate the things his body already knew. As the importance of clock time receded, it was replaced by the time of routine; the time of morning-coffee-making, and the time of taking pills, and the time of unrolling his hammock and securing each end to a tree. It yielded, little by little, to physical time, determined by the body's need to eat and drink and move and defecate and sleep. There was the musical time of the forest, which began each day in the highest canopies of the trees and slowly lowered itself down their trunks, to hover near the ground by nightfall. There was the time of parrots and the time of toucans, the time of moths and of frogs. Most of all, Larry found, there was the time of walking, the slow rhythm of his pack rubbing back and forth against his shirt, leaving a deepening brown stain as a condensed record of the impact of his feet against the firm or marshy ground. At the end of the day, when the walking had ceased and Larry lay back in his hammock listening to the pulsing swell of the cicadas, he knew that his own pulse was stitched into their hum, and that somewhere inside himself, his heart was still taking step after inevitable step.

XLVII

THE FOREST HAS its own ways of inducing dreams and of disrupting them. In a town surrounded by streets and people and buildings, the night brings a gradual reduction of sound and activity, a communal settling-in, a sense of universal agreement that prevails despite the sigh of a lone car passing in the empty street, the howl of a cat in the alley, or the shouts of some drunken men leaving a bar. Everything is on the side of sleep, and the rest go about their business, or toss and turn in their beds, unable to forget that they have somehow transgressed, or been forsaken. In the forest, however, it is the traveler who, upon securing his hammock with the aid of a flashlight, finds himself moving against a rising current of activity as he arranges himself with his head against a pillow made of rolled-up clothing, his jacket resting on his shoulder, its arm across his chest. Larry was as tired as he had ever been, and his head was as heavy. He let himself sink into the hammock's embrace as though he were a child, secure in its grasp, watched over by the trees that held it. He turned onto his right side and grabbed the jacket in his arms, holding it tight against him. He adjusted his makeshift pillow and felt it unroll all the way down to his leg. It was then, just on the verge of sleep, that the forest came for him, calling with grunts and whispers and cracking branches to announce the dawn of nocturnal day.

At first he resisted, fearful of the exhaustion within him and the voices of unknown presences outside him, from which sleep had thus far offered him protection. But a scraping sound on the ground beneath his hammock made him jump for his flashlight, which he wielded like a machine gun, sweeping its beam wildly over the walls of his forest room and back and forth across the floor. As his spotlight passed the place where the scraping sound was coming from, he caught sight of an armadillo nosing its way along the ground, oblivious to the light, moving as clumsily and imperviously as a toy tank that a child could not quite operate correctly by remote. Larry watched it shuffle back and forth, pushing up dirt and leaves, until at last it turned and disappeared into the depths of the forest. Then he shut off his flashlight and lay in the dark, listening. There were croaking noises and whirs and raspy, belligerent cries. There were repetitive, insistent, careful tones, and sharp, indignant screeches. There were the calls of the howler monkeys, so loud that they echoed in the treetops and shook the sky, and worst of all, there was the constant, high-pitched buzz of mosquitoes, a number of which had infiltrated his netting, as though to guarantee the futility of his attempts to sleep.

As he slapped ineffectually at his arms and his ankles, Larry thought to get up and search for his repellent, but held back for fear that by taking a step outside his flimsy shelter, he would leave himself vulnerable to an even more vicious attack. He remembered when as a child, he would awaken in the freezing house at night and look longingly into the darkness toward the place where he knew a spare blanket was kept, unable to convince himself to move for fear of dispersing the thin layer of heat that was all he had against the cold. He tried to tell himself that his situation was no different on this night than it had been on the others, that the forest was no more active or threatening, the insects no more fierce, and the mesh on his *mosquitiero* no less dense than it had been before, but still he felt exposed, for the first time, to the forest. In the place of stars in the night sky, he saw a hundred pairs of eyes like constellations in the firmament of leaves. He feared, with a shudder, the interest of the *jararaca*, which he imagined twining itself among the branches above his head like a serpent weaving in and out among the engraved figures in an antique map. He listened as hard as he could to what the forest was saying about him, dreading that he might discover therein a clue to his terrible fate.

As Larry was beginning to discover, a given terror grows in proportion to its capacity to stir the memory of earlier terrors, to invoke a childhood fear of the dark, of the ghoulish faces hidden in the patterns in the wallpaper, or of the rustling among the shoes beneath the bed. Larry remembered clearly the forest nights he spent waiting for his uncle's snoring to start up, confident and unrestrained and loud enough to chase away the jaguars that prowled the periphery of every darkness. Even at home, there were times when, terrified for no reason at all, he would call up the memory of that sound to carry him across the treacherous passageway to sleep. Such experience had taught him that the fears whose roots extend deepest into the past can only be dispelled by forces just as deep. He closed his eyes and tried to reach as far down as he could to find a trace of his uncle inside himself, whose presence in the hammock beside him he had every reason but one to expect. He fell through a succession of layers of sound, from the highest-pitched buzzing of insects through the nasal retorts of the tree frogs, down into a low hum that could only have come from the throat of the earth itself. By the time he found what he was looking for, it was well after midnight, and he clung to it so tightly that the mosquito's buzz was no longer audible, nor did the brush of the spiny rat over the face of his backpack bring him any further unease.

XLVIII

IN THE EMPTY apartment, the ring of the telephone leapt from wall to wall, amplified by tension and neglect. Mrs. Tomoio, in the flat downstairs, sensing the loneliness of that echoing ring, added the comment of the end of her broomstick, while old Sr. Arterrio from next door, roused from his nap by the commotion, contributed to its rhythm a repetitive string of invectives. No doubt that complex pattern of sound traveled a thousand miles to Rio, where it gathered in Silvio Amanza's handset. When Jorge crossed the threshold at seven minutes past midnight, he sensed that the walls had been saturated by vibrations, which explained the shaking of his legs as he set his bags beside the table in the hallway without unpacking them and made his way towards the bedroom, unbuttoning his shirt as he went.

XLIX

AS LARRY LOOKED back, he had a hard time remembering the previous day, or how it differed from the one before. As he maneuvered around tree roots and tangled vines, he tried to remember what day it was, and suddenly realized he couldn't. He had started off on a Sunday, and had crossed the clearing on a Tuesday, but after that, everything had blurred together until the cycle of day and night felt like a wheel, spinning without end. He had assumed that it was Saturday—leaving three more days in a trek of supposedly just under ten—but his conviction wavered as soon as he tried to justify it. He thought about counting his pills, or his packets of instant food, but he wasn't sure how many pills he had started out with, or remembered to take, and he hadn't been eating the same amount every day. Then he remembered his water purification tablets, which he had used without fail, since he hadn't taken the time to boil the water. He took out the box and poured them into his lap, counting them once and then, more slowly, again.

Some of the packages were missing, so he pulled out the contents of the pocket in his backpack where they were kept and piled everything up in his cooking pot. There were six extra flashlight batteries, and two jackknives and a second compass, and a roll of electrical tape. There was James's miniature ax in its sheath, and a roll of fishing line, and a small plastic box containing fishhooks and tackle. There was a metal file and a box of nails, and a tiny notebook with a matching pen and metal covers that were held tight together with miniature magnets. But he found no wayward packages and no crumbs of disintegrating tablets lodged in the canvas seams. As he emptied the pocket and then filled it again, he sensed without conscious calculation that since two hundred and sixty one tablets were accounted for, thirty nine were missing, more than two weeks' worth. He knew the numbers in the same wordless way that he knew, in the pit of his stomach, what they meant: That with all his estimations, his endless compass readings, his maps, his hours of research, he was like an arrow hurtling past its target. He had missed his mark.

The thought was more than he could grasp. That his compass, so precise, with its needle as thin as a hair, had offered him unreliable counsel was a thought that, strangely enough, he had never stopped to consider. Last time, he and James had seen to their left, as they approached, a hazy cloud of light that announced a clearing in the distance, and in that brightening cloud they had caught glimpses of silhouettes flickering across a brilliant screen. There had been signs in the dirt since the morning before, and twice James had pointed out logs that had been deliberately felled and laid across their stumps. Thinking back over the past few days, Larry remembered no such signs, and feared in his heart, that he had become so lost in time that he never allowed himself to look for them. He zipped up the pocket in his pack and sat down, seeking, in immobility, escape from the reality of his predicament, and protection from whatever in the forest has the sharpest nose for fear.

There is no loneliness like that of someone who has sought it out, whether knowingly or not, and found it. Jorge had called him ill-prepared, but he had got it wrong. Larry knew how to collect condensation in a metal cup, and how to build a shelter out of rope and sticks. He knew how to tell the *jacu* from its tracks, and how to light a fire with a bow drill. Most of all, he knew that finding one's way involved more than following a compass, or a set of instructions, more than being led by a map, or by a guide. But everything he knew was clenched up, like a fist inside his heart, grasping something hard and round and silver in its palm, something that displaced Sara's coin and the concern behind it. Larry didn't remember how it got there, but sensed it had been there forever, a perfect, lifeless, reflective sphere in which, looking in, he could see only himself. It was the thing that had indentured him to the needle of the compass and its impulsive, twitching whims. It was the thing that made time unbearable. It was the thing that had stopped him from swiveling in his fiberglass seat in the airport in Belem and telling James—what? He couldn't begin to know. No amount of preparation could dislodge it, not even the sight of a lone figure in the forest, crying into his hands over the losses he had brought upon himself, yet still clinging in terror to his lonely fate.

From high in a treetop, a macaw turned its head to look down at the seated figure, its bright plumage and serious expression giving it a comical demeanor. An agouti stopped in mid-step and stood up on its haunches, its nose and whiskers quivering. At the thick base of a kapok, in a dark indentation between two knotted roots, a tarantula stood like a shopkeeper at the door of his establishment, looking out at the passing traffic with an air of detached ennui. None of them could know of the effort it took on the part of the figure to rise, to wipe its eyes one last time with the corner of its shirt, and to reach into its pocket for its compass. Larry flinched as he shouldered his pack, feeling an ache in his neck and his knees, from crying, he thought, taking a long drink from his water bottle. Overhead, the macaw took off with a flash of red and green, and on the ground, the tarantula shifted slowly backwards until it disappeared into its doorway, as though it had been summoned back into its shop by its assistant but was in no great hurry to respond. Only the agouti, who froze at the sight of Larry's upright presence, might have understood that the cold internal thing that had so often rendered Larry immobile, that had commanded him so often to rebuff the world's advances, that told him, in almost every situation, to play dead, was, for all its coldness, driven by a wish to live and not a wish to die.

Larry stood and pushed himself through the heavy air with the sort of frantic, reflexive effort that one might see in a man who, contemplating suicide while walking beside a lake, accidentally falls in and finds himself thrashing furiously and gasping for air. After an hour, his legs began to shake, and he remembered that he had forgotten to eat. He pulled out a handful of nuts and a piece of jerky and moved on, feeling less revived than he had hoped. The undergrowth seemed to thicken as he went; he hadn't remembered encountering so many thorns, or such dense vines. At last, he was forced to pull his hunting knife from its leather case, wielding it like a scythe, carving a tunnel through the hanging lianas. The compass was undaunted and cheered him on, promising that he had merely taken a small detour through a rough outcropping of branches and would soon find his intended path again. "Look," he commanded himself in desperation, almost shouting at himself, and what he saw was his own shirtsleeve, cut to tatters by the thorns, and through the strips of fabric, a spreading stain of blood. He thought of reaching into his pack for bandages and ointment, but knew that he couldn't afford to stop. Instead, he tore one of the strips of fabric from his sleeve and knotted it tight with his other hand and his teeth around his forearm, level with the center of the stain.

He carried on until his breathing became labored and his heart pounded in his ears, and then finally lowered his pack and sank down onto it, knowing he could go no further. "Look," he told himself weakly, though he saw nothing but thorns and brambles close about his face. All the joints in his body ached, the small ones in his fingers and toes no less than his knees and his elbows; his eyes ached from trying to squint through sweat and vines. Apparently, this was how one died in the forest, not violently, but of hopelessness, languishing due to weakness brought on by despair. He drained the third of his four water bottles in one long breath and put his head down on his knees, pulling himself in close. He wished he had a shell, or a blanket, to draw over himself despite the relentless humidity, a barrier to protect him from the stings of the nettles and the taunts of the mosquitoes he was too tired to try to slap away. As he drew in all his senses but listening, the hum of the forest seemed to expand, until it pushed from all sides against his imaginary blanket, until it became the blanket itself. The world ended at the edges of that blanket, Larry sensed, beyond which there was only emptiness, endless space in which his doomed frigate floated off to meet the darkness and the stars. He felt his body move unimpeded through a nothingness devoid even of sound and yet, as he glided on, he was surprised to notice that he did hear sound, a soft but unmistakable muffled breathing noise of the sort one might hear by holding a shell to an ear. He stood up and listened, waving away the mosquitoes. What he heard in the distance in front of him, though still far off, was the sigh of water rushing over rock.

As Larry shouldered his pack and pushed on, he let himself be guided not by the compass this time, but by the stream's beckoning call. What drew him forward was not so much the allure of water itself—having started off on the tail end of the rainy season, the way had been laced with tiny veins, and he had not yet developed a fear of water's scarcity—but the promise of a clearing, of a place to string up his hammock, to replenish all his stores, and think, and sleep. He no longer told himself to look, but to listen, and as he did, he heard the stream's breath swell. The undergrowth began to thin until he could walk upright again and then, suddenly, the forest gave way and he stopped short at the threshold of a gleaming praia, an opal crescent of sand nested between the green hand of trees and the blue hand of water.

L

LARRY COULD FEEL the shadows cover him over as he slept, as his own weight pulled him down into his dreams. But someone was trying to get his attention, and as he stirred awake, he realized it was the chill of twilight that was tapping on his shoulders and pressing at his sides. He sat up and brushed the sand from his face, looking out at the shimmering purple river and the darkening curtain of trees. As he strung up his hammock at the edge of the forest and cleaned the cut on his arm with antiseptic and ointment, he felt relieved but still weak; his arms and legs still ached when he moved them. He went to the edge of the river to bathe, but when he put his feet in the water, a shiver ran through him, and he decided to wash just his face and fill his bottles before returning to sleep. He knew he should be hungry but wasn't, so he pulled only his flashlight and his jacket from his pack and then crawled between the layers of netting, wrapping the jacket around him. On his descent into sleep, he felt a sudden pinprick of relief at the thought that he hadn't tried to bathe in the river with an open cut on his arm, which would have drawn the attention of piranhas, as it did, that night, in his dreams.

LI

KAMAR SODEIS WAS a principled man, although it would have been hard for an outsider to discern the particular set of principles to which he adhered. He himself would have identified it effortlessly in a word: progress. Against those who would decry Brazil's push to become an economic power worth reckoning with, Sodeis understood the necessity of commerce, of capitalizing on available resources, of self-determination, of modernization. Yet he and Diego Melo, his former partner, managed to disagree as vehemently as they embraced their shared credo. For progress, as it turned out, it was a far more difficult concept to put into practice than, in the eagerness of youth, they had at first believed. Where Sodeis had come to appreciate the native population as one more among Brazil's bounteous resources which, to the extent to which it could be helped to assimilate into the modern world, could be fruitfully exploited for the benefit of all, his partner was far more impatient as regards the native question, and eventually left prospecting altogether, abandoning Sodeis with a few allies, a pile of contracts (most of them untenable), and an even deeper allegiance to an investment in idealism. Meanwhile, Melo found his second career in politics to be far more satisfying than his first, and could soon afford to be generous to his old friend (who was, undeniably, a repository of certain unflattering facts regarding his history), and protected him from some unfortunate constraints of law, particularly regarding the Indian question. But Melo could not, as it turned out, protect Sodeis from the difficulties that arose from the even deeper principle to which he adhered unwaveringly: that every hard-won victory, every effort to find his way, was to be undermined, undone, wrecked, blocked, quashed, drowned out, sacrificed in tribute to those harsh ancestral Gods in whom, in his wish to view himself as powerful, as enlightened, he refused to believe that he believed.

LII

SOMETHING WAS WRONG with Larry's having arrived at the edge of a river twenty yards wide and slow-moving and deep. He was, at most, four hours from the place where he turned around, four hours in which little distance had been covered. The rivers he had encountered thus far were more like streams, and he had crossed them without incident, using sticks for balance, filling his water bottles at their farther banks. None had been wide enough even to necessitate a parting of the crown of trees, nor deep enough to harbor fish of any substantial size. Larry lay back in his hammock, trying to envision how a bend in a river might protrude into his path. He closed his eyes and the sun pressed on the lids, creating flickering shapes that confused his efforts to plot out in his imagination the river's twisting course, or the one he would have to take to get around it. Whatever path he took, though, would necessitate his re-entry into the tangled undergrowth in order to move forward.

Larry couldn't say exactly how he decided not to move on that day; he simply performed all the rituals of the morning as though he were planning to stay. He ate his breakfast slowly, without once looking at his maps. He changed into his shorts, and then put on his zinc ointment. He took out his pants and his underwear and his shirts and washed them in the river, hanging them from the branches that overhung the sand. Then he untied his hammock and strung it up farther from the sun. Soon, he gave himself over to a sleep so deep that he awoke from it only infrequently, for minutes at a time, over the following four days.

The sleep of fever overflows with dreams, which appear not intermittently, serially, but rather in a rush, as a waterfall can draw from many rivers at once, crashing them together on the rocks below. Larry tried to elude them as they swept over him from all sides; in his tiny world of praia fringed by forest, he clung to what he recognized, and then saw it eroded and transformed again and again. In the mornings, his dreams confined themselves within the banks of sleep, whose surface they only gently, occasionally ruptured, but by mid-day, both he and the world had grown torpid with fever, and their boundaries, and especially the boundary between them, began to shimmer and blur. He lay in his hammock with his water bottle in one hand and his sheathed knife in the other, raining sweat onto the sand beneath him, and watched as the scene outside himself, while still glistening with a fantastic beauty, began to grow untrustworthy, its sublime aura of stillness disrupted by a sinister displacement of solidity and color.

As he drifted off at sundown, he would always make one last attempt to reach the world as he remembered it. He would plan the route he would take the next morning after the fever had lifted and he was rested, not so much to be prepared to start off as to counteract the fear that he would never start off again. He would imagine himself turning back at the threshold of the forest to look one last time at his shimmering mirage of water and sand, and then moving on with great vigor and authority through the tunnel he had cut for himself on his way in. But that tunnel, he found each night as he crossed its threshold in his mind, brought him not to the heart of the forest, but to the center of his own dark thoughts, in which the undergrowth had rewoven itself even more densely than before, its tangles covered over with even sharper thorns.

In those dreams of the night, Larry could not afford to sleep. He patrolled the confines of his praia like a military guard, shouldering an imaginary rifle, alert to signs of immanent intrusion by any number of known and unknown enemies. He saw eyes glowing all around him, and feared they were the eyes of wild boar, who roam in packs and eat a man to the bone, clothes and all, in half an hour. He looked up in the sky and saw an infinity of eyes leering down at him from the very ends of the

universe, pairs of eyes and Cyclops eyes, all pinpointing him for some terrible, impersonal fate. He heard a rustle in the sand near the shore, and
bolted up to see a giant, gray-green train moving inexorably toward him,
guided by an engine decked with two yellow lamps as unnaturally bright
as a train's headlights. As it came into closer view, Larry saw in horror that
the train was a snake, an anaconda long enough to stretch from the shore
to his hammock, with a girth far wider than his, on which a hundred pairs
of diamonds shone. It moved toward him with the kind of rustling, chug-
ging silence that a train makes in the night as it passes sleeping towns.
Larry watched its slow advance for a minute, paralyzed, mesmerized by
the glint of its scales in the moonlight and the rhythm of his own pounding heart, and then reached for his knife, training his gaze on the soft parts
behind the snake's two level glowing headlights. As it approached him, he
slowly pulled aside the netting with one hand and cocked his other arm
like a trigger. For an endless moment, their eyes met and locked, and all
the sounds of the forest hushed; the river itself fell silent. Then suddenly
he snapped his arm with all his might, hurling his knife through a foot
of flesh, pinning the serpent to the sand. Its thrashing filled the clearing;
it threw its tail to the tops of the trees and sent it crashing down again,
writhing and furling. Exhausted, Larry sank into his hammock and slept
so soundly that by the time he awoke, the sun was already glinting off the
knife blade that stood erect a few yards from his hammock, piercing the
soft skin of the sand.

LIII

THOSE WHO APPROACH the Museo at Alter de Chao can't help but shudder at the masks lining the walkway, the skulls and shrunken heads and garish, growling visages of the fiercest of the fierce. They warn all comers: *Enter if you dare,* and they compel all to enter. But Martina's anxiety as she stepped through the doorway and looked around in the dank foyer was even deeper, more immediate. And Martina was not easily cowed.

"Sara Moretti?" she asked in a low voice at the desk, as a woman with white hair rose to scrutinize her.

"And you are?" She shuffled off slowly, leaving Martina among the shards and spear-heads, sharp as thoughts, lining the walls in their glass vitrines.

"Martina! I was thinking of calling you," said Sara, approaching. She led Martina back to her office, which was strangely cheerful, brightly lit and filled with variously colored objects. "But I wasn't sure you'd want to hear from me."

"So what is it with your son?" said Martina. She and the other makers of masks shared an appreciation for the power of an aggressive mien to vanquish their own fear and doubt.

"I'm worried too," said Sara.

"I'm not worried," said Martina. A lie. "I'm disgusted."

"I know," said Sara.

Martina grimaced, not wanting to be known.

"This has happened before," said Sara. "When the news came about his father, he took it like a little man, ran the show, hosted all the SPI who flew in, took care of me to a fault, and then withdrew to his bed for months, and refused to go out, or talk to anyone." Sara paused for a minute, regarding Martina. "And then again when he was in his late teens, and his first girl broke his heart. That's when he started to fly." Martina's face contorted to a smirk. "He thought the world of his father. Always at his heels. Only wanted to be like him."

"Well, my father was incinerated," said Martina. "What good does it do to dwell on it?"

"I'm not so sure," said Sara, looking at Martina intently now. Surrounded by broken vessels, Sara caught the tension in Martina's voice, and understood that she was one. Martina had turned her back to her, and was studying the pots that lined the shelves on the back wall.

"So how can I help?" Sara asked, restraining herself from approaching her.

Martina pushed aside the sudden wish to throw herself at Sara, to cry in her lap. "Here," she said, carefully drawing a few earthenware cups and hardened clay balls sheathed in dry, crumbling leaves from a worn canvas bag. "Do you have a way to analyze these?" She put most of the pieces on the table, but then turned to put the last one, an offering, in Sara's hand. "For lead and mercury, other contaminants?"

Sara put the cup and balls onto a tray. Then she approached Martina. "Let me introduce you to Sam and Bella, and show you the lab," she said, lifting the tray with one hand while she grasped Martina's arm with the other, drawing her ahead through the doorway.

LIV

ON THE MORNING of his fifth day by the water, Larry began to consider, in earnest, the fact that he might die. He could no longer insist to himself that his fever was imagined, and finally acknowledged that some action was required. He pulled out James's medical guide and began to read through it, looking for a list of symptoms that matched his own. He rejected the possibility of Chagas, since he hadn't been housed under thatch, and of dengue, as he had no rash. He doubted that he had filariasis or leishmaniasis, nor did he suspect schistosomiasis or typhoid or yellow fever. The obvious diagnosis, of malaria, he at first rejected outright, as he had taken his pills at least off and on for the past six weeks, but as he ruled out one illness after another, he was left with no other choice. He closed the book and began digging in his box of medicines. James had arranged them while they were still in the States, the label on each bottle covered over by another blank one on which James had written in his awkward print the names of various diseases and the dosages prescribed. "Diarrhea. Use as needed, not too much," one said. "Misc. infections. Some VDs. 3x/ day. Use all." A vial said, "Snakebite. Inject 1cc at site." Finally, he found a large bottle labeled "Malaria. 4x/day." and swallowed one of the pills with water. Then he crawled back into his hammock, which was still moist with sweat, and closed his eyes, trying to imagine a wall between himself and the throbbing behind his temples.

Despite himself, what Larry wished for most at those times was some benign indulgence on the part of the world. He pictured in his mind what his room at home used to look like, his desk and dresser covered with the artifacts of childhood affliction—comic books and boxes of chewable aspirin and tubes of Vicks Vapo-Rub and half-eaten bowls of Jell-O. His mother would suddenly take notice, her face revealing a kind of diffuse panic overlaid by an outward air of competence that he remembered seeing only at those times. It disturbed him that he had never managed to eradicate fully enough his longing for that distinctive combination of frantic interest and neglect, although he used to avoid it as best he could by refusing to acknowledge ever being ill. As he lay in his hammock, looking up at the leathery undersides of leaves, he felt his old longing creep in opportunistically, having sensed that he was weak. Even more than the mosquito's sting or the swipe of the *jacu's* paw, Larry feared that in the grip of his own lonely death, he would hear his voice call out to his distant, childless mother, and that she would finally hear him, and respond.

Larry shifted to one side in the hammock, as though to move away from the edge of that precipice in his mind. Like other sufferers from vertigo, he was less afraid of falling than he was of his impulse to jump, and pulled back instinctively, knowing that the danger was internal and therefore not to be tested. Out of fear, he forced his gaze outward, breathing hard with the effort, as though moving something physically heavy. "Look," he hissed to himself, willing the word itself to carry him to safety. He surveyed the shore, and saw a kingfisher hold up in its beak a silver sliver of light, but no longer knew how to find the sight remarkable. He watched the way the river clung to the ends of the vines and tried to carry them off, the way the wind brushed the branches and rippled the sun on the water. But for each time he pulled himself outward, something stronger pulled him in; for every leaf he saw above him, there was a bit of pain inside himself overlapping endless others like a shingle in a roof as big as the forest itself. Finally, he relaxed his grasp and fell—into death, he was sure—and lay wretched in his own fear and sweat for several hours, until shadows brushed the trees on the far side of the river. Then, rousing himself and noting tentatively that he hadn't died, he sat up and began his evening routine, leaning on his pack as he unzipped the front flap to reach his pills.

As he held the tray up to fit the bottle back in its place, he accidentally fell forward onto his pack and pushed aside a rolled-up shirt to reveal a stack of books, the titles of which at first seemed unfamiliar. He read them aloud, squinting through his pain in the shadowy half-light, and was flooded with relief bordering on joy when he realized that the life they represented was his own. Each one contained a story, but it was a personal story, about when he had read it, and what it had meant to him, and how it had made him what he was. It was as if all his shattered parts had been collected and bound in a few orderly if somewhat worn and unmatched volumes he could read in sequence to reconstruct himself. As he lifted them one by one from his pack and laid them out in his hammock, he could feel a growing conviction that he wouldn't die after all. He picked up the volume nearest his hand, a copy of Van Gogh's letters, and walked slowly down to the water, carrying it under his arm. He sat down on a rock, pushing his feet into the cool, wet sand, and read: "Well, even in that deep misery I felt my energy revive, and I said to myself: in spite of everything I shall rise again, I will take up my pencil, which I have forsaken in great discouragement, and I will go on with my drawing . . . ." Larry closed his eyes, flooded for a minute with his own determination to go on, followed by a second wave of shame and confusion at the thought that he didn't know what he needed to go on with. He sat looking out into the water, as though to discern beneath its surface, among the colorful, swirling schools, the dark presence of his own obscure vocation. At last, when the buzz of mosquitoes began to disrupt his thoughts and the light had thinned, he put on his heavy clothes and returned to his hammock to sleep, holding the faded blue volume to his chest. A wall of night sounds began to swell behind him at the forest's edge, and behind it, another, softer voice whispering, *"akama ua jata,"* don't leave me alone.

LV

THE DECISION TO forsake the most fundamental and communal aspects of life, the cultivation of the fields, and the smoking of fish, and the boiling of manioc, in order to pursue the more rarified or specialized ones, was not to be taken lightly. It was easily interpreted as an act of arrogance, especially on the part of someone younger than a hand-and-two of rains; most especially on the part of someone *rajora*. Yet one day, without telling her mother, Aran simply refused to accompany the other girls to the garden plot, choosing instead to slip off the path and spend the day among the looming, vine-covered *chajans* of the ancestors that spread deep into the forest behind the clearing to form interlocking ghost villages. The next morning, while the same girls were assembling for the hunt, she took her place among her peers without explanation, and kept an even greater distance around herself on the trail. All morning long, the others seemed undecided as to whether these actions on Aran's part were to be ridiculed or admired. But when they reached the first circle of felled trees that marked the end of what exists, at least as far as girls were concerned, and Aran alone refused to turn around, they whispered among themselves for a while and then, cautiously, turned to follow her out into a world that they had never seen. Aran pretended to pay them no attention, but she knew that somehow, her life had changed at that moment, and more by their decision to follow her than by her outrageous act.

LVI

THE NEXT MORNING rose like a luminous curtain. The grating and buzzing of insects and frogs gave way to birdcalls and the sound of water, and the fierce chill of the night was suffused with a gentle, spreading warmth. Overhead, two parrots flew off side by side, their bright green plumage reflected in the smooth unworried river, leaving in a stream behind them the muffled echoes of their cries. The vines brushed the water's edge with long, pliant fingers, without thinking, as a mother smoothes the hair on her child's forehead as he passes. Nothing was troubled in the forest, nothing on the sand. The deaths that were taking place in every corner of the landscape were quiet deaths, private, serenely inevitable unfoldings, in which fate showed itself as a modest, unobtrusive presence. Larry stirred in his sleep and muttered, but his expression was calm and lucid, his brow as unfurrowed as the river's. When the dark hand extended itself towards him, it was only to brush away a few unruly strands and then to lead him out to the threshold of the day.

"*Mboa*," he said to himself, at first silently and then out loud, as he climbed out of his netting and looked over at the deep green wall of forest on the far side of the river. At first, the sound of the word struck him as uncanny; he knew he had heard it only recently, but it took him a long time to remember that he himself had spoken it, for reasons he hadn't been able to pin down. The word had had a history with him; he could recall the day that he learned it, with the indelible clarity that always marks an instance of shame. Not long after they had arrived, he had been trying to hold up his end of a conversation with Dabimi and Daja and Amakar while the four of them were running together around the shelter that served as a smoke house, around poles and piles of sticks, trying to chase a lizard with green and purple scales. Larry had wanted to make the simple comment that the lizard was beautiful, but he stumbled looking for the word, and then again when he tried to describe what he meant. Their play came to a standstill. The boys walked over and recited a string of words to him again and again in a sing-song pattern, none of which he recognized. At last, he asked them to come with him to find his uncle, but when he started off towards the clearing, the boys stayed behind, laughing at him and mimicking the way he kept his hands in his pockets as he walked. When he caught a glimpse of James coming towards him, he ran to him and burst into tears within view of the boys, which only added to his shame. Later on over dinner James explained to him that Pahqua didn't contain a single word for beauty, but many, each of which made reference to its source. There was beauty from the animal world and beauty granted by the living. There was beauty given by the leader among men and beauty whose source was dreams and beauty from the dead. *Kuruna, tuara, ima, awa, mboa,* Larry had heard over and over in his head that night. After dinner, without telling James, he had forced himself to walk back to Dabimi's house and call from outside the *kaawa, "Pachi do kuruna! Pachi do kuruna!"* as he paced back and forth in the dirt. At last, one of the brothers, Amari, stepped outside and stood beside him, looking at the ground as if he too were ashamed. *"Makar nara an pachi,"* he said softly. Tomorrow we'll catch him.

Larry shook his head and tried to shrug off the thought. He took his pills and washed his face and folded his jacket and shirt. He was unsettled by the vividness of the memory no less than by the vividness of the day, by water so clear he could see striations on the stones in the riverbed, and air so clear he could make out individual feathers on the herons who stood preening themselves at the water's edge. It occurred to him that the clarity of his senses and his memory might be due not to the kind of day it was but to an improvement in his condition, so he paid attention to his shoulders and his elbows to see if they still ached. They did, and his knees still hurt when he walked, with their dull, more bearable morning pain. But something was lighter in his chest, he noticed, and his legs didn't seem quite as heavy as before. He still had enough energy after his chores to put on his ointment and sit beside the river with his book in his lap, watching and reading and eating the leftovers of a camp meal out of its foil pack. The ripples on the water were delicate and even, like the scales on a snake. The snake knew its path, and moved at a deliberate, leisurely pace, carrying time on its back.

Larry had read stories of men who had washed ashore and stayed, whether by choice or necessity or lack of will. He knew of the Lotus Eaters, and of Robinson Crusoe; he had heard about lost missionaries, crazy men, and half-men who tended isolated plots around their makeshift, palm-roofed huts, and kept monkeys on their shoulders as companions, and came to dread the rescue for which they had so desperately prayed. Larry pictured a pitched-roof house of cane-stalks, in which a few worn remnants of a former life—a few rusted pots, a pocket-knife, some frayed bits of paper and clothing—rested on stumps or hung from loops of *juco*. Unwittingly, he envisioned himself as its inhabitant, with a long, unkempt mane and madness in his eyes, crouching beside a low fire, his bony knees protruding from the faded tatters of his favorite blue pants as he scraped bits of meat from a desiccated bone. The image, he knew, was a warning, a caution against his urge to stay. He shuddered at the thought that whether he moved on or not, despite his barely having eaten for the last several days, he would run out of food in less than a week, leaving him, like the mangy, scraggly-bearded version of himself, to beg the forest for what it would provide.

The future had become a maze, a labyrinth of false starts and blind turns, in which, each time, he met the Minotaur before he found his way. That there was a center, a treasure or even a refuge, he had never stopped assuming, and yet had never allowed himself to envision what it could be. He had rarely pictured deliberately the place he longed to arrive at, but instead had focused all his determination and imagination on the task of arriving itself. What was more, he knew when it was that he had lost the sense of a goal. It was before James had died, while they were sitting in the airport with Joaquim, watching his uncle's outsized hands fumble with the tiny vials and needles. At that moment, Larry knew for certain the danger of hope, and resolved to do what he could to save himself from danger. The curtain fell and was not to rise again, but the metal point of a dagger appeared at a seam, threatening to rend it up the middle with the single word, *mboa*.

LVII

AS LARRY LAY miserable in his own sweat, there was no deluge through that tear in the curtain, no rush of evil into the world, no flood through a collapsing river bank, no angry mob streaming through a gate. Whatever rend there was, was thin and small, no bigger than a word, and memories slid through it slowly, as blood beads at the site of a small wound. The passage was so narrow that often the senses had to slip through one by one—a smell, or a color, or the gesture of a hand. A thought would well up slowly, like a tear in an eye, and hover quivering for minutes or hours before falling silently onto the sand. Yet behind the one word, there were others, pushing through at intervals, a halting and uncertain speech. If one were in a hurry, one would imagine there was little to be said, but Larry lay still for the entire afternoon, and barely moved from his hammock in the evening. By nightfall, the bucket had begun to fill; the level in the hourglass had risen, swelling with bits of memory, flashes of color and bursts of human sound *"Mboa,"* he whispered to himself as he felt the hammock cradle him, the first word of Pahqua he had spoken since James died. He sighed as he said it, blowing out the final "oa" sound as though it were a candle. *"Mboa,"* he said. "Beautiful from the dead."

LVIII

THERE WAS NO doubt that Silvio had had his share of disappointments, a few but not all of which he had brought upon himself; he had likewise succeeded in disappointing others in equal measure. From boyhood, his parents had simply assumed that he would be a doctor like his father, not merely earning a good living and bringing pride to his family and to Jews everywhere, but able to assume the mantle of his father's research, as soon as the elder Amanza was no longer able to carry it himself. This assumption on his parents' part served to prepare Silvio for a lifetime devoted to the innovation of newer and better ways to shirk responsibility, to avoid routine, to call his own shots, to escape. Thus, when approached by a stranger as he sat gazing out over the top of his open biology text at *Le Cigale*, holding his half-drained coffee cup halfway off the table at a precarious angle, he was more eager than he should have been to engage in conversation with someone who already, even then, bore himself with an air of self-possessed exoticism.

"You're a scientist?" Joaquim had asked him, motioning first to the book and then to the empty chair across from him.

"Nope. Just a student," Silvio replied, moving the chair back to make room for Joaquim to sit down.

"Well, science is a good thing to study," said Joaquim, motioning to the waiter. "There are so many things you can do with it."

Silvio gave a little laugh. "What can you do with it? I guess there's medicine, and research, and teaching," he said. "No more possibilities, really, than in any other field."

"I don't know about that," Joaquim said. "I've been looking to hire a scientist myself."

"What for?" said Silvio, closing his book, moving to the edge of his chair, poised now, like his coffee cup, to either jump or fall.

"Have you heard of the SPI?" said Joaquim nonchalantly. "We go tromping though the forest, trying to build ties with Indians." He leaned back to allow the waiter to place before him a tiny espresso cup. "It hasn't worked out for us, hiring just anybody who's willing to go. My idea is that we'd do much better with people who really know their biology, and their chemistry, their sociology, their anthropology and the like. I've newly signed on a geneticist, a fellow from the States, guy by the name of James Ardmore. You've read Comte?"

"Never heard of him," said Silvio, sensing incipient disappointment.

"Really? I'm going to have to talk to my dear friend Professor Oliveira, to find out what he's been teaching his students these days."

"Professor Oliveira? I have him now for . . . !" Silvio started to interject, stopping in mid-sentence when his eyes met those of his dark-skinned companion.

"Tell him I send my regards," said Joaquim, setting his cup down and standing up. "Here's my card," he said.

LIX

THE NIGHT WAS interminable. Even the moon gave up and left, folding itself into the pockets of the river like a stowaway and flowing off. Each time Larry woke up, he remembered a different dream, but when he took out his flashlight and swept the shore, the landscape was always the same. He clicked off the flashlight and tried to reposition himself in the hammock. When he closed his eyes, he could see one of the houses in Pahquel. In his dream, someone had been shut up inside the house, which was fitted with a door and a padlock like the shack near the airport outside Itatuba. The prisoner was trying to get a message out by writing on bits of paper and sticking them through the cracks in the walls. No one noticed the white scraps fluttering down the sides of the house, and Larry tried not to draw attention to himself as he shifted his body slowly toward them. He tried to catch them without being seen by reaching his hand out behind him, but the papers crumbled when he tried to grasp them. *"Tikima pattaa noa abaka,"* he whispered to himself unwittingly as he slept, sensing even in sleep that what he said was determined as much by which words he could recall as by their meaning. "They're falling into a hole."

And so his dreams fell, each bearing a message scrawled in transliterated Pahqua, which crumbled and blew away as he awoke. He dreamed about the sight of Banata's rough hand resting on the blue checked fabric of James's shirt. He dreamed about the smell of *mopa* soaking in a wooden vat. He dreamed about the day he had been missed, when he had gone off with Amakar and Dabimi to gather muruci without telling anyone where he was. They had wandered the whole day with their baskets on their backs, until the baskets overflowed and the juice dribbled out through the woven bottoms, running down their legs and staining them orange. Amakar had been protective of Larry; he knew he couldn't climb, so he told Larry to sit at the base of the trunks and guard the baskets while they shimmied up, wearing their *riris* around their waists. Larry had felt so happy at his task, even though he suspected that Amakar was only pretending he was needed. As it turned out, he had done a better job than any of them had expected by spotting a scorpion in the weaving that held the shoulder strap to Dabimi's basket. It had been almost dusk by the time they returned to the village. At the entrance, Amakar had made a commotion, singing out *"Liroko do amik. Liroko do amik,"* while James and Karad rushed to meet them, forgetting their anger in relief. Only, in Larry's dream, he hadn't made it back to the village because of the scorpions crawling all over his own pack. He turned in his hammock and brushed the back of his neck with his hand, and then jolted up and checked the woven ropes by the light of his flashlight while sleep stood patiently by, awaiting his return.

It was as though each time he tried to set off for the morning, some other task called him back to his starting place, some other tentacle of night. He dreamed about small things, the texture of boar-skin blankets and the taste of grilled river shrimp, and then of the more important things, of Anok, who used to grind her dyes in rows of wooden bowls, telling him stories as she worked.

Despite all his months of preparation, and his years of being tutored by James in Pahqua, Larry at first understood almost nothing she said to him. He would nod at her narrow, misshapen back and make lines in the dirt with a stick while she rocked back and forth on her heels, pushing the pigments with the *maata*. At first, she was the only woman he spoke to at all, because when she didn't have her baby in her arms, she would sit with her back to him and keep her eyes on her work, freeing him from confronting the embarrassment of her nakedness. He rarely blushed in her presence, as he did when he tried to talk to the other women and girls. She would tell him the same story many times over so that he could learn the words, changing her voice to indicate the different characters.

Occasionally, she would tip a few of the bowls toward him, and he would pretend to admire the colors, which looked to him like lumpy, dull versions of his tempera paints from grade school, and smelled distastefully pungent in the hot, still air. She covered the bowls with sapucaia leaves and lay flat stones across them, pushing them into the shade of a miniature lean-to that was built into the side of her house. After she rinsed her hands in a wooden trough, she would walk off without saying goodbye. As Larry got up to leave, he could usually hear her baby crying and her voice offering it the comfort of her stories.

Once, when she was in the midst of grinding *caba* in a wooden bowl with the round, grey stone, the baby started to cry inside the house. She stood up and handed the stone to Larry, gesturing to him to continue. Larry sat by himself, turning the *maata* in his hand to the tune of "I've been working on the railroad," the only song he could think of. The pigment smelled somewhat more tolerable than the others, like fruit mixed with mint and sour milk. It stained the stone a dark, blackish red. He leaned into his work with the full weight of his body, imagining that if he did a good job, she would ask him to help more often, an honor he longed for in a world in which many of his efforts, his triumph with Dabimi and Amakar notwithstanding, were regarded with subtle condescension. As the dark substance grew thicker, it clung to the sides of the bowl and took on a glossy sheen that made it look like tube paint. He tilted the bowl back and forth, and his face was pulled long and then pushed squat as his reflection ran over ripples in the surface. The trees stretched and thickened around his head like knotted locks of hair.

When Anok came out again carrying the baby in her arms he showed her the bowl, looking for her approval. She smiled at him broadly, nodding at him to put it on the ground in front of the lean-to. She motioned for him to put the *maata* into a gourd beside the water trough she used for hand-washing, and then, without warning, thrust the baby towards him. At first he tried to refuse, insisting that he didn't know how to hold it, afraid he'd make it cry. There was something shameful to him about babies. He felt uncomfortably girlish resting it on his lap, watching Anok as she shredded bark with the sharp edge of a stone. When he heard Dabimi and

Amakar approaching from the far side of the house, a wave of panic hit him, and he felt the impulse to lay the baby down and run off before they could see him. As he stood up, they came around the corner and stopped directly in front of him, watching in disbelief as he lifted the baby and placed it over his shoulder. "I was helping Anok," he tried to explain, his voice shaking as he held the thin leg against his chest. A smell like that of rotting fish passed in the air between them as Anok spooned a whitish, lumpy substance into the bowl that held the shredded bark. He felt a flush spread over his face and fumbled in his mind for words, until at last the silence was broken by the shouts of the two boys, *"Anok, tika sapat ina marana!"* "You never let me hold her! Why can't I have a turn?"

Anok answered without looking up from her work. "He does what I ask him to do," she said. "He does a good job, but you never listen." She crouched over the bowl, holding it steady with her feet. The idea that two boys his own age would fight to hold a baby was unheard of to Larry. When Anok finally gave them her permission, he was unsettled by the eagerness with which each one cradled the small head in the crook of his arm, singing, drawing invisible designs across its chest. "They're hidden in the corners of your house," they each sang in turn, almost in a whisper, to a tune he had often heard Anok hum over her work. "They are the *Ark Pol*, who steal your children away."

Larry stood to one side and watched the child smile and reach for their faces. "It has no diaper," he said in English.

"Okay, you take her," said Amakar. *"Wan, wan,"* said Larry, holding his hands between them as though in deference.

"What's her name?" he asked as a distraction.

"Name? It's obvious she's not old enough," said Dabimi, as though he couldn't imagine a more stupid question. "You know she's *rajora?*" he whispered to Larry.

"Rajora?"

"She has no *jitana*," he said, leaning towards him, his voice still low.

"Mmm," said Larry, nodding. Despite his embarrassment, he looked down at her to see if there was anything missing, but since nothing obvious was out of place, he concluded that a *jitana* wasn't a body part. He repeated the word several times to himself, hoping to remember it long enough to ask James about it. As he broke it into syllables in his mind, he absently held out a finger for the baby to hold. She brought it to her mouth, scraping at it with her two teeth. The three stood around her and she pulled their hair. Despite himself, Larry was reluctant this time to give her up, and allowed her to grab his nose and push her feet into his collarbone. He said "diapers" to her again and again, and she laughed with him at the absurdity.

Such was the beginning of their love affair. Larry had come upon a sense of purpose that obscured the nagging shame that flooded him whenever he allowed himself to remember that he had become a nanny. He would sit in the shade, bouncing the baby on his legs to the rhythm of Anok's story-songs and the boys would call his name from across the yard. When one day Anok had to meet with some other women in the far village, Larry kept the baby all evening long, and for once had as many after-dinner visitors as James did. He would follow Anok to the site of a new *chajan* and people would nod at him, both men and women, even those he had previously feared. Most of the other babies were carried by women or girls, though Amari often came out to play Kari after lunch, clutching his infant sister carelessly, Larry thought, like a football, under his arm, and Atwa, with whom James was so close, sometimes sat on the log in front of his house smoking a thick roll of *kikara* while he balanced his infant son on his knee. Nearly a month had gone by when one evening, as Larry sat with James on their stools of lashed cane stalks beside a dwindling fire, James turned to him and asked, out of the silence, "So you want to be the *jitana*?"

Larry looked at him through the rippled film of heat and tried to remember where he had heard the word. "At first I was a skeptic," James said, "for their sake and yours, but as I've thought about it, it does make sense. Especially since we're coming back."

"Am I supposed to know that word?" Larry said defensively.

James paused for a minute, and then laughed so loudly that Yamara came out of his hut across from them and ran over to see what the joke was. He had begun to laugh too, even before he reached them, but when he heard James spit out what he could, *"Kokoru do Liroko nara alo jitana,"* he too was doubled over, unable to choke out words. Horrified, knowing that the joke was on him, Larry stood up and stepped backwards through the doorway and started pacing back and forth across the hut with his hands jammed into his pockets. After a while, he started to feel dizzy, so he slumped in a corner without turning on his flashlight to check the walls for reduviids. The last of the light receded from the doorway, leaving the room in complete darkness. Outside, the voices grew even louder and more numerous, and then slowly faded and thinned, as a fire stretches itself out into embers between stones. At last, the embers flickered out and the forest's voices flooded the empty space. James turned on his flashlight as he bowed to get through the doorway and fixed its beam on the ground by Larry's right hand.

"I think there's been a miscommunication," he said, sitting down beside Larry and switching off the flashlight.

Larry turned his head away, allowing the cicadas to answer in his place.

"I thought you knew what you were doing," said James, unfurling his legs in front of him. "And like I said, it made sense."

"What are you talking about?" said Larry loudly, trying to pass off his humiliation as anger.

"In retrospect, there's no reason you should have known, but I assumed that one of your friends would have said something, Dabimi, maybe, because he's older, or even Anok."

Larry thought back to the time when he had first spoken with Dabimi and Amakar at Anok's. "You mean about the baby?" he said with the inflection of a retort.

"About the baby's needing a *jitana*," said James.

"*Jitana*," said Larry, suddenly remembering.

"You've heard the word?"

"Maybe," said Larry. He tried to imagine what his error might have been, but could only assume that his punishment would, as usual, involve a measure of shame far greater than the extent of his previous contentment.

"Do you want to know?" James asked.

"I was just trying to help Anok," said Larry, getting up again to resume his pacing. "It likes me." He took a few steps before he realized he couldn't see to walk, and sat down where he was, across from James.

"A *jitana* is a second father," said James, speaking on faith into the dark. "When a man's *kaag* has a baby, he can decide whether to allow a second father to be named, who will care for the child as best he can and protect it with his spirit if the real father ever dies or leaves. Anok's *kaag* wasn't so generous. He forbade all the men from going near his child. So the child pays the price for the father's bullheadedness."

"I can't take care of a baby," Larry blurted out, "and we're leaving in another month anyway."

"You're already caring for her, just by carting her around. You've done more than enough, especially since Anok is *Ak* so she's taken care of in that way. The most important part is in your agreeing to it. The child'll have an easier time finding a *kaag* herself if she has a *jitana*, just an easier time in general getting around."

"I'd be the father?" asked Larry, unwilling to make sense of James's words. "I can't be a father! I'm only eleven!"

"More a protective spirit, really," said James, sensing Larry's panic. "It makes sense, because it's clear by now that none of the older men intends to do it. Most people are scared of Anok, I think, with or without the curse on her."

"So I'd be married?" said Larry, in the same panicked voice.

"No, of course not—you're an honorary father, not an honorary *kaag*. There's a big difference. No one is going to let another man marry his wife, but almost all men want their child to be well cared for."

"But why should it be me? A lot of people could do a better job." Larry thought about Dabimi's easy manner, the way he swaggered with the baby on his hip.

"I have a theory about that. First, it's because Anok trusts you and thinks you're hardworking. Also, she'd resent giving a boost in status to anyone else who stepped forward. And despite her stubbornness, she does feel the pressure. But . . ." James paused for a while before going on, "I think probably the biggest reason has to do with the fact that the *jitana* has the first claim to marry the child if it's a girl. If you leave, she can block somebody else's claim by using you as an excuse, or not."

James stopped talking. Larry watched as his uncle lit the camping light with a match and strung up their hammocks from the corner-poles. He pulled out their netting and their flannel-lined sleeping pants and the cotton sacks of wadded-up clothes they used as pillows. Then he went out with his toothbrush, leaving Larry alone in the flickering light. Somewhere deep in the forest, an owl monkey called out to announce itself, and Larry imagined it scurrying over broken branches with its baby clinging to its chest. He could picture its face with its huge, nocturnal eyes, which gave it an eternally terrified look.

"How would it affect me?" he said as James came and sat down again beside him. "Will anyone be mad at me?"

"Only if they're jealous," said James. "Most people see it as your shouldering a burden on their behalf. It's a way to be someone on your own here, rather than through me."

"I'm not old enough," said Larry.

But the next day, she spoke his name, *"Ro"* for *"Liroko,"* and the next, he won his first game of Kari in the clearing beside the center house after lunch, and they all went swimming in the river, Larry and Amakar and Dabimi and Amari and Karar, and spent the afternoon trying to catch fish with their hands, and threw sticks like javelins from bank to bank. On the following day, Larry and James sat in the shade and watched as Anok worked on a new section of Tarana's *chajan,* listening to the stories she was painting as they passed the baby back and forth between them, and a week later, they sat together again, watching Anok paint the story of her baby's *jitana* into her own *chajan,* so that when the child reached the age of six moon cycles and was given a name, they saw, in varnished images of yellow and orange and blackish red, how Liroko had come from out of the trees with his own *jitana* to become the *jitana* of the child, born of Anok and a dead man, whose name was now Aran.

LX

FOR SIX YEARS, Larry had worked to condense what was most meaningful about his first trip to Pahquel with James, into isolated phrases, into facts about which he had no personal interest; he would ask James about the range of the tapir, but never about his friendship with Asator; about the Pahqua word for kneecap, but not about the reason he was chosen as *jitana;* about which kind of palm leaves had been used in the roof of their hut, but never about why James wept as he said goodbye to Warari—a woman Larry had barely been aware of—and held onto her shoulder at the end of the path. James too had found his own private method for distilling a thousand stories—those he had told many times and those he had loved too deeply to tell—into a single plot whose ostensive subject was his fight to preserve the only words that might have captured otherwise untold thoughts. Whole dramas dried up before their eyes; that moment under the *chajan,* in which they stood together beneath the accrued histories of the living and the dead, sticky in their body paint, their smells blending, became "The *Jitana* Story" and then no story at all, never mentioned by either of them, even to each other, to the point that four years later, when their relatives fussed over an infant at a distant cousin's wedding, no word was spoken between them as Larry awkwardly declined to hold the child, saying he didn't like babies.

If James had lived, perhaps he too would have been reminded, during that seemingly endless night on that tiny strip of praia, nestled in the crook of the river's arm, that what remains unspoken floats in a certain well-appointed antechamber in the mind, living quietly amid the damask and the mildew, as in Sr. Catalpa's house, until it is taken up for use as a prop in one or another instantly forgotten, never-forgotten drama. On that night, the main character was someone who looked like Larry only younger, with a shorter haircut and a brighter, more open expression, carrying a baby in his arms. The figure entered the dream, taking his place on the riverbank beside Dabimi and Amakar, holding Aran on his lap.

"You're not holding her right," said Dabimi, positioning her head more securely. His concern was warranted, for when Larry turned aside for a minute, the baby fell into the river and was carried off by the current, which grew stronger and more violent as his dream was pulled downstream. Again and again, Larry managed to rescue her, by ever more desperate means—by fishing her out with a stick, by building a dam downstream, by jumping in and carrying her aloft with one hand while trying with the other to keep his body from being battered against the rocks. He groaned and twisted in his hammock. His body was feverish with the effort, pulse racing as he tried to push her up onto the shore. He struggled to catch sight of his friends, but they had left him alone to thrash against a current far stronger than he. At last, her arm was pulled from his grasp, and he could only watch in horror as she was swept downstream towards the rapids. He ran along the bank beside her, shouting her name again and again, but his voice was lost in the crash of water against rock, and her small body plummeted down into the foam. "Aran! Aran!" he shouted, grasping at the sides of his hammock. Finally his screams awoke him to a morning dazzling with sunlight, and the placid, innocent river, and turtles sunning themselves on rocks, and a small voice speaking in clear, slow tones, *"Pani, apa tanaa."* "Person, I am here."

PART

TWO

LXI

THE WORLD APPEARS confusing and unreal when one's vision is clouded, but often no less so when one's vision is too sharp. When Larry raised his head and pulled himself up in the hammock, he saw everything around him in exaggerated detail; every leaf on every tree, the veins in every leaf, every knot in the fabric of his netting and, as he threw the netting off and turned to look behind him, every strand of dark hair on the heads of the women who stood side by side, watching him. He squinted as he returned their gaze, not to make the image of them clearer, but to blur it so that he might buffer himself from a reality too immediate to allow him the wherewithal to see. Through the thin openings between his eyelids, he scanned the line of silent figures, and when he turned away, he caught a glimpse of some essence he recognized, as one sees the furthest stars in the night sky only out of the corner of an eye. What he saw, in the form on the far right, in the shape of her eyebrow, or her mouth, or her shoulders, or some other feature he couldn't pinpoint, was Anok, only a different Anok from the one he thought he remembered, unbent and smooth-skinned, wearing a necklace of painted beads and feathers that nested on her chest against a woman's breast on the right side and on the left side, a girl's.

Larry opened his mouth and closed it and opened it again. "Anok, I've been looking for you," he stammered at last, mixing English and Pahqua in a chaotic jumble. He stood up and reached instinctively to button his pants and zip his fly, as though frightened of offending with his undress. They stood in silence as he struggled with the zipper. "I got lost," he said, feeling his pulse in his ears, so loud he could barely hear himself. "I think

I've been sick." One whispered to another, and Larry strained to catch the words. The figure standing next to Anok grabbed her arm to hold her still. The slightest breeze touched their hair and the feathers that adorned it.

"Did I make a mistake?" he said, looking from one to another, shaken as much now by their silence as by the shock of their appearance.

"*Patiri!*" called the tall woman at the head of the line, and they all turned at once and set off in single file towards the mouth of the forest, almost in a run.

"Anok!" Larry called desperately, reaching out for her arm as she passed at the end of the line.

She shook him off with a scream and ran to catch up with the others, but as soon as she stepped into the thicket, she turned back to face him, holding a branch in front of her. "Why did you call me?" she asked Larry, glancing back over her shoulder as she spoke.

"I've been looking for you," Larry said again, helplessly, in Pahqua. "I needed to be with you," he said.

"I don't know you," said Anok. She took a step backward and her face was lost to shadow.

"But you do! You do!" pleaded Larry, fighting tears. "I'm Liroko! Liroko! I took care of your baby! I mixed your paints. Jarara is dead, and I have no home, and I'm lost and I'm sick. Don't go," he said, unable to stop himself. "Don't go. Don't go. Don't go. Don't go." He searched for her face among the dark branches, and a dozen pairs of eyes looked back. They were the eyes of the forest, of James, of the old Anok, of a tiny orange monkey throwing off the rind of a *piquia* and skittering away. They looked out at him from the semi-darkness and rendered their judgment and moved on, crushing mounds of dark green scrub as they went, leaving only Anok as a sentinel behind them. Larry paced his shimmering, desolate corner of sand, wiping his tears on his shirtsleeve, and the eyes of the sentinel followed him, and saw what had to be done. They watched as he untied his hammock and rolled it up, straining with the knot while his legs trembled with weakness and pain.

When he had finished gathering his clothes and cramming them into his pack, he pushed his books down on top. By the time he came to the last one, his thoughts had grown so shrill that he could hear them being shouted in his own voice, in English, punctuated by howls and gasps and the sound of a rasping cough.

"What do you want?" he yelled out, startling the forest. "What do you want? I'm done. I can't do any more. Do you want to win? You won. Are you happy? I'm done!"

The forest swallowed the words as they appeared, dulling their impact and absorbing their echoes. When he finished packing his books, he took his pills with shaking hands, not bothering to count them, and pulled out a box of raisins, slipping it into his pocket. He filled his bottles and shouldered his pack. His knees buckled under the weight. When he fell, the pack came forward and hit him on the back of the head, and he collapsed onto the sand. The blow didn't hurt him, or cause him to black out. Its only purpose was to mark the end of his efforts, to delimit the far boundary of hope. He slipped off the straps and curled up between the burning surfaces of sun and sand, ready to be crushed between them. Instead, he heard a rustling behind him and, despite himself, jolted up. Before him stood the vision of Anok with his pack on her back, leaning slightly forward to balance its weight.

"*Pakara ano jajata?*" she said, when she caught his eye. "Does it fly?"

"Are we going?"

"*Pakara,*" Larry answered. "It flies." He got clumsily to his feet and they walked to the place where his two smaller bags sat. She waited with her back to him while he pulled one strap over each shoulder and then she started off without looking back. As Larry stepped after her into the forest, he was suddenly tempted to turn back, at the very least to pay his respects to a place that, in leaving, suddenly felt more like home to him than any other he had had, or could imagine having. But he pushed himself forward after Anok and the door closed behind him with the crack of wood against stone.

The route was uneven and dense with branches, but less impenetrable than he had remembered it; there was no need to reach for his knife, or to keep his arms over his face as he went. Despite the ache in his joints and head, his body fell into the rhythm of walking, and he was able to keep the bright orange cover of his pack in view, though the body that carried it often vanished into the mottled brown walls that framed them on all sides. In fact, without the sight of that saturated patch of fabric to guide him, he would have been helpless to follow, as his eyes had grown used to the light during his timeless stay on the praia, and he had lost the ability to discern the subtle variations of muted color that marked the forest's contours. He saw only a blur of camouflage and darkness, pierced by a small orange beacon that blinked and danced at the far end of a sinuous tunnel.

Only after he began to feel accustomed to walking did it occur to him that he had finally been saved, or captured, or both. At first, he imagined the latter, and felt weak and ashamed, more naked than Anok. He pictured arriving at the village looking foolish and ineffectual and sick, not worthy even of pity, but as he walked on, his fear of being seen as diminished was gradually overtaken by the even deeper terror of his having been forgotten altogether. There was genuine confusion and defiance in Anok's face at his insistence that he knew her, and he couldn't help but picture himself surrounded by a crowd of people he thought he loved, each one bearing the same demeanor, threatening in its blankness, offering proof that the place that he had secretly called home had never really existed. He put his hands in his pockets, feeling, against his palm, the smooth round face of the compass, which there was no longer any reason to draw out.

They might have walked for an hour or a day. At times, Larry could barely stagger forward but at others, he felt his strength return in an agitated rush. As he walked, he ate raisins and nuts from his bag, and tried to drink from his water bottle without choking or tripping. When he saw her crouch down and stopped at a respectful distance to urinate against a tree, his arms and legs retained the feeling of motion, pendula that had forgotten how to be still. His limbs moved not to propel him forward, but because the entire world moves and breathes, expands and contracts, oscillates, paces the length of its confinement, even in surrender. He stared at the neon patch and his eyes reeled him forward while his arms and legs flailed in the air like a beetle's. They rounded a bend in the path, and he made out a lone felled trunk which lay off to their right among some brambles, half-covered by moss and ivy, its trunk propped up on its stump.

Larry walked quickly by it and then stopped short. It was James's hand that caught him by the shoulder and turned him, and pointed, and James's voice that whispered, "Look!" It was James's voice that tried, unsuccessfully, to quell the panic that rose in him at the sight of that hewn log. It tried to remind him of their first glimpse of one of those logs together, of his excitement and the thousand questions he had had, and his urge to run up to touch the marks the stone ax had left in the exposed cross-section of the trunk. It offered a gesture of reassurance and then disappeared, leaving Larry alone to gasp for breath in the thick, still air. Every aspect of the forest had grown heavy, sounds most of all, which refused to evaporate; the cries of birds and insects, the leaden pulse of his own footfalls, even the sharp snap of twigs under foot, were blunted and engorged and hung like overripe fruit from the ends of the vines. High cackles became low, booming voices: Sodeis, repeating in a distorted baritone, "there's no room for anything personal," and Sr. Catalpa inviting him, again and again, each time more slowly, to refill his glass tumbler with wine, and the nasal drone of the customs agent in Rio, asking James over and over, absurdly, how long they planned to stay. Music changed key; the slow movement from Beethoven's seventh played in his head, ponderous and dirge-like, pitched so low that it threatened to dissolve into vibrations. Sound itself came, for a minute, to rest, and motion drew inward. As he trudged on toward the place where Anok had been standing, he knew that his only refuge from fear was in time's capacity to thicken and set, causing an eternal postponement of his arrival. For a minute, he ceased to cover ground as he walked, while wasps hovered in the air as still as hummingbirds, and a spider's web turned to spun glass. But even then, on the horizon, the spaces between the trees began to glow, rippling the air, reaching their thousand hands toward him, gesturing their infinite need.

"This way," she called. They took a sharp turn to the right and then another to the left, and came out into a clearing that overflowed with light. Before Larry had a chance to shield his eyes, he felt a hand on his back, and another on his head, pushing it down, guiding him through a low doorway into a darkened, foul-smelling room. As he straightened up again, he heard voices coming from a corner behind him and turned quickly to see

Anok pointing at him, gesturing as she leaned in towards a woman with long thick gray hair and uneven, sagging breasts. As the two came toward him, he felt his legs give way, and they ran forward and caught him by his arms. They slipped his bags from his shoulders and eased him onto a low platform of split logs lashed together, covered with a spongy sheet of what looked like moss but felt more like the dried inside of a gourd. Larry sat on the side of the platform and looked from one to the other in confusion and disbelief. Before him stood two versions of Anok, young and old; one wearing Anok's characteristic stern expression and the other, her familiar guarded smile.

"He called to me, mother, by my name and yours," said the younger of the two, glancing toward the other.

"Do you have a stick for your face?" said the older one, motioning with her hand against her chin.

Larry looked at her in disbelief, watching the movement through blank, confused eyes.

"For your face!" she repeated, sounding impatient. She motioned to his pack, which lay where Anok had set it, just inside the door.

Suddenly, Larry remembered. He reached a hand out towards the pack, and the young Anok brought it over and set it down against the platform. Larry dug through it and pulled out his razor and soap. "I need a bowl of water," he said, and one was brought. As he began to shave, slowly, his hands shaking, without a mirror in the dim half-light, the older one sat down beside him and began to sing in a soft, low voice. The song was soothing and, as he allowed it to cover over the chaotic whirl of his thoughts, familiar.

"So I'm here," Larry said at last, as though in a daze, to the older one, almost forgetting about the younger, who, after retrieving the bowl, had backed away and now stood in shadow watching them from the corner of the dark room.

"Liroko," said the elder when he had finished, holding his head under the chin and turning his face toward her.

"Anok?" Larry said at last, searching her rutted face in disbelief. Suddenly, he was engulfed by a wave of relief that was narcotic in its power.

"Can I rest?" he asked, and she gestured him down. He pulled his jacket from his pack with shaking arms and tried to throw it across his legs, but she took it from him and covered him instead with three soft animal pelts that had been lying in a pile at the end of the platform, after shaking each one with a firm, jarring snap. He balled up his jacket and pushed it under his head.

"Where is Jarara?" she said as she pushed the edges of the pelts under his legs.

"*Napata.* Dead," said Larry, overcome with exhaustion and misery and relief. He closed his eyes and began to sink into the dark pool of his dreams, but caught himself and pushed with all his might to bring himself back to the surface.

"Who is that?" he said, gesturing weakly with his arm, already drifting downward again by the time the answer came.

"Shame, *jitana!*" said Anok from above him, at the surface of his thoughts. "Don't tell me you've forgotten Aran!"

LXII

BY THE TIME Larry's head came to rest in the matted arms of his jacket, word of his arrival had already spread. When Aran ventured out to empty the wooden bowl of shaving water, she had to push her way through the crowd that had gathered in front of the painted doorframe of her hut, blocking her way to the trough.

"*Pin ano Jarara?*" they whispered to her as she bent down to pour the water into the dirt beyond their *kaawa*. "*Napata Jarara?*"

She stood up haughtily, glaring at anyone who blocked her way.

"*Pin ano Jarara?*" Dabimi asked loudly, standing in front of her. "*Pin ano jitana?*"

"*Jara ka,*" said Aran in exasperation. "I don't know." She tried to maneuver around him and the empty bowl fell into the dirt. "Move away" she said in a fierce whisper while she bent to pick it up, and he did, flashing a mocking expression to the man beside him as she disappeared through the hut's doorway.

Once inside, she squatted beside her mother and they leaned in against each other, shoulder to shoulder, watching Larry sleep. In the silence, the murmur of the voices outside swelled like the rest of the forest, wrapping the tiny hut in a thick blanket of questions and assertions, of pleas and demands and laments.

"*Pin ano jitana?*" she herself asked at last in a hushed voice, averting her eyes from the direction of her mother, even in the darkness.

"*Ibo jitana,*" said Anok, nodding into the blackness. "That's your *jitana.*" Her tone was firm but emotionless, as though she had made a wall of her voice. "I have to go now and talk to Asator," she said. She stood and shook out her legs, turning her back to Aran.

LXIII

JORGE GRABBED AT the receiver with annoyance, and fought back the temptation to return it to its cradle before finding out who had disturbed him.

"Moretti" he growled, already angry at Silvio for calling him three times in one day.

"Jorge," said his mother on the line.

"That's my name," said Jorge, shaking his head.

"Martina's been calling. Silvio's been calling. It seems like you're making things worse for yourself."

"Is that so?"

"So you have a choice," said Sara. "I can come over, or Joaquim can, or you can have both of us."

"How about if I just call Martina and get you all off my back?" said Jorge, reuniting, violently, the receiver with the phone.

LXIV

WHEN ANOK APPEARED at the mouth of the doorway, the crowd, which had grown by now to a hands-and-feet and more, gathered around her as though speaking in unison an obvious question. They pushed forward onto the *kaawa,* but stopped at the threshold, *chajan* of the ancestors, and didn't cross. Torches had been lit, and light flickered above their heads.

Anok stepped forward, and they backed away.

"Pin ano Jarara?" Napata Jarara?" people whispered, more to each other than to her as they followed her through the clearing. When Anok arrived at Asator's house, she stood outside his *kaawa* and called to him. While she waited, the mass of bodies behind her untangled and scattered around the front of the house. Finally, Asator emerged.

"Pin ano Jarara?" said Asator, after lowering himself slowly onto the log by the door, taking his time to arrange his wooden cane across his thighs. Coming from his mouth, the question sounded as gentle as it had sounded harsh in the mouth of Dabimi.

"Napata Jarara," said Anok, after a silence in which she considered whether or not to tell him. James is dead.

"Napata?" he said, lifting his stick again and pushing one end of it into the ground between his feet. "Who told you that?"

"Ibo Liroko. Ibo jitana."

"Buka jitana?"

"In my house. Aran found him by the river, calling her. They were out beyond the world, which is something else I have to tell you. I'm sure it was Aran's fault." She paused for a minute. The penalty for venturing

167

outside the perimeter of logs that demarked world's end was significant, a moon cycle's ration of smoked meat, but that was the least of her problems. "He's sick," she went on, looking over Asator's shoulder to address his son, who had emerged behind him. "Go and get Panar." Pahquel was made up of three separate centers that were positioned in a row, and Anok was asking him to walk to the farthest of the three to bring the curer back with him.

"Not now!" said the son, eager to hear the story that would emerge through the singing.

"He's still sleeping, but I don't know for how long. I want Panar Ak to be there when he wakes up."

The son scowled and kicked at the dirt, but when Anok broke off in mid-sentence and nodded at him again, and Asator elbowed him lightly on the thigh, he exchanged a glance with the old woman and headed off, calling out as he went to alert the forest to his path. After he'd gone, Asator's daughter stepped out of the hut into his place. She moved closer to her father and put a hand on his arm, patting it softly as he began to sing the names of those whose death-images had been added to the *chajans* since the rain. When he came to those who had not yet been given names, he referred to them by the names of their mothers, Katura baby and Jajata baby and Jun baby and Aparan baby.

Death songs are common songs, familiar to even the smallest children. Many who weren't even Ak could have sung most of the parts themselves from beginning to end, given their symmetry: The story of the departure from the world of the ancestors and the birth into the world of persons resembles word-for-word, in reverse, the story of the return. But in James's case, there could be no singing of his birth out of the body of a woman, but only of his *ritaXa*, his sojourn. There could be no first-hand account of the death, of the visitation of the ancestors, and their joyful reception of his spirit; no darker story either, of James's suffering and removal as a result of their vengeance against him. As Asator sang, Anok strained to listen for clues as to how the death would be regarded, the outcome of which would determine Larry's status in the group forever. Were he the holder of an ancestral curse, the results would be devastating for Aran.

"They are reaching down," Asator sang at last, and Anok's shoulders relaxed as she exhaled outwards. That was the reassurance she sought: That Jarara would be welcomed by the ancestors as one of their own. Anok was less concerned about the question of which line was rightfully his; given their long history together, Asator would no doubt claim him as one of his own, despite all the claims shouted out from every corner. But these were not questions to be answered by men; it was Asator's privilege to sing not his own decrees, but those of the ones who came before, who could no more afford to be indulgent with the truth than their descendants could. "They're waiting now to hold him," sang Asator. When a person went to join them, the ancestors would welcome him by gathering him in their arms, rocking him like a baby. Like the others, she began to rock, closing her eyes, as they all did, to better feel the motion. She swayed forward and back, and yet opened one eye from time to time to keep track of Dabimi, who sat off to the right outside the circle defined by the arches of the torchlight, staring. In the silence that surrounded Asator's voice like an aura, the torches cracked and spat, as though to remind them that they were all born of fire, whose claim transcended theirs, and would prevail. Asator's singing contracted to a hiss, the sound of breath escaping, a wheel turning with some effort. Between phrases, as the crowd muttered their parts, he leaned over and whispered to Anok.

"What?"

"Nothing," said Anok.

"Liroko has his claim," whispered Asator, so that she could barely hear him. "And Dabimi's too young for a second." Others were singing now too, beating out the rhythm with the ends of their torches, calling out the names of those they'd lost.

"You know Dabimi hates Liroko for it. I heard him talking outside my house."

Asator turned away. The song began to fade, moving more and more slowly, like a wheel grinding to a halt. When it stopped, he turned to his daughter and motioned to her to help him up. Low voices started to swell again, but stopped short when he raised his hand. "The *chajans* walk in their father's paths." He paused again and then went on, over the general murmur. "In four days, we'll burn wood from the house of every man, and those pieces are his body. And we'll do the dance and spread Jarara in the house of his line, over the roof and under the *chajan* of Dabimi."

LXV

ARAN SAT CROUCHED in a corner of the hut, listening to the swooping of the bats outside the doorway, and to the sound of Larry's slow breathing. Before, when so many people were gathered outside, whispering about her and calling to her, she had tried to stay calm by reassuring herself that they would soon be gone. Now, as she sat alone in the darkness, surrounded only by the cries of the night, she would have wished them back, if only she might not feel so utterly alone. Somewhere, far away, there was a circle of torchlight filled to bursting with the sound of human voices, but she was well outside it, beyond the touch of the longest fingers of the light. That she imagined herself to be the topic of their conversation was of less than little comfort; rather, the thought was like a sign that even her own fate had been stolen by the others, leaving her bereft. In a moment of weakness, she found herself wishing even for Dabimi, who, despite his bullying, might have reassured her by his mere presence that things were as they had been. But just then, Larry groaned in his sleep and shifted his position on the ledge. The sound of his breathing was raspy and sad, the muffled cry of someone dying, or of someone equally alone. Gradually, her fears about his claim on her subsided, pushed aside by the dank smell of pity, odor of sickness and solitude alike.

LXVI

FOR TWO DAYS and nights, Larry thrashed on the narrow wooden ledge, which was hard despite its covering of skins. People came and went, Panar Ak and Anok and Aran and two young nieces of Panar's whom he brought to assist with the cure. They crouched beside the palette and caught the pieces of bark that fell from Larry's mouth as he slept and held up hollowed-out gourds for him to urinate into while he clung to their shoulders with sweaty hands and called them both Aran. Panar Ak swayed and sang as he ground roots in wooden bowls that looked like the ones Anok used for paints, and produced liquids that, to Larry, smelled equally repulsive. Even in his sleep, he grimaced when Panar Ak began mixing, pushing himself into the wall and covering his nose and mouth with his arm. In a lucid moment, he had explained his pills and had handed them over, and Panar Ak ground some in with the rest of the strange mixture and held the bowl up for him to drink from. Every time, he would choke and sputter and gasp for breath, insisting that he needed only the pills, and would try to push the bowl away. From her corner, Aran watched him squirm and fight and then finally wipe his eyes on his sleeve and give in, taking down the mixture between deep, labored breaths, as though it were a pool he were drowning in. Sometimes, Aran would have to fight back the urge to save him, but at other times, she sat alone on her shore and watched impassively, feeling nothing as he struggled for air.

On the third morning, Larry woke up early, in time to see the first strips of light, thin as reeds, slip in through the spaces in the walls. They fell across the bodies of mother and daughter on their rattan mats, and wove themselves into the threads of softer light that laced the hut's far wall. When Anok stirred and sat up, they shimmered over her like ripples in a shallow pool, and when she reached out to put her hand on Aran's shoulder, they lapped at the edges of the floor.

"Are you awake?" Anok whispered, shaking Aran's shoulder gently.

Aran mumbled in her sleep and turned over.

"You can sleep, but I have to get started." Every morning, Anok offered her more rest, and every morning Aran understood that the offer was really a threat. She sat up and rubbed her eyes and then looked over her shoulder to see if Larry had moved. Larry lay still with his eyes shut.

"Asleep," whispered Anok, quietly rolling her mat.

Aran got to her feet and picked up her own mat. "Will he live?" she asked, turning her back on the answer.

"What do you want?" asked the mother, unwrapping the protective covering of leaves from a wooden bowl. Larry could hear her scratch her head, crumble something in her hand, move towards the door with small, precise steps. She stood even with him on the outside of the wall, and he could hear her breathing. He felt the air stir as she moved. She lit the fire and soon it had consumed the more subtle of the sounds, as her peculiar smell dissolved into the heavier aroma of palm starch flour and cassava leaves frying in rendered boar fat. She sang as she moved a stick across the smooth, round stone, stirring the meal as he had watched her do so often in the past. In those days, her baby would cry and she would give the stick to Larry, motioning to him to continue. He half-expected to hear the same cry, but instead, Aran's voice startled him back to the present.

"I don't know," said Aran, bending down and taking the stick. She pushed the stone off the fire and stood up again, looking down at her mother's hands. "*Jara ka.*"

Larry heard footsteps as Panar Ak approached them at the hearth with his nieces scrambling after him. "Is he still sleeping?" Panar said in a low voice to Anok.

"Aran will wake him now," said Anok in a tense, clipped tone. "She has his breakfast ready."

"*I* bring the breakfast," said one of the nieces, her feet pounding in the dirt.

"No," said Anok. "From now on, Aran's going to tend him, and you can help Panar with the mixing." "*Patir*," she said, pushing Aran forward toward the door.

Inside the hut, Aran stood by the palette and looked down at Larry. Even though his eyes were closed, he could feel her watching him, and fought back the urge to pull his jacket over his head. She looked at the mesh of greenish veins that laced his hands, and his hair the color of dead grass, and the stubble that had already begun to show itself on his chin and upper lip. She looked at the narrow outline of his chest beneath his clothes and his pale, translucent eyelids that betrayed the contours of his eyes. What she saw, she found distasteful, like everything that has been stripped of distance. If, from across the room, she had felt occasional bursts of sympathy, or curiosity, or concern, now when she stood beside him, she saw what the life she had even whispered to the ancestors to save consisted of: a blue pulse lodged between the sinews in his neck like a membranous newly hatched bird in a lizard's jaws. She cleared her throat and tapped her nails on the side of the bowl, and Larry opened his eyes and looked up at her.

"Hungry?" she asked distractedly, as though she barely had the time to look in his direction.

"Maybe so," said Larry, pulling himself up. She didn't try to feed him, as the girls had done, but instead held the bowl out so he could take it in both hands. He ate as the others did, by gathering up bits of food between his thumb and two middle fingers, with the bowl held almost at his chin. Meanwhile, she stood back and directed her eyes to the beams in the ceiling of the hut, as if to search for reduviidae nests. He ate as fast as he could, to shorten their uncomfortable silence. When he finished, he called to her tentatively, afraid to interrupt her, and she took the bowl without speaking and went out. It was the same for each of the day's meals, the sense of being watched as he slept and the silence and her determined examination of the ceiling beams. It was the same for breakfast the next morning, a ritual established with a haste in proportion to the awkwardness they would have felt without it. It was a private ritual between them, of the sort that binds an intimacy into an abstract and impersonal transaction, on which one comes too quickly to depend.

As he finished with the bowl and was about to let Aran know she could take it, Panar Ak appeared in the doorway.

"How is the troubled one?" he said to no one in particular.

"You're late," said Aran, taking the bowl from Larry and stepping backwards, away from both of them.

"*Ibo Napata Ara,*" said Panar Ak, squatting alongside the palette. Before he could hold his own bowl to Larry's mouth, Larry reached for it himself and rested it on his crossed legs. Panar Ak was startled by the gesture, since medicines had to be given by another person in order to work. But he stuck to his purpose, and while Larry gulped the mixture down, Panar explained to him in a slow, deliberate voice about the *Napata* as though he were talking to a child, about wood being bone, and the dance, and the fire. "We'll carry you out, so you can see him. We'll leave you by Dabimi's house, and when they come back with the ashes, you can help throw them under the *chajan.*"

"But I need to be there," said Larry, terrified suddenly that they would leave him behind and take James as their own. The rivalries of mourning surpass in their depth and desperation the rivalries of love, and Larry could not afford to let himself be vanquished. He imagined planting himself in the midst of the dance, a tiny scrap of stillness against a whirling backdrop, who would capture their attention through the intensity of his silence, testifying by his presence in their midst to the privacy of loss.

"You can't be at the dance," said Panar Ak, shaking his head. "You're not strong."

"Of course I am," he said, swinging his legs to the edge of the palette and sitting up. A wave of dizziness moved over him and passed. He pushed his feet squarely into the floor. "The dance will strengthen me."

"We'll see," said Panar Ak, taking the empty medicine bowl and heading towards the door. "Persons are already starting to get ready, painting their patterns and cutting pieces of their house-beams for the fire. Anok has been gone all morning, working on the *chajan.*"

"I haven't seen her working," said Larry, motioning toward the doorway. He was aware of Panar Ak's irritation at his challenges, but couldn't stop himself.

"That's what I said," said Panar Ak sharply. "She's been working, at Dabimi's."

When Aran came in to carve a piece of wood from the thick beam at the far side of the room, Larry was too impatient to watch her in silence as he usually did.

"Why is Anok at Dabimi's?" he called out, in a louder voice than he expected. "Shouldn't she be painting?"

Aran cringed at the sound of the name, but Larry couldn't see her well enough to notice. The beam she was carving was the one from which their household possessions were suspended—large baskets of pelts and small baskets of jewelry; an arrow-quill empty of arrows; and clay pots filled with lard and manioc flour and palm starch flour and fruit, sealed over with beeswax and leaves. She stood behind the basket that held their sleeping mats, so only her hands could be seen. They held the hammer and chisel stones up to the lower surface of the beam, but kept slipping when she tried to carve into the wood. The baskets jiggled back and forth on their leather straps and jute strings.

"Can I help you?" said Larry, unaware that he was on his feet. It wasn't until he reached the far wall that he realized he was walking unassisted for the first time in days. The effort seemed a miracle, the moment when the cripple throws his crutches off, or the blind man finds his sight. They looked at each other for an instant, riveted by their shared terror at the prospect of his recovery, and then looked quickly away again, up to the place where Aran had made a mark in the beam. He held the sides of the sharper stone tightly with both hands while she slammed the thicker one against it, and a strip of wood pulled away from the beam and curled down towards the floor. Larry knew no miracle had taken place, that he had thrashed on the ledge not only out of sickness, but because he couldn't bear to be well. Even now, as he pulled at the wood and cracked it back, he longed for his cocoon of immobility, for the few predictable gestures that sufficed for a sick person's life. "*Ibo Jarara*," she said as he turned the wood in his hands. He suddenly felt nauseated, not so much by his illness as by the thought of the bone in flames. He walked back to the palette and sat down, laying it beside him.

"Where do I go to prepare?" he asked as she tested the straps on the baskets. She pretended to be absorbed in the task, and didn't answer. "Why is Anok at Dabimi's house?" he asked again as she re-rolled the sleeping mats. "Don't you need this?" He held out the sliver of James, and she came at last and lifted it from his hands.

"*Ibo Jarara napata kawar Dabimi*," she said, holding the piece of wood like a rifle against her shoulder and turning on her heel to leave.

Larry started after her, but stopped himself. He knew that he couldn't let himself be seen without shaving, so he went to get some water in a bowl. The sunlight was painful on his eyes, and burned away the detail from the day. As he relieved himself at the edge of the forest, he squinted into the clearing next to the house, unable to detect any movement. There was silence everywhere, an uncanny emptiness that reminded him of something. He filled the bowl and went inside, stumbling in the darkness. His hands shook as he shaved, though he somehow avoided drawing blood. After he put away his razor, he took out a bar of soap and washcloth and bathed as best he could, using the rest of the water from the bowl. On his way out, he poured the soapy water onto the dirt just outside the *kaawa*, and the ground hissed and whispered at his back.

LXVII

MOVING BETWEEN THE houses that were scattered around the clearing like leaves, past doorways bright as turning leaves, whose color the sun didn't fade, but rather intensified, Larry felt pale and ghostlike, or like a pale survivor among ghosts. Each of the houses was empty, save a macaw or a parrot nesting on a perch, its head turned backward on its wing; save a dog whose eyes glowed red from the inside of a doorway, or who scratched in the dirt beside a hut. Larry stopped to rest on a stump at the end of a long *kaawa* and slowly surveyed the deserted grounds. The space was still warm from human use, and the silence bore the echo of high-pitched voices. Birds scattered; a tiny garden snake slid by, provoking the excitement of the dogs. Far off in the distance, he made out a lone stooped figure crouching in a doorway and knew it was Anok. With a sigh, he stood and plunged himself forward, toward one of the larger huts at the far edge of the clearing.

When he came upon her, he startled her.

"Where is everyone?" he said, dreading the answer he knew.

"Why are you here?" she said, regarding him. "We were going to come for you when the dancing was done." She turned back to the *chajan* and began to pound out an outline with a sharpened rock. "You might as well sit down and wait for them to come and get you."

He remained standing, watching her. After a minute, she turned around again and glared at him.

"If you're not going to answer, at least you can mix," she said, and handed him one of the bowls that sat at her feet. His first reflex was to drink from it, but he stopped himself and began to crush the leaves in it with the *maata*. His right arm shook when he turned the stone, and his left arm shook as he tried to hold the bowl from beneath, so he crouched on the floor of the *kaawa,* behind Anok's back, and set the bowl in front of him on the ground.

"Is this Dabimi's house?" he asked, already certain of the answer.

"It's Dabimi's" said Anok, "and now yours." Behind her voice, Larry could make out a clatter of sticks, overlaid upon an ascending wail of voices. He jumped to his feet and started off in the direction of the noise, but stopped in mid-step and turned back to face her.

"What do you mean, it's mine?" he said. The wailing grew higher and more rhythmic, as though coming for them through the trees.

"From today, this is the house of your line. It's Jarara's, so it's yours."

For the first time, Larry looked up at the painting on the *chajan,* and made out a large, pale oblong shape containing a greenish eye, with a smaller one beside it.

"No!" he blurted out. "I want to live with you!"

"You have a brother now," said Anok without looking at him. "It's good. You have a line."

"No!" Larry shouted again, taking off in a run towards the source of the pulsing rhythm. But he wasn't used to running. By the time he had reached the last house in the row, he was sweating and gasping for breath. He helped himself to a drink from the water-trough built into the hut's far wall, using the wooden ladle beside it as a cup. They had got it wrong, his thoughts shouted at him as he started off again. James hadn't shown Dabimi any special interest; they had never stayed in Dabimi's father's house. Nothing in the arrangement made any sense, nor could any explanation justify the fervor of his rage. It pushed him beyond his strength, along the path that wound through a thick patch of forest towards a separate, smaller clearing. It pushed him on until, suddenly, he came up short on the brink of a blazing column filled with swirling, brownish smears which, as he drew closer, became knots of moving bodies. He stiffened, transfixed, and stepped off the path into the thicket, where he became another of the forest's pairs of eyes. Leaves clung to the sweat on his arms like hands trying to steady him, and brushed his forehead lightly, eager to smooth away his rage and fever with their palms.

Not twenty feet in front of him, a small group of older men stood with their backs to him, beating sticks against a long, hollow log. He could make out the colors on the handles of the sticks, and the painted trim on the edges of the log. He could see the sweat on their backs as they played, and could hear them calling to each other over the din. The wailing women stood beside them, or walked around the pile of wood at the center of the clearing, considering it, adjusting it, adding to it from the pieces at their feet. One by one, as they finished being painted, others came to join them, so that their collective wail grew louder and more piercing by increments. Some were painted from head to foot, while others had only their legs and faces covered, and still others, especially the younger ones, only their faces. At the left edge of the clearing, some of the stronger men worked together to raise three enormous woven masks that were at least their height. Larry could tell by their gestures that they were shouting to each other, though he couldn't hear their voices. In another corner, men were squatting in a circle, drinking from a wooden bowl that was being held for them by Panar. In every corner of the scene, there was activity, someone marking the ground with a painted staff, someone tying feathers to a woman's ankles. He saw before him a painting by Bruegel, a canvas painted to its very edges with dark and random purpose. He wanted to watch the scene with the same detachment with which he might have viewed the painting, with an abstract sort of horror from which he might have turned away. Instead, despite himself, he leaned forward in his hiding place and strained his eyes, desperate to identify Dabimi.

A few of the men had begun to walk the periphery, singing together loudly, as though to drown out the women's wailing. Each time they passed, their line was longer, first ten and then forty and then a hundred, walking in single file. The young ones hung back at the end of the line until the snake swallowed its tail and the stooped man at the head of the line put his hands on the shoulders of the last boy. The two circles moved against each other, the women's nested within the men's, with the prone body of sticks as a hub. Face after face passed him, so close that he could see eyes gleaming against the saturated colors of the paint. He searched the strange masks without recognition, seeing no one as familiar; seeing none of them as men. Their anonymity emboldened him, made him feel invisible, and he stepped to the edge of the forest, straining to make out the words of their song. They passed in a trance, their eyes as fierce and empty as the eyes of the huge woven masks. They reached up with their left hands and gestured toward the sky, and stretched their right hands out toward the trees, but a single hand kept reaching, farther and farther through the thicket, until it had grabbed him by the sleeve of his T-shirt and pulled him out. For a minute the song stopped, and the wheel of bodies slowed. There were whispers up and down the line, from which Larry tried to turn away. Then a voice cried out and the wheel began to move again, and the song drowned out his panicked explanations.

"*Tapara ki satay*," an apparition hissed, pulling him aside while the others in the line moved forward, turning their heads to watch him as they passed. "You're not painted." It drew Larry to the place where the paint gourds had been stowed, in the thicket behind the towering masks, and held his head by the hair to steady it when his legs shook too much, and painted a rough design of teal and crimson across his ankles and forehead. Then, before the paint had time to dry, it pushed him into the line and waved him forward, into the motion of the song.

"*Tarima pota taranop tur, tarima kaawa pataj toti*," they sang, over and over, while the sun plodded forward on its own path, to the drone of its own relentless chant. Larry feared fainting; he feared dying of the heat; he feared the glare of those stark, bright faces that judged him so harshly, and betrayed no human concern. His first thought was to run, and his heart pounded as he approached the mouth of the path. He tensed his legs, poised to jump when he came up to the gap between the trees, but the music sensed his intention and tightened its grip, and the hand that held his shoulder clenched it. He turned to look behind him and saw the opening recede, and knew he wouldn't try again. Without being aware of it, he began to chant, tentatively, and was carried forward on the stream of sound. Soon the words themselves blended together; they too formed a chain that tightened and reeled in the sun, which, as it filled, tipped and spilled itself with a whoosh, igniting the body of Jarara. At the roar of the flames, at the sudden gasp that arose from James as he sucked their air into his blazing lungs, they all jumped back. The line of women pressed itself into the line of men, and the mass of bodies shook with a collective tremor. Then they were no longer standing in a double line; they were whirling around; they were shaking themselves with their arms outstretched; they were embracing wildly, as though the fire's eruption had flung them into chaos. A few of the men were holding each other by the shoulders like a line of Russian dancers and vomiting into the thicket. The women held each other and wailed. Whatever absurd message he had been so desperate to give them, about the irreducible privacy of mourning, was submerged, before he remembered even to speak it, by waves of heat and sweat and sound. He stood back at the edge of the forest and clung with both arms to a knotted branch that jutted out at chest height, and wondered whether he too would vomit. The body of James groaned and twitched on its bed of flames, throwing off sparks from its pores.

Yet little by little, as the fire burned, it began to contract and grow quiet, as though its shouts of rage had grown internal; it began to speak intimacies of resignation in soft, measured tones. As, in dying, heat leaves the extremities first, the whirling and writhing bodies that had been the fire's extension grew still and shriveled, crouching down, rocking and muttering in the fading light. A stump was rolled in and Asator was led to it and seated. The song he sang was low and monotonous; Larry could as little make out the words as he could the words of the fire, though he strained for the meaning of each. When one voice started up, the other would interrupt; the fire would assert itself with a crack, and the old man would counter by pounding his stick into the dirt. Larry moved forward and peered into the embers, but he jerked his head up when he heard, at last, among the sung names, the one he sought: Dabimi.

The group of bodies crouching closest to the fire parted to make a path for the ones who had been called. They came forward as they were named, Dabimi, and his *kaag,* and his son, and his daughter who bore, like Aran, one breast each of a woman and a girl. They were joined by two *jitanas* and the sister of the *kaag,* all rocking back and forth together as the old man mingled the name Jarara with each of theirs. Larry watched the scene in horror, as he knew James was watching, with the hatred smoldering in his ribs. For a minute, the song stopped, but then Larry's name went off like a trigger and he hurled himself at Dabimi, arms outstretched, trying to knock him to the ground. He rammed himself against Dabimi's chest with all his might, but at the moment of contact, his legs gave way, and he fell instead into Dabimi's arms. Like a series of steel doors slamming, the others began to throw themselves at them from all sides, embracing both Larry and Dabimi together, and then the backs of the ones who embraced them. A mass of bodies pressed them to each other, all swaying as one, a ship as wide as a barge, bobbing on the widest of rivers. Larry wept into the shoulder of the body that held him, made intimate by his hatred, and wept again when they carried him up to the *chajan* to scatter his handful of ash. He was weeping as sleep overtook him on his mat on the floor of Dabimi's house, and as, in his dream, the body of sticks rose to its feet, uncharred, and knelt beside him in the night. When morning broke, he was surprised, for a moment, not to see it next to him as he drew himself up to a sitting position and rubbed his eyes in confusion, scattering the ash from his cheek.

LXVIII

JORGE WAS STANDING at the sink shaving when the phone rang. He pulled his mouth to one side to get at his cheek, and then attacked the nascent mustache, the fruit of his isolation, an experiment gone wrong. He had always wanted to try it, but not in public. He had hoped that it would make him look older, but surprisingly, it seemed to have the opposite effect, making him look more like a boy than ever, a serious little boy walking around in his father's facial hair, to comic effect. The phone stopped ringing. He rinsed and dried off with a towel.

"What's gotten into you?" His mother's words, echoing in his mind, didn't help him in his effort to distance himself from the borrowed-mustache boy. Nor did the fact that he didn't know. The obvious answer was that he had harbored, for all those years, the belief that his father was alive in Lamurii, waiting until his only son had grown brave enough to free him, and that that fantasy had finally been shattered by the truth. Or the obvious answer was that he hated himself and Joachim in equal measure for abandoning yet another innocent to the forest's brutality. Or the obvious answer was that he couldn't live with the feeling that he had humiliated himself in front of Martina, had proven himself to be less than he needed to be in her eyes; if nothing else, she was a woman, and she had seen him cry. Or the obvious answer was that he had realized that the mission to which he had devoted himself, to which he and his father before him had devoted themselves, was doomed, ill-advised, counter-productive, destructive, wasteful, ultimately inhumane. But as Jorge was in no position to notice the obvious, he dressed slowly while nursing the sense that

Martina had somehow betrayed him, through some subtle condescension that demanded action on behalf of his honor. He stepped out the door and closed it behind him, turning the key in the lock just in time to hear the phone start up again, echoing down the hall.

LXIX

BECAUSE THERE WAS a man already in the house, Larry wasn't given the sleeping ledge. Instead, he had a floor mat and some of the largest of the skins, and a coarse blanket, made from the bark of a milk tree. He was treated with an uneasy deference; Dabimi's *kaag* and daughter called him *"paar aXata,"* "brother of honor," when they handed him his food, and turned their heads quickly if they came upon him shaving. He rarely made eye contact with them, or with anyone, but sat for long hours on a stump on the *kaawa*, cradling an open book in his crossed legs. Two weeks earlier, Anok and Aran had appeared in the doorway carrying his bags and had placed them in a pile in one corner of the hut. He had been so relieved to see them that he reached his arms out to them. "I need you . . ." he called out in desperation, but Anok merely nodded to him and hurried Aran out the door in front of her, pushing at her daughter's back when she lingered. He waited until they were gone, to cry, and then put his hands over his eyes and leaned his head forward. The tears swelled in the cracks between his fingers and fell through, translucent messages falling through walls. Each afternoon, sitting cross-legged in the shade of the *kaawa*, his book open in his lap, he saw in his mind an image of Anok's hand pushing firmly against Aran's back, and felt the same emptiness again, and stained the pages of his book with his tears. Only on occasion did he let himself imagine that Aran had hoped to speak with him; that Anok had pushed her as hard as she had for a reason.

When his mind wandered from his Henry Walter Bates one day, it occurred to him that he might have lost his status as Aran's *jitana* when he joined the new line. When Dabimi came back to the hut at midday looking for a meal, Larry cleared his throat and called to him for the first time.

"Am I not to talk to you?" he said, his voice shaking from fear or lack of use.

"You are my brother of honor," replied Dabimi, sounding impatient.

"Am I still Liroko?" he asked.

"Um," said Dabimi, jerking his head.

"Am I still Aran's *jitana*?"

"Um."

"Then why didn't she talk to me?" said Larry, closing the book and stretching his feet to the ground.

"How could you speak to her in your own house, when you don't give her a thing?" Dabimi asked in a harsh tone. "Some people want the honor without the work, but there's no honor to their line in doing that." He turned on his heel and headed toward the cooking area. When he left, Larry sat for a while, looking out over the tops of the trees, and then got up and dragged his pack onto the *kaawa* by the straps, leaving two thin ruts in the smooth dirt floor. As he began to dig through the outside compartments, Dabimi's daughter came and handed him a bowl. Then she returned with a dried-grass broom and swept away the tracks his pack had made. He rummaged through the small pocket on the front of the pack and came up with the black leather change purse in which he kept his American money. He felt for the coins on the bottom—the ones with buildings on them wouldn't do, nor could he give them an image of a bearded man. He looked at the *cruzero* from Sara, but knew he couldn't give it in any case. Instead, he picked out two quarters and slipped them into the pocket of his shorts. Then he tried to lift the pack to put it back in the hut, but it was so heavy that he put it back down, and ended up making ruts in the floor again. As he lowered it to the ground, he nearly dropped it, but caught it at the last second by the two small pockets that stuck out on either side. The right one held only a few wadded up dirty socks, but the left was stretched taut over what felt like a smooth-sided box. Only when he had unzipped the pocket and peered at the top of the box did he remember what it was: the reticule containing James's ashes. For a minute he thought about sprinkling them on the floor with the others, but he caught himself and shuddered and pushed the box back into the pocket, zipping it shut. He kept his eye on the pocket as he ate, as though to be sure no ashes would escape from it. As he walked to Anok's hut, turning over the quarters in his hand, he felt a renewed sense of strength in the thought that he alone possessed the real James.

As he approached, he could see Aran and Anok squatting side by side in front of the lean-to, bent over their paints. They looked up when they heard him coming, and Anok rose to her feet and greeted him warmly, holding onto his arm as she called him by name. Aran stood shyly off to the side as though he were a stranger, and cast her eyes downward when he looked at her. Their friendliness was relieving and unsettling at once, since it made him doubt that they had been cold to him before.

"You seem well," said Anok, looking him over, holding him away from her in order to see better. "Panar Ak made a good cure," she added, pulling him around toward a log and motioning for him to sit.

"He doesn't come to see me any more."

"You're well now, and Tapata baby is sick."

"A sick baby," Larry said in an unconvincing voice, trying to sound sympathetic, when in fact he was distracted. "Why haven't you come to see me?"

"Listen," said Anok, shaking him by the arm. "It's not good for you to move into Dabimi's house and a baby gets sick next door."

"They think it's my fault?" he said, suddenly alarmed.

"I can't say what they think." Anok trailed off as she turned away and stood up. She motioned to Aran, who stood and came to her side. The two whispered for a moment, and he imagined them disparaging him in low voices, shaking their heads solemnly while they plotted to betray him. He imagined the entire village turned against him, as he knew had happened once, in his first year in Pahquel, even to James. That was why they hadn't visited, he suddenly realized; why they hadn't spoken to him; why they had looked away. He leapt to his feet and reached into his pocket for the coins, holding out one in each hand.

"Dabimi said I had offended you by not giving you gifts when you came," he said hurriedly, as though to patch over the more disturbing thought with the less disturbing one. They looked at the coins for a moment and then quickly away. Neither moved to take one. He pushed his hands toward them, and they moved back slightly.

"What did I do wrong?" said Larry, returning his hands to his pockets. Anok nodded to Aran to bring the food. While she was gone, Anok leaned toward him and whispered, "It's not time now to make your claim."

"Huh?" said Larry in English. "What are you talking about?"

Aran reappeared for a minute. She passed a bowl to her mother and then left again. Anok offered some dried greens in honey from the bowl.

"I'm not making a claim," said Larry, pulling out one of the greens by the stem. Anok took the bowl and set it on a log. "I just want to know why you haven't been talking to me."

"You can't make a claim just because you want to leave Dabimi's, or because some men are blaming you. It shouldn't be for such a reason." Anok shook her head and stared at him. "You should at least wait."

"I'm not making any claim," said Larry, holding up his empty hands. "I need to talk to you. I need to see you. No one talks to me."

"They say you still do nothing but sit and look at your legs."

"What else can I do?" he asked, making fists in his pockets around the coins.

"I thought this conversation was for two hands of days ago," Anok said. She looked up at him to see if he understood her, but he looked lost. "Asator's not going to tell you what to do. You'll have to figure it out for yourself. Why aren't you helping Xaper with the planting, or Lanon with gathering honey? They always need help with the skinning, but I don't know if you're even skilled enough."

"Not skinning," said Larry, stalling for time, knowing that he had no skill for any of them. "Not honey."

"There's gathering medicines with Kakap. Amakar's son is good with the bees anyway."

"Why can't I work with you again?" said Larry, remembering the feel of the *maata* in his palm.

"I already have Aran. I'll take you tomorrow to Kakap," she said, patting his shoulder. "He's Ak. You'll be good for him." She left him for a minute to help Aran with the food. He drew lines in the dirt with his toe. When they came back, he forced himself to eat what they had brought, even though he had just had a meal at Dabimi's. He felt full and stiff as he headed back towards his hut, but his mouth held the taste of their food, which was different than the food at Dabimi's, despite its being made of the same few ingredients.

As he approached Dabimi's house, he slowed down as he passed the *kaawa* of Tapata. One of Panar Ak's nieces was coming out through the doorway and ran to him, greeting him as *"Rara,"* "patient," or "troubled one." The word eddied in the air, creating an emptiness.

"How's the baby?" he asked her, steeling himself for the worst.

"He is better now," said the niece, holding out her cupped hand. "We're giving *pikar.*" In her palm, she held strips of bark like the ones he had been given at Anok's. "But he doesn't have any teeth, so we have to chew for him."

"That's a hard job. It doesn't taste good," said Larry.

She seemed to find the comment funny, and ran back into the house laughing, looking over her shoulder.

He stood and watched as she disappeared through the doorway. The front of the house was wide and even, and looked back at him with a stare as blank and anxious as his own. The *chajan* was painted only to a child's height, and the ring of thatch that grazed its brow was trimmed neatly across, like the niece's. From time to time, he sensed movement beyond the doorway, an indistinct roiling of the darkness, but no one else emerged. On the sides of the house, to the right and the left, were two long covered troughs, the smaller one for manioc flour and the larger filled with water for drinking and cooking. As he passed by on his way back to Dabimi's he caught sight of a thin-handled ladle resting on the side of the water trough, and suddenly remembered that he had drunk from that smooth, oiled cup, had held it with both hands and felt the stalk of the handle graze the hair above his ear. His upper lip, beaded with sweat, had left its mark on that pale wooden bowl, which he had set down in the trough, to bob like a dinghy in a pond.

LXX

ALTHOUGH SR. CATALPA dressed each morning and went upstairs to his office to sit at his oversized desk with its hand-tooled leather blotter and its hand-blown glass inkwell, there wasn't much for him to do since most of the business of running the prefecture had already been relocated to the central office. He might just as well have arranged for the move to Brasilia earlier, but for the characteristic way he had of drawing out every process, a habit that had paid off exponentially in his work as a government official. He felt the need to close files, to confirm arrangements, and to pack boxes with exceptional care, personally supervising the cataloging and wrapping of each of his mementoes and antiques. Occasionally he had a visitor, a fellow paper-pusher from downriver, who came in search of an antidote to the monotony and isolation which the promise of a pension demanded, as well as a bit of cheer from the Prefect's well-stocked store of brandies and liquors. The Senor was known as a generous man, so long as what he shared was not of value to him personally. He lived by a few simple precepts, the guidance of which had never failed him: Retain the service of those in your employ, and never hire natives for tasks that can be done by loyal, Portuguese-speaking long-time dependents; curry favor with indigenous elders through the judicious distribution of well-timed gifts; never share hard drink with children, women or natives; and never overindulge yourself. In his choice of goals as in his actions and decisions, Sr. Catalpa appreciated pragmatism over ambition, safety over risk, stability over change, a greased palm over conflict. Thus, he owed Joaquim Rocha a greater debt for having fired him than he did for hiring him in the first place, and a greater one still for having situated him in a position so compatible with his character.

Most of all, Sr. Catalpa was not used to strong feelings, so he had been surprised by the sense of deflation he felt at the departure of his four visitors, and particularly of Larry, who was so close to his eldest son in age and degree of apparent naiveté. His guests' disappearance upriver played over and over in his mind as he arranged and rearranged his files, and mingled with the remembered scene of his three children floating off around the same curtain of walnut trees, propelled by his least favorite brother-in-law's oar. This foreign sense of longing, noticeably absent after his wife's passing, was only exacerbated when one evening he came across a file of his old correspondence with James, chronologically arranged and indexed, and settled in to read it in the parlor, accompanied by a glass of Merlot and a plate of tinned smoked oysters. At first, he was distracted by the day-to-day interruptions of the household, and by the disagreeable fact of being forced to sip his Merlot from a tumbler, as the stemware had already been packed. Every so often, his maid Ana would walk through to adjust the draperies, or her husband Gabriel would straighten pictures or remove insects with a long-handled dustpan and broom; both had learned well from their employer the art of keeping busy by attending to details, creating an infinite array of new tasks in the process of completing old ones.

"You're a man of deep integrity," James had written in one of the letters, dated the same year the Senor had been removed from the SPI, obviously in response to some bid for reassurance on his part. James's sincerity obviated the shame of accepting a compliment, even from a dead man, and Sr. Catalpa read the line several times, reluctant to put down the letter in response to a knock on the door. Before he could stand up, Gabriel had already ushered in the stranger, who stood surveying the opulence around him while the Prefect collected himself.

"Eduardo Catalpa. Welcome," he said, extending his hand with particular graciousness, as he was still under the influence of James and his compliment.

"Kamar Sodeis," said his visitor, grasping the Prefect's limp grip in his firm one.

"What can I do for you?"

"I have reason to think you can help me," said Sodeis, seating himself, in response to the Prefect's gesture, on the divan. "I'm with Q. P. Comercio Ltda. Let me give you my card." He extracted one from a tooled silver case and put it on the table.

Sr. Catalpa ignored the card, his attention drawn to the inlay on the case. "Lovely," he said under his breath. He motioned to Ana to come over. "What can I get you? A glass of wine? A whiskey?"

"I suppose just a drop of whiskey, if you're offering," said Sodeis, pulling papers and maps from a zippered case and setting them on the table on top of the card.

"Of course," said Catalpa, pausing for a minute, mesmerized by the impossible blue of Sodeis's eyes, before shooing Ana away.

"I'm recently back in these parts, after some time away," Sodeis set in, accepting the glass tumbler Ana offered him. "In my previous incarnation, I was an independent mineral prospector, with years of experience in claim staking, soil assessment, mapping, geochemical assay sampling and the like. I've been administrator for the Clarante and Duorios Agreements, and I've created the most current and up-to-date maps of activated and deactivated logging roads in Para state."

"I see," said Sr. Catalpa.

Sodeis drained his glass and spread out one of the maps on the table. "This is mine," he said, gesturing towards it. "I compiled this one myself."

Sr. Catalpa distractedly refilled Sodeis's glass and bent his head over the map in front of him, nodding. "So how can I help you?" he repeated, feeling suddenly exhausted.

"I've always said that if you want to know the area, ask the people who have lived there the longest," said Sodeis, raising his glass as he scrutinized the Prefect's lined face. "I thought you might have a sense of which of the natives in your area might really know their lumber. I'm especially interested in hardwoods, you know, Ipe, Cumaru, Angelim Pedra, the most popular, but also the rarer ones. I thought you might know of a native or two who might allow me to use my time more efficiently," he said, intuiting that his phrasing might appeal to his audience of one. "For your information, I speak fluent Tupi and several other native languages, as well as half a dozen European ones. Foreign service brat," he said with a tinge simultaneously of derision and pride. He drained his glass and set it on the table within reach of his host, who refilled it.

"I'll certainly give it some thought," said the Prefect, to close the discussion. "Efficiency is always to be wished for."

"Yes," said Sodeis, holding his glass to the light. "This is fine stuff! Where did you come by it?"

"By courier from Scotland," said Sodeis "Can't trust the mail boats for that sort of thing."

"Exactly," said Sodeis in English, with a brogue. He began to struggle with his map in an attempt to fold it. Sr. Catalpa reached for it and began to pleat it neatly, realizing with a start that his visitor was drunk. He had a deep distaste for all forms of inebriation, and stood up to indicate the end of the conversation, but Sodeis reached for the bottle, pouring another for himself, and topping off his host's glass, which still contained the Merlot, as well.

"How long have you been at this particular post?" he said, clearly showing no inclination to leave.

"It's been about twenty years now," said Catalpa reluctantly.

"A veteran! I've been at it for thirty, off-and-on, since I was sixteen years old, though I spent the past ten or so out west. I've done pretty much everything." Sodeis said sloppily. "A woman in every village, maybe two, you know how that goes, been shot at ten or a dozen times, the whole bit. Never got caught in the government service trap, though!"

Sr. Catalpa nodded glumly, aware that he could not, in good conscience, rid himself of his guest in his current state so easily. He sank down beside Sodeis, trying to figure out his next move.

"Never shot at them myself, though. That's no way to get your work done. No, that's not the way to go about it," he said, shaking his head with a drunkard's certainty. "They're always going to outnumber you."

"So how do you do it?" said Sr. Catalpa, stalling for time.

"You have natives do it for you," said Sodeis, leaning back. As he did so, a silver pistol slid noiselessly from his portfolio onto the divan's cushioned seat.

The Prefect stared at it in horror for a minute and then turned his gaze quickly back to Sodeis. "Is that so?"

"They're an excitable bunch, in general," said Sodeis. "And they don't like being interfered with. Makes sense! I bet you don't either," he said, laughing conspiratorially in the Senor's direction.

Senor Catalpa riveted his eyes upon his guest while he slowly slid his hand across the divan and grasped the pistol, pulling it behind his back and transferring it to his other side.

"No, that's the important thing to remember. They do make sense, like everybody else. That's why I get so far with them. I understand that. Just basic respect. What's good for me is good for them."

Senor Catalpa pushed the gun between the bottom cushion and the frame of the divan without interrupting the rhythm of his bobbing head. At that moment, Gabriel entered the room and the Senor threw him a distraught, silent appeal. "I'm wondering if we can offer you a bed tonight," he said, now bowing as well as nodding. "We've got plenty of spare rooms."

"I might take you up on that," said Sodeis, still showing no sign of moving. He poured himself another, allowing some of the whiskey to overflow onto the carved table. Sr. Catalpa grabbed the rag from Gabriel's belt and blotted at the table. "Ask Ana to make up a room for Mr. Sodeis, if you don't mind," he said loudly over his shoulder.

"Yeah, if you're forced to take action, it's best to enlist one of their trading partners to set them right," Sodeis continued. He had started alternately to drool from the corner of his mouth and to draw his blue shirtsleeve back and forth across his lips. "And that goes for the hired guns too," he went on, "your meddlers, your surveyors, your SPI, your *seringais*,"

"Why don't you help me show Mr. Sodeis to his room," said the Prefect, pushing back a wave of nausea as he stood and offered his arm. With Gabriel at his other side, they lifted Sodeis and guided him to a bedroom in the back of the house, and then returned to the parlor. Almost instantly, they could hear the sound of snoring echo in the hall. Sr. Catalpa slid the gun from between the cushions of the divan and tentatively held it out to Gabriel. "Do something with this!" he said in a low voice, handing it over. "I'm wondering if we should send Joao to the mission."

"I don't think he's dangerous right now," said Gabriel, who was perhaps the only man in the region other than his employer who could count himself a stranger to the hardscrabble world of guns and schemes and immoderate drink (except second-hand and for only a short period, during which he had had some trouble with his eldest son). He added hastily, "I don't think we'll need to shoot him."

"No, no!" said Sr. Catalpa with a shudder.

"Do you want me to sit up with him, sir?" Gabriel asked doubtfully.

"That would be perfect, Gabriel. Come for me when he wakes up," said the Senor, turning from him to the folder of correspondence, which was now slightly sticky from the spilled whiskey.

LXXI

KAKAP WAS SO short and thin that from a distance, he gave the impression less of a person than of a short, gnarled tree. His hands, especially, were oddly knotted, with long, tapering fingers, one of which was missing a tip. He had a strange way of holding them, splayed apart like claws. Larry's first thought when he met him was that he had been chosen to gather medicines because he was too eccentric or too delicate to be sent with the other men to hunt. For that reason, Larry sensed a distasteful kinship between the two of them, and imagined they'd be regarded derisively, all the more so by association, like the queer kids at school. He stood with Anok off to the side while Kakap darted back and forth across the hut, rifling through his rows of clay pots, throwing up dried leaves in bursts as though his fingers were mice. *"Pararan!"* he called out, holding up a specimen. *"Tatar!" "JaXaca!"* From time to time, one of his daughters would wander in and he would test her, barking out a name and then jerking his head up and down impatiently as he listened to the story she sang. When she finished, a smile would spread across his face, slowly drawing back his lips to reveal an outcropping of teeth as wayward as his fingers.

"I can't remember all that," Larry whispered to Anok when Kakap turned his back to speak to one of his children.

"You'll be very good," said Anok, touching him on the arm. Before he could protest, she nodded to Kakap and backed off through the *chajan*, leaving them alone. When she had gone, Kakap turned to study him, seeming taller and more formidable as he approached. The yellow of his eyes and teeth deepened, and became more prominent in his face.

"We'll go tomorrow, huh?" he said in a low voice, as though it were a confidence between them. He leaned forward and studied Larry's face, reaching up without warning with his index finger to brush the hair from Larry's brow. Larry froze for a minute, horrified, and then shuddered and stepped backwards into one of the diagonal beams that held up the roof. It hit him on the shoulder blade and he jumped forward, grimacing, while the baskets that hung from the crossbeams danced on their strings.

"Where will we go?" Larry managed to choke out.

"Out," said Kakap, "for two days."

"I can't," said Larry, backing toward the door.

"No?" said Kakap, looking puzzled. "Are you working on the skins?"

"I might be," said Larry, trying to turn away.

"They're not doing the skins for another hand of days," said Kakap, amused at his own trick.

Larry ran all the way to Anok's, swearing loudly in English as he went. When he came upon her sitting on her *kaawa*, he nearly broke into a sob, but choked it down.

"You don't think you can do it?" said Anok, looking up from what had apparently been an afternoon nap. For as long as Larry had known her, she never slept during the day. "You're sick again?" she asked, rubbing her eyes and then looking at him more closely.

"I am," said Larry, putting his hands over his temples. He waited until they were sitting side by side on the log in front of the lean-to to try to speak to her.

"Is Kakap a . . ." he started in, reaching wildly in front of him for the right word, finding nothing but emptiness. At last, he resorted to the English word, as though, through force of desperation, he could make her understand: "*Ebo Kakap* . . . a pervert?"

Anok looked at him, puzzled, repeating the unfamiliar word.

"Does he . . ." he trailed off again, realizing he knew no Pahqua word of any sort that had to do with sex.

"Does he . . . try to make a baby with a man?" he choked out, turning his head away.

Anok shook her head and moved closer to him on the log. Without thinking, he leaned away and turned his back to her.

"Did I make a mistake?" she said in a serious tone, moving away again. "I thought you would want him to *pajaX*"—the word was unfamiliar to him—"but James must have done it already."

Larry tried not to listen, but the strange sound rang in his head. The thought behind it sickened him. He leaned down over his knees.

"So James already did it?" she said, more insistent.

"Um," he said, still horrified at whatever it was.

"That's good," said Anok, standing up. "I'll tell Kakap, and you'll go with him in the morning."

"Um," he said again, standing up because she did. His head swam, and he rocked a bit on his legs.

"I'm sorry. I didn't know," she said again, touching his arm.

When they parted at the head of the path, before she went off to the left to speak again to Kakap, and before he continued on up the rise to Dabimi's, she turned back and called to him, reaching out with her hand for his arm.

"Don't be afraid," she said, as though he were a child. "You'll be very good. He'll come for you tomorrow."

LXXII

MARTINA HAD SLIPPED into that state of timelessness which the wheel offered, and didn't hear the creak of the heavy glass front door. Jorge found her bent over, singing to herself, unaware of him as she reached out without raising her head for her stick and sponge. He stood as still as the shelves behind him, as still as the bench, inhumanly still for a long time, and then he cleared his throat.

Martina looked up but didn't respond. She cut off the bowl with a wire and lifted it onto a wooden slab covered with cheesecloth. Then she threw another ball of clay onto the wheel with a heavy slap.

"So, how are you?" said Jorge.

"You're kidding, right? You know that Moretti? He's a real joker," she said with her heavy accent, turning back to the wheel.

"I didn't realize until recently that you were so given to mockery and insult!" Jorge said tensely, "But now I'm finding out that those are your specialties."

"I have never insulted you and you know it," said Martina forcefully, stopping to look up at him. "I suppose I should wonder what's gotten into you, but I'm out of curiosity right now. I'm having a good time working, and I'm having a bad time talking to you, so why don't I get back to what I was doing?" The act of kicking was not that much different from the act of running. The stone made a scraping sound as it moved the wheel.

The trick was, as usual, to be able to tell where a thought came from, whether in through the senses or up from some dark underground abyss. "So now you've found out what you were getting into with me," Jorge started, "and it's not what you expected, so you're not even going to bother to show me the door. I'm just supposed to infer that I'm not what you had in mind."

"Where did you get that from?"

"And you just get out of my car and don't even say goodbye!" It was true that she had done that when he had driven her home from the hangar, but it was what she always did.

"I'm working now," she said. "I don't consider this a conversation." She turned back to her lump of clay, which had grown dry from too much spinning without purpose.

Jorge watched her for a minute and then turned and walked out. To say that she was right, even to himself, would have been far too painful, particularly at a time when his disappointment in himself was like a lead cape compressing his shoulders and his chest. He stood for a minute on her doorstep and then set out, knowing only that what had happened was gratuitous, and not at all what he had intended, and that it meant his life.

LXXIII

THERE ARE NIGHTS when the trees and the sky and the sounds of the forest draw around, cocoon-like, lying easy on the skin, and others when the forest offers only a rough cloak of brambles, a hammock of thorns, a damp, infested blanket against the creeping chill. The stars had collected in one corner of the sky and glowed softly like a snow bank in the moonlight; the moss that draped the rocks by the edge of the small lake worked like a baffle to soften the harsher sounds. There was Kakap's breathing, wispier than James's, but reassuring still, predictable and steady like the pace of walking, and the occasional soft snap of an ember from the fire. Their baskets, which hung like orioles' nests from a branch alongside them, conveyed a human presence in the darkness, eight thick bodies standing by, heavy with tubers, crowned with reeds and ivy sprigs for hair. Larry couldn't see their eyes, but knew that they were made of soft red berries and shiny pakara nuts. They twitched with interest when they heard a splash in the water, or the crack of a branch underfoot, or the creaking of Larry's hammock as he turned onto his side, trying to convince himself that he was safe enough to sleep.

The two stories of Larry's life, the one of the night and the one of the day, seemed to portray two different people from two estranged, if neighboring, lands. The book that was opened to him now, as he curled himself around it in the darkness, was the night book, whose chapters told of his years in his bedroom growing up, the night terrors and the reading under the covers with the flashlight, and his months with James, being lulled by his snoring and his ease. So many of the nights were haunted; the ones at Sara's, the ones by the river, or at Dabimi's, and worst of all, there was the first night with Kakap, in which the forest, with the darkest of intentions, reached in through the spaces in his netting from every direction to smooth his hair and stroke his skin. All night, he sat crouched in his hammock with the netting pulled taut around his shoulders, his hands clutching penlight and penknife, drawing his jacket around his knees. Kakap's inert body beside him barely stirred. When at last he caught sight of dawn shimmering in the distance between the treetops, he ran to her and wept, and she closed the night book gently, and hid him for an hour in her skirts. His gratitude was boundless, extending even to Kakap, who suddenly opened his eyes and looked at him, unfurling his ragged smile.

"Did you sleep well?" he asked in a kind voice as he rolled his mat and stowed it in his basket.

"Well," Larry said, feeling, in his rush of exuberance, a sudden urge to embrace him, struck by how small he was, fragile as a bird.

There had been other chapters since then, each shorter than the last, describing the shrinking interval between wakefulness and sleep. Some contained unexpected moments of contentment, when the chirrups and breathing and trickling water all came together in the darkness and soothed him, and made sense. Were an editor to read the book of night, Larry knew, he would no doubt look with disapproval on its extremes of tone and atmosphere, on its inexplicable disruptions of plot. He showed it to no one, however, and let it fall slowly from his hands onto his chest in the dark.

LXXIV

SARA SWITCHED ON the light by her bed and reached for her book, pulling herself up by the elbows. She never would have turned on a light in the middle of the night when Marietto was alive; he was one of those urban-light sleepers who relied upon the hum of the forest to lull them, and regarded mechanical noises and electric lights as sources of tension and foreboding. Such were the fruits of loss; without Marietto, she was free to turn the lights on and off dozens of times in a single night. Indeed, without James, she was freed from the haunting thought that if she had only chosen differently at the outset, Jorge might have grown up with a father at his side, resulting in a very different outcome. Without Jorge, she need not limit her time at the office so as to be at home when he stopped by on his way to and from the airport to take out or repay the one cruzero loan. In fact, she need not act like a mother at all, and could even resort, during one particularly challenging evening, to dining at midnight on beans, served straight from a can. She didn't need her son to remind her of the ways in which loss resembled a form of flying, of transcending all that was familiar on the way to the breathtaking emptiness above.

LXXV

ON EACH OF the evenings when he was in the village and not out gathering with Kakap, Larry pulled his date book from the pocket of his travel bag and crossed off another day, adding days for his time in the field. In Pahquel, time was marked by the seasons of fruiting and flowering, by the rise and fall of the rivers and the stars, and most of all by the presence of the rains, whose furious blessing was dreaded and awaited during the dry time. The years were recorded on the *chajans* by the slow creep of color up the thick lintels, but only Larry counted days and parceled them out into weeks; despite himself, he privately commemorated his approximation of the fourth of July and his birthday and even his mother's birthday with sudden bursts of homesickness. When he had first arrived, the time seemed not to pass at all, and the Xs had inched imperceptibly across the expanse of the stark white grid. Lately, however, the days were passing faster than he could count them, and he carried an image in his head of the calendars in movies whose pages fly off in a stream, leaving a single date exposed. In his version of the movie, the date that held the camera's focus, surrounded by nothing but stark, blank walls, was the fifteenth of September, when he had, for some forgotten reason, told himself he would set off for Sr. Catalpa's, for the trek back to what he called in his mind "square one," rather than "home." He shut the book and stared into the fire, scarcely blinking when the *kaag* nearly stepped on his hand as she passed him on her way out the door.

Larry sought in the fire what he suddenly missed most, the chance to ask James what he should do. He called to him silently, in the recliner chair in his parents' living room, in the seat beside him on the plane, in the small hut they had shared during their first visit together to Pahquel. He called to him in his funeral pyre, and in the enamel box of ashes, and in his hammock in the darkness, from where, although invisible, he could still be heard. He tried to piece together an answer from odd bits of phrases spoken in his head in James's voice, "atta boy," and "look at this here!" and "so you *can* teach an old dog new tricks!" He posed the question over and over again, as though to make it sharper by rubbing it back and forth against a stone in his head, and it glinted in the firelight, revealing no sign of James's answer. A spider staggered from the edge of a burning log and crept off into the darkness; in the center of the fire, the stones remained steadfast. The night world of the forest overflowed with creatures who said "go," or "stay," with those who hurried over fallen tree limbs and those who nested in their hollows, listening every evening to the rhythm of feet overhead.

That night, after the children and the *kaag* had gone to sleep, Dabimi came and sat with him beside the fire, squatting at an angle so that he could see him without facing him directly.

"You're good at gathering," Dabimi said at last, poking at the fire with a stick. "Kakap came up and said so, without my asking." "Um," said Larry, suspicious of the compliment. He pushed the embers around with his own stick, startling at one point when it lightly tapped Dabimi's.

"I hope I'm bringing enough to my line," he said.

"Of course," said Dabimi, waving him off with annoyance. "Our troughs are filled with flour." He paused and cleared his throat before he spoke again. "You're doing well. You'll want a *kaag*, and children," he said, glancing sideways at Larry. "I know a nice one over in the far village. She is a mother's niece of Kura"—he nodded towards his *kaag* in the hut—"and would bring credit to our line."

"How do you make a claim?" asked Larry, as though he hadn't heard him.

"Of that woman?"

"Of anyone." He was careful not to mention Aran's name.

"Speak to the father first," he said, standing up and looking down at Larry. "Always, a gift to the father."

Larry stopped himself from reminding Dabimi of what they both knew, that there was no father to ask. He turned his face to the fire so Dabimi couldn't see his expression, but his reaction was clear from the way he jabbed at the ashes with his stick. He waited for him to leave, but Dabimi merely stepped back and stood behind him in the shadows.

"This hand of days was good," he said at last to Larry's back. "Four pigs, two for now and two for later. You don't need to bring in any more."

"You're the best of the hunters," said Larry. "You were better than the other sons even when you were young."

"Pataja guides my hand," said Dabimi.

"Even then," said Larry, "your hand could feel his guidance."

"*Um,*" said Dabimi and fell silent, leaving Larry to listen to the night. In the silences, there were always layers of sound, low rumblings and nasal croaks and high-pitched chirps placed like shingles, each overlapping the one below it, from the dirt floor to the ceiling of leaves and stars. Between any two objects in the darkness, there were strands of sound tying them together, and also, in their sheer density, pushing them farther apart.

"Or," said Dabimi, brushing away the strands like cobwebs, "you could press your claim through *pajaX.*"

"What do you mean?" said Larry, sickened at the word.

"You understand me," said Dabimi mockingly, suddenly turning to go.

"Wait!" said Larry, turning to face him.

"I'm tired now," said Dabimi, still facing the house.

"You don't like me," said Larry, unable to stop himself. "You didn't when we were young, and you still don't."

"You are my brother of honor," Dabimi said stiffly, his voice low and intense.

"What bad thing did I do?" said Larry.

"Don't make the wrong choice," said Dabimi, disappearing into the hut.

Larry waited, staring into the darkness into which Dabimi had vanished, and then gave up and turned back towards the fire, which was dying softly into embers. Leaning back, he grabbed some branches from a pile by the end of the *kaawa* and tossed them on it, fanning the flame with his datebook. The fire was a more responsive companion than Dabimi had been, and flared obligingly. He sat back and listened to it crack and hiss, trying to sort out all the pictures in his head. There were the ones of him leaving, announcing his plans to Anok, trying desperately to explain himself to Aran's turned back. He saw Dabimi gloat as he forced himself to give a tribute to his generosity. He imagined, with a shudder, setting off into the forest, and arriving at Sr. Catalpa's half alive, having been lost again, or chased by those he had betrayed, or attacked by boar, or swarmed by bees. He saw himself writhing with fever on the same perfect crescent of sand and never arriving at all. Then, he was on the plane looking down on Florida, on D.C., on Boston. He imagined going back to school, sitting in the Dean's office trying to explain his failure to inform him that he wouldn't be returning for the fall quarter, or locking himself in his bedroom at home, playing the same sequence of chords again and again on his guitar until his parents threw up their hands in despair and turned him out. He thought about moving in with Sara and finding a job at the wharf in Santarem, or teaching English for money, or begging for a job at the museum, answering the telephones or making change at the front desk, listening with an empty interest for the familiar cadence of English. He couldn't picture with any vividness the possibility of Joaquim's taking him in, as he wasn't sure what his house looked like, or who lived there, or even where it was. His mind scanned the images he could call up one by one, in search of a setting in which he felt capable of living, and found only awkward situations, risks, disappointments, and dead ends. There were no real friends to miss him, no commitments unfulfilled; not even a dog the burden of whose care would be resented by his parents. In a way, he found it odd even to wonder about going back, given his assumption, which he had often stated without laying out his reasons, that he had wound up in Pahquel because he had nowhere else to go.

Larry would have said that Pahquel was his fate, except he was used to thinking of fate as something terrible and easy, as the place one slid into without longing or even effort after intending some other, more desirable outcome. In this case, the fact that he saw no other option lent his situation no air of inevitability, no sense of solidity, no opportunity for surrender. Part of him suspected that he had never intended to stay in Pahquel beyond the four months he had planned for, but rather had assumed that he would somehow figure out what to do next just by being there. As he consciously considered, for the first time, the thought of living in Pahquel forever, he felt a sudden rush of terror at the realization that if he stayed, he would have to fight even harder to protect himself. There would be no escaping Dabimi's hostile gaze, or its consequences; no means of forgetting Aran if she rejected him. He would have no choice but to face the wrath of anyone he wronged, to dance in all their dances, and to drink from the draught that gave them visions and caused them to vomit into the bushes, swaying in each others' sweaty arms. He would have no choice but to live as one of them, all his differences having become, over time, unremarkable, insufficient to exempt him from the cruelties of inclusion. Perhaps he had hoped to be absorbed by Pahquel, but only as himself, as a perpetual outsider whose every approximation of their gestures had a perpetually incongruous aspect to it and thus a notable charm, like a child's when he is playing grownup. To lose his identity as the strange one, he sensed, was to lose his right to a handicap, without which he despaired of getting by.

The fire had died down; he noticed not the darkness, but the chill. He stood up and shook out his legs, walking over to the edge of the forest to relieve himself before he headed into the hut, while images swarmed after him and buzzed around his head like gnats. As he unfurled his mat into his netting and shook out his skins in the dark, he heard the *kaag* moan in her sleep and shift to her side beside her children. From behind them, on the sleeping ledge, Dabimi's snores were soft but harsh, nothing like James's or Kakap's. "A connoisseur of snoring," he thought to himself with a kind of black amusement as he ran his dry toothbrush over his teeth, too tired to get up and walk over to the water trough. He pulled his jacket over his shirt and tried to get comfortable on the hard ground, against which the mat and skins gave little padding. Outside the hut, the forest was an engine revving up, proof that the night was not for sleeping.

To the insomniac, only two types of creatures exist, the ones who are already sound asleep and the ones who are awakening to action. There is the scurrying of the spiny rat, and the rooting of the possum, and the bat darting after its quick prey, just as at home there were the newspapermen, typing in a frenzy while the presses rolled behind them, and the revelers dancing in fast-motion like they do on newsreel tapes, and the policemen giving chase down dark, deserted streets. Meanwhile, the sleepers all but disappear into their own stillness, like rabbits curled in their holes, and shut-up flowers, and closed-up shops. The children and the *kaag*, for all their slow breathing, were as inert as the walls of the hut, and the village was scattered with others who were equally immobile. He knew Kakap was breathing slowly in a hut not far away, and that Anok and Aran were unresponsive, like two unsinged rocks in the midst of a furious fire.

Larry had long ago taken the insomniac's oath, which bound him to believe he was alone in his misery of muscle cramps and terrible thoughts and hypersensitivity to sound. In this, he was like all other failed sleepers, like Jorge, who knew that any return trip to Sr. Catalpa's would be fruitless, that there was no undoing the past, and tossed in his bed, certain he was to blame for yet another loss; like Joaquim, propped up on his pillows reading like all the other old men; like his mother, whose children were dead or gone, and husband gone overnight of a heart attack, and the house cluttered up with boxes to be sent ahead with the movers to her sister's in California. "Isn't it too soon to leave?" she wondered, her leg knotted up in the covers, when Larry could be returning any day to find the house locked up and empty, a For Sale sign in the yard. There was nothing protective in that oath; yet those who couldn't sleep would never had been comforted anyway by knowing that others suffered in the night as they did. Last year, while reading late for his European Lit class, he had had to put down the book by Proust that had been their first week's assignment, unable to go on after reading of the sleepless patient whose only hope of comfort was snuffed out with the light under the door. To know that other lamps were burning, that others struggled under the weight of too many thoughts, would have made his task of finding relief all the more hopeless. As it was, he turned on his mat for another hour and a half, crumpling up the skins and twice catching his zipper in his netting, before being sought out by the image of Aran, who turned slowly to face him, revealing the deep brown of her eyes and her newly symmetrical breasts.

LXXVI

EVEN THE WAN dawn light that crept in between the heavy curtains constituted an assault on the senses of Kamar Sodeis as he lifted his head and then lowered it; even his head's soft landing on the sweaty feather pillow exposed it to a sort of searing violence. In the chair at the foot of the bed, the Prefect's soft but burly bodyguard sat slumped over, predictably asleep on his watch. Sodeis had no memory of having entered that room, no memory of whatever useful information he had managed to glean from the Prefect, and no memory of where he had left the case containing his papers and maps, his favorite pistol and his tool kit and his brand-new blue Parker Jotter. He did have the memory of feeling the way he felt now on many other occasions, the raging, sick intuition of somehow having betrayed himself, though how badly in this case he couldn't venture to guess. He sat up again and tried to slide quietly to the floor, but the bed was higher than he thought, and he landed with a soft, jarring thud, waking the faithful Gabriel.

"Rough night, sir?" said Gabriel, sitting up and stretching.

"Something like that," said Sodeis, reminding himself that it was likely no harm had been done. The things you had to fear were the ones you did sober, since any witnesses to the other kind were no doubt equally drunk. "You too?" he said, smelling the front of his shirt.

"Let me take you to the Prefect."

"No need. I'm just going to take my things and go. Convey my regrets." He stood on wobbly legs and hobbled out into the hallway, relieved to find his case on the divan. He picked it up and began to make his way down the path to the river, halting and sliding on his way down. Gabriel stood on the verandah watching him pause on the path to relieve himself and then take off again toward the river, wondering if he should disturb the Prefect anyway but deciding to let well enough alone.

When Sodeis got to the water, he was surprised to see the Senor standing by himself at the end of the dock, in seeming contemplation of the steam that swirled over the water. He started to turn away, but his foot skidded on the rough sandy gravel, and the scraping sound, accompanied by the string of whispered curses that shot from him despite himself, caught the Prefect's attention. As he approached, he patted the canvas of his case in an effort to discern the shape of the pistol inside it, but couldn't tell whether the lump his hand found was his gun or just the top of his clipboard.

"Thanks for the bed. I'll be on my way," he said coldly, bypassing the dock on his way to his boat.

"I regret to say that you're no longer welcome here," said the Prefect, still obviously distraught, "and won't be until you can moderate your taste for drink."

"You seem to be a fan of the hard stuff yourself," said Sodeis, climbing into his boat, laying his case on the thwart and adjusting the oars.

"That sort of slight will not be tolerated either," said Sr. Catalpa, sensing that things could heat up unnecessarily. He glanced up the hill for Gabriel, and on not finding him began to pull on his fingers with even greater vehemence.

Sodeis stepped out of the boat onto the sand. When he leaned over to launch it, his head began an unbearable pounding, the effect of which was amplified tenfold by the strengthening sun. While he was hunched over, trying to subdue that pain, it occurred to him that his host's sobriety presented him with yet another unwelcome set of details to contend with. He stood up and approached Catalpa on the dock, scanning the top of the hill to make sure the old man's attendant hadn't followed him down. Suddenly, he lunged at him, grabbing one arm and twisting it behind his back. "You breathe a word of anything I said to you last night and you're a dead man," he hissed, throwing the Senor down on the dock. He walked to his boat and pushed off. "Remember that! I have ways of finding these things out, and I'm a man of my word," he said as the boat lurched out, seeking the current.

LXXVII

SARA FOUND MARTINA in the back of her shop, drinking coffee and reading the *Gazeta,* still in her robe.

"Am I disturbing you?" She stood in the doorway, framed by the low, harsh rays of the morning sun that streamed in through the display window in the front room.

Martina's first inclination was to turn away, to express her resentment at Sara's capacity to be kind, a capacity she had lately found lacking in herself. But her loneliness got the better of her and she looked up, folding the paper and laying it on the table beside her.

"Coffee?" she said.

"*A vontade.*"

Martina wiped out a coffee cup with the edge of her robe but then thought better of it and went to the sink to wash it. She poured the coffee and set it across from her, motioning Sara to sit.

"How are you?" said Sara.

"Tired." It was true.

"I have some information for you, from the lab, and then two questions."

"Information first," said Martina, refilling her own cup.

"Here are the numbers," said Sara, drawing a piece of paper from her bag and unfolding it on the table.

"Testing for lead is fairly easy, but getting an accurate read on mercury is harder—see here? Organic mercury?—so take that one with a grain of salt. But here's the surprise. Arsenic. Not a mining runoff. Smelting, but not mining. The only thing I know about arsenic in the tribes is from Marietto, from his stories about *latifundios* giving out sugar laced with arsenic when they were clearing their lands. So that's something to take note of, there.

"And the questions?"

"Easy one first, or hard one?"

"Easy one."

"Or maybe they're both hard. But the first one: Can I have a lock of your hair? I want to send it along for testing, just in case."

Martina went to a drawer and pulled out a pair of scissors. She grabbed a handful of hair and started to cut it at the root.

"Not so much!" Sara took the scissors and snipped off a small piece at the back by her neck. While she was holding Martina by the hair, she decided to bring up the second one: "If I could somehow convince Jorge to get back in his plane, if I could talk Joachim into going back for Larry, would you agree to go with them? Give it one more chance?" She put down the scissors and walked around to face her. Sara studied her face for a reaction, not expecting one. She understood that with Martina, even more than with her son, it was a matter of learning to read her expressionlessness for tiny signs of changes in pressure.

"I'm not on speaking terms with certain likely members of that party."

"You don't have to talk then," said Sara, pulling a garlic bulb from her purse. "Question three: Sam told me to ask you if you'd be willing to eat three cloves a day. Stop the arsenic from binding. So no one will get close enough to talk to you anyway," she said, placing the bulb in Martina's palm.

LXXVIII

ONCE LARRY HAD what he thought of as a job, he noticed a change in how the others treated him. He would go with Kakap to Panar Ak's hut in the farthest of the three interlocking villages and strangers would tease him and try to peer inside his basket. Panar's nieces began to call him by name, and the youngest one always clamored to sit on his lap when they all met under the *magno* tree to plan their next *nataja*. Panar Ak smiled broadly, without a trace of his earlier annoyance, as he offered Larry a drink of fermented acai. Whenever Larry was at home, Dabimi's *kaag* made him a drink of bacaba juice at the hottest time of day. Tapata, whose baby was still sickly and was sleeping on her arm, waved to him from her *kaawa* and held out a gourd of mucuri juice, and on his free days, when he followed Anok to whatever *chajan* she was painting, the owner of the hut, who might once have ignored him, spoke to him directly, and offered nuts and *tucuma* to them both.

The sense that he had only to work in order to be liked made Larry feel he had suddenly cracked a code that, in the end, had proven far simpler than he had ever imagined, and made him suspect that he had wasted the years of his life from childhood on in searching for a key that was unnecessarily personal and obscure. If, on his first visit to Pahquel, he felt accepted, sometimes even coddled, it was, in his mind, by virtue of his relationship to James, an illusion he nurtured all the more on his return, due to an utter inability to conceive of how he might be of value otherwise. Thus, what he feared most during his illness was the waning not of their memory of him, but of James, which would have left him stranded and exposed. Yet, sitting next to Kakap on his *kaawa*, sorting out the branches from the roots, he felt as happy as he had ever been, and hummed along when Kakap sang the song about how Nataji taught them to go on the *nataja*, how to cut the stems and tie them and present them to Panar. The idea that he had earned such contentment on his own, without James's intervention, was simultaneously exhilarating and, he suddenly noticed as he wound a bundle with reeds and handed it to Kakap, deeply sad as well. He tried to turn from whatever thought had brought on the sadness by listening to Kakap as he sang to the stalks and leaves.

Each plant was treated differently, tied with a different sort of tie and knotted in a distinctive way, according to its nature and its purpose and its place in the lineage of ancestors. Kakap would sing the specific story of each one as they worked, nodding for him to join in on the repeated lines. As he bound the stems of *panatan* with strings he had pulled from the rough coat of a *tatara* tuber, he sang of Pantor, his own ancestor, who had created the herb from a paca bone he had rolled in dirt and then dipped into the river. He leaned forward to show how the stem was so long because Pantor had been tall, and how the scent of the tiny yellow flowers, which were sheltered under the leaves, had been Pantor's scent. "It's a gift to us small ones," he said. The leaves glistened even in the shade, brighter than the crumpled bits of parchment that were its flowers, and when Larry turned the plant in his hands, it gave off a faint, musky smell. The story was told of how it had wandered until it found its home in the place where the soil around a decomposing log mixed with silt from the river; of how it became a plant; of how it had to be blended with the herb that was its *kaag* in order to soothe pain, of how only one cluster of flowers was to be cut from each stem. As he sang, Kakap referred to the plant as "he," and Pantor as both the discoverer of it and the plant itself. He lay the bundles on top of one another in a low basket, pushing the basket away with his foot when it was filled.

"Why did you say we're his smaller and smaller children?" asked Larry as they moved on to the next substance, the sap they had collected in painted gourds. There were four types in all, corresponding to the four aspects of the body: leaves and stems, trunks and bark, roots and tubers, and sap.

"We grow smaller with every birth," he said. "When our grandfathers lived, they were tall." He shook his head as he peeled back the leaves that were layered over the mouth of one of the gourds. "After two hands of sons, we have shrunken and bent, and after two hands more we will no longer be able to reach the tops of our *chajans*."

"How do you know?" said Larry as he stirred the sap with a stick, imagining Kakap reaching up with his missing fingertip. "Isn't your son taller than you are?"

Kakap waved him off and began to sing about the sap, which was the blood of the tree named Juru, after Anok's ancestor, who had discovered it. The Juru's sap was special, according to its song, because it hardened so quickly, forming a glossy shell over the *chajans* that kept their colors from fading. Thus, Kakap sometimes called it the guardian of the lines, as he sang and stirred, holding up the stick now and again to watch the thick amber resin run off the end, back into the mouth of the gourd. Also, in small quantities, it cured toothache. They pulled stray bits of bark and dried leaves and a few small beetles out of the viscous liquid and then sealed the gourds again with wax and leaves.

"Do you know the song of these?" said Kakap, holding up some tubers in his hands. To Larry's surprise, he could say their name and sing a few lines of their song, sure that he was getting the words mixed up and telling the story wrong. Kakap unfurled his slow smile and patted Larry's arm in time to his uneven chant. Larry didn't recoil, but sang a little louder, pleased at himself for having learned more than he thought. The song stayed in his head all the way to Anok's, and he began to sing it out loud as he approached her hut as a way of announcing his arrival. Anok came out and stood on the *kaawa* listening, leaning against the front of the house with her arms crossed and her head tilted to one side. Aran, too, stuck her head out of the door of the hut to listen, and smiled despite herself before withdrawing again into the darkness behind the *chajan*.

"I'll walk with you to Dabimi's," said Anok, clearly pleased with him and yet also clearly wishing to hurry him away.

The sun was low in the sky as they made their way up the winding path between the scattered rows of houses. Parrots swiveled their heads to watch as they went by, and some of the men from the middle village hailed them when they passed on their way back from a hunt with two pacas and an armadillo slung between them. Kinata leaned across the jagged line of sticks that defined the front edge of her *kaawa* to offer Larry a papaya, and Tapata called out an offer of mucuri as they passed. Lita offered nuts and Kanani offered tapereba juice, and Anok, as far as Larry could tell, offered him Aran, by leaning towards him while they were standing alone in the clearing, away from the doorways of the huts, and whispering, *"Jitana, press your claim."*

LXXIX

JOAQUIM ROCHA FUMBLED on his desk in Belem through the agglomeration of bark samples and talismans and papers and books which he referred to as his library, searching in vain for his reading glasses. Giving up, he bent again over the worn red notebook, squinting at the primitive script and scribbled marginalia and strange symbols and off-kilter diagrams of circles and squares. He was not an educated man in the traditional sense, but the past nearly fifty years spent among academics, bureaucrats, *garimpeiros*, politicians, tribal elders, *sertanistas*, cowboys, bootleggers, *seringais*; men wielding spears, clubs, machetes, shotguns and curses straight from the mouths of the most fearsome Gods, had left him with a belief in the power of patient, consistent effort to clear up the most difficult problems. And for the ones he couldn't cut through on his own, he had an endless file of contacts to whom he could turn for help, and an absence of the sort of pride that would prohibit him from using it them. The obvious choice in this case was Bruno Oliveira, who even in retirement possessed the scientific currency he sought, but also, and more important, the loyalty and reticence he required of those to whom he turned.

"Daniel!" Joaquim called out to his youngest son, the last at home, who at that minute was passing his open door.

"Father!" said Daniel, coming in and standing by the desk.

"Get me Professor Oliveria's number, would you?"

Daniel, shaking his head, began digging through the piles. He pulled out his father's leather binder of addresses. The son was perpetually amused by his father's disorder, and aware, at some level, that his father was returning his bemusement—the same look, but with sharper edges. The look signified Joaquim's disappointment in his son for being raised in a house, by parents, signified his disappointment in children everywhere, all of them, for having been softened by lives of ease.

"And while you're at it, can you find me my reading glasses?" said Joaquim, as the son reached over patiently and peeled them from atop his father's head.

LXXX

WHEN LARRY RETURNED at evening with Kakap after a day of sap-gathering, he found the village in turmoil. A crowd of people in body paint was gathered around a peccary roasting on a spit in the clearing, and another crowd milled beside a large trough of fermented Murcuri juice, stirring it with painted-handled sticks. Kakap led him through a clutch of children trying to play *kara* amid the swarms of men, past the women braiding blue and green feathers into each others' hair, and on to a hut at the far edge of the village where Aran and Anok were still at work. Kakap walked up to the *kaawa* and lowered his yoke of dangling gourds while the women caught them and propped them upright on the ground with sticks. He motioned for him to do the same, and Larry bent down slowly until he could feel his burden lighten as the gourds touched the ground. Anok untied the largest one from Larry's yoke, patting him quickly on the arm. She handed it to Aran, who pulled back the piper leaves that had been used to seal it and examined the sap that ran clear off the end of her stick.

"Can I start?" she asked her mother.

"Is it good?" said Anok.

"*Um,*" said Aran, turning to the *chajan* behind them, which was painted all the way to the top. Feathers had been hung from the center of the lintel overhead, like mistletoe, he thought. Aran started to cover the *chajan* with the sap, using a stack of *turpa* leaves tied together as a brush. She worked from top to bottom and then began at the top again, stepping on a log to reach overhead.

"See how quickly it dries?" said Kakap, catching Larry's hand in his broad net of fingers and holding it up to the wood. "That's why we waited until the end to get it, and then ran back. You remember, like I told you—Juru was quick." Aran looked down at them from on top of the log and said, "Your hand is going to stick." Larry made a face and pretended he couldn't pull his hand away.

"So what happens to this *chajan*?" he said.

"It goes back," said Anok, waving her hands towards the wall of trees behind the hut. "Asator will sing it," she said, reaching out to catch Aran's arm, "when Aran goes to tell him we're ready."

"Why should I go?" said Aran in a defiant voice, standing close beside her mother as though determined not to leave her alone with Larry and Kakap.

"*Patiri!*" said her mother, giving her a push.

"I'll go," said Kakap, heading off before Anok could stop him. Anok scowled. They sat in uncomfortable silence, Larry on the log and the two women squatting beside him, listening to the sounds of talking and laughing, and the shouts of children at the game. The smell of the roasting meat reminded him that he hadn't eaten since the morning.

"Kakap is good to me," he said finally, in an effort to make the silence seem benign.

"His father too, and his father's father," said Aran defiantly, following Larry's lead in avoiding her mother's distress. "Two hands of fathers, all the way back." She waved at the hut, or beyond it, into the woods, toward the river.

"It's good when children follow their parents," said Anok sharply. "Aran still has it in her head to gather, despite the change. Only Karun from her age group is doing that now."

"Change?" Larry said vaguely, trying to pretend he didn't know what she meant, in the hope of eliciting some more detailed explanation.

Instead, Anok came up and pulled Aran around, turning her shoulders so that she was facing him. Aran looked away, as did Larry, back up the path towards the clearing. Dabimi was coming down the path towards them, with his face frozen into a fierce smile, at the head of a large group.

Larry and Aran both caught his eye and quickly turned back again to face the more familiar danger. When Aran heard Asator's voice, she jumped up and tried to roll the stump forward. A few of the men, including Dabimi, helped her turn it upright so Asator could sit down. The space was cramped, and the press of bodies made it hard to breathe. The odor of sweat filled every crevice. Anok pushed Larry into the hands of some women who came up from behind the hut to paint him. While they smeared ochre into the indentations on either side of his shins, whispering to each other about the hair on his legs, Asator began to sing about the *chajan*, which had walked hands and feet of rain in a single stride. Between each verse, he left time for Anok to sing a part of the story depicted on the *chajan*, while the members of the audience called out or clicked their tongues or clapped their hands against their stomachs, smearing their paint. Behind Asator stood Taran and his family, who were rocking nervously from foot to foot, anxious to hear what was going to be said to their ancestors about them. Beside them, at the far corner of the crowd, stood Dabimi and Aran, paying no attention to the story. It looked to Larry like Dabimi was trying to grab Aran's arm, to whisper to her or pull her aside, but his view was obscured by the head of one of the old women, who had finished his ankles and now stood up in front of him and held him by the hair to paint his face.

"I have to go," he whispered, trying to shake off her grasp.

"You're not finished," she hissed back while the other woman drew a thick line with her finger across his forehead. By the time they released him, Anok was already singing of the births of Taran's children, who were still too young to hunt. Larry squeezed between the rows of sweating bodies, his skin making squeaking sounds as it caught skin. He got to Aran just as Asator was singing the last refrain. Dabimi was gone. The song ended in mass confusion, as everyone howled and clapped and streamed over Taran's old hut, stripping it of its walls and roof. Asator was being led out on the arm of his daughter up the hill to where the food was, and a line followed behind him like ants, carrying huge pieces of the disassembled hut on their heads.

"Wait!" Larry hissed at Aran as she started off into the stream of bodies. She turned to look at him, her gaze intensified by the concentric circles of paint around her eyes.

"What did he say to you?" whispered Larry when the last of the others had gone.

"Who?" she said, looking away.

"You know," he said.

She walked backward a few paces, stepping into the open space that used to be the inside of the hut, framed by the *chajan* that now stood naked, without its robes of lashed cane and thatch, its bare legs and feather genitals bright against the trees.

"He intends to press a claim," she said, "which is more than you intend."

Thus was Larry's decision made. "My claim will be the first," he said, walking towards her, reaching out for her arm.

"I don't believe you."

"I was going to speak to your mother tonight."

"Then you will be too late," she said, with sudden emotion in her voice.

"Why too late? Aren't I *jitana*?"

"Another *chajan* gone, and Dabimi's claim is ready now," she said, walking through the place where the back wall would have been, heading off into the woods. "And besides, my mother thinks you're too afraid to bring me to your father's house."

Larry stumbled as he followed after her, desperate and bedraggled, just as on the day she had first found him. His eyes smarted from sweat and paint, so that he had trouble keeping her in view. As she ran deeper and deeper into the forest, the brown of her skin faded into her surroundings, making it harder for him to see her at all.

"He can't do that!" he called after her in English, his voice sounding whiny and small. Vines hit him in the face, and scrub scratched at the paint on his ankles.

At last she stopped and waited for him to catch up, standing with her back to him. As he reached her, she began to pull, violently, at the vines that covered what looked like a stand of old tree trunks.

"What are you doing?" he said, fearful that it was him she was ripping to shreds before his eyes.

"Aren't you going to do anything?" she answered, without stopping. He reached forward and grabbed a vine, ripping it with a snap from its moorings. They panted and grunted and tore at the leaves side by side until their fingers touched wood and they both stopped at once, looking at each other, breathing hard.

"This is yours," she said, pointing to a space between the vines where the wood seemed to glow red in the dim light. Larry yanked hard and the vines fell away to reveal a painted surface, still shiny and slick to the touch.

"It's a *chajan*," he said, stepping back.

"It's yours, right?" she said, setting to work again. After what felt like an hour, the two of them stood back and looked at the *chajan* standing naked in a pool of black shadows, its dress of dull green leaves around its ankles. Where Aran pointed, Larry could see a triangle, James etched into its thigh at chest height.

"It's Jarara's, so it's yours," she said, walking forward until she stood within it, placing one hand on each of its legs. "See? You don't need Dabimi's—this is your father's house too."

Suddenly he understood her, and his heart began to race. He could barely look at her, let alone walk towards her, or touch her with his outstretched arm. She stood watching him, and in the silence, he felt his muscles go taut, as though his knees were going to crack. The paint on his skin was more oppressive and heavy in the heat than his shorts were, as though it were clogging his lungs. His stomach was knotted in hunger. His palms and his forehead were sticky.

"I need to lie down," he said, squeezing past her through the doorway on instinct, rather than walking through what would have been a wall.

"On the ground?" she said.

"Sorry," he said in English as his arm grazed hers, aware as though with heightened vision of the absurdity of their standing crammed together in the doorway of a house whose walls were nothing but open air. He pushed through and stumbled into the space defined by the imaginary walls, and lay face upward, gasping for breath. Aran stayed in the doorway and stared at him, a look of horror on her face.

"You still won't?" she said, in a voice full of disbelief.

"No, no," he said. "That isn't it. Come here."

She came and crouched beside him, and he pushed his hand out through the layers of undergrowth, of overgrowth and empty space, through confusion and shame, and took her hand and held it to his chest, where it tossed like a dinghy on the waves. He pulled her down next to him, and they lay together, still except for the rising and falling of her hand as he struggled for breath. At last, for no reason he could think of, his breathing grew more placid, as though a danger had passed, and he relaxed and stretched, feeling his spine against the dirt beneath his shirt. Even his hunger was gone. His mind, which had been racing, stopped at the point beyond which it couldn't bear to go, just short of replaying a scene from his first semester in college, when an awkward, drunken encounter with a girl from his Western Civ. class while his roommate was at the movies culminated in a spreading red stain on his bottom bedsheet. The stain was revealed to the world the next morning when his roommate's friends found him asleep and stripped his bed with him still in it, with a flourish that made concrete the indissoluble connection he had previously suspected between sex, humiliation, and betrayal. He even forgot, for a minute, that she was there, so that when he shifted on the dirt floor of what was once the home of his line and drew his hand up to his chest, he was startled to find her hand beneath it. After lying for a while in his grasp, she slowly lifted his hand and placed it on her own breast, where it could touch her heartbeat and snag in the tangle of her hair.

Had he not had certain memories to cling to, he might still have stopped at the *kaawa* of that small hut and paced back and forth in helplessness and fear, never entering through her body's unpainted *chajan*. His heart began to race again as he sat up and slipped off his shorts, more out of fear than with desire, as he tried to push away the thought that his failure to act would cost him not only her trust, but Anok's as well, and perhaps his survival in Pahquel. The memories on which he threw himself were not of his freshman year tryst, or stories from books, pin-ups at the barber shop, his eighth grade teacher, or the woman in Rio, beckoning to him from the doorway of a dingy house, pulling the hem of her skirt up to her breasts as he passed. They were, rather, the memories of holding her as a baby, when she reassured him, and he could make her laugh merely by shaking his head so that his hair fell over her stomach. It didn't matter that they weren't real memories; the one who lay beside him was surely older than he was, certainly not a girl of eight. He clung to them because he needed them, needed to remember the soothing whisper of skin on skin, the freedom of moving from place to place with her in his arms, the sense that he knew her, to whom he'd barely spoken a dozen words. He closed his eyes and remembered how she smelled, of must and sour milk. He remembered how she used to cling to him when Anok tried to take her back. "We're safe now," he whispered to her in English by way of love-talk as he stroked her hair and brushed her shoulder with his mouth, stretching out and entering, pressing his knees into the mud.

LXXXI

EDUARDO CATALPA UNDERSTOOD full well that he had no business in the forest, and that he depended for his very survival upon the illusion he had created in the midst of it of a world more suited to his temperament. Yet when he pulled himself to his feet at the end of the dock and began to make his way haltingly up the slope toward Gabriel, who was running towards him with his arms open, it occurred to the Prefect in a flash that his carefully crafted illusion had precipitously shattered, and that somehow despite this fact, he was still alive. The thought was not merely terrifying, but somehow intoxicating as well.

"Let me help you," said Gabriel, reaching him just as the Senor attained the crest of the hill.

"Thank you, Gabriel. I'm all right," said Senor Catalpa, allowing himself to be supported nonetheless.

They limped into the parlor, where the Senor collapsed on the divan. He opened his mouth to request a chardonnay and then closed it again, feeling a sudden revulsion at the thought of drink. Instead, he looked around as though to make sure Sodeis wasn't lurking, perhaps behind the bust of Apollo on its marble pedestal, or within the folds of the drapes.

"I'll send Joao to the mission right away, sir, and they can summon the police."

"Not yet," said Catalpa, testing his arm, finding it not broken or dislocated, but swollen and red from his hard landing. "First, get me a compress," he said, dismissing him with a wave of his good hand.

By the time Gabriel returned with the damp towel, Sr. Catalpa had reached a resolution the sheer audacity of which held him sufficiently in thrall that he had forgotten all about the pain in his arm. His reasoning had proceeded thus: Within three weeks, he was to be gone from Paruqu forever, closing a chapter that he could only regard as the centerpiece of his life. This chapter had unfolded thus far without his having accomplished anything whatsoever, other than the creation of a sort of vitrine of refined stasis that had afforded his children a relatively carefree childhood, despite the intrusions of the tutors, and his wife, two decades of marital disillusionment and boredom. But perhaps James had been right after all, that he had been an honorable man, capable of more, not merely of compliance, but indeed of something heroic, which might even allow his children, on his return, to see him in a new light. Of course he wouldn't have dreamed of pursuing Sodeis himself, or even of alerting the police, who, in his experience, caused more disturbance than they prevented. Rather, he sought a small act of defiance, which could allow him to defend himself in a way that he never had before, and would even have significance beyond himself, without putting himself in undue danger. He had to *tell,* in defiance of Sodeis, but tell what? And to whom?

When he looked up, he suddenly noticed Gabriel standing beside him with the towel. He unbuttoned his shirt and allowed him to place the compress, realizing gratefully at that moment that the arm that had been affected was his left one, leaving him able to write.

"Get my lap desk and some paper," he instructed Gabriel, remembering with pleasure that he had discovered, lodged between the cushions of the divan after Sodeis had been removed to the bedroom, an excellent blue pen, a ballpoint, the design of which was pleasing enough somehow to offer confirmation of the wisdom of his plan. He bent over the desk, writing quickly, and then sealed the letter with a flourish, addressing it and handing it off to Gabriel. "Have Joao send it now!" he said, suddenly overcome by deferred pain.

LXXXII

THE MOON HAD passed through four full cycles, and although she hadn't bled during that time, Aran's belly had barely swollen. All across the village, people had been whispering, and then talking openly, suspicious of her story and her mother's quick decision to embrace it. The new hut had been constructed on a rise behind the home of Piri and Karon and their baby, but it stood blank and empty, tempting the forest to re-claim it. Spiders cast their nets across the *chajan*, as though to confirm that the threshold was not, as things stood, to be transgressed. Disintegrating moths hung in the doorway, twitching in the forest's exhale.

Their life together began dramatically enough, with their return to the village just in time to interrupt Dabimi's efforts to press his claim to Anok by presenting her with a quiver of perfectly hewn arrows and a basket of folded boar-hide laces.

"That is not his father's house!" Dabimi bellowed, his voice steaming like ice in the heat. "They would have had to come to my house, where I would never have allowed it."

"Which wouldn't have done anyway," said Anok, just as coldly. "There's no consummation in the woman's father's home."

Dabimi stopped in mid-protest, his mouth and eyes wide open. Finally, he collected himself. "You don't know what you're talking about," he said firmly.

"I know my child's father," said Anok, "who left me nothing but the curse of his ancestors. And I almost cursed myself for you." She spat in the dirt. "I'm old now, and soon I'll have my own line to face."

When Larry arrived home that night, he found his belongings in a pile just outside the boundary of the *kaawa*. He stood and stared at the pile. He didn't hear Kakap come up behind him, and moved only when Kakap nearly fell as he tried to shoulder his pack. He took the pack and gave Kakap the shoulder bags.

Larry had hoped that by establishing his status as Aran's fiancée, he would be shown renewed deference, as when he first began to gather. What he found, however, was that there would be no recognition of their union until the birth of their child; no wedding, no painting on their *chajan*, no dancing, no greetings but giggles and whispers at his back. Without any public recognition of their status, he again found himself fearful that she would slip through his grasp. He was plagued by longing and foreboding when he was away from the village for more than a day at a time. After moving his belongings to Kakop's, he filled the days when he wasn't out gathering by helping Aran with the household tasks, especially the ones involving lifting. He soon began to haul the water on his own, and dig and mash the tubers, but still the baby didn't grow, and the talk around them became more apparent, and more dire. Aran began to turn away as they bent together over the cooking stones, and Anok hesitated before taking his arm as he left at nightfall.

"It takes nine moon cycles to make a baby," Larry would remind them, growing more and more unsure of himself each time he said it.

"Three," Aran would say firmly, turning away.

"Maybe even ten, two hands of cycles," he added one day when Aran seemed particularly upset, as he pushed the breakfast from the cooking stone into a bowl with his stick.

"You tricked me," she said, leaving with the bowl in her hands. She didn't come out again. He went up to the *chajan* and called to her.

"Do you want me to stay?"

"No," she said.

When Kakap returned from his visit to the far village, he found Larry weeping into the crook of his arm, leaning on his pack with his knees hunched up to his chin.

"Is something wrong with her?" he asked, his eyes searching Kakap's. "Isn't it ten cycles? Do you think I cursed her?"

"It's not Ark Pol," Kakap said cautiously, wiping a tear from Larry's face. Not a monkey ancestor's curse. But despite himself, he had wondered to Asator whether it was safe to allow Larry to sleep on a mat beside his children, given Tapata baby's illness, which he had dismissed until now as the result of an insult to its grandfather.

"We'll know in ten cycles, won't we?" said Asator, reaching his hand out and holding it still while Kakap brought his arm up to meet it. "Not so long now." The grasp was surprisingly strong; the pressure of the fingers lingered on Kakap's arm as he walked home. He greeted Larry with a special warmth, both out of his guilt at having doubted him and out of his sense of Larry's distress. "Let's do the *kina*," he said, pulling out the grinding stones and the furrowed wooden slabs. He began to sing the story, but then fell silent, and they sat together watching the juice run through the veins in the wood to collect, purple-red, in the bowls at the bottom of the slabs.

That night, as Kakap walked to Anok's house, the moon seemed to glow before his eyes, lighting the path. "So we'll wait ten moons," he whispered to her as they sat together on her *kaawa*. "That's not so long now."

"What else did Asator say?" said Anok, feigning disinterest but listening for something in particular.

"He only said to wait."

"Maybe he disagreed with my decision."

"He didn't say so." Kakap stood up and brushed the dust off his legs.

"Maybe you would have made another choice."

Kakap looked down at her still squatting in a corner of the *kaawa*. Even hunched over, she was formidable, even in doubt.

"We're two old *tiXaja*," said Kakap, starting to leave. Two old trees, the indestructible ones, the kind used for *chajans*. "You had no other choice." Anok nodded a grudging agreement as she watched him walk away, into the light of the burgeoning fifth moon.

LXXXIII

IT WAS CLOSE to midnight, his neighbors were outraged to notice, by the time Jorge picked up the phone. The call didn't catch him shaving, as calls used to do, but rather on his back on his sofa, with a damp towel pressed to his eyes. He rose and reached for the receiver not from a wish to hear from anyone, but from a desperate need to make the ringing stop.

"Alo, desconhecido!" said Joaquim's voice on the line. "Where you been?"

The obvious thing would have been to hang up, impulsively, and then to lift the receiver again and bury it under pillows forever. But Jorge remained frozen in place, pressing the earpiece to his temple.

"I'm calling to apologize. Will you hear me out?" said Joaquim, his voice muffled by skin and bone.

Jorge held the receiver more tightly against his throbbing forehead.

"I shouldn't have let it happen," said Joaquim, "and I'd like a chance to make amends and more. But now we have some real leads to follow. It would be your chance to right two wrongs at once." He paused. "No. More like seven or eight wrongs. Who could turn that down? We could be ready to go in two days."

"I'm not available," said Jorge finally, into the silence that held the place of a question. "I have a real job now."

"You had a real job before, and no one's been able to find you, short of camping outside your door, and you are obviously too slime-headed to care that the people who care for you are suffering while you've taken up residence under a rock with the rest of the reptiles."

The obvious thing grew more obvious and more impossible at once. "Maybe I can figure out how to right my own wrongs. Maybe I'm doing that now."

"Righting wrongs and creating others that are far worse. You don't answer the phone. You don't respond to anyone's concerns but your own. I guess you're not answering your mail much these days."

That was true; there was a stack of unopened letters by the door.

"It's all I could do to keep Silvio from coming over and killing you, which was maybe a good idea anyway, especially since you seem to be giving him a pretty good headstart yourself."

"He wouldn't be able to find me, even if he tried," said Jorge, getting up to warm the compress under running water. He lay the compress on the sink and took his glasses from his shirt pocket. He put them on slowly and walked to the window, squinting as though searching the night for his own approach.

"Do you really think we don't know where you are? Do you really think Mrs. Tomoio wouldn't have seen you walking back and forth in front of her window day and night for six months? Do you really think she wouldn't have taken pity on your mother?" Joaquim was deliberately not confronting him with the question of why it would be that someone who was supposedly so desperate to get away would move just two blocks from where he lived before, and keep his old telephone number, a feat that usually required a substantial bribe to arrange. He was right. Jorge was a failure even in his efforts to disappear.

"I need some time," said Jorge, squeezing out the compress in the sink and placing it again over his eyes. "I'm trying something different. Tell them all I just need time."

"I'll tell them all you're a stinking, reeking rat," said Joaquim, in a softer, resigned voice. "So how's the new life?"

"Stinking and reeking," said Jorge, pressing the compress to his eyes.

LXXXIV

WHEN KAKAP APPEARED in the doorway, the moonlight intensified around him, as the rays that escape from an eclipse contract and burn. If he noticed Larry looking at him, he didn't acknowledge him, but went about his nightly rituals: unrolling his mat, passing his web of fingers back and forth over his head as he sat on the corner of his sleeping ledge; singing to himself under his breath, a blessing on his family. One night not long after he had moved in, Larry noticed that Kakap had added his name to the roster of the living blessed, and James to the longer list of the dead. Since then, the sound of his name in the center of Kakap's song had always given him comfort, but that night, he half expected not to hear it. When he did, his eyes stung with gratitude, and he struggled to stifle the sounds he would have made by crying. After the song came to an end, he did his best to weave it again in his head from the noises the forest provided.

In his mind, things were encroaching and receding; the sun forced its way through the slats in the walls at dawn in rays as sharp as darts, and the rains, when they came, pierced his face like ice shards, and every whisper stung him, and every thought of Aran and Anok was like a splinter in his stomach. What fell away were the familiar things, the comforts; Jorge and Joaquim, long gone from Sr. Catalpa's house, stepping into their boat again and again and pushing off, heading farther and farther upstream. His uncle stood on the far side of the world and reeled in the string to which were tied the memories of his habits and the way he smelled and the sound of his snoring. Each night, his parents were dislodged from their house and flew off in a storm, and the house itself went spinning into the air, like the one in *The Wizard of Oz*. He thought of the *chajan* of Anok's house, in which he appeared as an odd, one-eyed icon, and the *chajan* of their old house in the forest, and Dabimi's *chajan*, and Kakap's, on which his children and his parents were joined at shoulder height by his two hands, depicted as two elongated brown finger-shaped objects reaching up and down along the right side of the wooden doorframe. He thought of his own *chajan*, picturing it only as a blur, its raw wood limbs forming a stark foyer to his and Aran's abandoned home.

Each morning, he dreaded word from Kakap as to whether they were gathering or grinding or meeting with Panar Ak in the far village or doing nothing at all. There was no comfort in going, and even less in staying, though worst of all was having to walk through the three villages one after another, greeted by fewer and fewer people, avoiding Panar's eyes while trying to remember which roots and leaves were to be gathered, in what quantities and from what distances and heights. Finally, he asked Kakap if he could stay behind on meeting days, and Kakap agreed, with apparent relief. After that, he used the time to do slowly what he otherwise, when he wasn't out gathering, had rushed each afternoon to finish. During the height of the day, while most people were away from the village or asleep or sitting together under the shade trees around the circle of logs talking in low voices, he would retrieve the empty gourds from behind Aran and Anok's house and walk down the thin, worn path to the river and sit for a while in the shadows, watching the water glide silently over the rocks. He would scramble down the steep wall of the channel, using tree roots as treads, and fill the jugs, tying their laces together across his shoulders before climbing up again. After leaning the jugs against the side of the house and returning to Kakap's, he would pull a book from his pack and sit down in the corner of the *kaawa*, hanging his head down over it so he wouldn't catch the eyes of those who passed.

He had come halfway around the world, he thought in misery to himself, only to take desperate refuge in the same books he had inhabited at home. There was *The Lord of the Rings*, and Henry Walter Bates, and a worn copy of the *Aeneid*, which a stranger had left on the train to Boston. There was the old leather-bound atlas, which he couldn't bear to open, and the thin volume of Van Gogh's letters, given to him by James so that "you'll always have someone with you—other than me—any time you want, who understands you." He opened the book to search for his companion, but today his friend seemed to taunt him by talking on and on about the miracle of birth and the inspiration provided to him by children. "There is something deeper, more infinite, more eternal than the ocean in the expression of the eyes of a little baby when it wakes in the morning," he read and turned the page. "Young wheat has something inexpressibly pure and tender about it, which awakens the same emotion as the expression of a sleeping baby," he read, and tried to turn away. "I think that there is no better place for meditation than by a rustic hearth and an old cradle with a baby in it," he traced unwittingly with his eyes. As he moved to close the book, with disgust and stifled rage, a single phrase jumped out at him, which he read again and again in a sort of joyful disbelief, with the uncanny sense that a prayer had been answered. "The nine months to childbirth . . ." said his friend, and Larry repeated him under his breath, first in a whisper and then out loud. "The nine months to childbirth . . ." When Kakap arrived home from the far village, Larry told him eagerly about the vindication of a claim he couldn't imagine how he had come to doubt, but Kakap looked with confusion at the passage he pointed to, and drew out the bowls and berries and gestured for him to start. Larry finished quickly, singing as he worked, nodding when Kakap sat down beside him to tell him about the next day's trip.

'He's happy now, and sings the songs again," Kakap reported to Anok after they had returned from the forest. "He is certain that the child is going to appear in two hands of moons, and showed me a thing that he said told him so."

Anok might have shaken her head out of bitterness and waved him away with her hand, but Aran's belly had grown, and that day she had said she felt a kick in her stomach after the morning meal.

What they both knew, Anok and Kakap, was that nothing could happen that hadn't happened before. Persons had been held back for a hand of days or more—had failed to return from the forest as planned, having been tricked by a devious dead relative, or singled out for instruction by a loving one. It was common to be held back, Kakap reminded Anok, and not always for the worst. This child has been held back in order to be taught to gather, Kakap told Mabara the next day, and Mabara told Jer, and Jer told his brother and his brother's wife while they were hanging the fish for drying. "That child is going to know more than we do; it'll teach us."

On his way through the village with the water jugs, Larry noticed that the older men nodded to him on the path again, and the women got up from their mats and poured out gourds of murcuri juice as they used to, and the knot that had tightened around his chest began to loosen slowly, allowing him to breathe. One day, while he was leaning the water gourds against the rear wall of Aran's house, she surprised him from behind, walking awkwardly toward him, looking puffy and unbalanced.

They stood in silence and then both looked away. Larry kicked at the dirt, and rolled a stone back and forth with his shoe, and played with the frayed hem of his flak jacket. When he finally looked up again, he saw her doubled over and ran to catch her as she sank.

"Are you sick?" he whispered, holding her by the arms.

"Let's go," she hissed back through gritted teeth. "To the house."

She limped off into the forest, gradually straightening as she went. Larry followed after her helplessly, his heart pounding, panting to catch up. His mind was a blur; could he have failed to count the moons right? Did he miss one? He tried to envision the pages of the notebook on which he had placed the checkmarks in a line, and nearly ran her down as she stopped again and squatted with her hands around her stomach. By the time they reached the old house and he had fashioned a dry bed on the muddy ground inside it with his jacket and shorts, the sun had withdrawn from the sky, replaced by a moon that gave nearly as much light. Aran lay on her side, breathing heavily, shivering and sweating, with her hair matted against her face. Larry paced back and forth in a panic, stopping every few minutes to stare into the semi-darkness behind him, searching the forest for intruders, sweeping the scene for a danger he knew to be close by.

"What should I do?" he whispered more to himself than to her, and received no answer from either. At times, she seemed to be asleep, and once, he panicked when he didn't hear her breathing. He crouched beside her and put his ear to her mouth, and thought he heard the faintest hiss, but not the rhythmic in-and-out of breath. He shook her by the shoulders, and she jerked her head up, hitting his temple with her forehead. The blow sent him flying backwards. His first impulse was to run, but she groaned and he whirled around and slipped on the leaves into the mud as he tried to get up, jostling her as he landed. It was thus that his course was determined: to lie beside her as he had fallen, shivering in the chill of her sweat, holding one arm across her chest as a restraint while she writhed and thrashed like a snake shedding its skin. Finally, the thrashing subsided, and a minute passed, and another, in which only the smallest of movements occurred: his teeth chattering, and her breath in shallow gasps, and the fluttering of a tiny moth in the air above their legs. A pause in a universal frenzy, a glitch in the record, and then a sudden scream, an explosion that scattered fluid everywhere, as though her body were a gourd that had burst, and an unfamiliar cry, an accusation or a shriek or a sob.

"Get it," she cried, moving his hands downward. "Bite," she said, holding the cord up to his mouth in her slimy hands. Larry took a gasping breath and bit down hard, and felt his teeth tear through flesh. Again and again he bit, until the cord was severed, and then he turned aside and vomited into the mud. The mud received what came to it, sweat and saliva and vomit and ooze, and covered it in mosses. They fell back, pressed together on a skin of leaves and matted shorts, and the infant lay between them, wrapped in his muddy jacket, howling into the forest while they slept.

LXXXV

SILVIO'S ANGER WAS obvious. Unlike most people, who raise their voices or gesture aggressively, Silvio, when provoked, became still and quiet, in alarming contrast to his naturally belligerent presence. He sat at the edge of his battered desk without moving, glaring from beneath his owly brow at the map in front of him while through the receiver, Joaquim's voice floated out and fell around his shoulders like a densely woven net. If there was one thing Silvio couldn't tolerate, it was the threat of being ensnared.

"There's nothing to be done at this point," Joaquim said, taking advantage of Silvio's rare silence. "As far as I'm concerned, you don't know anything about it."

"Except that I've lost my best pilot over it," said Silvio through gritted teeth.

"We'll get to that later," said Joaquim. "I think he'll be back."

"You think? You think? Fuck your thinking! Your thinking is costing me plenty." Silvio's raised voice was a sign that, despite himself, he felt reassured by Joaquim's confidence in Jorge's return.

"There's more to it than you know," said Joaquim, equally unruffled by Silvio's silence and his bluster. "But like I said, I'd suggest you forget anything you know about it."

"All I know is that I made myself two promises: to do my job, which means to keep my men in line, and to look after the kid, and you've managed to ruin both of them. So just tell me what you're going to be up to next. Are you going back for the kid, or not?"

"I'm not," said Joaquim, "not for a while, and you're not sending anybody else, either."

"And a while is how long nowadays?"

"A while is until I get some inkling that Jorge is going to move on it."

"A sign! You're waiting for a sign? Maybe for some voodoo message or some mysterious wind. Maybe you'll find it in the bottom of your *caipirinha*. I need to know now when you're planning to get him."

"You should have come out, Silvio," said Joaquim, ignoring him. "I told you that. You should have come out when we were all together here. You should have given yourself a chance to say goodbye."

"You want good-bye?" shouted Silvio, slamming the receiver onto the cradle and holding it down like a victorious boxer. Only when he could be sure that the match was truly over, that his opponent was truly out, did he remove his hand in order to open the door and wave in Maria, his long-suffering secretary. "Take a letter," he barked to her, gesturing at her roughly to sit down. "Address it to Mr. Joaquim Rocha, 35 rua de Palestrina, Belem. Dear Mr. Rocha, colon. You're fired as of today, comma, 4 August 1967, period."

"You're firing your boss?" said Maria.

"And you!" said Silvio, glaring at her. "You're like one of those German inmates. First you write one for him, and then you write your own."

"Sure, boss," said Maria, turning back to her pad.

LXXXVI

BECAUSE OF ALL the time he spent before birth with his ancestors, the child of Aran and Liroko was expected to grow unusually quickly, but in fact when at six moons it came time for him to receive his name, he couldn't yet walk, or even crawl. They danced for him, and Asator sang his song and gave him the name Iri, but throughout the feast, the child seemed barely aware that the fire was for him, and spent most of the day asleep in his father's arms, sucking on his father's little finger and clutching and unclutching his still tiny fists. Larry could tell that the ordeal was terrible for Aran, who shrank from attention in any case, and for whom the public acknowledgment of her situation could only have added an extra measure to her shame. She betrayed no trace of her distress as they turned to face each other in front of their *chajan*, which had been newly cleared of cobwebs and painted at the base with Iri's birth, but he could sense a tremor in her hand as the song of their union was sung for the first time. He knew better than to try to comfort her in front of the others, but when they were alone, he approached her while she crouched with her back towards him and held her from behind, until she finally turned and lay across his legs, looking up at the hanging basket that held Iri asleep. She didn't say anything, but toyed with the hair on his leg.

"So the ancestors have blessed us today," he said.

There was a long pause. "Yes," she said.

In the midst of her sadness, he tried to hide that he was happy. Where she saw signs that the child was stunted and strange, he saw only a beautiful, good-natured boy who had her large, intense eyes and full cheeks.

Where the pity of those around them was a deep embarrassment to her, to him it was a reassurance against the return of their fear of him. Most of all, when he held the child in his arms and sang to him as he slept, he felt the same spreading joy he remembered from before, when he had carried on his hip a baby with an uncanny resemblance to Iri, whom he had called Aran. So deep was his devotion to the child and to its mother that its fervor shielded him from awareness of the outcome which some had demanded, that the perhaps cursed child be left in the forest as an offering for boar. He did sense that the child's possession of a name gave him a more definite character, but what he didn't know was that the name in itself meant that the child could no longer be killed.

In the tenth moon cycle following the birth, as he and Aran sat on their *kaawa* with the baby squirming on his legs, Aran broke off her gossip about an argument she had overheard between Piri and Atani to tell Larry she had missed her bleed. She hadn't been expecting to, with the baby so long on her breast, but within two hands of days, her waist had already thickened, and she began to sleep again in the afternoons, and stopped going out to help Anok paint the *chajans*. On the days when Larry was out gathering, Anok started coming to the house in the morning to make the root-flour pancakes and to be sure her daughter had rolled up her mat and begun the household chores, chiding her with the same sly comments she had used when she was a child. Panar would sometimes visit them at night to give Aran a drink that was intended, she knew but Larry didn't, to safeguard the child in her womb, lest that one be held back as well.

If the wait for the first birth had been inexorable, the second one moved like a rapid, glassy river. On the days when Larry stayed home, he waited on Aran with the tenderness of one stem that brushes another in a breeze. Encouraged by the growth of the child inside her, Aran began to show him little signs of affection, a heartfelt rather than impersonal gratitude. He would return from hauling the water and hold out the wooden ladle for her, and she would cup her hands over his as she took a drink. He would feed Iri the usual mash of tubers and fruit and she would rest her hand on his arm while he moved his hand back and forth between the child's mouth and the bowl. He would sit on the *kaawa* with the sleeping baby curled in his crossed legs, resting the spine of his book lightly on his arm, and she would bring him juice while singing, under her breath, the song women sing to ask their husbands not to go out to the circle of logs with the other men in the evening. Most surprising, her affection for Iri seemed to grow in proportion to the growth of the new child; lately, she had taken to whispering to him and stroking his cheek, even within sight of the others. Indeed, there were days when he felt that he could barely recognize himself in his new life, as though it were a coat too large and fine for him. He sat together with Aran and Iri on the logs that circled the place where meat was divided and chatted with Piri and Amakar while they waited for their share. He helped Aran ladle juice into gourds when Jarma came to visit and laughed as their guest described, comically, his wife's mother's way of cooking *laraj*. He sat with Aran on Anok's *kaawa* after he got back from hauling her water and watched the darkness seep in though the trees, and when they got home, he lay beside her and their sleeping child and felt the peace Van Gogh had promised him.

It was during one of those charmed moments, while Larry lay on his back with his head on Aran's legs, his ear nearly pressed to her huge belly, that he realized that the birth was imminent. The third moon had waned and he had reveled in the thought of seven more just like it, but when the baby kicked against his cheek, he seemed to see it in his mind behind its rind of skin, a perfectly formed infant whose small hands pressed against their walls of membrane, stretching them to cellophane.

"When do you think?" he asked hesitantly, pushing his words one by one through the thickness of her stomach. "Soon?"

"Maybe a hand," she said, and as if by way of illustration, her hand appeared at the top of her stomach and rested there.

"Of cycles?" he blurted out, more forcefully than he had intended, pressuring an old scar.

"Suns," she said with equal force, removing her hand.

His first response had been a wave of nausea as he remembered the feel of his teeth in Iri's cord, and then relief as he reminded himself that the second birth would be at home, where he could have his knife ready.

He imagined sterilizing the blade in the fire and then holding it up for the night air to cool.

"*Kam, kam,*" he said with an attempted lightness, trying to pass off his earlier reaction as one of joy instead of horror.

Aran struggled to her feet and went inside. She unrolled her sleeping mat and dragged it toward the ledge. He picked it up and laid it on the wooden platform, and set his own mat beside it on the ground. Then he untied Iri's basket and placed it next to her. She drew it to her side with the inside of her arm, and he imagined resting there in Iri's place, burrowed in the crook of her elbow, washed in her scent and her heat and the shadows that slipped in through the walls from the fire that still smoldered on the *kaawa.* After he had curled up in his jacket and the blanket of bark and the one skin she wasn't using, he reached up to her arm and held it, relieved when she allowed his hand to stay.

LXXXVII

AFTER SO LONG, if Jorge had called, Martina wouldn't have talked to him. Her anger at him manifested itself as cheerfulness, and her cheerfulness, when she waited on her customers, mostly foreigners so eager for contact with the natives that they were pleased to mistake her for one, netted her a marked increase in sales. In the evenings, she embraced the wheel with a misplaced passion, and the clay did not disappoint in its capacity to neutralize all manner of tragic impulses and memories. It offered contact, a world outside herself, and the promise that everything in that world was in the process of transforming itself into something unexpected, and beautiful, and useful. It offered, in short, an alternative to asking questions, to the wish to know, which had proven so harmful in her dealings with Jorge. She had always been susceptible to the dangers of that inclination herself, but now the feeling in her hands was enough to distract her from the clay's message, which she was not anyway ready to acknowledge: that the constant effort to restrict oneself to what is solid and noble and hearty tends to yield, in the end, only a container for something else, a receptacle, a thin-walled emptiness, a void.

LXXXVIII

AS THE FIRE dimmed on the *kaawa*, the light of the third moon appeared in the doorway to replace it, accompanied by fanfare from the swallows and the toads. Amid that noise and the clatter in his head, Larry slept poorly. Several times he lifted Iri from his basket and held him, as though to keep the new child from wedging itself between them. When he dozed off with Iri on his chest, he dreamed that his hands had become enormous spiders that hung balled up from the limp ends of his arms. A small boy poked at them with a stick and they thrashed their black tentacle-fingers, shaking him violently from his feet and dragging him off into the trees. He awoke panting and shivering, startling Iri so he cried. When he fell asleep again, he dreamed that his pack was full of spiders, so that he couldn't find his knife to cut the cord. Then, he dreamed that the new child was itself a spider, with eyes that bobbed at the ends of fleshy black protrusions like a crab's. He woke to find that the moon had gone. He sat up and leaned his back against the sleeping ledge, where Aran lay on her side holding Iri's empty basket in the crescent of her arm.

It was not that a disturbance hadn't formed in his mind out of the spider-laden blackness, but rather that two troubling thoughts had taken shape from the same dark matter, such that his mind darted back and forth between them all night long and never settled. By the time day broke, his whole body ached from running that distance again and again in his head, so that later when he tried to follow Kakap over a rocky outcropping, he felt his legs give way and he slid down over moss into the scrub, scraping his calf and his elbow and crushing one of the baskets that hung from the yoke across his shoulders. Kakap knelt beside him and held his leg still while he looked at the cut, stanching it with a few *riti* leaves from one of his baskets, which were absorbent and smelled like moldy eucalyptus. Larry tried to push the broken belly of the basket straight with one hand while he used the other to catch the ooze of berries from the puncture, but its woven sides kept collapsing inward, and the torn edges kept sliding from his fingers as he tried to hold them together.

"Forget the berries," said Kakap, standing up and shaking out his legs. We can sing to Tur, and he will not be stern with us. There are more by the mogno logs. Forget the basket."

Larry stood up and looked at the cut on his leg, but was distracted by a small movement near his foot. He leaned forward to watch as a brown spider struggled across the cragged scrub, rocking as though slicing a rough sea. For a minute, he felt nauseous as the after-image of the spider swam in the blood on his leg, but he shook off the vision. He took the leaf Kakap held out for him and pressed it to his leg, and felt his other foot sink into a bed of moss, planting him in the marshy ground.

"How old are you, Kakap?" he said suddenly as he pulled himself out. "How many rains?"

Kakap laughed at the question. *"Pitarin a katir,"* he said. Hands and feet.

The answer was meaningless, as he knew, because in Pahquel there were no numbers higher than twenty. He had expected that answer, and perhaps even the laugh, and yet his heart pounded as he asked it, because it was a prelude to his asking Aran, which he had always told himself he didn't need to do. To distract himself from his unease, he asked Kakap the second question, which, now that he had formed it, was by far the easier to confront.

"How many children do you think a woman can have?"

"That's not good to ask," said Kakap, pushing at the leaves.

"Um," he said, peeling a few from his leg.

There were more berries at the mogno logs, as Kakap had said, and the basket was mended later that afternoon by Tikuna, and by the time he reached his own *kaawa*, he had made the prospect of too many children to support on his ration into his only fear, and then into a distant unlikelihood, since Kakap had been provided with plenty for five. When he stood for a while outside his door and listened to Aran call Iri, he imagined the hut crowded with children, each of whom he barely knew. He could hear Aran move from one corner to another, coaxing Iri to follow, and her image seemed to thin and fade as though the layers of his sense of her, of the way she threw her hair back, of her defiance and her loyalty, of her elusiveness itself, were being worn away by the friction of so many small bodies against her skin. He moved into the doorway and mother and child came forward from opposite sides of the hut to embrace him, in gestures that seemed oddly incongruous with his sense of his imminent loss of them.

"Iri's walking," Aran said, with excitement in her voice. The child had been so slow that she had come to doubt he'd ever start.

"Let's see that walk!" Larry said, forcing gaiety, lowering himself to the edge of the sleeping ledge. "Have you felt the baby much?" he said, reaching his hand to her stomach. She squatted beside him, and her belly forced her knees to the ground. He took Iri on his lap with one hand and moved his other to her arm. She caught his hand in mid-air and pressed it to his face, her sign for him to shave, which he did as best he could with his hand so unsteady, using boar fat and a blade he had tried, unsuccessfully, to sharpen on a rock. He was used to drawing blood. This time, he stanched it with one of Kakap's leaves, which he peeled from his leg. Then they sat together on the *kaawa* and let Iri stumble back and forth between them. Larry knew Aran wanted those who passed by to see him walking. He tried, but couldn't manage, to muster Iri's triumph as a reassurance against his own fears.

When Piri came to say that he had made a vat of *nir,* sweet peccary stew, his uneasiness intensified at Aran's eagerness to go with him.

"You go," he said, waving Piri on. "We'll be there soon, after Iri goes to sleep."

"I'm hungry now," said Aran when Piri left. "And Iri's hungry too. We were waiting for you."

"There's something I need to ask you first," said Larry, his voice wavering.

"What is it?" she said, as Iri fussed in her arms.

"How old are you?" he said. "How many rains?"

"Why are you asking?" she said, laughing, nervous at his intensity.

"Do you know?" he said. "How many were you when you found me?"

"Hand-and-three? No. Hand-and-four," she said, and let go of Iri. He ran into the house and she followed him, with Larry behind her.

"So now you're two-hands, or two-hands-one?" asked Larry, sounding dazed. It was starting to get dark, and the room was full of shadows that brushed across them as they moved. Iri let out little yelps of excitement as he ran, so that it was hard for Larry to think of what he wanted to say, or to remember that he had her attention. Finally, he grabbed Iri and carried him under his arm back out to the *kaawa*, calling for Aran to follow.

"We could have many more children at this rate, eh?" he said, trying to sound disinterested.

"Not so many," she said, suddenly concerned. "Why all the questions?" She came up in front of him and looked into his face.

"How do you know it won't be many?"

"I mean, because I'm so old." She searched his face in fear. He wasn't used to seeing her afraid. For a minute, her expression matched his, and then turned to something more like shame. "You're disappointed," she said, looking away.

Despite, or because of, the hard fist in his own stomach, Larry spat a gasping laugh onto the ground. He held her to him with his free hand and gripped Iri more tightly with his other arm, shaking, his eyes brimming with tears.

"No *jibimi*?" she asked him, still unsure. No second wife?

He couldn't answer, but just shook his head, pressing his forehead into her shoulder.

"It's not making sense," he said at last in English, pushing his mind against it. He put Iri down and took him by the hand. Then, he wrapped his other arm around her back and allowed himself to feel the soothing sense that had always come to him when he had held her as a baby. "No *jibimi*," he said, allowing the feeling to seep through his arm and his chest into his stomach, and to pool there.

"We're hungry," she said, laughing with relief.

"Ready," he said.

The smell of the *nir* poured down the path towards them, ahead of the sound of voices.

"I know—you brought Iri with you," said Piri, coming towards them, "so we can see how strong his step is."

Aran didn't seem embarrassed by the comment, even though it was true. She ate two gourds of *nir* in the time it took Larry to share one with Iri, and laughed while everyone watched Iri waddle to her across Piri's *kaawa*. To Larry, the vision of her bending down over her belly, extending her hands to Iri, was an image from a movie, or a dream. It played in slow motion, upon a rippling, diaphanous screen. When it was time to leave, he walked beside her with an unsteady gait, the three of them sharing, comically, the same uncertain waddle. He watched Aran tuck Iri into his basket, which she did with special tenderness, and then sat beside her, rubbing Iri's arm in the dark while he slept.

"He's snoring," he said, trying to distract himself from his reeling thoughts.

But the sound was Aran clutching her stomach, gasping as she rolled on her side with her back towards him.

LXXXIX

KAMAR SODEIS SLIT the top fold of the elegantly embossed envelop (the soft onion skin of which bore the letters Q. P. C. L., for Q. P. Comercio Ltda., in a rich burnt-ochre) with a snap, as though it were a man's throat. He was the sort who shouldn't have had to contract himself to any outside entity, individual, or creed, and yet the missives that arrived monthly, each of which contained the instructions for some additional project, some set of directives, some demand for submission on his part, only served to intensify his rage at the realization that he had not become what he had wished to be. Specifically, he had not turned out after all to be the infamous bandit, the lone prospector, the sort of Robin Hood who achieved such a profound justice by robbing the undeserving world of its riches that he need not even take the final step of sharing his fortune with the poor to be a hero. He shook out the letter, contemplating all the while the enticing thought of ripping it to shreds. He read:

Dear Mr. Sodeis: This letter is to inform you that your tenure as a contract employee of Q. P. Comercio Ltda. has hereby been terminated. The enclosed Incident Reports are included to substantiate our claim that your unprofessional conduct stands against the policies and interests of a 73-R Corporation such as ours. We will pursue no further charges against you, and all claims of misconduct have instead, (here Sodeis let out a soft, snort-like laugh), been turned over to the proper authorities for prosecution. Please note that the final installment of your contracted remuneration was deposited into Intercontinental Bank account #23814 on 17 July, and no further monies are due you at this time. Your replacement, Mr. Joao

Menenda, will arrive in Lamurii on 25 August. You are expected to familiarize him with all relevant protocols and to act as liaison until he gives you leave to depart, upon which you will vacate Lamurii province for a period of no less than five years from the date of this letter. Sincerely yours, Alejandro S. Jiminez, Corporation Council, Q. P. Comercio Ltda.

Sodeis leafed through the half-sheets on which the supposed incidents of his misconduct were detailed, curious suddenly to see which of the highlights of his career had come to his employer's notice. But he found only a description of a barroom brawl involving himself and the Mayor of Karoyo, a dusty village of no account an hour upriver from Lamurii, in the course of which injuries were sustained; a report on an unfortunate fatal encounter with a lone Mururi Indian over a small patch of land on which he and a crew of a dozen men were prospecting (this was proof that someone had it out for him, as crimes against Indians never merited censure otherwise); and an observation report filed by one of the sniveling, rodent-like clerks in the Q. P. C. L. office in Rio that addressed his pilfering of six boxes of office supplies. No doubt the chief had received the same letter, but Sodeis knew that didn't matter; without his help, he couldn't read it. He folded and pocketed the letter, rubbed his face vigorously a few times, as though to shake himself awake, and made a beeline for the chief's hut, hurling himself with a vengeance toward the clearing, into the clutches of the mid-afternoon sun.

XC

THE SECOND BIRTH was nothing like the first. Between Aran's contractions, Larry ran to find Anok, who brought in Panar and Amara and two small girls from Panar's village whom he had never met, different than the ones who had cared for him. Iri was fretful and kicked at him when he tried to stop him from running off, and the girls, when they weren't needed by Panar, made the child harder to quiet by teasing him. He sat in the far corner of the hut as people came and went, feeling desolate and useless, while the distance grew between him and Aran. He imagined leaving, taking Iri under his arm and walking off into the trees, but Anok came and carried Iri away to sleep with her in her hut. Panar lit the fire on the *kaawa* and then unrolled a sleeping mat beside it for each of the girls, and they finally settled, tentative as flecks of dust, while their uncle crouched beside them, grating keli nuts into powder against a stone. Amara went home, and Piri placed a gourd of *nir* inside the door of the hut and left, and at last the hut grew quiet, and the chasm between Larry and Aran began to fill up with the forest's noisy silence. He moved his mat over to the ledge and slept without intending to, with one hand wedged beneath her thigh. He awoke once and found his arm tingling and his fingers stiff. Aran was gasping on the ledge, and he sat up with her and brushed the hair from her forehead until she stopped. Then he fell asleep again despite himself. The next time he awoke, the hut was streaked with daylight and Panar and the two girls were hovering above him, holding Aran as she pushed.

"You almost missed it," said Panar, laughing in a way that Larry resented. He could hear Anok pacing back and forth with Iri on the *kaawa*. Aran was sitting on the edge of the sleeping ledge doubled over, dripping sweat into the dirt. Larry jumped up and sat beside her, holding his arm around her shoulders. A bloody fluid was dripping out from between her legs into a wooden bowl. Suddenly, the voices around him rang tinny, and the bodies blurred together, shadowy and tilting, and he vomited into the bowl that held the blood. The baby came out at that moment in a rush, and one thin strand of the vomit wrapped around its arm. Panar brushed it into the bowl and held up the cord for him to bite. Larry started to get up to get the knife from his pack, but found he was too dizzy to stand, and bit down through another wave of vomit as he fell back onto the platform, and felt the gristle lodge between his teeth.

"I see you don't crave the taste like some men," said a familiar voice, laughing. Larry opened his eyes to see Anok leaning over him, wiping his face with her hand. One of the girls was rolling up his sleeping mat, which had red blotches on it from the blood, and carrying it out. His head was pounding, and the light hurt his eyes. He squinted and tried to look around for Aran, but a pain gripped his skull and immobilized it. Anok brought another mat and helped him lie down. Without opening his eyes, he reached up to the ledge for Aran, but, not finding her, his hand waved wildly in the air until Anok took it and placed it on her daughter's arm. Aran made a noise, but didn't move. People were walking in and out around him, talking in low voices. He tried to remember whether, in the blur of sound, he had heard a baby cry, and suddenly panicked that it had been stillborn or sick, or had never existed at all. He pulled himself up and called out to Anok.

"The child?" he said, forcing out the words.

"It's big," said Anok, coming to kneel beside him, resting her hand on his forehead.

He wondered whether she was telling him the truth. He wanted to ask whether it was a boy or a girl, but knew enough not to curse it by giving it a sex before it even had a name.

"Can I see it?" he said.

He heard a groan from behind him as Anok slid the basket out from under Aran's arm. He sat up and Anok placed the basket in his lap. The child looked like Iri, but larger, its huge head covered in thick black down. It was sleeping. Its mouth was twitching, and it rested its chin on its fist. He didn't feel an impulse to pick it up, but just sat silently, looking down at it. Somewhere in the room, the two girls whispered to each other, and Anok led them out, sending Iri off with them to play. Larry sat alone in the hut with the basket on his legs and Aran behind him on the ledge and an enormous sadness that suddenly poured out of him like a second birth, like rain over the sleeping child, like all fluids everywhere, runoff of loss.

XCI

SODEIS WALKED THE short path to the chief's house deep in thought. As he arrived, the chief, in the company of assorted wives and children, had just begun to address his afternoon meal, and was clearly displeased to be interrupted.

"I'm going away for a few days," said Sodeis in Tupi, waving away the chief's half-hearted gesture toward the bowl in front of him.

"That so?" said the chief with his mouth full. "Something happen?"

"No. I'm just going to meet a few former business partners who are staying at the mission at Xitipa. Good friends of mine. A few days and I'll be back. I'll talk to Roberto, give him instructions, do all the monitoring before I go. I think things should be fine for a couple of days."

"Your boss know you're stepping away? You send a letter out with the mail?"

"All taken care of."

"Roberto better keep a close watch on his men. That's your job, you know. Whatever happens."

"I do my job, you do yours," said Sodeis. It didn't take a genius to conclude that since the visit of Joaquim Rocha and his group, the chief's suspicion of him had evolved into a restrained but unmistakable hostility. "So three, four days," said Sodeis, bowing and turning to go. As an afterthought, he turned back. "Can I bring you anything from Xitipa?" There was a flash of eagerness in the chief's eyes, quickly extinguished. Sodeis bowed again and headed back up the path towards his shack. While he was walking, he half considered the idea of actually hiking the four miles to the mining camp to speak to Roberto, the foreman. He was supposed to have done so daily, but in truth it was rarely even once a week, a fact he considered a key element of his smooth relationship with Roberto. "I do my job, you do yours," was a more general creed, which had proven itself many times over.

If he did talk to the foreman, he could either smooth the way for Mr. Joao Menenda, a total stranger, which would have been a generous and honorable action that might lend him credibility in his efforts to defend himself against the charges against him. On the other hand, he could also offer guidance to Roberto on how to make life as difficult as possible for his successor, as a form of revenge. The second possibility pleased him more than the first, but he opted instead to return to his hut to pack his bags, careful to take with him anything he, or the employees of Q. P. Comercio Ltda. might find of future value.

XCII

AT FIRST, LARRY assumed that it was only Iri he missed, and all of his longing trained on the image of him being led away crying, looking back over his shoulder as he clung to Anok's hand. He would take a few steps and then turn back toward Larry, eyeing him with uncertainty until Anok pulled him on again. His small form thus dissolved only very slowly into the gray-green evening light, leaving a blurred silhouette against the fading backdrop of the wall of Jikra's hut. In Larry's mind, he saw a hole in the wall the size of Iri's shadow, like a cartoon character would make. When the dark erased the image of the hole, he got up and went inside. Aran was sleeping on the ledge.

Larry was used to the sound of her breath, used to feeling its rhythm on the back of his neck as he sat up and leaned against the ledge, and finding comfort in it. That night, he knew that there was something missing even from it, some timbre of intimacy that, in his sudden loneliness, he craved. He thought of trying to climb onto the ledge beside her as he sometimes did, but knew that the baby's basket was resting in his place, and remembered too, his anger at having been betrayed the baby in some way, though he wasn't sure exactly how. It might have been by Aran's rushing the pregnancy or allowing intruders at the birth, or forgetting him among so many others. He knelt beside her and she stirred and reached out for his arm.

"Are you happy?" he whispered after some time had passed. *"Akara eta tuara?"* "Is your house beautiful from the living?"

"Beautiful," she said, holding onto his shoulder as he lay down. Leaning back with her hand on his arm, and later, helping her out to urinate, holding her in the dark by the armpits, standing with his legs wide while she squatted down, he felt suddenly that they were as close as they had ever been, and couldn't remember why he had convinced himself that she was lost to him. They held the basket on their laps with their legs touching, and she nuzzled his neck with her face, and teased him gently about having thrown up again into the *tira*. Larry forgot completely the despair that had gripped him so shortly before with its eight black tentacle-arms, and lay back on his new, strange-smelling mat beneath his jacket and skins, and felt the warm, black waters of sleep lap at his right side. It wasn't until a howler announced the distant light from his treetop perch like a man in a crow's nest calling out land that he felt a chill grip him, and imagined a dark shore looming, and knew which one it was.

He had awoken from a dream about which all he could remember was the image of a small stone resting in his open palm. After lying awake in the darkness, trying to hold the image in his mind, his hand became Aran's curled body, the stone in its center the child, which now lay embedded in its basket in the space beneath her arm, a small thing suspended in the center of an expanse: a pearl in an oyster, a drop of water on a leaf, a cruzero clutched in Jorge's fist, a colony of huts barely visible, nesting in the faintly veined palm of the forest. He repeated to himself the word that had accompanied the image in the dream: "*Mboa*," and knew with a sickening sense that the stone was Aran, and that he was the hand that held her. He worked out the numbers in his head: She had been newborn the summer he turned eleven, and now, eleven years later, she was afraid of being too old to bear more children. Asator and James had seemed, on the first visit, to be roughly the same age as his parents, but on the second, Asator was fragile like his grandfather, and even Anok was gray and stooped, with knotted fingers like his grandmother's. Worst of all, the child was carried for only two and a half months to Iri's nine; it too was a stone, which he could clench in his palm with all the strength he had, and yet, inevitably lose. He sank back onto the mat and her hand slipped from his arm. It hit the side of the sleeping ledge with a soft thud and she started awake, jerking the basket. The baby cried once and then settled again, rubbing its face in the moss lining. Aran pulled herself to her elbow and looked down at him. A diffuse light like a dry fog had filled the room, and she could see it reflected in his open eyes.

"Are you happy?" she said at last. "Is your house beautiful from the living?"

"*Mboa,*" said Larry, shutting his eyes. Beautiful from the dead.

XCIII

KAMAR SODEIS HAD nothing in particular in the forefront of his mind, and only a vague itch for revenge in the back of it, when he set out for the river with his pack on his back and bags crammed with papers dangling from his shoulders. He had stowed his boat well upstream from the camp, far enough upriver to render any concern about using the motor unnecessary, though that made the trek to it a mile longer than it would have been otherwise. The sun was high by the time he threw his bags into its hull and began to reach around for the shovel he kept under the seat, with which he used to bury his extra gas cans. The cans required holes nearly a meter deep, and in a shady spot so the heat in the ground didn't ignite them. That tended to make the digging arduous, through dirt rather than sand, even when the holes had been excavated many times over. He waved his hand around, kneeling in the wet silt, and then swore loudly when he realized the shovel was gone. On the bank that jutted out at waist height behind him, he could see the handle of the shovel protruding from an empty hole. When he got to the hole, however, he realized it wasn't in the place where his cans were buried. There was nothing in it, so he pulled out the shovel and excavated the three cans, which sloshed reassuringly as he carried them to the boat. Digging something up was always a lot easier than burying it in the first place.

The cardinal rule of the river was "Never mess with another man's boat." Although he hadn't always obeyed this rule himself, and in fact had been quite liberal from time to time in his use of craft he had discovered in opportune places, no one had ever tampered with his own boat before.

As he pushed out into the current, the sense of another man's hands on his oars left him feeling strangely uneasy. He shook off the feeling by yanking the cord decisively to start the motor. Then he took off upstream, in the opposite direction from Xitipa.

XCIV

DURING THE FIRST hands of days after the rains, the forest was a flower, newly opened, moist, its perfume dripping from pistons as numerous as stars. The men returned from the hunt bearing yokes that were overhung and bent, and the baskets of the women overflowed with fruits and tubers. The low ground that lay towards the West was always flooded then, swarming with mosquitoes and parasites, but in the *jacu* direction, to the right at the end of the path behind Anok's house, the water stayed within its widest borders, and moved forward with a compressed intensity, carrying cities on its back. Tributaries that until two moons before were only furrows in the cragged hide of an expired beast were thriving with algae and fish and shards of sunlight. Larry sat with Aran and Iri and Karina and Piri on a thick log that ran parallel to one small inlet and watched as Oji and four other boys waded knee-deep in the brackish water, beating a vine they had laid on a rock just beneath the surface with stones the size of *kipa*. A few other children stood ankle-deep on the gray shoulder of the stream and shouted insults and advice to the older boys, bouncing their empty baskets on their backs and stirring up the water with their sticks. When the fish, stunned by the poison, began to bob up, sparkling like bits of green and blue foil on the surface of the water, Iri jumped to his feet with a howl and tried to slide past Larry along the log, but Larry restrained him and pulled him onto his lap.

"Soon," he whispered in his ear, but the boy kept squirming, trying to run to Oji. "Next rain," he said, and held him.

The boys at the shore were holding their baskets between their knees, grabbing the fish with both hands. When the baskets were full, the older boys and the men, Larry among them, shouldered them and they all walked back up the path together in a triumphant parade, stopping every now and then to retrieve a fish that had come to and thrashed its way out. Larry held Iri by the hand as they went, but Oji, who was already the height of Aran's shoulder, took her arm, as he was too big to be led. They sang to the vine, and to the rain, and to Asator, who offered them the guidance of his line, but who now lay dying in his hut.

Back in the village, people were speaking in whispers, and a few were already painted. When Larry's group burst into the clearing, they immediately smelled the last breath and stopped short so that the ones behind pushed up against the ones before, and the song was jarred to silence. Larry and Karina and Piri dropped their baskets and ran towards Asator's hut, untying the bands from their arms as they went. In the distance, they could already hear the drum beating out the heartbeat of the deceased. As they approached, they were met by smoke from the fire on the *kaawa*, by the smells of sweat and rot and wet twigs struggling to burn. The son and the daughter were there, the daughter now wailing, now drifting like a stunned fish, unable to comprehend that she was suddenly *rajora*. Panar Ak was still inside, filling Asator's mouth and nose and anus with sweet-smelling herbs that would announce him to the ancestors as he burned. People milled around, sweaty, pressed together, waiting for word as to when the dance would start, whether tomorrow or even today, as they whispered among themselves, although the fire for smoking the fish was already burning, and the fish were waiting to be smoked. Panar came out, his hands stained from rubbing the herbs, and told them to come to the clearing at dawn, and dispersed all but the family and the painted men who were to guard the body during the vulnerable time between death and immolation. Larry moved off slowly with the others toward the fish-fire, but when he glanced behind him, he noticed Anok crouching with her back against the *chajan*, holding her head in her hands. He went to her and sat cross-legged beside her while the backs of twenty men faded into the mud on the path.

"Have you painted yet?" he finally said, seeing clearly that she hadn't. "Can I grind the pigments, mother, or go for Aran?"

"Don't," she said, moving one hand from her face to his arm. Her breasts rested on the insides of her thighs, two abandoned oriole's nests, heavy with water from the rains. Larry could see the movement of bodies out of the corner of his eye, but he didn't look up until two legs stood before him, two familiar feet, with toes as long as fingers.

"I have the berries," said Kakap, and helped Anok stand. The three walked together to his hut. Between verses, Kakap addressed her in a low voice, with the epithet used for the kin of the dead. When they arrived, he held up the berries in a reddish bowl, but pressed her to him for a minute with the bowl out of reach before he handed it to her.

When she left, Kakap took Larry's arm and pulled him back into the house. "You know she was *rajora*," he said, "and she was his."

"She had no *jitana*?" said Larry, confused.

"Not that kind of *rajora*," he said. "A woman with no husband or father. A woman who can go to men."

The thought stabbed at Larry, who had convinced himself that Anok and Kakap and Asator and Panar Ak formed a secret society of elders who guided Pahquel with an abstract, benevolent interest that precluded their more personal involvements. In his mind, he had relegated her encounter with Pitiri, Dabimi's father, to the status of a small irrelevancy, a means to the end of having conceived Aran, and her connection to Asator as a form of partnership, rather than as a passionate entanglement of any sort.

As though he had a sense of Larry's distaste, Kakap spoke to defend Anok before he had a chance to reply. "It was a great comfort to Asator to have her when Kapora died. Because of your protection of Aran, she was able to endure Pitiri's revenge and go to Asator without regret, or danger to her line. And she was *tuara*. You gave her that."

At home that night, Larry struggled to shake off Kakap's words in an effort to keep the loss impersonal, in an effort to rob it of its power to invoke the loss of James. But when Anok appeared on their *kaawa* with the dye still wet on her hands and allowed herself to be led to the fire, when she crouched with Aran and wailed, Larry knew that he wouldn't be able to escape its power, or to protect James from it. By dusk, there was wailing from every *kaawa*, and from the dark pores between the trees, and from the sky, reef of stars, and he could no longer deny that it came from inside himself as well.

"You need to comfort Jarara now," said Anok, taking his hands in hers. "You sing to him."

Larry pulled his hands away and walked past her into the house. He stood beside his sons as they slept, shifting his weight back and forth from leg to leg, listening to their long breaths, which were thin enough to slip into the silences between the human cries. At last, as though he had found what he had come for, he turned and went out again. He sat down next to Aran, leaning the back of his head against the wall of the hut with his eyes closed. Aran and Anok stopped wailing.

In their silence, Larry numbered his miseries; the misery of knowing that no loss was impersonal, and the misery of knowing how quickly he would lose the ones he loved the most, and the misery of knowing that no one ever recovered from such loss. The dead were shell and bone, but the living, too, were porous. Looking at his own hand, he caught a glimpse of Asator's hand resting on his painted stick, with its cracked thumbnail and its knuckles that were round and raised like coins. The image of the hand seemed suddenly solid, more substantive in memory than in life, and the cries he heard from distant *kaawas* were bubbles of air escaping from the bones of underwater reefs, the relentless exhales of time.

XCV

IT WAS NOT Jorge Moretti who hiked each day the cluttered urban trail that stretched from *72 R. Sen Augusto Meira* to the austere main branch of the *Banco do Brasil* at *R. Barbosa 794*, through the imposing bronze doors to a back office just large enough to hold a desk, a chair, a few metal filing cabinets and a hat rack as bent as a man twice its age. It was not Jorge Moretti who, in his precise, tight script, filled lined index cards with the serial numbers of the stock certificates of some seventy-five Bovespa-traded companies, as brokered by Dannie and Roberto, "our men in Sao Paolo." No matter how closely the figure who hunched over the stacks of cards might have resembled him, and no matter that he was always dressed in one or the other of Jorge's two gabardine suits, with his father's heavy watch sliding up and down his arm, the real Jorge would have been hard-pressed to recognize him as the same person who had greeted him in the shaving mirror every morning for the first two decades of his manhood. The other two fellows in the unit, who were both named Marco, a coincidence which attested, in Jorge's mind, to their interchangeability, spent more of their time at luncheons, boasting of conquests and discussing boxing, than they did in actual work. They regarded Jorge as an oddity, an awkward old woman, a humorless, dusty sort who no doubt never scored with the ladies, and ironed his underwear.

"You coming?" they shouted into the open door of Jorge's office as they slipped out an hour early, knowing full well he wouldn't. Then Jorge would be left alone with the soft click-click of his ballpoint pen and his stacks of cards and the occasional echo of footsteps in the hall. Jorge knew that the footsteps would never belong to his boss, who was more likely to be out with the Marcos than patrolling their stuffy back suite. That he made more money at this job, which demanded nothing from him, and in fact reduced him nearly to some kind of automated transcribing machine, than he did with SPI had a certain irony to it, but was beside the point. Rather, the point was that in this job, he never had to think; his mind had endless open space in which to wander, but no need or inclination to go anywhere at all. Only twice thus far did any of the names he inscribed in his indexes, along with their addresses and identification numbers, belong to anyone he knew. Once, he jerked up in his chair when he noticed that he had just finished recording the purchase of 1,000 shares of Gerdau (siderurgy and metallurgy) by one Silvio Amanza onto one of his worn index cards, and, several months later, he again felt the tension in his stomach as he attributed the purchase of twice as many shares of Fibria (paper and pulp) to a Diego Melo, since 1960 of the BSB. Neither of those occasions prompted in him any urge to look further into the finances of either man, although he did pull the latter of the two cards, on impulse, and place it face down in the inbox on his desk. For the most part though, he understood that when one's primary investment is in the passage of time, it was numbers, and not names, that moved the great wheel forward.

XCVI

ASATOR WASN'T WITHOUT Anok for long. After the fire had devoured him, and the dancing had consumed his survivors, after the two dreamlike hands of days in which chaos reigned and Larry hid in his hut for fear of coming upon people having sex in broad daylight in the clearing, or upon bands of men painted to look like animals wandering in and out of the forest, or upon people eating to the point of sickness, or drinking the *katiro* until they vomited into the stubble at the edges of the paths; after the feather had fallen, and it was not Dabimi's, and the world had fallen into order again, Anok dozed on her *kaawa* one afternoon and fell as softly into death. Larry had been fetching her water and hadn't noticed that she didn't look up as he poured the gourds into the trough. The paints were already mixed, not just the pigments, but the pigments with the liquids, indicating her intention to work that afternoon. The paint gourds stood in a neat row against the side of the hut, and the sun swam in them and suffused them with intensity.

The day had been remarkable for its ordinariness, and for that reason beloved by Larry. He had loved the ease with which the gourds filled in the high water, and he had even loved, without fear, the spider's patience as it waited in the corner of the *kaawa* for its prey. He loved the gentle, awkward greeting he had received from Jin, who, only a moon cycle before, had been wandering the clearing, shouting obscenities and beating back invisible intruders with a painted stick. He loved the way Aran had touched his arm to wake him, and the silence on the path, and the diffusion of the light in the treetops. There was order in the day's unfolding, and reason in the veining of the leaves, and the stillness that seemed to have been revealed everywhere as the madness receded was pervasive enough to determine that death was ordinary too, and thus suddenly all the more worthy of fear.

In fact, he didn't stay to be sure Anok was dead. He only noticed, for a fleeting moment, that she was changed, immobile in a sickening, familiar way, before he dropped the gourd-yoke and ran to Kakap's fast enough to leave, for a time, the possibility behind him. On the way back to Anok's he ran behind Kakap as though to use him as a shield, and turned away as Kakap wailed, as though to deny that the wailing was his own. When Kakap stopped, Larry turned around again to see him sprawled across her lap. She looked down at him like an empty, serene pieta, draping him in her granite robes. Both had forgotten he was there; the moment was intimate, unbearable, which made the intrusion of so many people, who heard Kakap's wailing and pressed onto the *kaawa,* all the more violent and confusing. There were women to lead Kakap away, and men to run for Panar Ak. Atani set out the bowls for the herbs, and Kita and Tanar lifted Anok's wooden body onto the sleeping ledge inside her hut. Kajar, toward whom Larry had felt nothing but an intermittent, mild dislike, took his arm and walked him up the path to his house, standing beside him on the *kaawa* as though expecting to be invited in to witness Aran's first cry. Larry stood for a minute, confused, unsure of what he had to do to get Kajar to leave, and then finally dismissed him with a nod that shattered the lacquer that had seemed to spread over the skin on his face and neck and arms.

Larry watched himself turn and walk into the hut, as though from a great distance, or from another time. Aran and Oji were leaning side by side against the sleeping ledge, grinding tubers for the flour, while Iri was playing pick-up-sticks in the back corner. Larry pictured them all in a glass vitrine in the Natural History Museum, in an exhibit on Indigenous Man, marred only, made ridiculous by, the remnants of his tennis shoes.

"What's wrong?" Aran asked, putting aside the nuts.

He came to her and held her.

"Mother," someone said at last, using his voice. He feared that she would understand or need him to say more.

She did understand, but didn't wail. She only fell back on the ledge, taking him down with her, sliding with him between the two transparent panes through which they could see, but not hear, Iri and Oji, and also Anok, and Pahquel, and the effigies of themselves clinging to each other on the ledge, moving their lips without producing sound. They slowly stood together, as though the pressure of the glass had fused them; they leaned against each other on the path to Anok's with their faces contorted, stumbling forward like Masaccio's innocents expelled, because the ground itself had suddenly become untrustworthy, and their legs were no longer their own. They jostled each other against the sides of Anok's *chajan*, not knowing how to let go, and the crowd of people milling and talking on the *kaawa* split apart to make way for them as they fell towards the ledge inside the hut. When they came up to Anok, she looked surprised to see them; indeed, her expression was odder for the absence of its usual wry grimace than for the fact that she was dead. Larry wondered when she was going to start on the *chajan*, feeling a sudden urgency lest the paints dry in their gourds. Aran leaned down and adjusted her hair, frowning as though its lack of symmetry disturbed her. Panar came and scattered the persons on the *kaawa*, shaking his head while he worked as though annoyed by their idleness. Kakap returned with the herbs and set himself to crushing them with his strange, staccato gestures, frowning tensely at his hands as though irked by their unruliness. Larry felt Anok's blank eyes on him, and knew how sensitive they had become to movement and light and feeling, and how quiet and small he needed to be to conform to the scale of her silence.

Over and over, without end, it turns out that the dead are bored by sentiment and repulsed by suffering, and are absorbed instead, with an intensity that can only be called fanatical, in the search for signs of how the loss of them has changed those who have survived them. They look for the odd curl of the lip, the slant of the shoulders, the settling of old scores, the bearing of children, the acts of cowardice or bravery, the unselfconscious gestures that they regarded once, foolishly, as their own. They study the *chajans* with an inexhaustible interest, and thus they identify the ones they must protect with their very names, with all their tools of memory and distance and fate. The funeral dance is always the same dance and the fire is always the same fire, yet no one who has died or who still lives can refrain from the impulse to comb the stream of faces or the simmering pool of ash for whatever they alone can recognize of themselves. Not even for an instant did Anok look away. That evening, when she had been fully prepared by Panar, and the others had gone home, while Larry sat beside Aran as she painted Anok's *chajan*, Anok searched their faces and their hands, as, no doubt, in her loneliness she always had, anxious to see her reflection even before they understood that she was gone.

The moon was as eager as Anok to see itself in them, and climbed up into the treetops even before the sun had finished climbing down. It hung behind their shoulders while Aran etched her mother's image into the old muscle of the house and carved her mark, a smooth, brown crescent, into its bone. It lit the path so Oji and Iri could find them, the younger leaning over the older protectively, whispering comforts and stories and songs, leading him forward by the hand. It asserted itself and refused to leave, even when the fire sent smoke up to obscure it. The moon barely feigned interest in the rambling chant that was offered by Tirinat, Asator's successor, whom it deemed unfit to lead, but it mourned Anok relentlessly, flinging its tears, out of season, onto the half-bare *chajan* of Anok's empty house.

XCVII

WHAT IS TIME to clay? That was what Martina valued most, the fact that although the wheel made a scraping noise at regular intervals like a ticking clock, and the clay rose and fell back, and despite the fact that her hands on the clay had their own pulse, distinct from the pulse of her heart, repetition had the power to vanquish time entirely, each minute like the one before it, forever. There were interruptions, of course; she could list them: There were the coffees with friends, first just her and them and then, in the course of only a very few years, her and them and their babies in their arms, their toddlers, squirming to get down, yanking on the table cloths, dropping their dingy toys and teething them, always eager to leave. There were a few half-hearted dates with friends of her friends' husbands, the most sensible of whom didn't call again. There were the two unfortunate nights when her loneliness got the better of her, followed by disastrous mornings. There were the books bought and read and stacked in piles on the nightstand and the dresser and the floor. There were the movies and the trips to the grocery, nearly every day, in fact, since she now avoided the market, and once, unexpectedly, there was a visit from her Cousin Tighe, whom she had never met, but who was ten years older, passing through on an air tour of the tropics, bringing memories of her parents and her aunts—Aunt Jantje and her mother and their three other sisters—and their old house in Amsterdam, of which she had no recollection at all. The Cousin left behind a stack of photographs, images of a serious child in the arms of strangers who resembled more closely the couple in her one photograph than they resembled her as she knew herself to be. That was another truth about time: When it did come to rest, it was as vulnerable to sliding backwards as forwards. So that was what the clay was good for: it insisted, in the face of disruptions like the appearance of Cousin Tighe, that whatever was done could be undone, could be re-rolled and re-trimmed and mashed up with a few drops of water. It told her how pliable it was possible to be, and it told her you could always start again. Yet even as she worked the wheel and felt the clay breathe in her hands, she understood that a vessel, once fired, would relentlessly endure, and that she too, had emerged from the kiln hard and empty, immune to time.

XCVIII

IN THE FOREST, sounds and the creatures that make them can be catego-rized along a continuum, reflecting their places in the stratigraphy of time. At the base of the column are the hums, the buzzes, the low rumblings of choirs whose members press together, whose voices do not rasp with age, who are ignorant of rhythm, of measures and stanzas, and capable of singing as they breathe. They crowd the air at dusk, threading their strands through the roots of the trees, weaving the warp of trunks into seamless bolts of sound. In the strata of such density, voices are laid down tight as bricks, with no space for mortar, breath, between them. These hums and buzzes quickly become monotonous, and then tormenting, and then nearly inaudible, affording, as they do, no opportunity for mourning. They play the part that in the urban world is played by the vibrations of trucks in the streets, by machines, and by certain interminable sorts of speech. One might even say that the members of those choirs are not scathed by death, since when one voice ceases, it is replaced so quickly that not even a hiccup, the skip of a needle on a phonograph record, can be heard.

At the crown of this column of sound are the cries of monkeys, and of parrots, and of persons, which come only intermittently, with stretches of longing between them. In Pahquel, persons were blessed three times over: by the *chajans'* capacities to hold them, and the songs' ability to sing of them, and by the breadth of the spans between them, yawning crucibles of silence, in which memories were created in an instant, so that people could be mourned no matter how briefly, or long, they had lived.

XCIX

IF PEOPLE FALL into two groups, the poets and the scientists, then Sara Moretti would, without hesitation, have counted herself among the latter, even as she was smart enough to know that the distinction was nonsensical. In her role as scientist, she brought order to the laboratories at Alta de Chao; standards were imposed, specimens were labeled and catalogued and stored under precise conditions of temperature and light, data was codified, procedures were spelled out clearly in manuals, and occasionally, employees were let go for their failures to follow protocol. No one expected such discipline from an Italian, let alone from a woman, and when she inherited the post from Loardo, who had previously chosen her to be his assistant from among a pool of men with titles and credentials, she was at first regarded with outright hostility, with protests, with resignations *en masse*, with projects deliberately ruined and once, with a dead rat left inside a file folder neatly labeled *"Rato"* and placed in the center of her desk. But if Sara felt distress at her reception, she didn't betray her reaction to her adversaries, or even to her few allies in the lab, but only threw herself into the task of bringing order to the world outside herself. It was a further testament to her scientist's nature that her two closest colleagues, a married couple named Sam and Bella Selman, were Jewish immigrants from Warsaw, a fact which her mother, in particular, would have found blasphemous, and to which that old lady would have responded with sputtered anti-Semitic ravings which were easily overheard by the neighbors, from whom Sara learned very early to distance herself. Fortunately, Marietto was passionate in his support of her, and a constant source of wise counsel. Even now she consulted him, asking him for guidance from beyond the grave. Even now, she allowed herself little rituals, sillinesses, she thought, and strained to see his influence in the myriad tiny clues that, unbeknownst to her, she gathered constantly and analyzed and re-analyzed and obeyed.

There are premises that scientists consider fundamental: that things change in accordance with the law of cause and effect, that the answers to important questions emerge only slowly, and that these answers must be replicated many times over in order to merit even provisional acceptance. For instance, outside Sara's awareness, she couldn't help but think of the disturbing events of the past few years—James's death and Larry's disappearance, and Jorge's resignation from SPI, and the loss of Martina and, for all intents and purposes, of her only child himself—as the somehow expectable results of specific misdeeds of hers from the past, the most significant of which had been a long-time disorder in her feelings for her late husband's closest friend. And indeed, the answer as to how to address such a painful state of affairs was long in coming, just as the specimens that were gathered by the lab—donated to the museum or acquired from other institutions, if no longer purchased from private collectors, who no doubt came upon them by questionable means—waited in queue in boxes sometimes for years before her few chemists, Sam and Bella and two other Fellows from the University of Sao Paolo, her two Indianists, her staff paleontologist and his interns from the university, and even her three lab assistants, were able, at last, to lift them from their cartons, to set them on their tables, and to enshrine them in temporary vitrines. There they would sit, like birds newly hatched and hungry, like interrogation subjects, like immigrants just arrived, trying to find their bearings in the brightly lit and bustling world of the lab. And so the question that had festered, packed away for years, took its turn on display under the twin spotlights of grief and inevitability: If only she had avoided James after Marietto's death, if only she had attended more to her son's suffering, if only she had married James in the first place and provided Jorge with a father who could actually have seen him into adulthood, at least, might her son then have proven himself equal to life, able to marry, able to pursue what was clearly his calling, able to forgive them all?

C

IT WAS OBVIOUS to everyone, and most of all Anok, that Aran had grown to fill, more and more completely, the outlines of her mother. Her tendency to hang back in conversation, to busy herself with some solitary task while the others sat drinking Mucuri juice and talking on their *kaawas*, which had always been viewed by Larry as a form of shyness with which he felt akin, turned out instead to be the first step towards that detached, ironic stance that had made Anok formidable, even to her line. During the years in which Aran had assisted her mother more invisibly, even, than the succession of Panar's young nieces had assisted with the cures, she had committed to memory not merely the songs and the patterns on the *chajans* and the formulas for pigments, but an aspect of authority that was unmistakably Anok's. Her own children were perhaps the last ones to notice the change, having always confused her hermetic restraint with its more elevated form, longing and admiring her with an intensity that persisted in proportion to the distance she maintained from them. Thus, when Oji returned, after the hand of days in which his initiation into manhood was accomplished, during the hot season after his fourth rain, he saw nothing new in his mother's chiding Iri for the way he rolled the mats, or in the way that Iri pretended unconvincingly to resist her but then rolled them again with exaggerated care as soon as she turned away. Only on the night of his first *chajan* ceremony, when he sat with the other initiates and watched as even Tirinat deferred to his mother and called her Aran Ak, did he begin to suspect that she was held in unusual esteem by others than himself.

For Larry, the realization hit with full force on the day he returned with Kakap from an overnight gathering trip, exhausted and nursing an elbow inflamed by a tocandira sting, and was startled to see Anok crouching at the *kaawa* of Ananda's house across the clearing, carving a newly-named child into the barely painted *chajan* while Ananda and his wife, Tari, looked on.

"Oh, mother," said Larry, without blinking, coming up behind her. "That painting at the ankles is too hard on your back. Leave it for Aran."

Perhaps the moment was as terrifying for Aran as for Larry as she turned slowly to face him. Perhaps she looked into his eyes and knew that he could see that she was beyond the time of children, with her hair already half-white. Perhaps she, like Larry, shuddered inwardly at the vision of him holding her as she died, in the same arms that had held her as a child. Or perhaps she was proud of the mistake, understanding as she did that time was of no interest to the ancestors who move the sun and bring the rain and settle disputes between persons and teach the jacu to hunt. Tari giggled nervously, as though still unsure if Larry had made an error or a joke. Aran showed nothing in her face to suggest she thought the one over the other, though she frowned at the crimson liquid in the bowl in her hand, and pulled a large beetle from it with a stick.

As Aran and Larry walked home, he would have apologized for his mistake if he thought he could have done so without causing an even greater offense. He might have told her that he needed to be gone again because Kakap had walked so slowly that they hadn't found the *Xira*, or the *Tapiri*, or the *Laar*, but the words formed a dam in his throat, over which no stream could pass. To speak of Kakap's diminishment was unavoidably to speak of hers; to comfort himself with the recognition of her intensifying power was to acknowledge that such power was dependent on the proximity of the ancestors, who never loosen their grip on things they lend. The only alternative to talk was silence—of the forest's kind, built up of a thatch of voids, each filled to overflowing with movement and noise—and the friction of her shoulder against his, and her smell, mingled now as it often was with the smell of the paints that sloshed in the gourds at her sides. Slowly, as they neared their hut, the sounds of Pahquel at evening rose to meet them; the clattering of stones as Piri fixed the pancakes and the greens, the usual argument between Mabara and Katura, the indignant fussing of the parrot on Ciri's *kaawa* as it burrowed its chin into its feathers. The house itself was empty, but held echoes of the shouting of the children in the clearing, and also of Oji's singing as he approached the *kaawa* and said goodbye, with much laughter and teasing, to his friends.

Larry left to retrieve Iri from the *kari* field. When he came in again, he sat down next to Aran on the sleeping ledge and together they watched their children getting ready for bed, unrolling their mats, hanging up their ankle straps, singing, in registers an octave apart, asking the ancestors for guidance. Although he was well into his sixth rain, Iri was still afraid to urinate alone after dark, and whined until Oji took him out, as he did every evening, to the edge of the trees beyond the seep of the firelight. Often at night, Iri would try to crawl between Larry and Aran when they slept together on the ledge, or he would push himself onto Larry's mat on the floor, wedging himself between Larry and the side of the wooden platform, for which Oji would tease him the next day, and call him *pitiX*, a baby too small for a name. That night, there was the usual argument over where Iri's mat would be; Oji pulled it to the center of the room as he always did, and Iri pulled it back to within a hand's width of Larry's, and sat on it quickly, before Oji could pull it out again. Oji always unrolled his own mat on the far side of the room, and made a show of lying down, as though to inspire his older brother by virtue of his mocking example, or as though to impress Aran.

The effort was, as they all understood, doomed to failure on both counts; on the one hand, Oji's show of independence succeeded only in intensifying Iri's fears, while on the other, it only drew attention to the fact that he was still coming home alone at night, without a woman. Larry might easily have chastised Iri for his timidity, just as Aran might have teased Oji as the other mothers did, who called their sons *pitiX*, or sometimes weak-penised, and even turned them out of the house until the morning. But the tug-of-war in front of them, like the ones that took place on the clearing every feast day between the strongest men, was not to be dismissed with irritation, or resolved through any powers of the living, even Aran's, for the combatants were pulling on the pure strength of their fear, and the rope that was stretched taut between them was the tautness of time itself. In the same way, Larry could feel the rope between himself and Aran growing longer and tighter and thinner with every quarter-moon, as each attempt to pull the other closer only drew out the span of years between them, and forced a wedge between their fates. They leaned into each other's shoulders; they stretched out together on the ledge, and, like their breaths, which met in the gap between them, pushed themselves against each other with all the force they had, until their pulses knotted, though the rope quivered and strained.

CI

JOAQUIM ROCHA WOULD have been outraged at anyone who dared to suggest that there was any relationship whatsoever between the act of sending off Daniel, his youngest, of putting him on a plane for Boston, *os Estados Unidos*, of all places, and the growing anxiety he felt about what he had come slowly, over years, to recognize as his abandonment of Larry. Yet the sense of vulnerability of the lone traveler haunted him as he watched, from his vantage point across the concourse, as an intense young stranger paced the length of gate 9, smoking and scowling at the ground. Cora was preoccupied, as she always was, with small things: whether the part in Daniel's hair was straight, whether he had remembered to bring the letters from the Admissions Office, whether he had remembered to call his grandmother before he left. She fretted that he wouldn't write, that he wouldn't eat well, that he would fall for some crass, high-living American girl. She smoothed and ruffled and smoothed again the hair on Daniel's forehead while Joaquim followed, with growing interest, the senseless, determined stride of the lonely young man across the corridor.

Several times he caught the young man's gaze, although he was unable to meet the eyes of his son, who stood directly beside him and loosely rested his hand on his father's arm. Of his five children, only Daniel, their surprise, had remained as close to him in deed as in feeling; the others had reciprocated their father's constant absences by likewise being always elsewhere, at the homes of their friends, or at the movies, or more recently, with their own families in distant cities, their awe of their father amplified by the breadth of the emptiness between them. Only Daniel sat at his father's feet, engrossed in his stories, spent long hours examining his arti-facts while his father worked, and cried for hours, days, Cora told him with an accusatory inflection, when he left again for the field. But even Daniel had always evaded his father's invitations to go with him, to experience the life of the *sertanista* first-hand. The refusal was devastating, though Joaquim would have never admitted it. It had left a slight tarnish on their bond, which had largely been buffed away through years of contact.

A woman's voice came over the loudspeaker announcing flight 154 to Rio and a crowd formed at the door to the tarmac—men in suits and women in heels and white gloves and children in uncomfortable traveling clothes, shrieking with fear and excitement. Then the same group re-formed beside the plane, each one in that clump holding a hat in place against the fierce gale from the engines. Father and son stood together, hatless, both resting their hands on the oversized valise between them. Together they pushed it forward toward the baggage men who were throwing suitcases back and forth in a jagged trajectory into the hold of the plane.

"I'm going to miss you, father," Daniel shouted, his hair now complete-ly disheveled. He knew full well his father's investment in claiming never to miss anyone, and also that his father wouldn't answer him for fear of betraying a hint of tremor in his voice. The one thing this family knew well was how each of its members said goodbye. Thus he could picture, without having to look up, his mother's expression as she stood inside the terminal with her face nearly pressed to the window: equal parts pride and disapproval, equal parts profound grief and irritation at the failure of her husband to keep her son's hair in place.

"Harvard's supposed to be an okay school," said Daniel, with a forced laugh.

"Is it?" said his father into the wind. This was a joke between them, between the son, with his preparatory school education, and the father who, despite all his reading, his erudition, his intense collaborations with professors from all over the world, had never managed to graduate from high school.

"Don't let mother get too lonely," said Daniel, regretting the comment as soon as he made it.

"She'll tire of me soon enough," shouted Joaquim above the engines. "In another month or two, she'll think I'm around way too much. Remember, she's not used to me!" Daniel had heard his father's threats to give up "the work" forever, but lately they had come with a different inflection, a discouragement he hadn't heard before. He found himself constantly brushing off the thought that his own growing up, his plans to leave for college and his actual leaving, were somehow to blame for his father's corresponding loss of vitality and once-fanatical sense of mission.

"I have about one more run left in me," said the father. "A short one." "But you've got a lot of running ahead of you. I hope you're ready for it."

"I am ready, father," shouted Daniel into the din, extending his hand as, behind him, people began jostling up the metal stairs that led to the door of the plane.

The father embraced his son. "I *will* miss you," he said into Daniel's ear, his voice cracking. He turned away quickly and walked towards the gate, turning his back as Daniel mounted the stairs. Always having been the one to leave, it was the unfamiliarity of the moment, he wanted to believe, that was unbearable. Cora came towards him and they embraced while people milled around them. "Rio, New York, Boston by train, and then a taxi," Joaquim thought for a minute, tracing Daniel's itinerary. "Rio, New York, and Boston." For a fleeting second, he entertained the fantasy that Larry had returned to Harvard after all, and that the two were destined to meet there. He remembered with a sudden sting that he had never told his own father even that he was leaving. He had only left a stack of bills wrapped in paper in his father's bedroll. It's true that he had sent him payments every month via Abarta, twice as much as he was used to, with just himself to feed, and that he trusted Abarta to see that the money made it to his father's hand. But then there was Abarta's note returning the last of the payments. Over Cora's shoulder, Joaquim could see that the young man had stopped pacing, and was rifling in his pocket, searching the depths of his trousers in a muted panic for his lost cigarettes.

CII

WHEN WORD PASSED through Pahquel like a ripple on a river that Tirinat had been mauled by a boar while out hunting with his brothers, the news was met not so much with shock as with a sort of sad relief, as though it offered proof of the collective suspicion that preceded his reign that he was fragile, somehow too weak to sing or lead. Even in the first nights after his death, few of the moans from the huts outlasted the dawn, and his fire seemed to burn down quickly, to collapse into itself, snuffed out by its own ash. The liminal time of interregnum passed without the force of frenzy, while the intensity of the debate over who would succeed him, over which feathers should be granted a place atop Tirinat's *chajan*, seemed to grow in inverse proportion to the intensity of mourning. By the time the decision was to be made, arguments had broken out, fissures that ran between houses and even villages like cracks that split the dirt in a dry time, and the number of feathers had grown to seven. They covered the top of the doorway and seemed to pin each other there, suspended in a tension as brittle as *chajan* lacquer.

As the sun reached its high point, people started to show their restlessness openly; men paced back and forth in front of the *kaawa*, children cried, men and women squabbled over small things, bereft of guidance. Crowds gathered around the ones whose feathers were in contention, whispering advice, singing songs of their line, passing bowls of juice and crumbled fish between them. Larry stood off to the side alone, eyeing the clumps of people, walking back and forth with the other solitaries. As the afternoon wore on, the groups seemed to draw together as people clung even more tightly to their lines. He weighed what might be gained or lost by going to stand with Dabimi's, among those with whom he still technically belonged. At last, he concluded he would gain little in exchange for an act that could be seen as adding weight to Dabimi's claim. Instead, he stepped to the perimeter of Kakap's circle and stood slightly behind him, until Kakap swiveled towards him as though he were a door and beckoned him to enter.

"*Kawano ti ni taparo parak,*" the oldest of Kakap's three sons whispered to him, "A bird-filled sky," and they laughed together at the irony of the phrase.

No one remembered such a circumstance, in which the ancestors expressed only hesitation, and the feathers only twitched, as though a finger had touched them and withdrawn. Kakap didn't remember, and shook his head at all his children, and laced and unlaced his fingers, and closed his eyes as though to concentrate more closely on the ancient, inaudible songs. Larry knew those gestures well—they were all Kakap had ever shown of fear—and sensed the dread and the familiarity at once, the quiver in Kakap's hands and the reference, offhanded and unselfconscious, that he made to all his sons. Larry pushed his shoulder against the shoulder of Pitar, Kakap's middle son, and laughed despite himself, the anxious, collective laugh in which he was relieved to have a rightful stake.

As the sun grasped the branches and pulled itself behind them, the clumps began to disperse again, and the circles of bodies grew porous. Kakap left the group to speak to Panar Ak, to ParanX, and to Kinara, Asator's son, whose feather was once that morning lifted up and then set back down again on the top of the *chajan* with the others. He went to Piri, and to Taran, and to Dabimi, and while he stood in Dabimi's circle, Larry came over and joined him, grateful for the chance to fulfill his obligation under the safety of Kakap's wing.

"You've waited once before," Kakap said to Dabimi, in a voice that was pure of motive, despite Larry's presence behind him.

"That time the wait wasn't so long," said Dabimi, with a reluctant smile that betrayed his anxiety. He nodded to Larry without looking at him.

"There weren't so many choices then," said Kakap in a benevolent tone, shaking his head and holding Dabimi briefly by the arm.

Larry and Kakap sampled the *titini* Dabimi's *kaag* had made, and asked after her bad knee, which Panar was treating with a wrap of *rajiru* leaves. Kakap joked with Dabimi's daughter and son, and teased his son's two daughters about the interest they had aroused in certain recently initiated men from the far village, and then they moved on, stopping at several other circles before returning to their own.

Kakap's youngest daughter had joined her father's group while they were gone, and as they came up, she was mocking the anxiety of the others to distract herself from her own. She reviewed out loud the nervous gestures of the owners of the feathers, and her brothers laughed in whispers at Xosa's twitch and Dabimi's bobbing head. No one spoke of their real concerns, questions about who had shirked the tending of the fires, whose daughter had recently begun to menstruate, who had given too much or too little when dividing up the hunt, who had not sung well as he carried water from the river. No one spoke of the boar that had killed Tirinat, whose bones now rested with his ash and bone, but whose essence might still be raging among those the fire had already claimed, disrupting their ability to choose.

As if to give legitimacy to the need for such restraint, Kakap smiled his kindly, noncommittal smile as he surveyed the clearing, looking down on the swirls of activity and the glimpses of emptiness where the scrub showed through. He raised his hand to his eyes to blot out the one last, sharp ray that pierced the trees behind the clearing, and then let it drop to his side. As though in obeisance to his gesture, the light dropped too, and dusk swelled across the clearing. Torches were brought, and songs were sung, and the murky uncertainty was like a thick river that carried them out of the world.

"Oh, Taraptar, where are you now? Oh, Asator, is your left arm strong from throwing the heaviest spear? Did you show yourself in the current? Did the last rain fill your troughs?"

The number of things that Larry did not know about Pahquel was too great even to imagine; essential things, like the need to protect unnamed babies from the shadow of the *kipta* tree, like the significance of the lines that were painted on his legs before they danced, like the reason why a child of a mother whose name was comprised of two syllables would be given a name of two syllables as well; like the terrible ordeal that faced the ones who, long ago, after slaughtering their enemies, refused to eat them and thus forced the ancestors to strip them of their right to kill. He did not know that the world, contained within a perimeter of felled trees that could take a man four hands of days to walk, was taken from monkeys many *chajans* ago, after killing was forbidden, and given to persons to tend. He knew nothing of the Intrusion, and of its terrible aftermath, nor did he understand the group's cultivation of the capacity to forget it. And he knew even fewer of the small things, with which any child would be familiar; how to bow his head before the fire, and how to tell when a person was preparing to receive a second *kaag*, and how to weave his own wristbands, or arm bands, or ankle bands, or those of his sons. In short, he was like an animal, a dog who sat at his master's feet and drew in the world in quick, nervous whiffs, exquisitely alert to a few irrelevant scents. He knew as little as the dog of Pahquel, and yet he understood, with an intensity equal to that of anyone around him, what it was like to be untethered and forgotten and adrift. Kakap knew that he understood this, and thus kept him close by his side, forming an epaulet with the fingers of his left hand around his narrow shoulder, clutching his other arm with the bones of his right, submerging him whole in the scents of his body and breath. Just as water muffles sound, so Kakap washed them both in the humid grasp of his aura, and buffered them from the noises that moved toward them across the clearing, distorted and slowed them to a low hum, laughter and footsteps and whispers and finally, just before dawn, the shout that burst out like a parrot's scream to announce Dabimi's success.

CIII

THERE WERE THINGS about which Martina spent a great deal of time thinking and things about which, unknowingly, she refused to think. Curiosity was an inconstant friend, she knew, that could turn on someone faster than a snake in Eden, faster than a person could. When she bent over the wheel, the questions gathered around her head like insects, or auras, or angels, but she kept them at a distance mostly by singing. Usually she just hummed to herself, so quietly that the sound was lost to anyone other than her, covered over as it was by the rhythmic scraping of the wheel. But lately, she had come to rely on the more potent musical *mosquitiero* of the radio, which was turned up to full volume to be heard over the sound of steel against steel. For this reason, she didn't look up when Joaquim stepped in and approached her, sliding himself onto the bench beside the wheel. He said a few things that were lost over the swell of the scraping and the horns. Finally, he reached over and turned off the radio. She startled, gashing the lip of the bowl with her thumbnail.

"Damn it!" She pulled the vessel from the wheel and smashed it into a ball.

"Sorry," said Joaquim. "I was trying to be unobtrusive."

"If you're looking for Jorge, he's not here," she said absurdly, knowing full well that Joaquim knew about their estrangement.

"My point exactly!" said Joaquim, standing up and brushing the clay dust from his pant legs.

"What's your point?"

"It's that Jorge isn't here, where he should be, begging on his knees for . . ."

"He doesn't have any reason to beg, and I don't have any reason to forgive him," said Martina, cutting him off. "It's not an issue of forgiveness."

"That wasn't what I was going to say," said Joaquim, giving up on the pants. "I meant, begging you to come with him, because he's going to be away for a while."

There was that curiosity, swelling in Martina like a bruise. She fought it down. "Make sure to wish him *Bon Voyage* for me."

"I don't think he'll be able to do it without you," said Joaquim. "We need you to keep him going, because we need him. It's as simple as that."

"So you're using me to further some half-assed project of your own, with no regard for me or for him?"

"Exactly," said Joaquim, laughing. "No regard whatsoever."

Martina stared at him for a minute and then reached for a ball of clay, pushing hard with her foot to start the wheel. Joaquim stood beside her and watched the ball turn hollow as it grew. As she cut it off with a wire and transferred it to a slab, he stepped in closer as though to admire the finished product.

"The fact is," he started up, pointing to the open bowl as if to illustrate his words, "it's all personal. We're all in it for our own reasons, which you know more than anyone. Nothing has changed between you and Jorge, except for this wall of pride he's put up temporarily while he tries to figure out if he's worth anything, to you or anyone else. In the meanwhile, you can go on pretending it's all about him and no one's thinking of you at all, if that's what you want, but you're lying to yourself. You can't stand to think that you need him as much as he needs you, because it's the same issue of pride for you too, though you won't admit it. It's a great act, this pretending!"

Joaquim looked up and noticed a reddish tone deepen around her eyes, then fade. That was enough for him.

"So you've talked to Jorge about this?"

"No, he doesn't even know I'm here. This one is mine."

"So what's personal in it for you?" said Martina, defensiveness in her tone.

Joaquim was silent for a minute. "I suppose," he said, with the softest waver in his voice, "it's the same for all of us. Something to do with regret."

CIV

ONE MISTAKE MADE by almost everyone is to imagine time as something universal, known by all, and by each similarly. Few picture time as a man with a million masks, each of them threatening, yes, but each in a different way, and sometimes invisibly. If time seduces one with limitless promise, it shows another its fierceness; for one, it sweeps by in a seamless stream, and for another, it inches forward in an endless series of increasingly violent jerks. Silvio's time combined aspects of each of these; it flowed by without notice, immersing him in its amusements, fine wines and thick cigars and full-bodied women, and then it intensified into flashes of desperate impulse. "Get me commercial, tomorrow, to Santarem," he barked at Maria through the crack in his office door, just as she was adjusting her hat in the mirror, already in her coat and gloves.

CV

DABIMI WAS A strong ruler, who loved to lead nearly as much as he loved the sense of power leadership afforded. Only the ancestors might have thwarted him, but they remained strangely silent while he attributed to them mandates that did not, at least in the minds of the elders, bear their stamp. His decrees became increasingly specific, and over time, it appeared that they were more and more aimed at restricting the liberties of particular persons: There were penalties for families with five or more children, penalties for those who rebuffed the overtures of elders in line for *jibimis*, and penalties for the birth of additional children to those whose first or second had been held back or were otherwise of suspicious lineage. Also, he frequently disappeared, to prepare the way for successful hunts, he said, and no one doubted his expertise where such questions were concerned. Often, he was gone for days at a time, and in his absence, persons became increasingly bold, unafraid to mock him and disobey, in ways they wouldn't have dreamed of during Asator's reign, likewise without comment from the ancestors. Such was the limit of Dabimi's strength. They gave Kakap not a lesser but a greater portion for his five children, and no one said a word when Aran chiseled the bright commemorations of additional *kaags* into the *chajans* of Kiri and Porpora. Only the mandate to regulate the number of children of persons giving birth to *rajora* was followed to the letter, at least in the household of Aran, whose bleed had faded to an intermittent trickle, a thinning stream in a dry time.

CVI

"GOT SOMETHING THERE?" Silvio threw out his hand as though to yank away the letter, but Sara turned quickly, so all he grabbed was air. They were sitting at a table at the *Boutu Vermelho* instead of at Sara's dinner table because, despite her protests, despite the fact that he had just arrived, Silvio was too restless to take a meal at her home. He had been flipping loudly through the pages in a clipboard, jabbing at them with the tiny, chiseling motions of his pencil point, snapping them forward and then batting them down into place again.

"He was rock steady! I counted on him! Look at these runs! Look at these runs!" He slapped the page to make his point. "A person doesn't just snap, just like that!" Silvio knew full well that agents often snapped like that; that such breaks constituted the most common threats to the safety of his men, and were far more menacing than the formidable and constant dangers they faced in the field. Agents made sudden, glaringly bad calls, were beset by odd infirmities, became possessed, developed strange phobias, nursed malarial delusions, evaporated without a trace; he also knew that the seamless ones were the ones most likely to crack. Even Victor the Fearless, who, as of a month ago, refused to leave his apartment or answer his phone and sat in the dark with the shades drawn, neck-deep in sweat and isolation; even the invincible Ricardo, dead by his own hand. Even, at one point not so long ago, before he assumed his current position, himself.

Sara stared down at the letter in her hands, paying him no attention. She wasn't reading, but it was impossible, nevertheless, for her to raise her eyes; for a moment, even she was confused as to whether her absorption was due to the letter's intrinsic interest, the sense it gave of arriving from a past time (its date confirming as much), or to her desperation to find some reassurance regarding her son, even in distraction, and regardless of the source.

"Do you know an Eduardo Catalpa?" she asked finally, knowing full well that she would never succeed in keeping a secret from Silvio. The only choice she had was in how and when to reveal it.

"Catalpa? The worm at the end of Joaquim's line? That one?"

"I don't know," said Sara. "I mean the one from Paruqu."

"What of him?" said Silvio, craning now to see the piece of paper Sara still held out beyond his reach, still unaware that it was the letter itself that held her.

"I think this might interest you," she said, holding it up now between them, so that Silvio couldn't see her face. He could, however, see her hands shake, and hear her voice waver had he been attentive to detail.

"Dear Sara Moretti," the letter began. "Let me introduce myself to you. I am Sr. Eduardo Catalpa, Prefect of Paruqu Region, Dist. 1452, of the Federal Bureau of the Interior. I have been privileged to number among my dearest and most respected friends one Mr. James Ardmore of the United States of America, as well as your late husband, Sr. Mario Moretti of Santarem. I am aware of your husband's fate, and I send you my belated condolences, and now condolences are in order once again, to us both."

Silvio snorted, as though the bizarrely delayed nature of the Prefect's message regarding Marietto confirmed his estimation of the bureaucrat's ineffectuality. Silvio was always particularly condemning of bureaucrats, in an effort to reassure himself that he had not become one.

"I remember with indubitable clarity," Sara went on, "the details of your husband's demise at the hands of the Lamurii, who, as you may or may not know, are located a mere one hundred kilometers to the northeast of me, on an inlet of the Jamanxim. His death was like a knife in my own heart, which was recently ripped open once more as I learned of the death of our mutual dear friend. I had always been given to understand from our dear, deceased Mr. James Ardmore that the Lamurii may have unfairly inflicted their justified wrath on your late husband, who no doubt was a dedicated servant of all Brazilians, as am I myself."

"I need to take a leak," said Silvio, getting up and stretching his legs. "I'll be back," he said, heading into the restaurant. Sara kept on reading, either because she didn't notice he was gone or to express in her typically indirect way her anger at him and all the others for leaving.

"I have recently come across some information, however, from a secret but absolutely reliable source, that may shed new light upon the situation that preceded your husband's demise, about which I felt you should, by rights, be informed. I have come to suspect that the natives of the Lamurii region may have been incited by other elements with a vested interest in ridding the area of SPI agents and other government servants whose presence might have led to the exposure of unauthorized activities unfolding in that same or adjacent areas. If this indeed proves to be the case, then these elements are not only guilty of violating the laws regarding the disposition of Indian Lands, as these have been laid out by the Ministry of the Interior, but in fact, of your late husband's murder!"

Silvio came up and sat down again, picking up his clipboard, half listening as Sara continued.

"While not in a position to follow up on these allegations myself at this time, as I am in the midst of moving our offices from Regional to Central headquarters and will be gone within the month, I wanted to pass along the name of at least one of the individuals who may have been decisively involved in the tragic events that claimed the life of your dear, late husband. This man's name is Kamar Sodeis, and I have reason to believe that he has recently taken up residence in the area once again. I pass along this information under the greatest strictures of confidentiality, and at great potential risk to myself. I know from personal experience that this man is armed and dangerous. I ask that you destroy this letter, and remove my humble name from your mind, retaining only that of the potential instigator, should you decide to pursue the matter further. In the meanwhile, I remain your servant, Sr. Eduardo Catalpa, Prefect, Paruqu Region, Dist. 1452."

"What the hell?" said Silvio, finally attentive, snatching the letter from Sara's hands, looking it up and down. "Let's go!" he said, jumping up and pushing in his chair with his foot.

"Where are we going?" asked Sara in a voice tinged, uncharacteristical-ly, with panic. She grabbed at the letter, finally snatching it back.

"To Jorge's. Kill two birds," said Silvio, pulling Sara along by linking his arm in hers.

CVII

WHEN, AT HALF past six, Silvio and Sara approached Jorge's apartment down the long hall, they were surprised to hear voices coming from inside. His mother was instantly relieved, her fears of her son's disappearance, his isolation, disconfirmed fleetingly, in a flash, but the discovery seemed to make Silvio madder. He rapped hard on Jorge's door, and when the voices ceased, still without offering an answer, he pounded louder, with both fists at once. Finally, they heard footsteps approaching, and the door swung open to reveal Joaquim.

"You rat!" shouted Silvio, pounding now on Joaquim's chest as he had on the door a moment before. "You bastard! What are you doing here? You're always second-guessing me! Get out of here! Let me handle this! Go! Get out!"

Sara moved backward into a corner of Jorge's sitting room, directly opposite her son. Between them, the spectacle alternately blocked their views of each other and revealed bits of them, framed by a crook of an elbow or a knee. Punch swung at Judy, and then Judy at Punch, and the crowd in the square roared its approval. The expressions of the performers were outsized, exaggerated and therefore comical, and that reckless, slapstick aspect made their silence all the more imposing as they suddenly fell side by side into the center of the sofa. Sara and Jorge approached from the wings, taking their places at the arms.

Joaquim rubbed his chest and then his jaw, where a welt was rising, while Silvio held a hand over his temple. Jorge whimpered quietly, still holding in his hand a book that he was making a show of trying, absurdly, to read.

"Nice to know you can still swing a punch," said Silvio.

Joaquim tested the bones and sinews in his hand.

"Why are you here?" asked Jorge as Sara reached across the two in the middle for his arm. A silence hovered, fixing them forever, and then, without warning, Silvio and Joaquim erupted at once, laughing until they cried, doubled over laughing, laughing as desperately as the crowd laughed in the square, mesmerized by the puppet antics of the loud, small creatures who threw themselves into the same intimate fight again and again, and whose embrace was equal parts violence and love. Sara got up and went into the kitchen, returning with two cold bottles of beer, which she pressed against the wounds of the combatants.

Jorge buried his head in his book, allowing his tears to fall on the pages. "You need to leave. You're not my boss any more," he said in a choked voice. "I know I should have written a formal letter, but you already know I'm done with SPI."

"Not yet," said Joaquim and Silvio in unison. They paused to look at each other for a minute and then added, "Listen to me." They started again, paused, started, paused. Finally, Joaquim gestured with his free hand toward Silvio, who in turn gestured toward Sara. "Read it," he said.

Sara pulled the letter from her pocket and read as her son wept, keeping his eyes in his book. Joaquim leaned forward with his hand cupped around his ear straining to hear.

"We need you," Silvio said to Jorge when Sara was done. "We need to get ourselves back to Lamurii, and then on from there, and we need to go together."

"What do you mean *back* to Lamurii?" Silvio said, jumping to his feet. "Since when have you been to Lamurii?"

"Just stay right there," said Joaquim, slowly rising, putting his hand on his shoulder. "I don't think I could survive another round."

"Go fight this one out on the street," said Sara, who had slid behind them when they stood up, pulling herself up next to Jorge on the couch.

Joaquim looked down at them for a minute and then up at Silvio. "And then there's Larry," he said, heading towards the door.

CVIII

THERE ARE AS many types of trees in the forest as there are types of people: There are the ones who thrive wherever they are planted and the ones who are thrown out of sorts by any inclement condition or event. There are the ones who draw the interest of the birds or insects and the ones who recede. There are the ones who pulse with sweet sap and the ones who harbor only bitterness; the ones who feed only their favorites and the expansive ones who shelter all comers with equal generosity; the ones who provide for others and the dependent ones, who cannot live except off the bounty of their hosts. There are the ones who germinate and thrive and fall within the span of a hand of rains and the ones who live forever. There are the soft ones, who bear on their flesh the scars of all the minute details of their histories, and the hard ones, who are impacted by only the most dire or persistent of circumstances. And of the hard ones, there are those who, once marked, shatter into splinters and the others, the *chajans*, rare though they might be, who can remember and yet still remain whole.

CIX

"ENOUGH!" SAID SILVIO, turning and heading back down *Av. Altamira*. Joaquim reached out a hand to pull him back, as he had at five-minute intervals all evening long. It was like walking an ill-trained dog, with the pain it gave in the shoulder.

"Eight o'clock."

"No, now. I've had enough."

"They need time. Sara needs time with him."

"I don't need Sara to talk to him. He answers to me," said Silvio, stabbing the air with his index finger.

"Not any more."

"Oh? He hasn't resigned. I don't have a letter from him."

"You don't have mine either," said Joaquim, reaching for his arm. "On paper, you're still answering to me!" Silvio shook him off, gaining half a block on him, interspersing running steps between the steps of his surprisingly long stride. By the time Joaquim caught up, they were nearly at Jorge's.

"There's something you don't know," Joaquim called after him, slowing his pace.

As soon as Silvio realized that Joaquim was no longer pursuing him, he turned around to face him. The two of them stood for half a minute, eyeing each other at twenty paces, hands hanging shoot-out style at their sides. Slowly, Silvio took one step forward, and another. Joaquim looked down, but waited.

Silvio drew near, raising his hands and spreading them out empty, as though to ask a question, or to show he was unarmed.

"Sit down," said Joaquim, gesturing toward the curb.

Silvio hesitated and sat. When someone else was talking, he preferred to feign disinterest, all the more so when the conversation was important to him, but with Joaquim, he couldn't. He took this as a mark of shame, and hung his head while he listened to the man whose yellowed picture, torn from a newspaper, had sat in a frame beside his bedside table for twenty years.

"I think I know why James died," Joaquim began.

Silvio turned away.

"And I think I know his secret."

"You're just figuring that out now?" If Silvio couldn't pretend to ignore Joaquim, at least he could act like he had the jump on him.

"Okay. You tell me."

"You mean his sexual problem?"

"No, that's not the one I meant," said Joaquim. Silvio refused to unclench.

"Then just tell me!" said Silvio.

"I'm talking his genetics problem."

"You're talking up my ass," said Silvio.

"Or maybe I'm talking about a different person. The one I'm referring to is the one Joao Oliveira knew as Peter Harding, his mysterious second author. The one who gave him the data to write all those papers on the evolutionary effects of environmental toxins." Joaquim waited for a glimmer of a reaction, at least to the sound of his old mentor's name, but Silvio was determined not to gratify.

"Something happened to that tribe of his, and he was desperate to find out what, and when, and who, and the sad part is that he never even thought about himself at all, but I think whatever it was killed him too."

"If it did, there's no way to trace it now," said Silvio, hanging his head again and addressing the gravel at the curb. "I'm not a scientist any more, never was, and I'm not God either. I haven't read any medicine in twenty years, and we're already in the midst of one witch hunt, and I don't have a single medical man on my staff at this point," Silvio said, finding his old aggression and looking straight at Joaquim as though revived by the possibility of punching him again. "Hell if I'm going to let you pull me into this one."

"And that's where Larry is now," said Joaquim.

"You have no idea where he is," said Silvio. "You don't know if he's alive, which he most likely isn't. You just let him walk."

"He's there."

Silvio sat in silence, regarding the gravel again. "Okay, so say he's there," he said at last, looking up. "So we've got to go and get the kid before whatever it is kills him too."

"And hope he's still a kid when we find him."

"Right!" said Silvio, rolling his eyes.

"I'm serious," said Joaquim, above the chimes from the church. "But enough. It's eight now. So go."

By the time Joaquim stood and stretched his knees, Silvio had cleared the door of Jorge's building, having made no effort to prevent it from slamming behind him.

CX

AS JOAQUIM REACHED the entrance to Jorge's apartment, Sara came up beside him with a shopping bag in each hand.

"You didn't talk to him?" said Joaquim as they climbed the stairs.

"I did," said Sara. "But we also need to eat."

They opened the door to find Silvio in the living room alone, pacing between the bookshelf in the corner and the divan.

Each of them had made up their mind in an instant, without consulting the others, each in regard to a different question, so that the prospect of collating their individual pieces of four potentially unrelated puzzles was colored by their incommensurate anxieties. The fact that Joaquim and Sara had encountered Mrs. Tomoio on the stairs as they approached (who, like those around her had no interest whatever in the Indian Question, in the obligations of state, or in Comte's vision of a new social order, and only a passing and superficial regard for the love life of her one-time neighbor, or for the outdated story of a murder not even fit for the tabloids, though she did bring said former neighbor a vat of her stew on a semi-regular basis) did nothing to distract them from the tensions that each of them carried. As the two approached, they could smell the aroma of the stew emanating from Jorge's apartment, and indeed, from Mrs. Tomoio herself as she greeted Sarah and then moved on.

Once inside, they barely acknowledged each other. Finally, Jorge emerged from the bedroom and Sara pushed him toward the kitchen. He disappeared and returned with four open bottles of cold beer, two in each hand, which he passed to the others silently, without looking at any of them. Sara pulled cold cuts from one of the bags and set them on the table, still wrapped.

"This meeting is now called to order," said Silvio loudly, banging down his beer, as though to establish through priority that it was he who had called it, and had the upper hand. The beer sloshed out of the bottle and drenched his hand, which he wiped on the tail of his shirt. The others looked back at him in silence. "I'll tell you that Valerio and Lino will be here by tomorrow. They're going with you, and I'm going home."

"You're going *now*?" Sara addressed at Silvio with a look of confusion, which he brushed off.

"Things have come up. You don't know the eighth of it. But let's just think about now."

"Valerio sounds good to me," said Joaquim, looking up, straight at Silvio. "He's a mediocre pilot, but a good *sertanista*. Lino, we're going to have to leave behind."

"That's not your decision to make," Silvio said firmly, banging his beer on the table again for emphasis, after covering the top of the bottle with his thumb.

"My guess is that it's been ten years since you've been in the field," said Joaquim quietly. "It takes working with someone to know who they are."

"And you think you know everyone and everything? You've been out there so long that you don't have any idea what's been going on in the world. In *your* world!" Silvio made a move to get up and pace, but thought better of it and sat back down. "Besides, aren't you done with SPI?"

"Not even on paper," said Joaquim, laughing at himself. "Or at any rate, I can't seem to stay that way. This is my mistake, and I need to do what I can to undo it. But that's a different issue."

"I'm just going in to try to find Larry," said Jorge, cutting in. "That's all. You can come if you want to,"—here he addressed Joaquim—"but I'm leaving tomorrow morning, and I'll be back by next week." What he didn't say was that the bag with the Pahqua coordinates was still missing, and that thinking back he hadn't seen it at least since they'd left Paruqu.

"Jorge, you're not prepared," said Joaquim, without a trace of irony. "I've been going through James's papers, and I think I've figured out what's going on. I've spoken with Oliviero, and with Marcelino Benara at the University. There's a lot more we need to do." He stopped to appraise Jorge, who was looking at his shoes. "We're in sight of figuring out why your father died, and James too. Two different reasons, but probably connected in the end."

"I don't need your academic experts to anoint me," Jorge shot back, as though he was anticipating a different kind of attack, and it was too late to change course.

"You know it wasn't the Lamurii that killed your father. You're clear on that, right? Do you know how many outsiders were murdered by Indians in the last thirty years? Probably less than ten. And do you know how many Indians have been killed by outsiders?"

"As of last count, by which I mean yesterday," Silvio interrupted him, "about sixty more than the day before."

Joaquim turned to look at him.

"You have no idea what's been going on out there," said Silvio. "You just don't know."

Joaquim started to respond to Silvio, but then thought better of it and turned instead to study Jorge's face, which even in profile, betrayed his thoughts. "You don't need to know what happened to your father. But I do, and so does he," he said, with a nod toward Silvio.

"Know what?" said Jorge.

"And do you think Interior's going to jump in and apprehend him if we don't?" Silvio blurted out in Jorge's direction before Joaquim had finished. "Do you think he's going to do anything besides stir up trouble if we leave him out there? We're not talking retribution here; we're talking prevention, basic responsibility. We're hanging by a thread. He's going to make it look a whole lot worse for us!"

"But what authority does SPI have to arrest someone?" Sara interjected. "It's not law enforcement. It gets back to the mission of SPI."

"The mission of SPI is obvious, and it's been obvious all along, if anyone cared to see it," Jorge interjected. "The mission of SPI is to move tribes around to make it easy for Brazilians to take their lumber or their metals or their land without being killed. It's to make deals that protect the financial interests of Brazilians by bilking Indians in a way that makes us look good. It has no power other than the power of the outlaw, and if you want to fight fire with fire, go ahead. All I'm going to do is get Larry out of there."

A silence fell over the room, which was broken by Silvio's slow clapping. "I think finally somebody's getting it right," he said in a raspy voice, elated and angry and defeated at once.

Joaquim allowed the silence to set for a time before starting in. "SPI is about justice. You can't forget that. That's what it was about all along, and that's what it continues to be about, and we can't let the Kamar Sodeises of the world subvert that basic fact. If it turns out that protecting tribes means protecting them from us, so be it. But without us, they'd have nobody. Without Orland and Claudio, there'd be no secure demarcation. How many years ago was that? Three? That opened up the world for us, and if we close the door, we have only ourselves to blame."

The others looked at each other and then down. No one spoke.

While they were arguing, the room had grown dark. In their silence, the moon peeked out slowly over the roof of the house next door, throwing its beam across Jorge's wooden floor. Without thinking, Jorge placed his foot beside the beam, adjusting it to make it parallel. Sara laced and unlaced her fingers. Joaquim ran his hand over his chin, realizing without thinking that he needed a shave. Silvio reached out and unwrapped the food. He took a piece of bread and the others suddenly jumped in after him in a rush, four pairs of hands pushing across each other for lunchmeat, finally finding an outlet for their desperation. Sara turned on the lights and they ate in silence, two, three sandwiches apiece.

Finally, Silvio turned to Joaquim, his mouth still full. "You're not going to build your great system of justice from the field," he said, washing down his sandwich with a swig of warm beer.

"Or from a desk in an office, or over lunch with politicos," Joaquim shot back, toasting him with his own bottle. "Lino stays here."

CXI

DESPITE THE OPEN book on his lap, Jorge wasn't reading. Rather, it took all the energy he had to fight the waves of shame that broke against the pylons inside him, creating disruptions in his stomach. The elusive distinction between using others and being used was, at that moment, lost on him, with the unfortunate consequence that he was unsure as to the proper target of his resentment. While he worked his way down the list of people he knew, his mother, and Martina, and Joaquim, his father and his uncles and his long-lost grammar school friends, only James struck him as someone around whom he had never felt exploited, or had needed to make excuses. James had clearly relied on him—for his last ten years, he would accept no other pilot—but with a kind of delight in his skill that suggested pride rather than need. Perhaps his father might have felt that way too; perhaps by remembering James, he could create an internal sense of what a father's pride might feel like, or even discover a memory of it. But for now, the one he imagined feeling what his father felt for him was Martina, and the thought was unbearable. She was the one who had seen him waver; the one who had seen him cry. For that, he could never forgive her, both for allowing him to spoil her regard for him, and for allowing him to spoil his father's. He closed the book and sat up, looking around for her with red, angry eyes.

When he scanned the far corner of the room by the kitchen, however, the person he found wasn't Martina, her image or her voice or her smell, but Larry, whose presence made him even more nauseous, and filled him with an even greater intensity of rage. He could see him, bumbling and vulnerable, fighting for a life that anyone with a bit of perspective could see meant nothing, completely unprepared, if he wasn't already dead, to make any contribution of the sort that would be worthy of pride. To sacrifice himself to save someone who wasn't worth saving was the height of exploitation, its very definition. As it turned out, Jorge realized, he didn't need the twenty-four hours Silvio and Joaquim had given him to think through the question of how much he was willing to do; the answer was so obvious that further thought could only cloud it, as opposed to making it more clear. He stood quickly and headed for the phone, but on his way, despite himself, further thought caught up and flooded him. The further thought was of Larry again, not of his face this time, but of the tracks his tears had left in the dust on his shoes as they sat side by side in the courtyard of the Museo. In that Larry, the one who, Quichotte-like, hurled himself against his destiny at any cost, he had seen another vision of himself, and something of the nobility in fighting losing battles. That was the point, purely by chance, at which his hand made contact with the phone, and there was nothing else to do but to pick up the receiver and dial.

CXII

THE FOREST CONTAINS endless stories, far too many for all the ancestors combined to tell, but it is not kind to the sorts of stories that are
written in books. As if to avenge itself upon these usurpers, it attacked
the pages of Larry's few volumes with mold, their spines with mildew,
and their covers with layers of spores that threatened to obscure even the
most basic of their intentions in a spongy, foul-smelling slime. He spent
much effort laying them out in the sun during dry times, flipping through
their pages as though to inoculate them leaf by leaf, down to their darkest
crevasses, against the coming rains. Despite the fact that in Pahquel, persons were deliberate in their blindness to his possessions, betraying no
outward curiosity whatever toward his knife blade, obstinately looking
past him when he drew out his compass or twine or metal nail file, they
could not help but notice the way he treated those odd objects, with their
fly-specks arranged neatly in rows like crops in tiny, sun-bleached fields.
They mocked his way of turning pages, ridiculed his pacing eyes, and imi-
tated with exaggerated flourishes his ritual of laying out his volumes at
dawn like fish to be smoked and gathering them in at dusk. But of the fact
that he often shed tears when he sat with them, and looked so deeply into
them that he might as well have been studying the deepest part of the
river's floor, these things they didn't mock. As he sat cross-legged on his
kaawa, head bowed over the pages, they regarded him cautiously, and did
not address him, suspecting somehow, the involvement of the ancestors
in his absorption.

One evening, while he was bowed in his usual posture, immersed *in The Two Towers* while the fire waned, Iri stumbled over to him and reached for the book, snatching it from him and laughing. Larry pulled it away, but without returning Iri's laugh, which prompted a tantrum on Iri's part, as he reached out with greater insistence, nearly tearing the paper.

"*Po po! Po po!*" he shouted while Larry closed the book and held it aloft.

"*Pi pi,*" Larry said, "*Pi pi.* You you. I'll give it to you, but you have to be quiet and sit down."

At last, Iri stopped screaming and squatted beside him, sniffing and wiping his eyes. "This is a book," said Larry, using the English word. "Letters," he said, tracing Iri's name in the dirt. "Iri." He took Iri's finger and spelled out I–R–I, sensing as he did that he was crossing some unspoken barrier, some necessarily impermeable membrane, and feeling suddenly afraid. Thus, he taught his child to read in the way all parents teach their children; by mistaking their resentment of the objects of their attention for the interest that over time, it becomes; by giving them the tools with which they will, inevitably, be betrayed. Only in Larry's case, it wasn't so clear whether in the process of teaching his son to read he was giving his son the world or taking it from him, drawing him in or setting the course for his expulsion from the only life he had.

CIII

SILVIO SAT IN Sara's kitchen, drumming his finger on the phone, trying to get a connection to Rio. The Telepar was far more reliable, and vastly cheaper, but he refused to listen to Sara's advice, and so wasted half the afternoon on cursing and pacing and haste. At first, Sara sat with him, but when she realized how little inclined he was to include her, she left him with a card containing her office phone number and a note saying she'd be home at 6. It wasn't until an hour later that Silvio realized she was gone.

The truth was that despite his insistence, Silvio wasn't at all prepared to talk to Rio, or to Sao Paulo, or even to himself. The puppeteer was pulling too many strings, and was too tangled up in them himself to know which part would move when he pulled on any particular one. There was the prospect of losing his best agents and best friends, if not forever, then for what sufficed for forever in the context of his plans. There was the need to show that his agency was able to protect its own, and that he was able to monitor his men on the ground. There was the fact that he couldn't trust anyone any more, and had come to feel, over the past year especially, that he was losing control of the strings, that there was something rotten at the core of at least half of what he had going in the field. There were the personal commitments, the promises to Joaquim, and retroactively to Marietto, and to James about Larry, and there were the legal fights, and the recent pressure from congressmen, Garapar and Redondimo and Diego Melo and too many others to name. There were decisions about which authorities to involve and when, and there was the sinking feeling that whatever decision he made, he would end up losing, and alone.

When a voice came on the end of the line, he jumped and nearly dropped the receiver, having forgotten that he was still trying to place a call. He stuttered for a minute, trying to remember to whom he had been so desperate to talk, and then regained himself, relieved to find it was Maria, his secretary. Her voice was without its usual affectionate coloring though, and conveyed a sense of panic even from a thousand miles away.

"I'll be back on Saturday," he barked at her in an effort to regain the upper hand.

"No, now. You have no idea what's happened in the past three days."

"Say it."

"Arturo witnessed two flybys in two days, both infected clothing drops and their chief was on to it. You need to go see Arturo. He barely got out alive—two broken ribs and about twenty grazings, some of them agented. He was lucky. You need to get somebody here now."

Silvio was silent on his end of the line. He could feel his lungs folding in on themselves, as though he himself had taken the curared arrows, while his mind raced around his chest like gulls around a tall ship, binding its sails with rope. "I'm going to need an attraction team down here in Santarem," he said at last, summoning sufficient air to speak. "I want you to pull in Valerio and Lino, and have them out here by tomorrow. Tell them to come to *11 Rua Galdino Valoso* when they get here."

"But what about Arturo?"

"Pull in Marco and his crew. Have them ready. I'll be back tomorrow night."

Maria, at least, he could trust. He hung up the receiver and began to pace again, between the kitchen and Sara's front door, through the front room with its stacks of books, its artifacts and rumpled throw rugs. At last, he paused before an end table, which held an open book and a thick stack of photographs. He picked up a few off the stack and waved them in front of his eyes as if trying to get his own attention, in an effort to distract his mind from its sickness. When Sara walked in at a quarter to six, that was how she found him, transfixed on the spot by the sofa, holding before his eyes an image of another time.

CXIV

IT TOOK FOUR of the largest *barcas* to hold all the crates and furniture and servants and still leave room for the oarsmen to maneuver. Sr. Catalpa stood with difficulty at the stern of the last in that line of gilded elephants that bobbed and snorted and shifted impatiently, looking back at his already unfamiliar former home. From this distance, the house seemed more gracious than ever, as though it had in retrospect, finally attained the aspect of enchantment that had eluded it in service. He could barely bring himself to wave his handkerchief towards the clutches of natives gathered on the dock and at the shore who, he knew, would swarm that beautiful carcass as soon as the last of their caravan was out of sight. Instead, he raised his hand and brought it to his lips, blowing kiss after kiss at the cheek of a mistress as flattered by distance as the mistresses of his youth had been flattered by the dark. *"Adeus! Adeus!"* he cried, leaning forward as the *barcas* creaked and jolted, surprised at the clutch in his throat. Only when he reminded himself that the house had recently been tainted, and that the Sodeis problem had also been definitively left behind, did he pull his eyes from the shrinking gem at the horizon and avail himself of the limp bread-and-cheese sandwich that Gabriel stood offering him on a cracked Wedgwood plate.

CXV

JOAQUIM KNEW WHEN to press an issue and when to let it go, and also how to get his way regardless. When he heard Sara move around in the kitchen, he got up quietly, closing the door of Jorge's room, where Silvio still slept, as he passed by on his way down the hall. By the time he had pulled out a chair to sit down at the kitchen table, Sara had already placed a steaming mug of coffee in front of him.

"Sleep well?"

"No," said Joaquim, who was known as a good sleeper.

"Tensions are high," said Sara, sitting down across from him.

"From all sides," said Joaquim.

"Which sides in particular?"

Joaquim took a breath and then began to talk in a pressured burst. "Something tells me our old vision is fading, and then I catch myself. I push away the thought. I tell myself there's still important work to be done. I think of Xingu, even with its problems. I think we could give SPI a whole new direction if we really started to think in terms of *non*-contact, of demarcation *only*. There's been too much focus on intervention, and that's what's placed our men in situations of temptation. We need to re-think ourselves completely at this point, or we'll lose our way forever. And maybe Silvio's right. Maybe that can't be done from the field. Maybe we're doing more harm than good right now. And maybe he's the right one for the job, but it's just as likely that he'll be too wedded to the romance of taking action. He's not someone who has an easy time sitting still, or

317

letting his men sit still in the field either. It can take a year to make a solid contact, and it can take five to demarcate an area without it."

Sara studied Joaquim in silence, the muscles and sinews in his thin arms, and the dark skin draping at the collarbone. They were two old people, each, perhaps, still fighting for something.

"*Morrer, se preciso for, matar nunca!*" Joaquim said softly, and then fell silent again. Sara nodded. Rondon's motto: "Die if necessary, but never kill."

"And then there's Larry," said Joaquim suddenly, interrupting her thoughts. "I don't know what sort of contaminant it is out there, but it's there. And it seems that our little team has no interest in that part of the puzzle. James got too caught up in the details, in his strange preoccupation with words and dying languages and genetic theories, and Silvio can't sit still long enough to pay attention to any details at all. But whoever's responsible clearly sees the tribes as their own perfect laboratories, and is as dangerous as any of the worst *fazendieros* we've run into. Whether or not our mission needs re-thinking, we've still got a lot of work to do out there!"

"Of course we have work to do," said Silvio from the doorway, buttoning his shirt. "Got another one of those?"

Sara poured him a cup and set it on the table. Then she started in. "I know this isn't my job, and I'm an outsider in all of this, but it's clear to me," she said, "that this fighting on one front at a time, everybody on their own turf, isn't working anymore. Things have gotten just too complicated. If you're going in, you should do the whole thing, and do it the right way. I've gone ahead and asked Sam from the lab to go along, and I've approached Martina about acting as his assistant. She has good instincts, and she knows her soils. I was thinking of just assaying, but now we're going to need to get our hands on a whole suitcase full of phlebotomy kits. My guess is that one thing will lead to another, and that you'll run into that Sodeis fellow no matter whether you decide to follow him or not."

"Martina's in?" said Joaquim. "How did you pull that off?"

"I'm not certain, but I have a feeling she is."

Silvio stood up and pushed in his chair. "I need to get myself home," he said, "but I'm going to leave you with a present and then a question."

"I'll take the present!" said Joaquim, suppressing a smile. "You can give her the question. I'll tell you what I want for my present. Call Lino back to Rio."

Silvio shot Joaquim a look. Then he went to his room and retrieved his suitcase out of the front pocket of which he pulled a cloth pouch. He set the pouch in front of Joaquim and stepped back a few paces. Joaquim unzipped the pouch and pulled out three sets of handcuffs.

"Are the keys in here?" he said searching in the bottom of the pouch.

"Of course the keys are in there," said Silvio, straining to look over Joaquim's head into the pouch and then remembering he had put the keys on his own keychain. As he was unfastening them from their clasps and laying them in front of Joaquim, Sara asked, "So what's the question?"

"The question is," said Silvio, coming up behind Joaquim and putting his hand on his shoulder, "Why do I hate to listen to this guy? Like, why the hell didn't I take his advice and marry you when he told me I should go for you back in '54?"

"Joa!" said Sara, looking at Joaquim in mock shock, her neck reddening.

"Well, here's your chance to make up for lost time and listen to me," said Joaquim, pulling Silvio towards the door. "No Lino. Recall him as soon as he gets here. Give him the same gift you gave me, and make sure it's his size," he said, gesturing with each hand toward his opposing wrist.

"No Lino," said Silvio tipping an imaginary hat to both of them as he headed out through the living room, hailing a cab at the door.

CXVI

ONE OF THE realizations that grew on Larry only very slowly, over the course of years, is that homesickness is a far more complex malady, far more difficult to diagnose, let alone to treat, when one has never felt at home. Also, despite its reputation as an acute condition, he found that it became bothersome only after the time when it should have faded forever, as if what one was mourning was the possibility of homesickness itself. But when Iri read his first sentence, when Oji, at the age of two and a half months, took his first halting steps across the *kaawa* in full view of a hand of persons whose relief at his not having been held back only added to the intensity of their praise of him, Larry was aware, in the back of his mind, of a wish to share his excitement not only with James, but with Joaquim, with Jorge, and even, he was ashamed to admit, with his parents, who no doubt did not celebrate his own milestones with the same enthusiasm that was now being lavished on his children. His longing not only for people, but for places and things swelled up at odd times, and always surprised him. Still, after all this time, he could not manage to remember that he didn't have a camera, and fought the urge to rifle yet again through his pack to find it. And the worst of it was that there was no one he could speak to about his old life; from the point of view of those in Pahquel, the time prior to his appearance was thought of simply as the time in which he was held back, and the things he learned, talked about, experienced then were regarded as confidences between himself and the ancestors, and not for other ears. Thus he had no choice but to envy others their intimacy with the ancestors, and to look among these lineages for any signs of his own. There was some comfort in Kakap's insistence that he had as much claim as anyone, more, in fact, for his having been held back, to the ancestors both of Dabimi's line and, due to his having sired children, of Anok's, but the comfort was often short-lived, erased by a sense of shame at his hidden past, as though he were betraying the ancestors both of his own obscure lineage and of his new ones.

"Why does no one want to hear about my ancestors?" he asked Kakap one night while they lay in their hammocks with their gourds hanging beside them.

"Of course we do," said Kakap, "Your ancestors are ours, and we love them!"

"No," said Larry. "I mean, the people I knew before I came here. The ones who gave birth to my parents and to me."

"I said, we do." Kakap laughed. "We love them."

"No," said Larry, suddenly determined to be as insistent as Kakap.

Kakap was silent for a long time. At last, he said, "I can only say that the things that come to us from out of the world are bad, and they must not be in the world."

"How do you know that?" said Larry.

"The ancestors told us."

"Then why did you allow me and Jarara to live here?"

Another long silence, in which Larry suddenly became afraid that he had asked too much, that Kakap would suddenly see him as a foreign particle, an intrusion to expel.

"The ancestors told us," he said at last.

The night sounds swelled up, as though to concur with Kakap's summation. He listened, but remained unsatisfied. "What did the ancestors tell you?" he said.

The night itself answered, but in riddles, in noisy, coy, preoccupied exclamations: "The world is more than you thought."

"Should I not be asking?" Larry said at last into the cacophonous silence.

"No," said Kakap. "Our ancestors are our teachers." Then, at last, a long breath, and Kakap's story-telling voice: "Jarara was ours because he kept the bad ones out of the world. When they came in, he followed them. That was when we were hand-and-four of villages, not the three we are now. They made us get sick and die. They were going to take the *chajans* and all the girls and women, so that we would wither. But Jarara had a thing like the ones you look at. He made it himself, and he showed it to them, and it told them their children would die if they used our women. It told them they would die. And the *chajans* did not yield. The bad ones left, and he left with them. We did not throw one spear. He came back without them."

"Really?" said Larry, feeling a sudden stab as he remembered he had left James's notebook at Sara's. It occurred to him then that the longing for things was always a longing for someone. He felt ashamed not to have realized that before. "So what about that story of him and Asator being held back together?"

"Yes, that story is also true," said Kakap.

CXVII

JOAQUIM WALKED SLOWLY to the Telepar, not merely because he dreaded the call, but because he was as weighed down as the burros that plied the *Travessa dos Martires* with the spoils of the harbor on their backs. He had been feeling his age acutely lately as a burden among burdens, an exhaustion like a father's who discovers that his children still need him long after they should have been capable of living on their own. With his literal offspring, he was oblivious to a fault to their need for him, having learned a lesson or two from his father, who, especially after his mother's death, had all he could just to keep a roof on their tin shack. But with regard to the offspring of his dreams, Jorge and James and Marietto and Flavio and Heitor and a hundred other agents and, yes, Silvio too, not to mention all the forest people he regarded as his kin, he could draw for example and inspiration upon the memory of the great Rondon, who loved him like the son he never was otherwise; he could draw upon Orlando, on Claudio, on half a dozen of the native elders at whose feet he had been privileged to sit. Perhaps what pained him most was the sense that all around him, he could see evidence of the waning of Rondon's influence in the face of the modern obsessions with adventurism and greed, as though he were watching the disintegration before his eyes of a painting of staggering beauty in the torpid, mildew-saturated air, the last extant portrait of his next-of-kin. When the dial tone sounded suddenly, he shook off his thoughts with a start and recited the number quickly.

Cora's voice came on the line. *"Alo? Alo? Quim? A ligacao esta muito ruim!"* A poor connection.

Joaquim motioned with his free hand to compensate for the crackling on the line as though he were speaking to someone in front of him. "Cora, I'm going to be away again, but I think this'll be the last time."

"You told me that last time was the last time! How many last times are there these days? How do I know when it will be the last of the last times?" Cora tended to have one of two reactions to Joaquim's calls—either this explosive mock-rage or else withdrawal and resignation. Of the two, this was by far the best.

"I've done something I'm coming to regret. I have to make it right, and then I'll be home."

"What? You killed somebody?"

"It's James's kid. You know all those notebooks? I finally figured out what's in them, and I think I let him get into something he can't get out of. We need to go and retrieve him."

"Now? *Now?* After one, two, three years? He's probably dead by now!" Then, perhaps out of regret for that last comment, "So how long you going to take? Just because your kids are gone doesn't mean you don't live here any more."

"I know where I live, and I know who I live with," Joaquim said, "But this one's going to have to be open-ended. Not long, I hope."

"But the last?"

"The last."

"So give me the date." A ritual—Cora always asked him for a date on which to hold the wake if he hadn't arrived home by then. She knew it was all necessary, that he couldn't really live in their world, and that that was why she had married him.

"A date . . . a date . . . November first."

"Of which year?" They easily had as many rituals around absence as they did around proximity. Their rituals were everything, but not nearly enough. He had had plenty of time to figure out the difference between the things he could make right and the things he couldn't, between things that were true and those that weren't.

"*Te amo,*" he said.

CXVIII

"LET'S CHECK THE weight on these," said Jorge, pushing boxes one by one to the platform scale under the metal awning outside the hangar. Joaquim and Sam stepped forward to help him lift, and the three grunted in unison as they hoisted the cargo, marked it, and slid it off the scale.

Jorge was taking his time readying his plane, and the others were taking their time checking and rechecking their bags. In fact, the whole process of readying themselves had been extraordinarily laborious, due to the presence of as many forms of resistance as there were participants, and more. There were the packs to assemble, each of which contained a condensed version of its owner's life, including a few photographs to remind each of them of who he thought he was, the memory of which tended to fade quickly in the field. There were the three weeks it took the phlebotomy kits to arrive from Belem, and the multiple trips to the Mercado, and the prep work in the lab, and the paperwork, and most of all, there were the arguments, in person and over the phone, and the ones that took place privately in the thoughts of each, often just before sunrise. There had been the confusing search for Valerio, of whom Silvio had apparently lost track, and then the waiting for Lino, who didn't show up for a week and finally arrived, inexplicably, and clearly with rancor, on a flight from Belo Horizonte, and the long, dangerous hour in which Joaquim told him that Silvio had recalled him at the last minute, a fact that Lino would have known had he been where he said he would be.

Lino stood off to the side, still arguing with Joaquim in a low but intense voice while Sara milled aimlessly, fingering the *cruzeros* in her pocket, unsure as to how close to get to Jorge while he was working, as at any other time.

The passengers, Joaquim and Sam, jostled each other and made hooting noises as Jorge moved them together onto the scale, and Joaquim grabbed Jorge's pen and threatened to write their weights on their stomachs. They were off the scale and starting to lift the boxes into the hold when Martina walked up, carrying a pack on her back and a book under her arm.

"So what time is liftoff?" she asked them while they were still facing away.

Jorge turned on his heel and stared at her in silence.

Sam came up and shook her hand. "Glad you're in," he said. "I can use you."

Jorge moved his stare from Martina to his mother, and then to Joaquim. Then he turned to Joaquim. He reached into his pocket and handed him the key to the plane. "Have a good trip," he said, heading towards his car. Martina followed him and pulled herself up onto the hood of Jorge's Aero, dangling her legs. Jorge weighed the advantages and disadvantages of blowing the horn, of getting out and pulling her off, perhaps by the hair, of driving away with her still on the hood, of swerving or not as he drove. As none of those options seemed plausible, he sat immobile for nearly an hour, sweating in the hot car despite the hangar's shade. Martina took off her pack and leaned against it with her knees up, reading her book. Finally, Jorge heard the groan of a metal hinge as Joaquim opened the passenger door and got in. They both sat with their eyes straight ahead, as though they were driving together on a particularly demanding stretch of road.

"Ready, captain?" said Joachim, keeping his eyes on the road.

"Ready for what?"

Joaquim took a minute to answer. "Ready for you to grow up and take control of your life."

"How the hell am I supposed to do that," Jorge exploded at Joaquim, rising up in his seat, "when every time I turn around, other people see fit to manipulate me, and pander to me, and think they can make decisions about how I'm supposed to live?" He pulled his eyes from the road and turned them on Joaquim recklessly. "You don't want me to live my life—you want me to live yours. You want to keep me a child so everything works out according to your plans!" He took off his glasses with a snap and began to rub them frantically on a corner of his shirt. Then he put them on again decisively and turned back to the road, as though intending to drive fast enough to forget that the others would inevitably be speeding along with him.

"You know when I quit SPI?" said Joaquim slowly, as though they were touring on a pleasure ride with time to reminisce. His mouth betrayed a flash of a wry smile; they both knew that he had quit and also that he likely would never quit. "It wasn't directly after I lost your father. Those things take a while to hit home. It was when I realized *why* I had lost him, and what it said about me." He turned to see if Jorge was listening. Jorge was still staring straight ahead, into the distance well beyond Martina. "Ever since I left home at fourteen, I was always trying to prove that I could make it on my own, and then suddenly it occurred to me who I was trying to prove it to, and that was a punch in the gut. It occurred to me that all I was doing was trying to win over the people I was closest to by showing that I could live without them. It was a point of pride, and I sacrificed your father to it, and now I'm worried that I may have sacrificed Larry to it also. I think I've sent too many men out there to fend for themselves, without the background, or the backup." He turned his eyes back to the road. "In short, I should have listened to you. I'm trying to do it right this time, trying to learn something in my old age. And," he said, the twinge at the corners of his mouth hovering now, "you see how hard it is to change things."

Ironically, the only one Jorge could imagine wanting to hear from at that moment was Larry, perhaps because he was the only one Jorge knew who was even more lost and pitiful than himself. He pretended not to listen to Joaquim, but he knew he had no other choice.

"I'm not saying you're a child," Joaquim continued. "I'm only saying that it takes a grownup to rely on people, and to let others see it." He motioned to Martina's back.

It occurred to Jorge for the first time that Martina could probably hear everything they said, although she, too, was pretending not to listen.

"Why don't you talk to *her* about it," said Jorge, *sotto voce*, motioning with his head. "She's the one who's so willing to close doors and just move on!"

"Good idea," said Joaquim, and stuck his head out the window. "Martina, can you come in here a minute?"

Martina looked at them through the windshield. Then she closed her book and slid off the hood. After walking slowly around the car, pausing at the back door, she finally came up to Jorge's window. "Welcome to Bob's! Can I take your order?" she said. "Burger and fries?"

Despite himself, Jorge couldn't suppress a smile, for which he hated them both.

"The deal is you get your mustard and ketchup on the side. No, the deal is we don't have to talk to each other," she said. 'That's what your mother told me."

Jorge got out of the car and walked past her toward the plane. "The deal is if you're man enough to go through with it, you'd be doing something decent for a change. At least then all those fathers of yours might be able to admit to being proud of you again," she said after him, shouldering her pack.

CXIX

IT WAS LATE by the time Sodeis hauled his boat onto the sand at Paruqu and tied it off to the side, to one of the trees by the bluff. In his haste to leave Lamurii, he had neglected to pack food, so he was no doubt driven in part by hunger to summon to mind the well stocked and poorly defended larder of Sr. Catalpa, as well as by some perverse need to revisit the scene of his latest crime. From the dock, he could tell that the house was in darkness, a fact that might have portended either well or ill. Too tired to bury his gas cans, he left them with the boat and made the climb up the bluff nearly on his hands and knees, balancing his pack. When he arrived at the door, he pushed at it tentatively and it opened with a creak. He felt for his revolver in the side pocket of his cargo pants, but he could tell even before the door had opened fully that the house was deserted; the Senor had vacated his post. He set down his pack in the parlor where the Senor's coffee table had been and headed off to the kitchen to scout for any well-sealed canisters the help might have abandoned in the pantry. He found a can of soup but no opener, and debated, for a moment, shooting a hole in it, before putting it away. He found a bag of what tasted like sugar and licked a spoonful out of his palm. He found a large sack of dried beans, which he shook out on the table. A scorpion fell from the sack onto the floor and skittered off into the corner by the back door. He put a handful of beans into his mess looking around for water. To his sudden elation, he found an entire cabinet stacked chest-high with bottles of water, and containing as an added bonus, a large tin of chocolate bars. He unwrapped a bar and sucked on a piece of chocolate while he uncorked one of the bottles to pour it onto the beans, jumping back when he heard a sudden whoosh and looked down to see the beans hissing in the pot; he'd forgotten about carbonation. He covered the beans tightly and made his way back to the parlor with the bottle in hand, taking big swigs from it and belching loudly as he untied his bedroll and spread it across the floor.

CXX

NO ONE SAID a word as they entered Sara's car, each by a separate door. Out their windows were separate habitats of thought, into which they each disappeared for several minutes, until Lino broke the silence by swearing.

"So what are your plans?" asked Sara, trying to assess whether it would be safe to have him in the house.

"You can go call the bastard and ask him," said Lino, "He'll tell you one thing, and you can figure out the opposite, and that's what he's going to give me."

"I thought they said you were needed in Tarampa," said Sara, knowing full well why Silvio'd excluded him.

"He needs me, he needs me," muttered Lino, swearing under his breath and staring out the side window of the car. From the back seat, Bella leaned forward and put a hand on Sara's shoulder, to indicate that she was talking only to her.

"So yesterday I ran those numbers while you were out, and I never got a chance to tell you what I found!"

"Yes," Sara undercut her. "You'll have to tell me when we get back." There was anxiety in her voice. Lino straightened as though to listen better. "But in the meanwhile, you're both probably hungry. We should stop at the market," she said, pulling into a space in front of a small grocery. She got out of the car and motioned for Bella to come along. Lino started to get out also, but she patted him on the shoulder. "Let the women wait on you. Your day's been hard enough. You'll eat, and then you can call Silvio and work it out."

While the butcher was slicing the ham, Sara leaned towards Bella. "No data, no information, nothing until we get him sent off," she said, nodding at the weight on the scale. They approached the car with the bags in their arms, just in time to see Lino straighten in his seat. Sara tried to catch a glance at what he'd been looking at. There was a sheaf of folded papers jammed into the space between the run and the rise of the seat, but the outermost layer was blank. Clearly, the three were too suspicious of each other to engage in small talk, so the women entered the car in silence.

"I'm getting the feeling you don't care much for Joaquim," said Sara at last, resigned to learn what she could.

"That *vaqueirito?* What would I like about him?" Lino thought for a minute, filtering what he said. "And everyone knows, that other rat, Silvio, is in the palm of his hand."

"You think so? They were both here for two weeks before you got here, and it seemed to me like they couldn't agree about anything! I wanted you to tell me why they fight all the time."

"What did they fight about this time?" said Lino, with obvious false disinterest.

"About everything! Whether to go at all, whether just to leave Larry alone, whether it was Joaquim's fault that Larry was out there in the first place, what to bring along. I don't know. I don't know the details."

Lino seemed to brighten as Sara talked, as though he had begun to suspect that she really was an outsider.

"That guy has his nose everywhere!" he burst out, as though Sara's ignorance had given him permission to talk. "He's busted up most of my best contracts. I get something set, he busts it up. I go do something else, get it set, he busts it up. He should have quit twenty years ago! He's an antique. He's stuck in some dark age, and he's costing me my bread and butter, and he's smug! Smug, holier-than-thou, thinks-he's-an-old-wise-man, skinny little bastard. Now I have to live with the regret that I didn't at least rough him up for his trouble!"

They had pulled up in front of Sara's. "Ready for lunch?" she said.

"I'm ready to make my calls," said Lino.

"They're about five hundred percent cheaper at the Telepar," she said, knowing he'd realize they were cheaper still when you could leave somebody else with the bill.

Sara and Bella headed for the kitchen table to lay down the cold cuts while Lino strode to the phone and stood with his back to them, swearing and twisting the cord. "I'm done with SPI," he said, turning to them briefly while he waited for the operator. "Just for your information. You've just witnessed the birth of Lino Araujo, LLC, Prospecting, Brokerage, and—this is the best part—soon-to-be *Private* Corporation!"

CXXI

AS LINO HUNG up the phone and turned to them, Sara and Bella could see he was a changed man. "If you don't mind, I'm going to pack up and go," he said, whistling to himself as he set off down the hall. He came back ten minutes later with his leather-trimmed suitcase and its matching leather attaché and set them by the front door.

"So that's quite a bit of time you were on the phone," said Sara.

"I'll send you a cheque," said Lino, "as soon as I get myself settled. But in the meanwhile, I may need a ride to the airport," he squinted out the front window. "Although I guess there's no shortage of cabs. You heard that call of course," he said. Sara and Bella had feigned interest in their own private chat, but they had both listened carefully to Lino's end of various conversations, with Sara paying particular attention to the expense he had incurred on her behalf in placing his extended calls from her house.

"This is going to make me wonder why I stuck with SPI for so long," Lino said brightly, reaching for a slice of ham, rolling and eating it without bread. "So it turns out that my friends have friends, and a few of those friends are politicians, and a few of those politicians have influence, and it looks like I have a golden opportunity right in front of me and I'm going to reach out and grab it. You can tell your friend Joaquim Rocha that despite his best efforts, I seem to be landing on my feet, which is more than he's likely to do," he looked at Sara and checked himself, remembering that her son was out there with him, "tramping around after some fool kid! Now there's a waste of time and men!"

"Did you call Silvio and let him know you've quit?" said Sara, moving toward the kitchen counter and leaning on it, facing Lino, obscuring the pad on which he had been jotting notes as he had made his plans.

"Let's let him guess!" said Lino, shouldering his pack. "Thanks to you ladies for your hospitality," he said, bowing slightly at the door.

CXXII

SINCE LARRY REGARDED himself as someone who had never had a childhood, the daily lives of his sons filled him with wonder and confusion. As quickly as Oji had overtaken his older brother in height and weight, the two had seemed to form, before his eyes, their own sensibilities and roles vis-à-vis each other. Oji, for his own part, still seemed to revel in the fact that he could run faster, climb higher, and throw the spear farther than Iri could, and Iri's regard for his brother seemed equal parts resentment, admiration, and dismissal. But most of all, Iri would cleave to his father, joining him in singing to the plants, or in reading the smaller words in Henry Walter Bates, or listening to the stories he brought with him after gathering trips, some his own and some that Kakap had told him. Where there was an ever-present sense of distance between Oji and his father, the connection between Larry and Iri was undeniable, despite his efforts to care for them equally. Others often remarked on the resemblance between Oji and Aran, but never between Oji and his father. Larry had to continually push aside the urge to tell Iri stories about his past, about his life outside the world, an urge he never felt with Oji.

One night when Aran was out visiting in the far village, he knelt on his mat to hug Iri and then approached Oji, kneeling beside him.

"I'm too old now, father," he said, loudly enough for Iri to overhear.

"Are you?" said Larry, trying to hide the hurt in his voice.

"How old were you when your father stopped?" said Oji. Iri sat up and leaned forward on his elbow, listening. "How old were you when you moved to the men's hut?"

Larry sat without speaking for several minutes, not sure how to answer. "My father never hugged me," he said at last.

Iri got up from his mat and put his arms around his father. Despite himself, Larry could feel sudden tears roll down his arm onto his leg, and then unexpectedly, a hand on his knee. It was Oji's hand. He took it in his own, and held it against a wave inside him at the thought that what had been missing between himself and Oji might not have been Oji at all, but only a part of him. When Aran came in later that night, she found him asleep between his two boys, having moved his mat to the ground.

"Are you feeling well?" she whispered as she shook him.

"*Tuara,*" he whispered back. "*Tuara, mboa, tuara.*" "Beautiful from the living and the dead."

CXXIII

SODEIS BENT OVER his maps and lists, squinting in the dim half-light of a kerosene lantern to read his hand-drawn numbers and symbols, his lines as thin as razor-cuts. Whatever perversity there was in his nature that always led him to return to the scenes of his various crimes, that drew him back to Catalpa's, the thing was not so reckless as to lead him to fire up the electrical generator, which anyway now within six months of Catalpa's leaving, was already overgrown with moss and ferns and home to several colonies of swiftlets. He felt convinced that he could make the trek without a map at all; it looked to be a good ten days' hike in as the spot was unusually distant from any consistently navigable river. But ten days was time he did not have. What he needed was a shortcut that could trim four from that monumental ten, allowing him to scratch the unbearable itch of those two faint numbers and still have plenty of time to set himself up on his next logging venture before his impatience got the better of him.

He mulled over ways to optimize his time on the river as he walked to the kitchen, lantern in hand. There were at least twenty boxes in the pantry he hadn't even looked into yet; he pulled them open one by one and stacked them off to the side; a dozen bottles of bleach, an entire carton of mop-heads, a case of red wine of an inferior vintage if the price on the box was any indication. To his delight, there were several cases of still water and some tins of tuna and mackerel, an odd find in a house on the river with men right there to fish it. It occurred to him that with all the opportunities he had no doubt had over the past days and weeks, in bars and villages, he still hadn't remembered to bring a can opener. He piled the cases of fish on top of the ones with the bleach and put a pot of the water on the kerosene stove. The only thing to do, the water in the pot somehow told him, was to follow the river south in a light canoe (like one of the dull silver fish that lay beached, clearly unused, by the pier) and then portage the thirty miles—two days' worth of misery—to catch the Aramaya headed north. Five days at most, he told himself, even though most of the rowing would be upstream.

After downing two bowls of rice and beans, nicely spiced, thanks to the Senor, Sodeis strung his hammock from the same hooks that had once held Joachim's and lay nursing one of the disappointing but nevertheless drinkable bottles from the Senor's stock, staring deep into the noisy tangle of darkness. If he had been a man to know peace, he would have known it then. But Sodeis had never possessed an apparatus to detect that gift of the forest, and his longings were so deep as to be capable of satisfaction only through harder more definite forms of contact, of the kind that could be found only in conflict. As he dozed off, the images in his head had little to do with the forest itself, with friendships from long ago, or with any of the women he had known, all briefly, from a time some years back. Rather, the story that unfolded as sleep overtook him was confined, tragically to just two characters: himself and Joaquim.

CXXIV

ONLY AFTER THEY had hung their hammocks on the deserted verandah of Sr. Catalpa's faded manse did Jorge admit to Joaquim that he'd lost the bag containing Larry's envelope. Joaquim got up without saying a word and shook his head, heading out into the forest.

"Where are you going?" called Jorge as the others unpacked their bedrolls.

"To take a leak," said Joaquim heading up the trail behind the house.

They were digging out their toothbrushes and stuffing their pillowcases with rolled-up clothes when Sodeis sprang at them from the doorway, wielding his revolver.

"You're squatters in this house!" he shouted. "Get out! The house is mine now! You have no right to be here!"

"How is it yours?" said Martina, betraying no fear. "It's Catalpa's!"

"He left it to me," said Sodeis with a smirk.

Joaquim came up behind Sodeis swinging a thick branch. "I doubt it," he said as Sodeis went down. He stood with his foot on Sodeis's outstretched arm while Jorge kicked the gun away. "I can't imagine you're the sort Catalpa'd choose as an heir." Then he turned to Martina. "Would you mind looking in my case for a purple velvet pouch?" he said while he stood straddling Sodeis. Sodeis began to squirm, and Joaquim fell on him. The two rolled over each other, and Sodeis squirmed out from under him and jumped to his feet, heading for the water. Jorge grabbed the pistol and took off after him, with the rest of them trailing behind.

At the pier, Sodeis seemed to consider taking their boat, but looking up at Jorge, who was training the gun in his direction, thought better of it and jumped into his own rig, starting the motor with a snap.

"Should I shoot him?" Jorge asked Joaquim.

"*Morrer, se preciso for, matar nunca!*" said Joaquim, while Sam and Martina in unison shouted, "Shoot! Shoot!"

"I thought that applied only to Indians," said Jorge, lowering his gun as Sodeis disappeared upriver.

"*Mierda!*" said Joaquim under his breath.

CXXV

LARRY HAD ENTERED their hut the evening before as the father of an only child and a stranger, but he awoke as the father of two. Whatever had happened that night was not erased, as were most dreams, by the light of dawn, but rather lingered in the swirling fog that bathed their *kaawa* as they squatted together, eating their root pancakes and handfuls of dried cashews. Oji whistled as he collected his darts and rolled some of the pancakes in dried leaves, and when it came time for him to leave with his hunting group, he embraced each of his parents in turn, keeping his hand on his father's arm as he stood to face his mother's usual litany of admonitions and orders. When he left, and Iri had gone off gathering with his own group, which now consisted of sons who were three rains younger than he was, Larry squatted beside Aran at the side of their hut, grinding her pigments while she mixed them with the oils. As he turned the *maata* with his palm, he was surprised to find that his hand was moving in time to *"I've Been Working on the Railroad,"* as it had long ago, when his only other job had been to cradle the infant Aran. Still under the spell of the night before, his reunion with that old song from childhood only deepened his sense that the scattered and half-buried shards inside him had revealed themselves as the pieces of a puzzle which, if only they could be turned and positioned just so, might someday fit together into a whole.

"Do you want to hear about my ancestors?" he said suddenly to Aran, surprising himself as much as her.

"You want to sing of them?" she said, confused as to why he felt the need to ask.

"No, I just want to say them," he said, putting down the *maata* and disappearing into the hut. When he came back, he had a stack of books in his hands, which he placed gently in a pile on a stump.

"You're going to lay them out already?" said Aran. "The ground is still wet from the fog."

"No, I just want to say them to you," Larry repeated, lifting the first one from the top of the pile and opening its cover. The sudden sense he felt of impending danger made him pause for a minute, and then impelled him on. "All these people were hunters," he said, grasping for words in Pahquel that could capture the slightest essence of what he meant. "They were hunters, but not of animals. Of worlds. Of worlds they'd never been to." He started to falter, and turned to his pile. "You see, this one, it tells the story of a man who travels across the world to find a new home. He ends up in a place called Italy, which his line will someday come to rule." She looked at him, confused, frowning pointedly when he spoke of the outsider who becomes a chief. He put the book down and turned to another. "This one, it's about this boy who teams up with a runaway captured person and they jump on a raft like our gathering boat and find out about the world." He looked at her for recognition, but finding only confusion, put the book down. "This one," he continued on, now with a tremor of uncertainty in his voice, "is about these persons, called Hobbits, who must capture this ring"—he used the English word, wrapping a finger of one hand around the ring finger of the other—"and take away its strength, and this one," he said, laying Tolkein atop the pile, "is about a person named Henry Walter Bates who walks through the forest and tells stories about all the animals and plants." She nodded at that one, a gesture of approval that seemed to diminish, for a moment, the growing expression of concern he had begun to sense in her.

"Only living things tell stories," she said at last. "Only persons, or animals, or ancestors, or plants."

"Yes," said Larry, suddenly desperate for her comprehension. Then he had an idea. "These are my *chajans*," he said, drawing symbols on the ground with his finger.

"They're too weak to be *chajans*," she said, reaching up to touch one, pulling on a page. "They're leaves, not trunks."

"Where I was born, they last forever," said Larry, increasingly frightened. "Hands and feet of hands and feet." He turned, his posture one of supplication now, and picked up the dearest of his companions, his friend Van Gogh. "Listen," he said, and began to read, stumbling over the effort to squeeze the English words into Pahqua. This is my favorite: "Well, even in that deep misery I felt my energy revive, and I said to myself: in spite of everything I shall rise again, I will take up my pencil (my brushes), which I have forsaken in great discouragement, and I will go on with my drawing, and from that moment everything has seemed transformed for me." He looked at her, a question, and then flipped through the pages and went on: "This person was a painter too. Listen: When the grass is fresh, it is a rich green, the like of which we seldom see in the North (the *jacu*, he said), quiet. When it gets scorched and dusty, it does not lose its beauty *(tuara)*, but then the landscape gets tones of gold of various tints . . . . And this combined with the blue—from the deepest royal blue of the water to the blue of . . . the bluest flowers . . . ."

She looked at him in silence for several minutes, studying his face, unmoving. Only the wind toyed with wisps of her hair, fingering them gently, and then leaving them as they were.

"*Um?*" said Larry quietly at last, over the din of his heart in his ears.

"*Mboa,*" she said, coming to crouch beside him, understanding at least that she was grass.

CXXVI

WITHOUT ITS OVERSTUFFED sofas and its imposing buffets with their
settings for twenty-four and its pedestals set at odd angles, exhibiting rep-
licas in marble of the highlights of the high Renaissance, the Senor's house
began to breathe again, its lungs expanding and stretching, its exhalations
pushing the walls outward. As they walked through the echoing rooms
taking stock of what was left after the permanent residents of Paruqu had
no doubt stripped it, the broken furniture and piles of paper, the rusted
old desk and the shadows of pictures on the walls, Jorge and Martina acted
as if each was so preoccupied by the act of looking that neither noticed the
presence of the other. Jorge picked up a sack of rags carefully and shook
it, and Martina pulled at the drawers of a wooden dresser, rifling through
reams of used carbon paper. They came across stacks of empty file folders,
and cheaply bound books that smelled strongly of mildew and old clothes
and cartons of government documents, blank forms and completed ones,
some of which had already sheltered a few generations of mice. They
moved from one end to the other through the wing of offices and guest
rooms, whose hallway murals were even more triumphant than before, no
doubt at their perseverance. And then at the landing beside the back stair-
well, Jorge gave a shout and they all ran to surround him, Martina from
down the hall and Joaquim from downstairs, followed by Sam.

Jorge picked up the familiar travel bag and held it out at arm's length,
afraid to see what was in it, and what was no longer there. He pulled out
its contents gently, as though their preciousness at that moment had made
them suddenly fragile. Martina took the folders as Jorge handed them over

and laid them out along the wall, together with his clipboards, and a razor in a pouch, and a compass, and a bottle of half-disintegrated antacid tablets. At last, with trembling hands, he pulled out the envelope Larry had given him and turned it over. It had been unsealed, but the paper in Larry's hand was still inside it on which two numbers were written faintly in pencil. He handed the paper to Joaquim. "That's yours," he said, turning back to survey his possessions. "I think there's a folder missing, with the locations and dates of runs.

"Does it look like this?" said Joaquim, holding it up.

"That's it!" said Jorge, reaching for it.

"It's double-or-nothing day, I guess," said Joaquim, holding up a scrap of paper. "Found in Sodeis's bedroll." They all leaned in at once to see what was on it and in the process, Jorge could feel Martina's shoulder pushing against his and didn't step away. Joaquim pulled the bit of paper from Larry's envelope and they stood, comparing the numbers, which looked strangely foreign in Sodeis's flowery hand.

CXXVII

WHEN DABIMI'S *KAAG* breathed her last, slumping suddenly over her grinding stone one morning as she sat gossiping and singing with her two sisters from the far village, it was two days before Dabimi heard the news. It was common knowledge that he often stayed away at night, and no one was surprised that it was left to his children to decide on their own with which of the dried plants from Kakap Ak's stores she should be filled for burning, and when the burning would be. When Dabimi was intercepted by Kakap and Panar on his way to his hut on the second evening, Aran was already finishing, having painted the *kaag*'s transformation into the torso of their *chajan*, stooping slightly to put her work at eye-level. At the news, Dabimi hung his head, allowing it to droop just as the *kaag*'s had, like the falling of an overfilled gourd. But despite his distress, he stopped to stand beside Aran while she laquered the colors, leaning over to speak to her quietly before he turned and began to wail. Kakap and Panar came to squat beside him, and suddenly the entire village burst out, as though it had been waiting. Between swells, Kakap and Panar each spoke to Dabimi in turn about the particular plants that had been chosen, some from his line and some from hers, some to take away pain and others to teach her what she would need to know to take her place among the ancestors. The choices were of the utmost importance, for they would determine the course of her life outside of time and the world, but Dabimi seemed somehow impatient with the discussion, waving them off and moving instead to sit among his children and his *kaag*'s sisters, whose wailing was more heartfelt and filled in the voids in his own.

"He told me it's his right to claim a first *kaag*," Aran whispered to Larry after the boys were asleep. She was trembling in his arms, and her tears fell on his chest. "But that's not true. She was his first *kaag*, even though she died. I will never go to him. He has no claim on me. He has no claim," she cried again and again, in a hushed voice despite that she would never have been heard above the wailing that echoed from one end of the village to the other.

When she had quieted, he said, "Do you want me to go to Kakap and ask him? I can do it now or in the morning. He may still be at Dabimi's. I can go now and look for him." He lit a torch from the fire on their *kaawa* and began to head up the path toward Dabimi's house, but met both of the old Aks coming toward him before he had taken even a hands and feet of steps. In a hushed voice, he called them over and drew them into the hut, feeling already unsettled as he observed Kakap's unsteady gait and Panar's pronounced hunch as they came forward.

"He has no claim," hissed Aran, repeating herself so insistently that they had to quiet her before they could respond.

"Of course he has no claim," Kakap said first. "He has already had a first *kaag*. And besides that, aren't you *akarara*?" No longer able to bear children, which would render her unsuitable as a first *kaag* in any case.

She hung her head as she nodded, turning her face from Larry. He put his arm around her and drew her to him.

"He spoke so strangely," said Aran finally, turning to look at him.

"Many voices come out of a forsaken person," said Panar, standing up as best he could inside their small hut. At the door, he held both their arms for a minute. Kakap gave Larry a playful pinch on the shoulder as he squeezed past them onto their *kaawa*.

"And the other thing," said Aran as they turned to go, "is that he smelled bad. Not like a person," she added.

CXXVIII

JORGE WOULD NEVER have admitted it, but his anxiety tended to rise in direct proportion to the distance from his plane. As he went down the sloping path to retrieve Martina from the gathering of women working the clay, he remembered his previous encounter with her there and felt a sudden wave of shame, which was amplified by his distance from the Beaver's controls. At the moment, he wasn't so much embarrassed because of his prior outburst, however, but because the outburst at least implied a familiarity to which he could no longer lay claim. He was relieved to find her with a smaller group this time, which lessened slightly his sense of being observed.

"I think we're ready," he said, standing over Martina and the Indian women as they rolled.

"Can you talk to them?" said Martina.

"What do you want me to say?" said Jorge, his anxiety flaring at the prospect of a delay.

"Ask them where the other women are," said Martina.

Jorge asked in Ge, and drew his mouth and nose into a tight knot as he listened to the answer.

"She said two died, and the rest are sick," he said. "I'll give them our sympathy," he said, and did.

"What's their sickness?"

Jorge asked, and then translated for Martina, addressing her knees.

"They said it's falling sickness, that it's come to their village before. They seem to think it's not a white man's disease. Only Indians get it."

Martina held their forearms for what felt like minutes as she took leave of them, and followed slowly behind Jorge as he headed up the hill. When she reached the verandah, she motioned to Sam and to Joaquim. Jorge stood behind them pretending not to listen, playing with his pack.

"I think we should do bloods," said Martina to Sam. "I don't remember how many of them were there last time, but I'd guess ten or more. Now there are four. They say they have falling sickness. I don't know what that is, but we should track it."

"I have some guesses," said Sam, unlacing one of the boxes to look for his kits.

"They're not going to tolerate your just walking up and sticking them with needles," said Joaquim to Sam, putting a hand on his shoulder to slow him down. "I know you haven't been in the field before, but one thing you're going to learn is that taking blood is a threatening prospect."

"Let's you and I go and talk to them first," said Martina, walking over and pulling Jorge along with her by the arm. "Maybe we can explain it to them. Tell them we have a doctor with us who figures out illnesses."

"They have their own doctors," said Jorge.

"Don't forget the mission," said Joaquim. "That's where these Indians show up when they're ill. Catalpa liked to think that it was his diplomacy that was responsible for his good name with them, but the mission was here at least ten years before he was, and it's been relatively good to them. Also, the missionaries vaccinated, and they know how many of their trading partners got smallpox, while they stayed healthy. These Indians trust us at least to a point, and they trust the mission even more."

"Let's try this first," said Martina, pulling Jorge along.

Jorge glanced at Joaquim who shrugged. He hesitated for a minute and then turned to follow behind Martina with his head hanging, a chastened, obedient child. As he walked, he whispered under his breath: "Falling sickness," feeling the resonance of the phrase.

CXXIX

SINCE KAKAP COULD no longer shoulder the yoke or walk for long without resting, he gave Larry the choice of either going without him to gather, or of their going out together on one of the narrow, painted rafts that were used to bring in the *chajan* logs and the pirarucu from upstream. Long stretches of the river were nearly impassable even after the rains, and as neither of them was skilled at oars, Pitar, Kakap's middle son, was recruited as an oarsman, although the arrangement delayed his bid to undertake a *ritaXa*, the type of solitary retreat that prepared men for higher status. Larry hadn't expected Dabimi to approve their plan, which took Pitar from his hunting group and placed a greater pressure on his line, but when Kakap returned from Dabimi's hut, he could tell by the slant of his head that the meeting had gone well. Despite the likelihood that Dabimi had been pleased most of all by the postponement of Pitar's claim to a *ritaXa*, Pitar was eager to row, and spent his mornings on the river, learning from Sari and Xitot. On the day he returned from his first trip as a full-fledged oarsman, he strutted around the hut with an unselfconscious delight that reminded Larry of Oji, even though Oji was younger by five rains, and that Pitar was a grown man with a child. In his exuberance, he persuaded them to start within a hand of days, and threw himself into preparing and nagged his father to compile the song that listed the plants to be gathered.

They set off at dawn, when the chill was still sharp in the air, and the water could do nothing to warm them. The riverbed overflowed with rocks and grit, so that the raft had to be hauled for long stretches on its runners with their yokes and their hammocks tied to it. The hauling vines wore symmetrical red medallions into their collarbones, and fish bit at their ankles as they pulled the raft from the water. The mosquitoes were as dense as the air, and the mud was thick with half-buried stingrays, and caimans trolled for fish with their huge mouths gaping, so that conversation was often interrupted by the sickening snap of jaws. The sliver of sun was as sharp as its reflection, and the rocks were as sharp as the sun, and the waters were so thick with piranha that they had to haul Kakap onto the raft despite his protests and requests for a turn to pull. At those times, Larry tried to grasp the memory of James's voice preaching the blessings of Pahquel's nearly unnavigable river, which fed and protected them at once. He leaned into the vines and his legs shook with the strain, and sometimes after he and Pitar had maneuvered the raft onto level ground, they collapsed, panting, on top of it, pressing themselves into Kakap from either side. It would seem hopeless, and Kakap would declare, without accusation or self-pity, his intention to be left behind, and the weight of the impending loss of him would combine with the weight of the raft to leave them nearly paralyzed in the web of pulling vines.

Then, as they threw themselves forward, the rocks would suddenly give way and the raft would slide without effort through fine sand and clear water, leaving barely a ripple behind. They would enter a world without friction in which they floated weightless, untethered in time. Larry called himself Huckleberry Finn, and waved to the inhabitants of the shore—caimans that sunned themselves with their chins half-buried in the sand, and kingfishers, tentative and careful, and monkeys with serious white faces who turned their heads slowly to watch them as they passed. They would glide through clouds of iridescent butterflies whose reflections swam among tetras of the same shimmering purple-blue, and at evening, they were brushed by the slipstreams of egrets flying upriver toward the moon. They lay on their backs in the raft in slow-moving water and looked up through the thin, jagged deep blue seam that formed a part between the trees, across which toucans darted, and bats swarmed and wheeled. They beached the raft on slivers of sand barely wide enough to hold it, and ate their rolls of pancake and dried fish by the fire, and chewed on nuts and fruit from the baskets while Kakap sang to the plants, a familiar, soothing song that called on them to appear.

Over time, they grew more skilled at managing the raft, and memorized the riverbed, even in its changes, so that each three-day trip took them further than the last. Soon, they were able to go beyond where they had gone on foot, to the edge of the world, where even Kakap had never been. They learned which slips of sand afforded them easy entry, and marked out the paths with betel dye, and returned to the raft with their gourds overflowing, to the point that they could barely be sealed with the wax. Kakap mentioned, from time to time, his failing eyesight, but he could still discern from a great distance the distinctive hunch of the Karapta Cacao, which, bent and laden, he resembled, and the Laratir, which he greeted with a cry of joy, and cradled in his arms like a baby. Back at the raft, he placed it into its basket with great tenderness, as though he were putting it to bed. In fact, more and more, Kakap seemed to regard the trips as reunions with his plants. He would speak more often to them than to his own son, and seemed to have forgotten that Larry still needed teaching. Gradually, he became so lost in his songs, so oblivious to Larry and to Pitar, that they moved their attention for the first time from him to each other, and spent their days talking, about the living now more often than the dead. On the river, their conversations flowed freely, protected by a tacit agreement that their words would be left on the water. Indeed, in the village, they barely spoke, and acknowledged each other with a nod or at most a sly smile. On the boat, they poured out gossip, and talked about their children, and even made fun of Dabimi, sharing the risk between them. They spoke of Kakap in front of him, and then, all at once, were overcome and couldn't speak, and trailed their oars in the river, cutting parallel wakes.

One day, Kakap spotted an odd brown fungus growing at the base of a tree, and let out an overjoyed yelp as his eyes welled over with tears. It was Saptir, he sang, the great easer of pain. He hadn't seen it since he had gathered with his father, whose suffering it had soothed. He held it up with great excitement to show Larry and Pitar, but without looking at them, as though speaking only to his memories. Then he turned suddenly and set off toward the boat. They followed him in silence, feeling a chill spread up their arms. They emerged from the forest to find a thick wind blowing from the *jacu* direction, churning the water and jangling the gourds on their yokes. Then the rain came, rushing toward them, hurled on by the fury of the wind. They huddled behind a fallen log and clung to each other while the water pelted the shore and the gourds smashed against each other, their taut cords straining, and the raft shook, threatening to succumb. Then the thrashing grey curtain of the storm was yanked aside with a violent snap to reveal an unfamiliar landscape, quiet and still, strewn with branches and rocks. The water was as dark and as smooth as slate, in which a few dead fish were embedded like fossils. The forest was eerily silent. They ran to the raft and embraced it and, mindful of their bruises, soothed the gourds as they retied them. They pushed off and the raft groaned as it entered the river, still uncertain after its ordeal, nursing the stiffness in its joints.

After even the one rain, the boat rode higher in the water, so that the silence was less often rasped by the sound of wood on stone. Larry and Pitar squatted back-to-back across the rear of the platform while Kakap lay face-up at the center, resting his head on the tether-post while the gourds knocked together gently above him. Now and again, he would begin the song of Saptir in a muted, trembling voice and then break off, as though he had forgotten all but the first two lines. Saptir squeezed the molars of animals and persons, he sang, and the pain dripped out from their gums. "The pain dripped out, the pain dripped out . . ." and then silence, the whisper of water at the boat. Soon there was no song at all, and the boat became a cradle bearing them toward and away from the only place on earth that was their home. It jostled Kakap slightly as it was carried by the current, and only slightly more as it was hefted on its runners by Larry and Pitar over rocks and broken branches and set down. Kakap seemed not to notice where they were, and barely moved with the motion of the boat. Only the faintest, irregular quiver of his chest hinted that he was still alive.

Larry knew that the poet Virgil had spent his last years in exile, and had only been persuaded to return to the bosom of Augustus Caesar when he was so feeble that he could no longer walk the twenty paces from the top of the gang-plank to the sheltered cot that had been laid out for him like a velvet cradle in the hold. He lay in state, half-swallowed by the damask spreads and the pillows, beyond the reach of noise and quiet, oblivious to the attendants who tiptoed in and out not daring to look his way for fear the very light from their eyes would tax him beyond his strength. His body was inert, the one still point amidst a flotilla of great and small craft that rocked and bobbed in the gleaming harbor at Brundisium, and his head teemed with all that he had seen, the spires and the light-drenched blue of the sky and the relentless clustering of words into phrases, and phrases into songs without words. Larry knew this and couldn't stop knowing it no matter how hard he tried. After so many years in Pahquel, he still could not help but turn, when he was overcome, to the stories and the images from the books that had befriended him when he had been in greatest need and now that fact served to draw Kakap even farther from him into the embrace of strangers. He longed to tell him that he knew the last, fire-hungry loneliness of Virgil, that he had been intimate with him through the death of James, but Kakap's own last hours were anything but lonely, though he had slipped beyond the grasp of speech. When they arrived at the inlet downriver from the village where the boats were kept, Larry and Pitar lifted the runners and tied the vines around their shoulders. They carried Kakap down the narrow path as though on a litter to his hut, and set the boat down gently at the threshold of his *kaawa*. The setting sun glowed in the lacquer on the *chajan*, and the light from the fire drew out the colors that Anok had buried there, framing Kakap in what could have been, through Larry's blurred eyes, a brocade of crimson and brown, rimmed on one side by a golden cord.

CXXX

LIKE THE KOYRARE upriver, the Indians in Paruqu still insisted on sending the bodies of their dead on their way toward Xipiti in the arms of the water. They rowed them to the juncture downstream where the Paruqu empties into the bolder Arraroyo, placing their stone necklaces on them tenderly, releasing them into the infinity of currents for the piranha to clean and transport. For this, the Padres at the mission begrudged them, but restrained themselves from retaliating, choosing instead to create a compromise involving the farce of erecting wooden crosses over empty graves. Thus, despite the presence, on a bluff that was visible from the attic of the prefect's former house, of what looked like a tidy graveyard of recently whitewashed crosses, there was no hope of unearthing answers by exhuming the bodies of the dead.

Other sorts of bodies however, other hatreds, other tensions and terrors and regrets were easily disturbed by any misstep, any overturning of dirt. As Martina and Jorge crouched in the dark stench of a dying woman's hut, fumbling with the words that might allow them to defile her last hours with the assault of a needle stick, the added violation of a blade against hair, they were aware of the disaster a misstep could cause, of how quickly what they said could be turned around to mean the opposite of what they meant.

"Her spirit has already been chosen," her daughter whispered to them, "to inhabit my brother's first boy. That's not how it usually goes; the woman's spirit must be very strong to go to a boy. The news has eased her last hours."

"I'm happy for her," said Martina through Jorge, reaching for the daughter's forearm. After a long pause, she added, "But then that makes helping her blood even more important. The falling sickness must not be passed to the boy." If Martina's voice betrayed her duplicitousness, she couldn't detect it in Jorge's translation.

"Will it hurt her?"

"No. We'll do it very fast."

The daughter turned to talk to her brother and his wife in low, muffled voices.

"You can," she said when she turned back.

Martina stuck her head outside the hut, motioning to Sam. She stepped out to make room for him to enter. Standing outside the door, she could hear the muffled voices of Sam and Jorge explaining how the needle worked, and showing them the bag for the hair. There was a sudden high-pitched gurgle, followed by silence. Martina suddenly panicked that the shock of the needle had killed the old woman. To take a life, especially a life at its end, was a spirit-murder, an unforgivable crime that promised retribution. She stuck her head in the hut, and saw the daughter leaning over the mother, ear to her mouth, assessing her breath. The mother coughed and the daughter stepped back, sighing in relief. It was not the drawing of blood that was to carry her off, but the moon, who came in broad daylight to retrieve her.

CXXXI

ALTHOUGH MANY PROSPECTORS hired Indians to do their advance work for them, Sodeis always did his own. In fact, that was the part he liked best, allowing himself to get lost and then find his way again, often into new and lucrative situations. He had come across the largest unincorporated stand of cumaru on record just by waking up one day, putting on his boots and setting out, guided only by the compass of his own intuition. As he cleared the left fork of the Juruena, past the border of Nambikwara territory, he had felt that familiar sense of elation that always signified internal True North, a tremor on the water, or in the heat-rippled air. For a man with no home, that was as close as he ever got to a sense of having arrived. At those moments, his euphoria was marred only by the futility of the urge to tell someone, to share his accomplishment with one of the specters who always sat in judgment in the back of his mind, his father, or Diego Melo, or lately, to his irritation, Joaquim Rocha.

In the tiny tattered notebook he drew from a plastic case in his back pocket and held before him was a list of the leads he had gathered in his thirty-year career, thirty two pages in all, with twenty lines to a page. Of the more than six hundred entries, perhaps forty were still alive; a full two-thirds had been undermined by the procurement of negative certificates by others for a price or a return of favor, thirty or more had proven to be nothing more than fantasy or rumor, and fifty were unworkable due to the violence of nature or of *indios bravos*, who would take too much effort to pacify. Of those that were left, some were reports by *seringais* who were more concerned with protecting their stands of rubber from

Indian incursion than they were with liquidating hardwoods, some were based on information from nut-trappers or miners or SPI, many of whom would sell what they knew, if they didn't intend to use it themselves, for an avoidable cut of the profits. There were leads gathered from administrators like Catalpa (though it still irked him that he had acquired not a single line from the Senor), and from road workers, and from *vaqueiros*, and there was a whole sheaf of leads he had copied from the clipboard he had found among Jorge's papers. And then there were the two penciled numbers on a scrap of paper in an envelope in the same pouch, whose very ephemerality had rendered them most intriguing, as though a message in invisible ink were being held to the candle of his need, slowly releasing some forbidden revelation from the delicate obscurity of a crumpled quarter-page of onion skin.

CXXXII

SILVIO PUT HIS head on his desk and kept it there. Maria knew better than to comfort him. Instead, she brought a cup of coffee and silently placed it on the desk off to the side. When the phone rang, he nearly knocked it to the floor jumping up. *"Alo?"* he shouted into the receiver, rubbing his face vigorously, as though he were buffing a chassis. "Lima? Lima?" he shouted. The line went dead. Silvio slammed the phone onto its cradle, and then dropped his head onto the desk again with almost as much force.

"Better for us to do our homework first, anyway, before we talk to him," he said at last, lifting his head halfway off the desk, looking up at her at an angle. "Go get me everything you have." Maria disappeared and returned with a stack of files. She sat across from him and dealt them out into two stacks, a doomed hand for each of them.

"What do you want to see first?" she said as she dealt.

"I want to see twenty years ago," said Silvio. "I want to see Paris."

"SPI or other?"

"SPI. SPI. These are my men. But no more. From now on, I'm sending no one nowhere." He picked up a file and opened it. "Don't wait for me," he said, gesturing to the piles. "Dive right in yourself! Pull out anything involving one of ours and put it over there."

Five years, it turned out, was longer in retrospect than it had been the first time around. One or two denunciations a month had accrued behind his back into more than a hundred, ninety-five of which he didn't have enough men even to investigate, let alone resolve. Nearly all had been reported by Maria to the Federales of the relevant Divisional Areas, whose officers had no doubt filed them under O, for oblivion. That was how it went, he knew, having harbored, all this time, his own personal version of that unknowing limbo, a nether world that floated behind a curtain on which was emblazoned, on the one side, his father's face, and on the other, lifted straight from a faded newspaper clipping, the face of Joaquim. Taken individually, the stories had been tiny splotches, drops of blood that should have been quickly wiped away so that the painstaking work of contact, of planning, of gathering information, could go on. Taken together, now for the first time, the drops formed a river, an alphabet of infamy that spilled, with increasing intensity, across his desk: for the sin of administering Alcohol; for the sin of Burying Indians alive; for the sin of Child abduction; for the sin of Dismemberment; for the sin of throwing Explosives into villages from planes; for the sin of Fingernail extraction; for the sin of contaminated Gifts; for the sin of public Hangings; for the sin of toxic Injections; for the sin of abuses by Jesuits; for the sin of chaining Lepers to posts; for the sin of leaching Mercury; for the sins of Near and Outright starvation; for the sin of Poisoning sugar; for the sin of necessitating Quilombas, fugitive slave settlements; for the sin of Relocation by force; for the sin of Slavery, for the sin of Throwing Indians from cliffs; for the sin of Usurious financial arrangements; for the sin of spreading Venereal diseases; for the sin of Xenophobia; for the sin of the Zeal of a whole generation for torture for torture's sake. For all these sins, Silvio understood, there was no forgiveness and only a single possible response. He waved Maria away with one hand while, with the other, he stretched out his fist toward the phone.

CXXXIII

THE MAKESHIFT TAVERNS that sprang up around logging camps, upstream from mines, and sometimes even on the private property of the more benign or clever of the *latifundios,* who were clearing large tracts and thus had many hands to entertain, had always been places where Sodeis felt at home. It was that thing about being with people who were more drunk than he was that allowed him to relax. And he always found those establishments to be the most reliable sources of labor, if what you were looking for were men with expendable futures.

Also, you didn't enter them by doorways; rather, they were open structures, accessible from all sides, allowing him to slip in and out of them with ease, and to survey their inhabitants before making himself known. As Sodeis circumnavigated the bar at Yanarata to be sure he didn't recognize the clientele, he resolved to himself to give up on the mining interests altogether, which had always only brought him grief, as complicated as they were to administer, and to focus his efforts only on rare hardwoods, a resource that was unique to Amazonia, he reasoned, and thus was sure to retain its value regardless of what the world markets were up to.

At least that was the philosophy he espoused, loudly, to the three men whose table he came up to join, directly after overhearing that their contract with Findosino was almost up. The plan took shape as he described it to them: On the one hand, there was the possibility of brokering, which he could always pursue on the side. He had some leads, having heard about a few foremen who were experiencing problems with tribes and would find a smooth negotiator to be of use, especially one who was fluent in a dozen (a slight exaggeration) Indian tongues. Then, there were the situations in which a high bid could be undercut by a team of experienced loggers, "like us," he added, eyeing his companions, who generally needed to offer tribes merely a fraction of what their timber was worth, leaving a large margin for profit. And then there was the scouting, the prospecting for fine stands of hardwood in proximity to rivers to which they could stake an original claim.

"I'm asking your advice, gentlemen—since I'm relatively new to the area, and don't know how things are done here—as to whether you might know of some adventurous types who are out of work, men who own their own tools and gear. Don't suppose you know anybody like that."

"If you've got the contracts, I've got the men," said the tallest one, who was obviously also the smartest of the three. "There's a whole gang of us who are just about to finish up here in a week or two."

"Now that's fortunate," said Sodeis. "Because I just brokered a contract that's due to start around then." He rehearsed the faintly etched coordinates in his head as he reached for his cigarette case, but then thought better of bringing it out. He prided himself on his ability to gauge just how superior in social status he needed to appear in order to impress without crossing the line and stirring up problematic levels of resentment. He looked from face to face and suppressed a shudder. They were all coarse specimens, reeking of month-old sweat, and missing a clear majority of teeth. "So what are you up for?' he asked. "I know a man named Duarte Ochoa," he started to say, but then realized the man in question was SPI. While fleeing from Paruqu, he'd resolved to stay away from SPI for a while, to let his trail dry out. Meanwhile, the whisper of those two numbers distracted him, and he realized in an instant that that was where his intuition beckoned. "If I were to go out on my own, ahead, until you're ready, and set everything up, and wait for you, would you all be able to follow me in? Even if the trek is long and hard?"

The tall one looked to his fellows on the right and then left, and nodded a collective assent. "But we're API," he said. "They've got the plane, the generator, the whole kit."

"And what if you went for a little freelance venture, if they didn't have anything else for you for a while? What if you took a weekend, just on a lark, to make some extra money borrowing their kit?"

"That would depend on whether it was worth it," said Tall, looking deep into his glass, straining to see the few drops in the pit of it. Sodeis responded on cue, with a round for the three of them. "We'd be risking our contract. They do track us, you know."

"And as for pay, what are you getting now?" This was the part of the negotiation Sodeis strongly preferred to undertake with a pistol resting on his thigh, and suddenly felt exposed at the prospect of closing a deal without one.

"We're getting two hundred *cruzeros* a week," said the short one with the walleye, jumping a bit as he spoke. Clearly, Tall had kicked him under the table. "You're only getting two hundred? Why I'm getting two fifty . . . no, now it's three hundred! Findosino raised us last week, right? I think he has some other jobs for us, too!"

"Okay, then we'll make it six hundred for you and five for each of your men," said Sodeis. He had enough understanding of the economic outlook to see that inflation was accelerating like a boulder down a mountain, and that whatever deal he struck, it would be worth half again as much to him in no time. Anyone without at least a rudimentary mathematical aptitude was ripe to be played for a fool; he doubted that any of his companions could even count the zeros on the notes they passed back and forth between them, or could know whether they were making three hundred *cruaieros* or three hundred thousand. But in any case, the issue for him was never the money; in fact, there was quite a sum invested in gold overseas on his behalf through the Intercontinental Bank & Trust in Rio, of which he rarely skimmed the surface to fund even his more capital-intensive ventures. He would have been hard pressed to say what, exactly, the issue was. It had something to do with getting something away from somebody else, of winning at a game in which his gain was the loss of someone in particular, someone with a name and a face. It was a sense of vindication he sought, some capacity to prove himself capable of progress and even triumph despite those who would stand in his way, to prove his competence in the face of his obvious capacity to ruin things. It was the thing that made him willing to gamble on two numbers which, due to the very secrecy that veiled them, suddenly revealed themselves as the winning numbers in a lottery his gut commanded him to play.

Sodeis bought another round for all of them and drew out a map for Tall, scrawling the coordinates on one of his cards. He paid them each something up front, peeling the bills from the thinner of the rolls in his pocket, and repeated all their names, and shook hands indiscriminately, largely in commemoration of his fourth *cachaca* of the evening, and put his arm around a few, as though to take them into confidence and elicit their observations of the others. Then, without saying goodbye, he disappeared into the night.

CXXXIV

OF THE FOUR in their small party, only Joaquim appeared to bloom as the forest embraced them. Jorge seemed to grow more bitter with each step, clenching his face into a knot too tight to untie. Martina bore up stoically, the slight forward tilt of her body the only clue to her exertion. Sam, meanwhile, puffed behind them, stopping to set down his pack and his bags of specimen cups, jumping away when he saw movement out of the corner of his eye, reapplying his mosquito repellent hourly, complaining loudly that if he knew what he was getting into, he never would have come. At the head of the line, Joaquim disregarded him, utterly involved as he was in pointing out aspects of the forest with the ardor of a lover: Here clusters of sac-winged bats lined the buttresses of Kapoks, there was the spoor of the capybara, or the sublime Epidendrum, miraculously growing from bare rock, or an endless array of anoles, with their invisible tails and garish dewlaps, betraying their whereabouts with thrashing bursts as they scampered over twigs and half-damp leaves.

When the group stopped for lunch, Martina pulled Joaquim aside when they went off to hunt for firewood.

"You need to stop talking about lizards," she whispered to him while she kicked at a fallen branch. "You're going to make him sick."

"Didn't the American president say, 'If you can't stand the heat, get out of the forest?'" said Joaquim, pointing to a tiny grey anole on the tree trunk beside him. "Didn't another one say, 'There's nothing to fear but fear itself?'"

"Why are you throwing clichés at me? I'm trying to talk to you!"

Joaquim turned to face her.

"What are you trying to do to him? You know all about him and lizards."

"I suppose I do," he said slowly. "I suppose I'm trying to keep him going. I suppose I want to get him over it. He's like a woman, standing on a chair because of a mouse. He lives his life that way. How could I stand by and want that for him?"

"Like a woman?"

Joaquim laughed. "Like not a man."

Martina searched his face for fault lines, for scars, but she already knew where they were. "That American president understood you just fine," she said, still studying his expression. "There's no one more afraid of fear than you." The corner of his mouth betrayed a smile as camouflaged as an anole on a tree trunk. "You even sacrificed Larry to that fear, and now you're doing everything you can so you don't have to be afraid that he's dead, and that it's your fault."

The smile tightened and widened, as an anole betrays itself through movement. "I was right about you," he said, "but I also see why Jorge can't face you."

"Maybe we both pull our tricks from the same bag," said Martina as she turned and headed back to the others. He came up beside her and drew her closer by the elbow.

"No firewood?" said Jorge bitterly as they approached him.

"None at all," said Joaquim, smiling. "Since the menu for today's lunch is just nuts and fine imported chocolate, we realized there was no need for it." He drew from his pack a bag containing the foil-wrapped bars he'd found in tins in Catalpa's pantry and handed one to each of them with a dramatic flourish. The chocolate in the foil had melted, which didn't stop any of them from licking it off the wrappers. "I think we should press on a bit before we make any elaborate stops. We have a good two hours of hiking time ahead of us." Sam groaned. Martina shouldered her pack and then reached for the specimen bags. "My turn," she said.

Joaquim led the way, with Jorge behind him.

"It's been a long time since you've been in the field, I know," said Joaquim, hanging back, drawing closer to Jorge, who cringed as he came near.

"This is of a much different order than our jog in Lamurii." Jorge eyed him suspiciously and withdrew further into the isolation of those who cannot trust the ones they love. They walked on in silence, with Joaquim in the lead, but obliquely, so that Jorge could see his profile. In a soft voice, Joaquim pointed out orchids, and mountainous anthills, and the gossamer webs of spiders, but he made no mention of reptiles of any kind. "There's more here than any of us will ever live to know about," he said softly, "which is why I give my life to it." Behind the echo of his words, there was an echo even softer and more distant—that of Marietto walking beside a pale, cautious, impossibly thin little boy who had to skip to keep up with him. Suddenly, they were no longer colleagues, older and younger, with decades of respect and resentment between them; rather, they were a father and son, the one reaching, as he had never been able to do with his own children, to love the other by offering to him the world, while the other took up the gift in both hands, entranced and oppressed by his having been entrusted with it. "It's a matter of scale, Jorge," his father had said. "In the forest, there are monkeys that are smaller than spiders!" His father held his hand, subtly guiding him with it through a continuous series of small pushes and pulls. "Here, what's big is small and what's small is big!"

With the sound of his father's voice in his head for the first time in twenty years, Jorge found himself suddenly, unwittingly gulping down sobs, and choking on the waves of shame that came up behind them. Joaquim held back further until they were walking side by side. Jorge lay his head on Joaquim's shoulder and they bumped along like that, squeezing together through the forest's thin doorways and over its uneven floor, for half an hour before Joaquim stopped as they came up together before a wide clearing, a basin that swirled with the glow of sunset, a wind-blown, limitless sea.

"We'll park here for the night," said Joaquim, lowering his pack. He pulled Jorge to him one last time, and then held him at arm's length to address him. "Now we really do need firewood," he said.

CXXXV

KAKAP DIDN'T DIE either on that night or the next. Instead, he took the draught Panar had blended from the *Saptir* and the *Laratir* and sat up two days later on his sleeping ledge during the height of an afternoon storm. At first, Pitar, whose back was turned, didn't hear him stirring, and went on puttering with the bowls and the *maawas*, halfheartedly sorting them out into the baskets, but then Kakap called his name and he jumped as though he'd been struck. He seemed at first not to know where the voice had come from, but suddenly he realized and twisted around so quickly that his neck cracked. He ran to the ledge and squatted at his father's side, pushing his face into the skins that had been spread over him against the damp and the old-man's chill. Kakap dug in the skins and dredged up his son's head in his web of fingers, drawing it above the surface slowly as though it were a fish in a net, but without the strength to pull it from the water. Pitar straightened on his own and looked into his father's eyes, and his father looked back at him, seeming to see him, even in the semi-darkness, for the first time in a hand of moons. Larry watched the scene from the back corner of the hut, not daring to breathe or move. He pushed the fingers of his right hand into his left wrist and a current of fear he couldn't afford to be aware of moved around and around the loop of his arms and shoulders and chest.

"So when is your *ritaX*?" Kakap asked suddenly, in a voice of mock reproach.

"I couldn't think about that now," said Pitar, sounding confused, knowing he was being tested, but not what the right answer was.

"It's time. You need to arrange it," said Kakap, as though finishing a sentence he had started at that moment instead of moons before. "Bring Dabimi here, if he's even in the village, and we'll do it now." He made a motion to push Pitar away and Pitar stood up and hesitantly took a step towards the door.

"Pitar," called Kakap, and Pitar froze in place. "We didn't talk about Liroko," he said. Pitar turned and took a step towards him, glancing quickly in Larry's direction. In his corner, Larry stifled a gasp by digging his fingernails into his skin. "Do you think he'll gather well? Did he learn? Can he manage it alone?"

"He can manage father," said Pitar, although still with uncertainty in his voice.

"Good," said Kakap, shifting himself on the ledge. "Go and get Dabimi." He turned his head away, but then turned it back. "Pitar," he called out again when his son was nearly at the door. "Pitar, do you remember where Liroko came from?"

There was a slight rustling from the direction of the corner as Larry sank into a squat and lowered his locked arms around his knees. Kakap struggled to sit upright and rest his back against the wall. Pitar ran to help him. "Do you remember?" asked Kakap again, looking up and grasping his son's arm.

"Of course I know he's not from our line. He's from Dabimi's."

"That's right," said Kakap, in a voice that sounded almost amused. "And of course you know who held him back?"

"I don't remember," said Pitar, hesitating, ashamed and yet impatient at being questioned. He turned his head slightly as though expecting Larry to whisper him the answer.

"Of course you don't," said Kakap, pleased with himself at having tricked him. "I'm the only one anymore who knows that," he said, with no sign in his voice as to whether he intended to reveal the secret to his son. Pitar stood in the doorway, shifting the weight back and forth between his legs, uncertain as to whether to stay or go.

"It was Saptir," Kakap said at last in a low voice. He lay back on the skins and closed his eyes. Pitar hesitated for a minute in the doorway and then went out, leaving the hut in silence. Larry waited for a while and then let his hands fall to the ground. He pushed himself up slowly, terrified that Kakap would hear him brush against himself as he stood up.

"You can come out now," said Kakap with a weak laugh. Larry jumped as high as Pitar had, but started to laugh too, even as he stepped back and gasped out a muffled "No!" in English. He caught himself and came forward, still giggling, hanging his head down. He stood before Kakap, nearly doubled over, trembling with laughter until the tears ran down his face, growing more and more ashamed of his inability to stop. Kakap waited for a while and then cleared his throat, shattering him, so that only his tears were left behind. Larry wiped his eyes and moved a step closer in.

"Do you understand that it was Saptir who held you back?" said Kakap, his voice simultaneously more feeble and more firm.

"I'm not sure," said Larry, struggling to collect himself.

"I know where you came from, " said Kakap, "but what I need to know now is whether you'll go back."

Larry stood frozen, unable to speak. His tears began to fall again, along tracks that had already been laid. A minute passed and then there was a rustle in the doorway as Pitar came in with Dabimi.

"Dabimi!" said Kakap, weakly raising his hand to wave him over. Dabimi slid between Larry and Kakap, barely nodding at Larry. "What brings you to our village? We're honored you're here!"

"Kakap Ak," said Dabimi, extending his arm for Kakap to hold, brushing off the insult. "May the ancient ones hold your other arm," he said, and squatted beside the ledge.

"There are things to be arranged," said Kakap, pulling Dabimi even nearer, excluding Larry and Pitar.

"I'm not going to leave," Larry called to Kakap from outside the circle, trying to throw his voice over Dabimi's head.

Kakap didn't acknowledge him, and Larry began to wonder whether he had spoken at all. He looked to Pitar for confirmation, but Pitar's eyes were riveted on Dabimi and his father. Only Dabimi waved him off with annoyance, without bothering to turn around, and leaned in even closer to Kakap. After an interminable blur of time, in which Kakap and Dabimi whispered to each other, and Larry became more and more fearful that he had answered wrong, Dabimi stood abruptly and turned around to leave. He grunted towards Larry and Pitar and walked quickly past them. In an instant, he had stepped out through the *chajan* and was lost to the swirling sunlight that had followed the ebbing of the rain.

"Father?" Pitar said at last in a tentative voice, after they had stood motionless for some time. Kakap moved on the ledge and made a half-hearted attempt to push aside the skins. Larry and Pitar jumped forward at once and nearly knocked each other over trying to help him. Kakap reached down and grabbed each of them by an arm.

"You will *ritaX Ak* on the first day of the moon," he said, squeezing his son's arm, "and you," he went on, squeezing Larry's, "will go to Panar tomorrow and tell him you are *Ak*." He released them and they fell, made unsteady by the weight of their confusion. No doubt their pain at that moment was greater than Kakap's. In keeping with the law that a drop of white paint in a vat of pure black makes it blacker still and a drop of black gives white a fiercer glow, Larry and Pitar had no choice but to suffer their drops of fulfillment, gifts from Kakap to them and to Pahquel, as though they were the harshest of blows. They squatted with their backs against the ledge while the sun passed across them, so that Panar had to step around them that evening as he brought Kakap the draught. Only when Kakap's daughters arrived from the far village to sleep on their mats beside him did Larry stand and brush Pitar's arm with his hand. On his way out, he stood at the door weeping silently, bowing deeply to Kakap as he slept.

CXXXVI

ON THE EVENING of the seventh day, as they dropped their packs and sat on them, rubbing their shoulders and their aching feet, Jorge and Martina and Sam watched as the light from Joaquim's lantern intensified and spread as it came toward them in the darkness, a sun prematurely rising by increments.

"Let's break camp!" Joaquim shouted as he approached.

"What? Now?" Sam groaned, looking helplessly at the others.

"We're not moving," said Jorge.

"I found us a nice hotel. Luxury accommodations, plenty of running water, all rooms with a view."

Martina staggered to her feet and shouldered her pack. "Lead on," she said.

The others groaned behind her, but did the same. She had begun to notice that her actions held a sort of persuasive power of their own, second only to Joaquim's. They trudged on in the dark, none of them bothering to re-light their lanterns, following Joaquim's beacon through the blinding, shimmering dark. They could feel their faces brushed by webs, physical and other, by currents of air that held tinges of algae and the smell of dead fish, and by the slow crescendo of an approaching river.

When the forest gave way to a clearing, a crescent of sand that glowed like a mystical oasis in the moonlight, they dropped their bags and fell to their knees, already under the sway of its unreal allure. They tied their hammocks to the trees that surrounded it, and lit a fire in its midst, and ate their rice and beans as they watched the smooth movement of its inexhaustible resources of water and calm pour off into a distant, unfill-able sea. As the four travellers readied themselves for sleep, their drifting off resembled this drifting of water, a smooth, silent movement toward an infinite oblivion. And since oblivions have no history, nor particulars of identity or shape, they were unburdened by the need to suspect footprints in the sand that the winds had long erased, or to notice the exposed sore, just under the rope by which Joaquim's hammock was tied, where the bark of a tree had been worn away, or to recognize an empty tin of beans, nearly buried under dirt and undergrowth, that lay like a shipwrecked vessel just outside the circle of sand.

CXXXVII

SILVIO UNDERSTOOD FROM an early age that in the mandate to carry on his father's work, to celebrate his triumphs and build on them and move them farther forward toward some imminent denouement, there had always been a second, unstated demand: to undo the other's mistakes, to obscure the failures in the elder's efforts, to render them pale and irrelevant in memory's light. And perhaps it was Silvio's curse to have no son to do that work for him, just as he had abandoned his own father to the full truth of his life, and especially its limits.

How he had gone from who he was just ten years ago, he thought, surveying his old man's face in the mirror, good-looking still, but with no trace of what James had called his lothario swagger, to a man whose every facial feature sagged subtly with the weight of his own failures, was a mystery he could not bear to solve. Instead he merely bent toward his image, rubbed the stubble on his cheek with an intensity that brought with it a blush he could no longer have created from inside himself, and then turned away slowly from that visage, a quiet and resigned goodbye.

When he opened the bathroom door, he found Maria standing outside it, an immobile beefeater with a fresh cup of coffee in her hand. Silvio took the cup and kissed her on the forehead.

"Good news! You have the rest of the day off," he said, quickly waving her away.

"That's always a bad sign," she said, following a step behind him as he headed towards his desk. "Whenever you give me a day off, that's when I know I'd better call off my plans for the evening."

This time, Silvio raised her hand and kissed it. "I need to make some phone calls, and I don't trust you not to listen in. And I'll tell you something I want you never to forget: In this business, the less you know, the better."

"You know that's not true," she said, sitting in the chair by the side of the desk. "It's what got us all in trouble in the first place."

"From now on, I tell you nothing but the truth, and that's the truth," said Silvio, raising her up and escorting her to the door.

"What are you going to do if I go?"

"My dear, I am going to make my calls, and then I am going to go home, and make myself a nice big drink, and read myself some nice long fairy tales, and put myself to sleep."

"I'll go if you tell me who you're calling." She surveyed his face, and sensed without seeing it a flicker, fear, for a moment in his eyes. He looked at her for a long time, refusing to betray himself.

"Don't say I didn't warn you," he said at last. "You're in a bad spot already, given that you have not one but two sons still in the field."

Now the flicker was hers, but her eyes didn't move from his.

"First, I'm going to call Albuquerque Lima, see if I can meet with him, because I want to turn him into an ally, since we're going to need all the allies we can get. Start to work it from a power base. Then, I'm going to call some people in the press, but not ours. International. *The New York Times, London Times*. Then I'm going to call Diego Melo, slimy rat that he is, and see what side of this he's going to fall on, Mister *"Apresentador de Marionetas"* of the President's men.

He pushed her toward the door, bowing deeply as she pulled it behind her. Then he went to the phone. First, Melo, whose secretary said he wasn't in. "Bullshit!" Silvio shouted into the receiver. "I have a story that's about to break, and he's going to look like a fool if he doesn't know about it!" Before the secretary could even put down the phone to summon him, it was Melo on the line.

"You're going to owe me big time," said Silvio, wagging his middle finger in front of the receiver.

"We're not talking at my office," said Melo.

"Name your place," said Silvio.

"The bar at the Novo Mundo. Eleven tonight."

"I already have plans," said Silvio. "How about now?"

"Eleven at the Novo Mundo."

Silvio didn't bother to replace the receiver on the cradle, but only jabbed at the dial again. This time, he called Lima, whose secretary used the same old line. "First thing they teach you in secretary school?" he said. "I have an appointment to talk with him; can you remind him?" he said instead.

The phone went silent for a full five minutes, during which time Silvio wore another quarter-inch rut into the linoleum. After the second of those minutes, he began to bang the desk with his fist whenever he passed it, a slow drum salute to his effort not to slam the receiver down. At last, Lima answered.

"Amanza."

"Lima."

"What do you need from me?"

"I need five minutes. Five minutes, and then I resign." He sat down at the desk and positioned his stack of notes in front of him.

"Five minutes it is," said Lima. "Should I keep my secretary on the line?"

"Might as well," said Silvio, drawing in a deep breath before he spoke. When he unleashed himself, the words came like a spray of bullets, accompanied by a barely audible scratching sound on the other end of the phone as Lima's secretary struggled with her shorthand to keep up. The scratching sound had another function too, to mask the sound of scratching from Maria's pencil as she leaned in with her ear to the outside of the door.

After seven of the five, Lima cut in. "So how much more you got?"

"Maybe a hundred or so pages."

"Can you bring them over?"

"I can do that," said Silvio, holding the receiver between his shoulder and his ear as he patted the pages into a pile.

"Then we'll plan for your arrival in half an hour or so?"

"Right. So do I resign, or am I fired?" Silvio shot in.

"You don't go anywhere. We need you right where you are."

"You need my boot up your ass," said Silvio, as the click of the receiver masked the softer click of the lock on his office's front door.

CXXXVIII

ALL HAD NOT gone as planned. A portage of two days had dragged on for nearly four, leaving Sodeis with the question growing constantly louder in his head of when to cut his losses and turn back, of how much good money to throw after bad. The undergrowth had been unusually thick, and the number of scratches requiring iodine had thus been disproportionately large. Had he brought a mirror, he would have struck himself as an odd mulatto indeed; his face especially, even though protected by the outsize helmet of his canoe, bore the blotched appearance of the map to which he had, for the past five days, refused himself reference. But the iodine was necessary, his secret talisman against the seething cities of microbes that had, several times, felled him for weeks on end, curtailing his freedom to move freely, to flee.

When he came upon the riverbank at last, at midnight on the sixth day, the most rational thing would have been to spend the night there, to string up his hammock and wait at least for morning's glow. After losing so much time, however, urgency trumped rationality, or else sleep-deprivation had allowed rationality to mutate into new, exotic forms. As Sodeis slid the canoe down the rocky riverbank and launched it, the moon barely blinked, as though refusing to acknowledge their shared understanding. He threw his pack off behind him and tested the oars. The sound of the canoe gently sluicing the water was the sound of a sigh, a smooth relief, humid and quiet. The current was so slow that there was almost no difference in the pull of upstream versus down, and the rhythm of the oars lulled him, so that several times he found himself and the craft alike drifting backwards, into the dark past. In all, the repetitive movement of his weight against the oars, the inaudible hiss of steam on the water, the tinkling sound of fish trailing drops as they broke the surface and fell back, created an aura that was better than sleeping, the world being rocked by a reassuring hand. The dramas that were playing out beyond the inert, dark bodies of the riverbanks seemed of little consequence, ephemeral as dreams. The frenetic grunt of boar, the soft grating of snakeskin on rock, the cries of frogs and the shrieks of swallows, all were shed as effortlessly as memories. For it was not land that held his attention, but the river itself, that body he longed, through the reach of the oars, to embrace. Thus, he did not turn his head, let alone think to stop, when his canoe slid wordlessly by the sandy crescent on which the four were sleeping, four whose names he knew, and who were supposedly beings of his kind.

CXXXIX

THE NOVO MUNDO wasn't Silvio's sort of bar. He liked the dark ones, to be sure, but preferred the rat holes, the ones with the sticky floors and yellowed mirrors, where he could trust the bartender to keep confidences as much as he could trust the offerings of the establishment to loosen them. At five minutes after eleven on a Friday night, the Novo was packed. In a far back corner, someone was pounding a shiny black upright, and the neck of a bass craned above the crowd, moving from side to side, scanning for fish. It took Silvio a full five minutes to locate Diego Melo, who was leaning against the bar in his shirtsleeves, his necktie dangling at an angle, nearly untied. One of his interlocutors nudged him, and Melo pulled himself away from a group of men in dark suits and greeted Silvio with a choreographed embrace.

"My man!" shouted Melo above the din. "How many years, huh?"

Silvio nodded, feeling suddenly a bit woozy, hanging as he was over the abyss between what he had to say and the place he was saying it in.

"What're you having?"

"A scotch, straight up," said Silvio, looking around for a corner, or at least enough open wall to prop himself against.

"Well!" said Melo, ordering himself the same. He handed one over to Silvio, and toasted the last decade, and the decade to come. "I've been keeping track of all your hard work, man. You should know that. I see that you haven't had a raise in five years, and I'm putting you in for a big one." He looked over at Silvio with satisfaction, his glance more period than comma, as though he had succeeded in foreclosing on their meeting in record time by simultaneously insulting his old acquaintance and making him beholden.

Silvio waved away the offer of the money, his hand barely navigating the narrow channel between his face and Melo's. He gestured toward a table by the wall, and Melo reluctantly followed him over.

"I'm not going to waste your time on pettiness," he said. "Even after all this time, you know me better than that!" It was true that although Melo had never been SPI, he had hovered on the edges of it long enough to have been caught, once or twice, in the strings the puppet master pulled.

"So what can I do for you?" said Melo, resigned to a real conversation, throwing an impatient glance towards his friends.

"I'm here to give you a warning, and an offer," said Silvio. "It wasn't my intention to take you down, and you don't have to go down with this thing. You can get on board and help us out here and help yourself plenty because we need a mouthpiece, someone who's willing to ride the coat-tails of change."

"I'm not following you," said Melo.

"What I mean is that I've been waking up, sorting through all the deals we've made in the past 10 years, and I'm seeing some disturbing patterns, and I'll be handing the whole thing over to Lima, but only after I've had some long, fruitful talks with the press."

"You nuts?" said Melo, no longer concerning himself with the pretense of friendship. "The only one you're going to take down is yourself! I'm watching you light yourself on fire here!"

"I don't have profits at stake here. You do."

"You've got the wrong guy. What I've done for SPI has built this town, has fed a couple thousand of our own, and has made businessmen of a bunch of uneducated savages who wouldn't have a claim to their names without my influence." He looked at Silvio straight, pushing the hand with the drink aside so he could get in closer. "I'm beginning to take issue with your tone. So what are you offering me?"

"Take the reins on turning this agency around. Make your name as a real reformer. Turn back an account or two to put yourself in good faith, and flush this thing out from the top. If it breaks in the international press, you'll have all the publicity and a real popular mandate behind you, and SPI will back you, if you're doing it right. It's your way on up!"

"Why me? You've never had the slightest appreciation for what I've done, and I'm the last person you'd turn to for something like this."

"Because you've been there at least, in the field, and on the other hand, we have a long and unflattering record on you we could circulate with no effort at all. But more to the point, because you have the power. Almost enough for a run, but not quite enough. We could be useful to each other."

"I need to give it some thought," said Melo, looking sharply around.

"How much thought?"

"How about five minutes with my boys?" he said, nodding towards the bar.

"Five minutes," said Silvio, looking at his watch.

Melo got up and was swallowed by the crowd and the noise and the heat. Despite himself, Silvio craned to catch glimpses of him amid the circle of grey suits, trying to read their expressions and their gestures without being seen. He watched them from the corner of his eye as they nodded to each other, their expressions impassive or sneering, and one gesture among many caught his attention, a thick hand that patted, repeatedly, an area of pressed gabardine beneath the left lapel of a well-fitting jacket. Silvio jumped up, pushing his way between the crowd and the wall, knocking down chairs and jostling the patronage. He slid between the upright piano and the bass, behind their black velvet backdrop, and out the back door into the alley. The air was cool and moist, thick enough almost to absorb the slap of a lone set of footsteps behind him. He dodged garbage cans and a wheel-less abandoned car, first panting and then gasping as he ran. He heard the footsteps slowing behind him, but pressed on even harder towards the place where the alley let out onto Altimaya Street. He embraced that aperture of streetlight and movement with his arms open, already hailing an oncoming taxi before he could even be seen. He waved frantically and then sprang forward with a mighty leap and fell, as the sound of a single gunshot echoed against the damp walls of the city's dank intestines.

CXL

SODEIS RUBBED HIS eyes and looked around in a state of foggy confusion. No doubt because he never stayed in the same place for long, he tended to have trouble, first thing in the morning, remembering where he was. He sat up and lifted his netting over his head with both hands. The world was new, filled with promise and growth. That some of that growth took the form of stands of Janka and other hardwoods he didn't even recognize, accounted in Sodeis's mind for much of the promise of the day, but even he could sense, in the forest's soft chill, the possibility of something else, something unforeseen, that might represent a turning point in his latest rather miserable trajectory. He slid out from the aperture he had made between his hammock and his *mosquitero*, splashed water on his face from one of his canteens, and took a swig from his hip flask, wiping his mouth on his shirtsleeve.

He hadn't bothered to articulate to himself a plan of action, but that didn't stop him from following it to the letter: He would attempt to locate whoever was in power, and catch him alone, and broker a deal with him that would allow him to transport some of the beauty and awe he saw around him to the river, with the help of a crew who would soon arrive to assist him. If the chief was never alone, Sodeis saw barely a wrinkle in his plan; he would then woo the populace directly with the watches and pen knives and fish hooks he carried with him at all times for just such occasions, resulting in a delay of two days at the most. He shook out his shoes and put them on, rolled his hammock, grabbed his pack and headed out, chewing on a strip of jerky as he went.

The only difficulty his march of conquest presented to him was to be found in the yawning lag between the formation of his goals and the time of their fulfillment. A hike of even three hours, as he estimated this one would be, was long enough to allow certain unwelcome visions to slip in, never mind the 12-hour marches he was used to, which simultaneously absorbed his attention and left him open to being blindsided by internal swellings of shame and rage and regret. Today, for example, the mere leaf of a Janka falling on his hammock had left him susceptible to thoughts of his old partner in crime, Diego Melo, with whom he had shared equitably the considerable profits of a deal for two thousand hectares of said hardwood twenty years ago. But still, it wasn't the money. The contrast between the life of power and prestige he imagined for his friend and his own life spent urinating into rotting logs and prying the muck from his boots with a stick every night stung him with particular viciousness, and as he went on, it sank him further into that reservoir of self-pity that had long been filling within him. As his earlier sense of promise eroded with the fall of each drop into that deepening pool, he slowed and more often looked around him, noting, off to his right, what appeared to be an artificial glow emanating from the arcade of tree trunks in the musty dawn. The faucet of regret closed suddenly, freeing him to move at his old pace, in small, swift steps toward the light.

When he was within a hundred meters of the luminescence's source, he could see that the glow was being poured from a vast cavern, a world of swarming activity, from which flowed voices and motion and the smells of burning fires and smoked fish. All day, he watched and listened, moving from one vantage point to another, in order to discern any signs of a chief, any isolated wanderers, any well-worn paths which could indicate to him where to leave his offerings, SPI-style, any signs of contact already begun. He saw that when the natives left their village, they did so only in groups, a fact that was not unexpectable to someone thinking realistically, but deflating to Sodeis. As he placed his bright cloth on a fallen tree trunk and laid out his wares, he felt resigned, suddenly, to the likelihood that his offerings would be wasted on bands of young Indians whose discoveries, should they decide to hide them from their elders, could take weeks to come to the attention of anyone in power. Perhaps he would even have to enter the village itself, a risky business given that the notebooks he had encountered at Catalpa's gave him no information at all about the tribe, and thus no reassurance whatever that these were *Indios Mansos*, tame ones. To make matters worse, he carried an unfamiliar firearm, newly purchased, with which he had not yet cultivated an intimacy. As he relocated his hammock and *mosquitero* at nightfall just out of sight of his display, he could barely hold back from reproaching himself aloud for having permitted himself to fall yet again under the sway of hope when he knew full well that what rose in him like dew in the morning was always burned off by mid-day. At last, he drifted to sleep, and the hum of his self-reproach was replaced by the whisper of light footfalls, by slow breathing, by the soft jangle of a silver watch-band as it was raised by a dark hand to the moon.

CXLI

JOAQUIM WAS UP before all but the river. As the sun ignited the water's far extremity, he watched as a cloud of light roared silently toward him down the length of the river's satin fuse. In the face of it, he stood his ground, holding his compass out like an offering, his map like a shield. Behind him, the sand exhaled drifts of steam; the whole inlet swirled and glowed pink, glossy as pearl. Were he not chained to the mast of his own determination, even this old adventurer might have been seduced to stay, to unpack his clothes and wash them in the river, to set up his makeshift hut and drop his line in among the schools that hovered, with the lucidity of dreams, on transparent currents. Joaquim was well acquainted with the dangers of beauty, however, and roused himself, moving from hammock to hammock, gently nudging his companions awake.

"The news is, we're almost there," he said as he lit a fire and measured out the coffee into their dented tin pot. "Maybe a day, maybe less. We seem to have stumbled into a shortcut. Turns out, this tributary isn't on my map." He knew that if he hadn't some assurance to offer, Sam, for one, was poised to give up and insist on turning back, running off hysterically, endangering them all. But their night by the river had refreshed them. Even Sam took a dip before breakfast; even Jorge and Martina consented to be photographed, together, drying on the rocks in coincidentally identical oxford cloth shirts. As they set off into the cool, humid dark, following Joaquim through undergrowth so dense he had, at one point, to unsheathe his scythe and hack a series of doorways for his companions to step through, they were aware despite these obstacles of the resurgence of collective hope, of a hunger whose object now seemed tantalizingly near. When they came upon the outermost marker, standing rigid and dispassionate as a beefeater, they fell against it, and ran their hands across its heft without regard for splinters or insect stings. In the solidity of the trunk, which was too hard to allow intruders of any kind a foothold, they found reassurance that they had arrived at their destination, and that despite the delay of years, they were in time.

"Let's set up," said Joaquim, lowering his pack.

"Here?" said Jorge, "We can't stop now! Let's at least find Larry. I thought we were going to get in and get out."

"You think we can treat this contact as any different from the others, just because of Larry? We need them on our side, and we're going to collect the evidence we came for, and we're going to do this one right."

"What? Make a drop-off and the whole thing?"

"The whole thing," said Joaquim, beginning to set up the first of their two tents. "Though I guess we have some clues already. I guess they don't need axes," he said, admiring the smooth, sharp point of the fallen tree, like a sharpened pencil balancing on the even sharper point of another.

"So who's going with me?" he said when they had finished erecting their city, and had sponged down their dinner dishes, and had cleared a small plaza between the tents, demarcated by strings on which lanterns were hung. "Jorge? Up for a stroll?" said Joaquim nonchalantly, sticking his head into the larger of the tents as Jorge began to unfurl his bedroll inside it. Jorge looked up in disbelief, but obeyed. As Joaquim scratched out a note on a piece of paper torn from a miniature spiral notebook, folded it, and pushed it into his front pocket, Jorge filled the smallest of his shoulder bags with a sample of the usual offerings—twine and a hunting knife, and a tiny bag of glass beads, a handful of matchboxes—and set off behind Joaquim's lantern, bowing slightly to Martina as he left. Sam, suddenly panic-stricken, began to protest, calling after them into the darker darkness that signified nightfall. Martina hushed him, pushing him quickly in front of her into the tent and zipping up the opening behind them.

"Wait here a minute," she whispered to him, stroking his arm like a mother, or an aunt, and then unzipping the opening again, facing him as she backed out to keep him from following. She knew what comforts the illusion of shelter afforded and the terror that ensued when that bubble of illusion was ruptured.

"Where are you going?" said Sam, a grown man, now clutching his bedroll to his chest like a child. "Are you coming back?"

"I'm just going to pee. A minute. No more," she whispered, stepping out and zipping the tent flap behind her. As she squatted at the far edge of their camp, a single word came to her: *exile.* It had been possible to lose Jorge without even a minute of regret in the context of her studio, when it had been her choice to push him out, but now, perhaps incited by Sam's panic or by something more remote and personal, she saw clearly that the loss was not bearable. She interrogated herself: Why this sudden weakness? It wasn't exactly protection for which she depended on Jorge, or on Joaquim, for that matter; if the last week had convinced her of anything, it was of her own competence in the forest, her capacity to lead, and to protect herself, perhaps not so much because of her marksmanship as because of her willingness to fire in her own defense. It might simply have been the sight of Sam's quivering lip, or the vision of Jorge's back receding into the darkness, jostling a vision she had pushed away, into a corner of her mind far more dense with undergrowth and menace than the forest at night, of her father's back receding into a roil of suitcases and dark overcoats beside a snorting, shrieking train.

"Marty?" Sam called pitifully. She knew to expect him to treat her coolly tomorrow, out of shame at what he was tonight.

As she returned to the tent and slid into her bedroll, Sam pushed up against her and clung on, grasping her in his hairy, heavy arms and pulling her in to him. At first, she started and pulled away, but then she relaxed and allowed herself to be held, as though by a child or a father, while the world whirred and screeched like an enormous engine starting up around them. It was nearly dawn, and Sam had long ago released her, when Jorge slipped in beside her and she rolled over, clinging to him with the same intensity with which Sam had held her earlier.

"We made a lean-to, and placed it all," whispered Jorge, as though to postpone the need to address her embrace of him. "And we hid, and we saw one of them take everything, and he didn't even look for us. He just left," whispered Jorge, at last pulling his arm from his bedroll and laying it against hers. "But someone else is here too—you'll never guess. We're both sure we saw him."

"You saw Larry?"

"No. Someone we didn't want to see."

"Sodeis?"

She felt Jorge nod. "What are we going to do?"

"Get some sleep," said Jorge. "With our pistols under our pillows."

CXLII

IT WAS RIGHT for Kakap to die as he did, clutching his daughter's arm with one hand and a piece of Saptir with the other. As a comfort to him, Panar added crushed Saptir to the mix with which he was filled, so that there would be no pain on his journey, and he would encounter no delay in finding his father's house. The death and the wailing and the burning and the grief and the absence went by in a blur, as though to Larry, time had become a train that went storming past him before he could even make out the passengers leaning their heads out of the open windows, let alone the darker faces pressed against the glass. As Aran worked, the paint climbed the two legs of Kakap's *chajan* like water rising in the river, and the river filled its banks and overflowed like the paint along the mantle overhead. The house was disassembled and left behind, two bare *chajan* legs against the backdrop of the living village, and no new one was built, as Pitar had been sent out on his *ritaX* and all Kakap's other children were settled and there was no *kaag* living to provide for. Larry and Aran and Oji carried the baskets of gourds and *maatas* and rough stones for grating to their own hut, where a ledge had been constructed beside the mixing ledge to hold them.

Because Larry was now *Ak*, he was entitled, as Panar had schooled his nieces, to one or two persons to whom he could teach the songs and the plants and the ways of preparing them. He had hoped that Oji or Iri could go with him, but last boy of the last boys, Iri was still not ready for an age group, and Oji was more preoccupied with hunting than with gathering, and was preparing to *ritaX*. Rather than choose the son of Kakap's daughter from the far village, whom he barely knew, he decided to go out on his own, as Kakap had done, until Pitar had returned and was ready to go with him, leaving a place for Iri to join them later. Larry prepared the songs and the bowls and the yoke as before, but a sense of dread overtook him as he packed the wax and the cutting stones, for the void where Kakap had been had cut so deep in him that it penetrated all the layers of his life in Pahquel, and reached down into his memory of James's death, and grafted itself to that still-growing vine. At that moment, what terrified him most was not the danger of the forest itself, for which he had been prepared through years of tutelage by Kakap, but rather the impending sense that alone in the forest's intense darkness, he would have no one solid to hold onto. That night, although Aran was restless with excitement because Oji had brought a woman to the house at last, he curled up beside her on the ledge, and was jostled as she tossed in her sleep. At dawn, he stood in the doorway and watched her, the way her breasts fell away from her chest to either side, and how the strands of white hair flowed out over the small dark agouti pelt beneath her head, and he was suddenly filled with a fear that she too would be gone when he returned.

The way in was treacherous; he wasn't used to leading. His call to the plants had a plaintive, desperate air, and in hearing it, they cowered and hid. He had only seven to gather, but after three days, he had collected only two, and felt himself sinking into a nearly forgotten despair as he lay curled in his hammock with his knees folded into his chest. It was his fate to discover again and again that he was unprepared, to ready himself and then to fall back, yearning for and fearing the forces that always appeared at those moments to lead him on. His own eyes, accustomed to seeking out these forces, were not so sensitive to the stillness of roots and leaves as Kakap's had been. He would come upon a curtain of brambles in the dim half-light and his attention would be drawn to whatever moved the fastest, so that he would miss the silent *Tapiri* watching him with its hundred knots like eyes from beneath a decomposing log, or the *Laar* that trembled only very slightly in its gown of overlapping leaves precise as fish-scales. Thus, as he turned in his hammock, he saw only what was fleeting, Kakap in retreat, and Anok and James, pummeling across the dark cranium of the

sky like comets, blinding him to the stillness of the roots and low branches, to the thought of how solid and heavy Aran had felt in his arms.

If Kakap had been there, he would have sung of the constancy of the
ancestors, of how rhythmically they trod in their smoke to the plants
and entered them; of how surely they became their sap. But these were
not Larry's ancestors, despite the story Kakap had made up to cover him;
they did not want to hear him sing their songs. His ancestors were an
undifferentiated clan of Scotch-Irish on his father's side and Polish on his
mother's, who had as little interest in him as he had shown in them. They
had taught him nothing about how to rely on them, or how to shoulder
the burdens of a line. In Pahquel, he had been schooled for years in the
songs and the stories, and had learned to distinguish between an untold
number of plants, but he did not know how to trust in their guidance, or
how to earn their trust. He thought of turning back, of walking all night to
the *kaawa* of one of Kakap's daughters, who had grown up hearing about
TaroX and *Mita* and *Ker,* and might be willing to teach him, or to take his
place, but he knew that such disgrace would reflect poorly on Oji, and
especially on Iri, who, like himself, had never been secure in his place.
Instead, he stayed out for two days longer than he planned, and forced
himself to scan the tree bark for the tiny bromeliads with the purple cores
whose spiked leaves contained the elixir *Xit*, and to dig for the brown
mushroom caps that, when fried with coconut, strengthened old men's
joints. He screamed at the rain when he thought it would break him, and
on his last day out, after spotting the *Kipa* and filling the final basket, he
turned back for home without even stopping to eat. As he reached the garden plots of the far village, a sense of elation overtook him and swept him
with a longing to show Kakap he hadn't failed. Panar sensed his growing
excitement as he revealed the contents of the gourds, and had his wife
feed him pancake and greens, and directed him to Irapat's hut, where Aran
was painting for the naming of a child. Aran's joy in seeing him caught him
up short, and as they walked home arm in arm, he skipped up and down
at her side, knocking against her like Iri would, forcing her to put aside
her usual reserve and laugh from embarrassment and relief. They stood
on their *kaawa* with their arms around each other's waists while Oji and

Katari were busy together in the hut, and Larry told her how Kakap had guided him to the *Kipa* by pointing to it with the bent *Para* stalks. In the clearing in front of them, there were people strolling and talking, and fires appearing out on the *kaawas,* and the smells of smoking meat and frying dough. There were the grunts and snorts from their hut, where their one son was copulating with a young girl, still only single-breasted, who would soon become his wife, and there were the cries from the field where their older son was playing Kara, and there was the brown-and-soft-green scrub, across which Dabimi suddenly darted on his way from Atira's hut to Piri's. On impulse, still in the grip of his elation, Larry called out to him, and he stopped and nodded curtly in Larry's direction, so that as he turned, the fire caught a glimpse of his right arm, upon which a gold and silver wristwatch gleamed like a jeweled armband, encircling the soft matte darkness of his skin.

CXLIII

AT THE PROSPECT of his next trip out, Larry had expected to feel less dread than at the first one, but was surprised to find the same sickening sense rising in his throat as he readied his gourds and his baskets. The hut was already empty behind him as he stepped through his *chajan*, threshold of time, and launched out into the teeming forest. His task, he knew, was to try his hardest to see as Kakap had seen, to hone his vision in order to be able to detect simultaneously what was great and what was small, what was moving and what was at rest, and to inform any of those ancestors who somehow hadn't smelled the smoke from Kakap's fire of his imminent presence among them. The task entailed his constant singing as he went, his announcement to all who had been alive, and thus were still living, of the fire and the loss and the reappearance of Kakap in the very rumbling and humming of the forest. It was after only half a day's walking that he heard an odd snap, a breach in the pattern of vibrations that held Kakap and the world, and turned on his heel to confront Dabimi, who now stood before him in his penis-sheath and wrist watch and arrow-case, carrying a basket that betrayed, by its labored swinging, some heavy object within it.

"My kinsman," said Dabimi, bowing.

"I see your hunt has been blessed, as usual," said Larry, gesturing with his head towards Dabimi's basket.

Dabimi opened the basket to reveal a ball of twine, a hunting knife, and a silver hip-flask, filled to the top with cachaca. "These are from your person," he said, gesturing deeper into the forest.

"What do you mean, my person?" said Larry, suddenly gasping as though he'd been punched by something he thought he had evaded simply by turning from it in his mind: That the watch Dabimi was wearing was not something that had been given to him by James in the past, nor was it something he had taken from Larry's pack during the time Larry had lived in his hut, but was in fact an irrefutable sign of contact with a world he had allowed himself to believe had ceased to exist, except within his own memory and longing.

"Where did you get those things?" he demanded, panic-stricken.

"Do you want me to take you there?" said Dabimi, with a sense of triumph in his voice at Larry's visible terror. "They are from my friend," he said haughtily, clearly enjoying the idea that he had the upper hand even with Larry's own kind. "I have had many friends like that, many, in more than two hands of moons." After standing for a moment, relishing the power he wielded, he added, "In fact, this friend says he knows you, and has asked me to bring you to him, you and other persons who are *Ak,* who will talk to him and see what he has for us. So you go home. Go home and get Panar and the others, and I will tell him you're coming, and I will come for you." He walked up to Larry as though to embrace him, in a mood of great expansiveness, but instead, turned away and disappeared into the forest.

As Larry ran home, his mind reeled with possibilities. At first, he imagined it was James who had come for him, and had to remind himself forcibly that James was dead. Only then did it occur to him that it was likely that the person Dabimi had encountered would prove to be a stranger, his kind only on the basis of their skin or dress or speech, that the person had asked only to see leaders, and not him by name. The only thing he was clear on was that this stranger was an intruder, threatening the life that, by sheer, fragile chance, he had managed to find for himself, the only life that was possible for him. The man might be a logger, he told himself, in search of easy Indians to woo for rights; he might be part of a team of installers of telephone lines, or, worst of all, a scout for a mining company, whose rape of the land would inevitably leave indelible, toxic scars. As he tried one possibility after another in his mind, SPI and Sr. Catalpa and even Jorge, who, he told himself, would never betray him, and at one point, crazily, his parents, he noticed that he was panting as he ran, shaking uncontrollably, so that his gait became uneven, causing him to weave. He burst into the village gasping and ran blindly to Kakap's hut, only remembering when he had reached that bare *chajan* that Kakap was gone. He turned on his heel and headed for Panar's, fearing in his confusion, that he would find in his house too, merely the leavings of the last of his Fathers, the clean, white skeleton of his past.

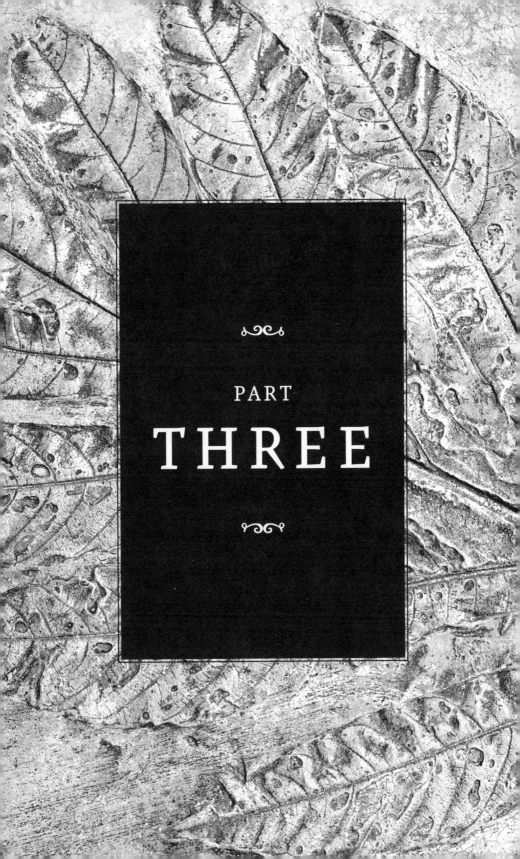

PART

THREE

CXLIV

THE RIVER WAS sated, as the rain was well aware. It pressed forward, robust and certain, eager and acquisitive, free of the memory of want. The river was sated, but the rain poured into it until it was filled to the point of disgust and disgorged itself into the forest. Thus all rivers flow from hunger to complacency to foulness; from decay to certainty to stone. When the waters finally receded from Pahquel, the three towns were like three turtles washed up on the shore, dazed and stranded, unsure of their direction. People began to move their arms and legs again, to visit each other on their *kaawas* in the afternoon, and to cure the meat and fish out in the open, so that the smoke no longer saturated the beams of the lean-tos, but stretched up in taut white columns to the sky. Breathing was freer and deeper, and the sun was sharper and more bold, and yet there was a tension in the air, an unfamiliar, high-pitched hum, a spider-thin reverberation of unease.

Dabimi was almost never in the village then, so that disputes went unsettled, and babies waited longer to be named, and once, when he was away without explanation for three days, a person was burned without the guidance of a leader, leaving his family to fear that he wouldn't find his home. Agitation and uncertainty crept into the greetings between persons; husbands and wives argued openly in their houses without so much as an attempt to dissemble, and even the parrots on the *kaawas* seemed testy and quick to outrage.

A hand of days after the burning from which Dabimi had been absent, Larry appeared on Panar's *kaawa*, shaking and wheezing, to tell Panar that

Dabimi's absences were not to prepare for future hunts, or for obtaining extra guidance; rather, they were to prepare for the end of the world.

"You'll see!" He has things from another world! Somebody's giving him gifts he can't repay!"

Panar looked at him soberly. "We don't know that," he said.

"I can show you! Will you come?"

They stared at each other in pulsing, humming silence. Larry knew that to enter, unbidden, the house of their chief, the one chosen by the ancestors to lead, the one whose powers were granted by the force of a hands-and-feet of *chajans*, and take his things, and see what they were, and what they had to say, meant another sort of end of the world. Panar came forward, the old man steadying the younger one, and Larry shivered with fear as he saw the fear in Panar's eyes. Even more terrifying was the fact that Panar turned to follow him, that Panar placed his trust in him when Larry knew that trust could cost him his life.

Dabimi's hut was empty when they approached. Larry and Panar gathered the baskets they found hanging from its rafters and ran towards Larry's hut holding them close at their sides, so as not to alarm the abducted objects inside them. On the path, they ran into Pitar *Ak* coming towards them, and motioned for him to follow. Aran appeared at the *chajan* as they came up, shocked to see them, clearly betraying her concern at Larry for appearing three days earlier than planned.

"Did the gathering go badly?" she said as she saw the stricken look on his face. She looked at the baskets, which were not the sort used for gathering, and then from one to the other of the men as they drew the things out and placed them at Larry's feet: A knife in a leather sheath; a pair of rhinestone cufflinks in a box; a pair of scissors; a small iron frying pan; a ball of gold-colored string; and a small vial of fishhooks with its cork stopper in place.

"He's taken these from someone and that someone's going to hurt us. I'm sure of it. They're coming for me or for us. They're going to hurt us!" Larry said in a mix of English and Pahqua, hysterically.

"Which of these things do you know?" said Panar in a voice of forced calm, holding them up one at a time before Larry's eyes. "You're sure they were taken?" He had used his flashlight every evening for the entire first year, and he had worn his clothes until they were nothing but ribbons and holes, and he had left his penknife open on the *kaawa* while he went for water, and he had used it for cutting leather and fish, but no one had ever asked him about any of the objects he had drawn from and returned to his pack. To steal from a person, as Dabimi had done, as they were doing now, was an assault on the ancestors, on time itself, the consequences of which they were already living beneath.

"They aren't mine," said Larry, "and they weren't Jarara's. But I know what they are and what they do and what world they came from."

At that moment, a comet shot across the evening sky, burning into the black udder of the heavens a scar so deep it did not heal, but oozed a yellow liquid into the moonless air. The light illuminated Dabimi's silhouette as he stood in the doorway, watching them.

"Yours?" said Panar looking up, stretching out a hand of sinew and bone, from which a striped basket swung.

"*Um,*" said Dabimi, shaking his head sharply. "The ancestors have only contempt for those who steal."

"*Um,*" said Panar, looking him in the eye. "And yet you stole these things," he said firmly, rising and taking a step forward.

"Those things were given," said Dabimi. "And they were given by someone you know. By him and by his friends!" He pointed at Larry and the others turned to look at him in horrified amazement, as though he had been suddenly unmasked. Without taking his eyes from Dabimi, Larry moved his hand around in the air, searching for Aran's arm, but couldn't find it.

"You need to tell me who it is. Who do I know? Who do I know? How do I know you aren't just leading me into a trap?" Larry shot back, thinking unwittingly of Jorge, and then reminding himself again that Jorge would never have betrayed him.

"You know a man with sky-colored eyes and thing," he said, gesturing toward what would have been a shirt. "He said that he knows you, and that you are his friend."

"I don't know anyone like that!" Larry shouted. "Is that who you're going to take us to? Some stranger?" he stammered, using the English word, as there was no such word in Pahqua.

"At sunrise," said Dabimi, triumphant, wild-eyed, as he added, "He'll be glad to see you. He's been asking for you." He took the basket from Panar's hand, and the two from the floor, and riffled through them. Then he slowly slid the laces up his arm like a taunt before disappearing into the darkness beyond Larry's hut.

When he had gone, the four stood paralyzed and silent, unable to free their eyes from the empty *chajan*. They barely noticed when the boys came in, beckoned by Aran to the back of the hut, and unrolled their sleeping mats on the floor.

At last, Panar turned around to face the rest. "So we'll get ready for the morning," he said, grasping Larry briefly by the arm as he went out.

When he had gone, Larry backed into the farthest corner of the hut and pulled the smaller of his two shoulder bags out onto the *kaawa*. He fanned the fire carelessly and in a single graceless gesture poured out the contents of the bag. There were batteries corroded almost beyond recognition, and a mess of fishing twine, and an empty bottle of penicillin, and a few small spiral notebooks, their pages bloated and fused by the damp. There was his own broken wristwatch, its face eaten away like a leprotic man's, and two others, preserved like mummies in decorated wooden sarcophagi, and some pairs of moldy socks, in which colonies of maggots resided. One of the batteries rolled off the pile toward the fire and he barely noticed how the flames singed the hair on his arm as he snatched it back. At last, he found what he was looking for—a few scraps of paper and an envelope sealed in a discolored plastic bag. As he opened the bag, he paused for a minute with his eyes closed, as though praying, or trying to read the papers by feel, and then drew them out slowly in the palm of his hand, leaves so fragile they were shaken by the very exhale of the fire. "These are *my* ancestors," he said to the air.

It was shocking to see how puny they were; because he hadn't allowed himself to look at them before, he had imagined them as squares of heavy bond paper, cardstock even, covered with strong dark letters like those from a fountain pen. Such fantasies are manifestations of the irony of time, variations on a universal theme: The son returns, contrite, to his father's house, begging for protection at last, when the old man is too frail to give it. The papers weren't merely flimsy but—although brittle to the touch—transparent, saturated by a dry grease that blurred the pen strokes into a network of blue veins beneath pale skin. The marks formed words, names and phone numbers, the legible passages as absurdly meaningless as the faded ones. There was the paper from Silvio, containing contacts at the consulates in Rio and Sao Paulo, and bearing the names of the leaders of the tribes that dotted the banks of the Xingu, the closest of which was two hundred kilometers away, along with a crudely drawn map that had taken on a topographic aspect due to the blurring of the ink. There was a chart from Joaquim containing Jorge's routine runs, roughly by season and coordinates, along with a list of which of his fellow agents could be trusted and which were more likely to inform on him. At the bottom of the pile was the letter from James, in a labored handwriting so intimately familiar that he nearly gagged when he saw it, the script uncannily faded and ghostly, as one would expect of a letter from the dead. In it, there was a phrase with which to reintroduce himself to Asator and a message to give to a woman from the far village of Pahquel, for whose daughter James had acted as *jitana*, but who had long since died, and an odd diagram of circles and triangles containing numbers connected by lines and equal signs, at the bottom of which was the formula 1:4.3, and an apparent warning that said "Thus they are more vulnerable to extinction if disrupted but also more threatening to surrounding populations."

Larry spread the notes on his palm and let his eye fall on the words that were illuminated by the fire. Light flickered over half a phone number, a first or last name, a word or two of a sentence. He stared at the changing pattern of light and dark as though it in itself had something to tell him, and was startled by a noise behind him. He jumped so that the papers were scattered in the dirt. He had forgotten about Aran, who had been watching him with a disturbed expression and about his boys, who were peering at him from just behind the *chajan*.

"Remember these names," he said to Aran, picking up the papers, reading off the lists three times in repetition in a whisper. "Now we can put these things back," he said, but Aran stood off to the side, unwilling to touch what wasn't hers, while he closed the plastic bag and threw the crusted batteries on top of it. He tossed the putrid socks onto the fire where they hissed and smoldered.

He didn't even try to sleep or to lie down on the ledge. Instead, he sat with Aran on the *kaawa*, awaiting the first stirring of the light. They were all fragile, each one a mesh of blue threads as pale as faded ink beneath a tissue of skin, the two sons inside, and the stooped, white-haired old wife, and the husband, tall and wiry, light-haired, his face still unwrinkled but scarred from shaving with dull blades. It was an unspeakable privilege to sit together, leg against leg and arm against arm, resting their backs against the side of their house, surrounded by the harmonies of the night birds and the insects. Before them, a sudden, unlikely perfection unrolled, the moment in which life emerged from the oceans and transformed itself, the moment in which all that was blurred, slurred, random and unformed drew itself together into a kind of sense, a single word resounding on the precipice of chaos. Perhaps every person bears witness to such a culmination, as a hand moves the lens of a life from one pole to the other through a fleeting point of focus. Nothing is revealed at such a moment, no object or person or idea, but merely the fact that the world is improbably sharp and real. Despite himself, Larry had taken his place in such a world and had been received. He was like a man who longs with such intensity to gain a woman's love that he cannot bear to be around her and wins her precisely as a result of his willingness to lose her. Only much later, years after the goal has been achieved does the recognition of it arrive, most often at the point at which its loss is imminent.

"Don't wake them," Aran whispered as the horizon lightened, barely waiting for a reply before disappearing inside and emerging again with a basket of food and water gourds.

"We should bring them with us," said Larry, standing.

"No!" hissed Aran, moving to block him. Larry turned to go around her, and she moved in front of him again. "What are you going to do?"

"Ok, I'm not going to wake them," said Larry, "but there are some things I need to bring along." He disappeared into the hut and emerged almost instantly, holding something behind his back, his hunting knife, which he buried at the bottom of the basket. Then he took her arm and they hurried out, following the path that ran behind the outermost huts of the village, which was rough with stubble owing to disuse. From time to time, a branch would reach out a hand to stop them, and once, they came to a sudden halt as the shadow of a man passed across the opening in front of them. They hung back until they saw that it was Piri, returning from his sister's house in the far village. He had with him a basket of dried fruit, which he had set on the ground while he relieved himself. When they saw him, they ran to him and motioned him into a stand of Sapucaia. "I'll be away for a day or two and Aran will be gathering with me," Larry said, aware that neither of them carried the yoke of gourds and baskets.

"Are Iri and Oji still asleep?" asked Piri, sounding confused. "Will they feed themselves? Is Kararar with Oji?"

"Their baskets are full," said Aran, "but they'll have to carry their own water in the morning."

"Tell them not to worry," said Larry, taking Piri by the arm, overcome by the sudden desire to embrace him. "I'll tell you about it when I get back, my friend," he whispered, forcing himself to let go.

Dabimi and the others were already gathered together behind his hut, stomping their feet in the chill, when they arrived. Without speaking, they turned and Dabimi led them out through the forest's towering *chajan* of trees, into its broad, cavernous rooms, in which the night still lingered. They passed the first circle of Pahquel, marked by a log resting on its stump, before the sun had cleared the treetops, and they reached the finger of water known as the *kiro akasa* long before the sun had reached its height. They stopped several times to drink, but they ate as they walked, swinging their baskets to their chests whenever they were hungry. Each one privately suspected that Dabimi had deliberately set a pace that would make obvious his superior endurance despite his age, and the realization made them even more determined. Pitar followed on Dabimi's heels, and Larry on his, surprised by the ease with which he kept up. As the sun touched the trees behind them however, he was aware, with a shock, that the other two were struggling. He could hear Panar breathing heavily at his back, and noticed that Aran's gait had become more and more uneven, until she almost dragged her left foot over the pack of dirt and leaves. He felt his throat tighten as he remembered her as she was when she had found him, agile and invincible, able, he had had no doubt, to carry the weight of two. He began to consider what would be lost in asking Dabimi to slow down, or whether he should try to pull Aran's arm over his shoulder, when Dabimi stopped abruptly in front of a thatched lean-to built into the side of a tree in a place where there had been a slight parting of the canopy overhead. The lean-to was empty but for a ledge that stretched across its back wall, upon which were placed a cigarette lighter and a ball of twine, a rolled-up fishing net, and what looked like a tarnished silver hip flask.

"So these things are not taken, but given," said Dabimi with a broad, gloating smile as he put down his basket and placed the things into it one by one, with the exception of the flask, the contents of which he swallowed in three loud, gasping gulps before replacing it on the ledge. "Given by my friend. Given by *your* friend," he said emphatically, looking Larry in the eye. "We'll sit and today or tomorrow he'll be here. And then, I'll take you to another of these places. They are all around us now. You just wait and see."

Dabimi dug among the things he had piled into his basket until he found a large dried Murcuri fruit and bit into it with an air of forced nonchalance. The others sat in a circle around him, watching him eat. All turned their heads at once as he tossed the pit over Aran's head into the scrub. Without the fruit to occupy him, Dabimi seemed suddenly aware of their scrutiny, and started picking at a nail with an expression of fierce concentration. Aran lay her head against Larry's shoulder, but didn't sleep. Panar did sleep, resting his forehead on his knees, while Pitar squatted in the posture of a runner at the block, leaning forward, his eyes fixed on Dabimi's face. As they sat, the light inched away so slowly that its retreat went unnoticed, leaving them unaware that they were only going through the motions of seeing. At last, they heard the crunching of boots on dry ground and started up, erect as prey.

"Sodeis?" called Dabimi into the blackness of the forest, eager to take charge of the strange reunion he anticipated.

The answer he received, however, wasn't Sodeis's, but Joaquim's, who stepped from behind a kapok with his arms extended. Larry froze and stared at him, unable to sort through the thoughts and impulses that fell in torrents around his head and threatened to overtake him.

"*Desculpe*, Larry," said Joaquim, approaching slowly, as one would a cornered animal. "*Desculpe, desculpe.* I'm so very sorry!" He stopped within ten paces of Larry and lowered his hands to his sides.

"What are you doing here?" Larry rasped out at last in English, amazed to see that his face too, was covered with tears.

"I know I can't ask you to forgive me," Joaquim went on. "And I won't insult you like that. But to see that you're alive! May I?" he said, stepping forward tentatively and pulling Larry in to him.

"Joaquim?" said Larry, dazed, over his shoulder, still not able to make sense of what he saw.

"We're here, Larry," said Jorge, stepping from behind another tree, pulling Martina along by the arm. "I'm sorry."

"That's not him, it's the other one! That's not the one who asked for you!" squeaked Dabimi, but no one turned to him.

"Why are you here? Why are you here? Why have you been buying him? Why are you his friend? Why are you betraying me?" Larry said again and again as he caught a fleeting glimpse, out of the corner of his eye, of what he thought was confusion, or even panic, on Dabimi's face. He turned from one to another while Jorge and Martina and Sam came up on all sides of him, excluding Dabimi from their circle. He looked at Jorge with sudden rage in his eyes, taking a step back, onto Sam's foot. "You told them," he said accusingly.

"I told them," said Jorge. "I betrayed you. And now it's too late to turn back. We're going to need to act quickly. There is no other choice."

"There is," said Larry, turning away. "I'm going home."

"Where?" said Jorge after him.

"Home and I'm begging you not to follow me." He gestured to the others, who sat motionless, staring in disbelief.

"Larry?" Joaquim called after him, taking a step to follow. He walked up and stood between Larry and Pahquel, looking straight into his eyes.

"*Mboa*," answered Larry before he had time to stop himself. "*Mboa, tuara, mboa.*" He glanced over to see Dabimi shaking his head, horrified to note that through this momentary, incongruous encounter, they had, for a moment, truly become kin. He turned and readied himself to run.

"Larry," Joaquim called again. "They're going to destroy Pahquel if you don't help us. We need you and you need us. Jorge is right. There is no other choice."

Slowly, with all their eyes watching him, Larry turned back and walked with Joaquim toward the rest of them, like a fugitive giving himself up. "What are you saying?" he said finally, unwilling to offer anything of his own.

"Larry, Pahquel's been noticed, and it's been noticed by someone in a position to exploit his discovery. About that, you can ask your friend here, who's been in contact with him, I'm sure of it."

The cord between Larry and Dabimi, formed moments before, was just as suddenly tensed and broke with a furious snap. "Who gave you this?" he said in Pahqua, pointing to the pan in Dabimi's bag.

"*Luma,*" said Dabimi. He did.

"Who gave you this?" said Larry, lifting the twine and dropping it back into the basket.

"*Luma,*" said Dabimi.

"This?" he said.

"*Luma,*" said Dabimi.

"And this," he said, pointing to Dabimi's watch. "Who is he?"

"*Ata patari*" Sky person, Dabimi answered, sensing the drama in the situation and now clearly trying to make himself the master of it.

"Who?" said Larry, turning to Joaquim.

"A guy named Kamar Sodeis. Mining, logging, hardwoods, burglary, extortion and more, a long list of accomplishments" said Joaquim. "And who's this?" he added, gesturing toward Dabimi.

"That *cabrao*?" said Larry fiercely, with hatred in his voice. "That's our *chefe.*"

"That's what I figured, and that's why Sodeis is after him. They've clearly made a deal, and you're going to have to convince him that that deal is off, and find a way to stop it." Joaquim turned to Dabimi and addressed him in broken Pahqua. "You listen to him and do what he says," he told him.

"How do you know Pahqua?" said Larry.

"You left the notebook," said Joaquim. "You left it behind. If you hadn't, you might have figured out by now that you're in danger even without Sodeis's interference."

"What?" said Larry.

"So can we go back with you?" said Jorge, interrupting him.

"What if I say no?" said Larry, eyeing him.

"Then we'll have to go with him instead," said Joaquim, nodding at Dabimi. "We've prepared for the possibility that you'd refuse us. But better for you to introduce us to your companions instead."

Larry looked from one to the other and then, in speech that was heavy and slow, addressed Joaquim. "I have two boys now," he said. As he spoke, they all noticed, at once, a glow on the horizon that, unlike the sun, intensified without rising. Slowly, the black silhouette of a man appeared, obscured, suddenly, blindingly as he came upon them, by the beam of a miner's headlamp.

"Look who's here! My dear friends!" said the figure in Portuguese, taking a step towards Larry and extending his hand.

Larry squinted into the light. He somehow understood what the man had said, although he couldn't identify the language. Joaquim and Jorge stepped forward, eyeing Sodeis, but waiting.

"Why are you here?" said Larry coldly.

"Sodeis. Kamar Sodeis," said the man, extending his hand again. Behind him, Aran gasped and Larry knew she had recognized his name from Silvio's list.

"What do you want with us?" The words seemed detached from him perhaps because they were in English.

"Us?" said Sodeis, laughing, gesturing first to Larry's chest and then to his genitals, which he had, owing to the disintegration of his last pair of shorts, only recently begun to sheath, mostly to hide his circumcision. "Us?" he said again, laughing and shaking his head.

"What do you want?" said Larry, envisioning his hand around the handle of his knife, still ignorant of the fact that the right to kill had been rescinded by the ancestors twenty *chajans* before.

Joaquim stepped forward, but Sodeis motioned him away. "This is for your little charge to deal with," he said. Turning back to Larry, he continued. "I've become good friends with your kin here," he said, with a nod towards Dabimi. "He's been teaching me Pahqua, in exchange for some tangible rewards." Dabimi half staggered to his feet but then squatted down again into a disappointed slump when he realized that his so-called friend intended to dispense with him now that the meeting for which he had been the catalyst had taken place.

"Just tell me what you want," said Larry again, taking a step towards him. His hands were shaking at his sides, the thumbs pushed out from the fingers as though preparing, on their own, to strangle him.

"And we've been doing business," said Sodeis, dropping the pretense to friendliness. "I think you Americans call it closing a deal." He pulled out a folded piece of paper and began to smooth it on the leg of his pants.

"I am not an American," said Larry, immediately ashamed that the man had been able to elicit a personal retort, unaware that what he said wasn't in fact true.

"You know, that's not quite right," said Sodeis, patting the front pocket of his flak pants. "I have reason to believe that you are here on an American passport and a visa which, I'd be willing to bet, have long expired."

"So you've come to turn me in?" said Larry, the thumbs straining out from the fingers, twitching like snake tongues, or like snakes.

"Turn you in?" he laughed. "Of course not. I've come to thank you," he said, reaching up and switching off the headlamp. Larry was as blinded by the darkness as he had been by the light, and stood with his feet planted until the swirling residue of lines and shapes faded.

"Why are you here then?" said Larry, "Just tell me and go. You have no business here."

"I have more business here than you do," Sodeis said, pausing for emphasis, "but mine will be done within a week, and then I'll leave for good, and so will you."

"I'll never leave," said Larry, turning to shoulder his basket, reaching out to grasp Aran's arm.

"You'll all be leaving," said Sodeis, gesturing with his hand around the circle, "thanks to the contract we've negotiated with your kin. I've told him he'll be blessed by all his people for securing, on his own, without you, the future of every last one of you."

"He said I stole from him, but look at how he stole from me!" Dabimi shouted drunkenly in Pahqua, gesturing toward Aran. Aran looked down and put her hands over her ears. Sodeis slapped him on the arm and he swayed in silence, as though collecting his strength to begin shouting again, pulling Larry back and forth with him.

"*Akara odama,*" said the man in halting Pahqua to Larry, pulling a piece of paper from his pocket. "A promise. You translate for your friend here," he said, switching on his lamp again. To each of the half-lines, spoken now in Ge but then elaborated in Portuguese, Dabimi nodded with a sharp snap of his head that suggested his sense of importance, and his desperation to seem as if he understood. Larry remained silent.

"You will vacate the land bounded by the Inhambu, Mental, and Arua rivers within three days." Dabimi's head bobbed like a buoy. "You will continue on to the area located between kilometers 45 and 50 on the eastern bank of the Mental, and will present yourselves to the Abbe of the mission at St. Girard, who will assign you to your villages and help you move into your new homes." Another nod and an attempt at a self-satisfied glance at Larry. Sodeis looked up from the paper. "I have described in drawings the living spaces to Dabimi, which will include kerosene lamps and blankets and comfortable beds and cooking pots and all sorts of amenities. You'll all, of course, have work."

"What are you talking about?" Larry shouted again, cutting him off. "Get out of here or I'll kill you!" He shook himself free of Dabimi, who fell backward and slumped into a squat with his back against the side of the lean-to, which collapsed under him. Then he turned to Aran and pulled her by the arm.

"You'll regret it," said the man without moving. "It's for them. It's the only way they'll survive. Anyway, you have no choice."

"Get the hell out of here," shouted Larry, dropping the bag and Aran's arm at once as he turned on his heel. The two snakes twitched at his sides, savoring their imminent fulfillment.

Sodeis placed the folded paper into his shirt pocket, and then drew out another. "I'm speaking now on behalf of Incorporated Timber which, as you may or may not know, owns the land you and your friends have been living on. We begin on that particular parcel in three days, and if you don't vacate, you'll be forcibly removed for your own protection. That's all. Your friend has been agreeable and we've arrived at something reasonable for everyone. Go home now and tell them all what they need to do. Make them understand how much better off they'll be, and then go back to where you came from, or else tell them it's your fault, that it was you who led us here, thanks to this note I found in the belongings of a friend of yours."

The snakes hurled themselves outward and found their mark. The two men scuffled in the dirt, throwing up clumps of rotten leaves while the light flashed and jerked and the others stood back in horror. Pitar rushed forward and pulled Larry off Sodeis, leaving him groaning in the dirt. Joachim stepped forward and put the handcuffs on him. "Come on," yelled Larry, and grabbed Aran's arm. They ran together, holding onto each other, leaving Dabimi and the others slouched over the writhing figure whose headlamp, still on his head, swept back and forth across the ceiling of trees like a spotlight scanning the sky. There was no hope of finding the path in the dark, so they stopped in an indentation between the trees and squatted in a huddle so close that each could feel the breath of the others on his knees. Larry leaned forward, panting and shaking, barely aware of the trickle of blood that dripped off the edge of his chin and down the side of his neck.

"The ancestors will punish you," said Aran at last, in a new cold, almost mechanical voice.

"I'll go back. The person isn't dying," said Panar, rising to his feet.

"What was he talking about?" said Pitar. Panar squatted down again beside him and waited with the others for Larry to speak.

At first, he didn't realize that the question was for him, knowing he had lost the right to make any sound at all, but Pitar jostled him, as though to start the flow of words through the pressure of his elbow.

"They're going to take our homes," he began, his voice cracking, and then corrected himself. "They're going to take *your* homes."

"Who?" said Pitar. "Which ancestor of yours is he?"

"He's no ancestor, and neither am I." Larry stopped and began to sob, and the tears flowed out and mixed with the blood, two rivers forming one stronger current in the dark.

"He's not a person?" said Pitar, sounding confused.

Larry squatted in his pool of bloody tears, unable to respond.

"*Ark pol,*" said Panar. A monkey demon. "His curse is on Dabimi. We all saw it. Look at what happened to him when he took those things."

Larry pressed his forehead to his knees. His body jerked first to one side and then the other, as though he were hurling himself against a row of doors, none of which would open. There was a door labeled Iri, and a door named for Aran, and a door bearing only the sign of his shame. There were doors for James and Oji and Piri and Panar and Kakap, for terror and the escape from terror, but not one would admit him, would so much as vibrate on its hinges from the impact of his weight.

"I think they'll come for us," he said at last. "They'll move us if we don't move ourselves."

"We always move," said Panar emphatically, referring to the march of *chajans*—who could say if it was fast or slow?—from the river to the top of the hill in the direction of the *jacu.*

"Not that," said Larry. "They're going to take the *chajan* trees and then most likely burn the rest for farmland. They'll burn our houses and us in them if we don't leave." The temptation welled up to tell them that it had been Dabimi who had led them to that fate, but the thought of him swaggering, drunk, utterly impotent, was enough to close up his throat again, and force the pressure to hiss out in a sound halfway between a moan and a sigh. The irony itself was enough to choke him, that Dabimi really was his kin, fellow member of the lineage of fools, deluded, unable to grasp the possibility that anyone outside himself existed, doomed to helplessness without reprieve. He stopped throwing himself sidelong against the row of doors and turned to face their unyielding blankness.

"There is no punishment enough for me," he said mechanically, "but there'll be time for that. Now, I'll do what I can. Go back and help Dabimi," Larry said, turning to Panar. "Wait with him until he sleeps it off. Then bring him here."

Panar obeyed without question, standing up as soon as Larry fell silent, disappearing in the direction they had come from. In his absence, the sounds of weeping from the various points around the circle were like the smoldering outcroppings of embers.

"We have no mats to sleep on," said Aran, her voice sharp with recrimination, her cold glare obscured by the dark. No person would ever stoop to sleeping on the ground like an animal, so they squatted with their backs against each other, or against tree trunks, Aran on one side of a thick Sapadura while Larry leaned against the other, unconcerned by the stinging ants that flowed in silent streams through the crevasses in the bark.

At dawn, Panar returned not only with Dabimi, but with them all, with Jorge pulling Sodeis forward by the chain between his hands. The group was unwieldy, a caravan of the wounded, limping and vomiting and swaying from chill and lack of sleep; it was afternoon before they even cleared the outer logs. They were starved and bitten and disoriented as they stumbled upon a scene that had the same aura of surreal nostalgia as the paintings of skating parties and family dinners on the Christmas cards Larry's parents used to send to relatives to whom they never spoke. There were clusters of people walking together, or carrying baskets between them, or sitting on their *kaawas* telling jokes about hunting and sex. There was the smell of cooking meat, and the sound of babies crying, and the glow of the fires, their smoke trails mingling with the halos of invisible stars. No one had spoken since Aran had made her comment about the mats; no one had asked the others to wait for him to eat or drink or defecate or rest, but had simply run to catch up after having fallen behind. Larry kept his back to Joaquim and Jorge at all times as though to deny their existence. The only constant sound had been Dabimi's whimper, the static agony of headache and despair and shame, which penetrated their bones more relentlessly than did the heat or cold.

"Gather them," Panar said at last as they stood together on the outskirts of the village, looking out onto a scene in which none of them belonged. As word spread from door to door, the assembly collected on Dabimi's *kaawa* and spilled out onto the clearing, filling it as the rain had filled the river, one person from each household, one torch for every line. They waited for Dabimi to sing, but for a long time, he only stood, looking back at them. At last he began, in a voice so low that even those standing on the *kaawa* could barely make out the words; what they did hear was nothing but a whisper that gnawed its way into the foundations of their houses to create tiny cracks which grew, at first only slowly and then in a rush, due to the press of fear and bodies, until the world collapsed around them with a sudden roar such as none of them had ever heard, burying them in great clouds of terror and chaos and debris. Words flew up, screams like burning timbers, the stabbing edges of disbelief, as people clung to each other, not knowing whether to run or stay. The wailing from every corner rose and fell like sirens, echoing amid the flashes of the torchlight. People ran and then stopped and then ran again. They shouted at each other, having lost the ability to hear. Dabimi waved his arms helplessly, but no one responded. Larry slipped away and returned without attracting notice.

Then, at dawn, they heard the nasal whine of a plane approaching overhead, growing louder as it circled lower and lower, almost grazing the tops of the trees. They watched it as though hypnotized, their bodies swaying as though it were pulling them into a vortex by a transparent rope. At last it rose and flew off in the *paca* direction, leaving an eerie silence in its wake. Dabimi stepped into that silence, standing on a log on one side of his *kaawa*, calling out words of promise and reassurance, impotently praising St. Girard, while Larry stood on the other side, shaking his head, waving the map he had retrieved from his pack, shouting out directions to the most likely tract of uninhabited land. The attempts by Larry and Dabimi to eclipse each other alternated with oddly rational debates about who should go, since there was only a hand of boats for each of the three villages, each of which could carry only a hand or two of persons. The land route was too treacherous, still flooded so early in the season. From these debates, the inevitable conclusions were derived; by the morning of the third day, when Sodeis appeared in the clearing, still wearing the cuffs, which had been sawed from their chain, flanked by ten men who looked like insects, wearing hardhats and goggles and pads at the elbows and knees, their saws dangling from thick straps around their necks, the engines growling intermittently like dogs who could barely be restrained, all persons had already thrown themselves to their task with such a collective desperation that the fearsome sight of that swarm of ant-men barely attracted notice. Under the row of goggled eyes, each person strained to dismantle his own house, pulling up the thick corner-sticks while the women filled the baskets with possessions, mats and straps and quivers of arrows and food. The women carried the baskets and set them together in the clearing while the men unlashed the rows of sticks that had formed the walls of their huts and carried them off in bundles to the burning ground, to be cast among the other bones of the dead. All morning long, the village folded in on itself, until at last, when the possessions had been gathered and tightly packed, and when the pyre had grown larger than it had ever been and set alight, they turned to the task of uprooting the *chajans* which now stood unclothed, surprisingly spindly, straddling the rubble-strewn ground. Men and women ran to join the teams, binding their waists with the pulling vines and hurling themselves forward with an insane abandon. In every instance, before the final groan, there was the same excruciating stillness one feels before a tooth is extracted, when opposing tensions match, and then a sudden violent rush as a line of persons toppled into a heap of legs and arms as a *chajan* gave way, dragging them through the dirt. The view from the plane, had it remained circling above, would have been of a battlefield of giants, broken limbs littering the ground, ornate, surreal, terrifying still, indeed even more so than before, like all fallen invincible things. In the midst of such ruin, the orderly flow of the *chajans* to the river, pulled along by vines by the living of their kin, the systematic way in which they were aligned and lashed together and sealed with wax, the smooth, almost silent launch of the finished rafts into the river, were more terrible than the chaos, than the roiling clouds of smoke from the burning ground, or the whining of the saws at their backs, or the frantic wheeling and screeching of the parrots, whose perches were upended for the masts. Persons streamed down the path as though it were itself a river that fed into the larger water, upon which gently bobbed a lengthening flotilla of ornately painted craft.

Joaquim and Jorge and Sam planted themselves beside the river, tying the rafts into a caravan, testing them, filling their cracks with wax.

Dabimi's raft was the first in line, and the first to push off upstream. He himself took the oar, shouting out in an intoxicated voice, as though the draught had not yet loosened its hold on him, the song of traveling to the hunt. He threw himself against the current, but the river, which had only been feigning indifference, sensed his inexperience as an oarsman and denied him easy passage. The sun glinted in the rivulets of his sweat, and his arms shook as he strained at the oar, until at last he handed the long wooden post, formerly the corner–post of his house, to his son-in-law, and positioned himself beside him at the bow, waving his arms as he sang.

As Larry looked down from the head of the path, the riverbank swarmed like a tree branch covered with ants, and shimmered like the river itself. Standing with his hand on Iri's arm, Larry remembered movie scenes of crowded stations, overhead shots of hats accumulating like rows of dark brown marbles against the muted grey torsos of trains. From above, he could see how the accumulation began to overtake the rafts, and he could make out his own raft, constructed of a gathering raft, pressed on either side by the legs of the *chajan* of his house, standing empty while the others filled. Intermittently, the whine of the saws would subside and he could hear wisps of Dabimi's shouted song.

"We need to go," he whispered to Iri when he found him, taking a few steps down the incline towards the rafts.

"Where's mother?" said Iri.

"I don't know," he said, speaking in a muted, emotionless tone.

"Where's Oji?"

Larry shook his head. He stopped walking, but didn't turn around to look. He took two long steps sideways off the path to avoid being carried by the stream of persons from the middle village pouring towards the river. By the time he finally allowed himself to glance toward Iri, he was gone. Larry stumbled down the incline, pausing before he stepped onto his boat. Everywhere, people were calling to one another, clasping each other, or standing together, hanging their baskets from their crossbeams, kneeling to press more wax into the crevasses between logs. Larry hung his baskets and then sat silent, cross-legged, looking out over the shoulder of the river.

"Did you see Oji?" said a voice beside him.

"No," said Larry, looking up, squinting, as though he barely recognized Panar.

"He's near the end, with Kararar's line. I'm three rafts down." Panar put one foot on the *chajan* log for balance as he leaned over to grasp Larry by the arm, but rather than providing an anchor, the pressure of his leg pushed the boat out from under him, so that it floated off into the current of the river. Panar threw himself forward and crawled up beside Larry, shaking off water, while Larry jumped for the oar and started maneuvering the raft back to shore. He heard a shout and looked up to see Iri waving frantically, holding up one of Aran's arms while Martina held the other. Larry reached the oar out toward the bank and Iri grabbed it, still clutching Aran with his other hand. The boat tipped precariously; the baskets thrashed on the crossbeam. Larry and Panar yanked the oar and Iri was flung onto the raft, trailing Aran in the water behind him. They reached the oar towards Martina and pulled her aboard. Then Iri and Martina grasped Aran's arms and together pulled her up. Her eyes were closed and she wasn't breathing. Larry turned her and shook her and breathed into her mouth, and she began to move again, coughing, gasping and writhing without opening her eyes. Panar and Iri tended her while Larry jumped up and grabbed the oar, throwing himself against it to avoid their being hurled by the current into the raft behind them.

It was a full minute before he could force himself to look up, to confront the three men standing even with his raft on the shore, whose existence he had almost forgotten, who were watching him, motionless in all the stir of activity. He was overwhelmed momentarily by the temptation to push off, as if by leaving them behind, he could obliterate the nightmare that was playing out in front of him, or could abandon himself to it along with them. He hesitated and then shouted above the din, "Are you coming or not?"

He pulled the raft even with the shore and Martina stretched out her hands to steady Jorge. Jorge did the same for Joaquim, who suddenly seemed weightless and shriveled as Jorge lifted him over the abyss. It took the three of them to drag Sam across and pull him in, as their craft listed violently and lowered in the water, threatening to sink altogether, or to throw the rest of them overboard. At last, they steadied and pushed off, with Larry at the oar, into a world made up of nothing but reflection.

By midday the rafts had cleared the *Rin* bend of the river without once having to be dragged or carried by their runners. The shore slipped away behind them, with its stands of Siritana and its turtles sunning on rocks and its intermittent cusps of sand. The river fanned out and shallowed, and the rafts bobbed on its sun-flecked surface like an unfathomable number of brightly colored Janka leaves. Larry rowed for a long time without pausing even to assess where he was, or to notice the rafts of the others jostling in his wake as he passed them. At last, he lifted his oar and looked around. There was no one in sight. On his raft, Panar and Iri and Martina were squatting beside Aran, who slept, breathing hoarsely, her eyes moving beneath dark, wrinkled lids. Sam clung to the mast, breathing heavily with his eyes closed. Jorge sat between Panar and Iri, staring into the water. Joachim sat alone at the front of the boat, staring straight ahead. Larry pulled his oar out of the water, securing the tip of it in a crevasse in the wood, and leaned against it, listening for any wisp of human sound. Just as he set the oar to row again, Pitar's boat appeared in the distance behind them. Larry waited as he drew up, and they went on together, handing the oars to their sons so they could squat as they used to, with their backs against the sun, watching the slow procession of the clouds. They were unchanged, but only sharpened, aware at some level that they were dreaming, certain that their illusions would betray them. When they assumed the oars again, they rowed in the same rhythm, two men who shared one breath. By afternoon, the *licaro* came into view, the place where the river divided. Without a word, they both took the left fork, away from St. Girard, and then waited while the other rafts came into sight. None seemed to hesitate upon reaching that rend in the water; each moved in a smooth, unwavering path, either toward them or away behind the wall of trees. He saw a metallic glint as Dabimi steered his raft off to the right, and started as he caught sight of Oji, with Kararar and her father and her sister, disappearing after him behind the dark green curtain. The stream of rafts was a body falling on a blade, and the blade split it as it split the water, into two quivering, ultimately unviable halves.

As they pushed off up the thinner strand, the crimson light of sunset spread down to meet them, blending them and the forest and the river together in a monochrome. Maroon-colored bats circled overhead, and dark red-purple monkeys muttered and fussed, and a huge, gray-rose caiman launched itself without a ripple into the glowing red river and disappeared. Larry passed the oar to Iri and squatted beside Aran, who, although her eyes were open, would not look at him, but only spat onto the wood near his feet. After watching her in silence for a while, he got up and knelt down beside Joaquim, squinting upriver into the sun's red eye. The rafts were gathered in front of it, a shifting black pupil around which its rose light sharpened and splayed. Their flotilla filled the corridor between the riverbanks, lodging between a towering wall of trees on the one side and a broad praia of glowing pink sand on the other, along which a sill of granite boulders formed a natural harbor. As they dragged their rafts, some into the harbor and others onto shore, Larry watched them from the water with a growing recognition of that levee of boulders, that shaded brow of sand, stirring within him.

When a leaf falls into a river and is borne away, it carries along with it a residue—bits of pollen, spores, bacteria, seedlings, some of which have already sprouted and are feeding from its veins, cultures in the broadest sense, the distillations of old habitats, dust of civilizations—awaiting reconstitution or dissolution by the rains. Lying awake in the sand beside Aran under the upturned bowl of the stars, amid the sounds of the forest and the river, of snoring and groaning and weeping, Larry could discern the shudder of her troubled breath, and curled his body around hers, pulling her back into his chest. Never in the past would she have stretched out on the ground like that, as an animal would, as though there were no difference between them. Now, it wasn't so much that the difference had been erased, as that, in the face of intolerable certainty, such symbolic confirmations no longer bore their familiar meanings, and would have to be constructed anew. For every expulsion, every act of flight, brings with it special obligations afforded only to persons: to name the lost world Paradise, and to mourn, in their steads, on behalf of all its creatures, and to bear the curse of memory, pulling the weight behind, the vines wearing marks into the skin. Larry curled around Aran and she hardened like a fossil within him, embedded as though within his rib, an unfathomably cold knot inside his bone.

ACKNOWLEDGEMENTS

I OWE SO much to so many, and so does this book. I would not have begun it at all were it not for Gene Borowitz, and would not have finished it were it not for the many people who have offered their help and encouragement along the way. Linda Sue Baugh read and critiqued all my early chapters as they were written, and offered much wise and sensitive guidance. Sigfried Gold's writing companionship was invaluable in keeping me on course. Joan Matlack believed in the book, promoted it, and pushed me to publish it when I fully expected that it would live out its life in the bottom drawer of my desk; I happily call her my unofficial agent and have her to thank for the fact that it did not. The members of my book club family of nearly 40 years, including Joan, Libby Ester, Laura Tilly, Alexa Hand, Barbara Beck, Beth Kaplan, and Karen Reeves (who went out of her way to keep my spirits alive during the hard times) were generous and supportive in their critique, and the late Sarah Hamilton went above and beyond book club protocol and gave the opening sections of the manuscript a thorough copy-edit. The late Barbara Muday was a mainstay of support. My graduation committee at the Chicago Center for Psychoanalysis, including Peter Shabad, Dale Moyer, and Lucy Freund, supported my final project towards graduation, which included a presentation of reflections on this book. I am forever grateful to Deborah Robertson and Gibson House for giving my novel the chance to see the light of day, and to Deb for sharing her vision of a literary/musical nexus with me. I am fortunate that the late Terrance Turner, perhaps the foremost anthropologist of the peoples of Amazonia, gave the book a careful reading and offered me many useful suggestions as well as enthusiastic support. I thank Steve Dawson for his encouragement of me as a writer and for his transformative role in my musical life. Poornima Apte's able editorial skills saved me from myself many times over, and I have been grateful to have the guidance of Mary Bisbee-Beek on those aspects of creating a successful book from which I am most likely to recoil. I'm grateful to Christian Fuenfhausen and Karen Sheets for their elegant design work and helpful image-sleuthing, and also thank the plant information people at the Chicago Botanic Garden for their research help. Many others have offered publishing advice or have read drafts of the manuscript and made hands-on suggestions, or else have offered general encouragement, including (alphabetically) Karen Smith Biastre, Jena Camp, Mark Caro, Kathy and Paul Davidson, Karin Deam, Bob Drucker, John Friedman, David Fuller, John and Joyce Fuller, Denise Gibbon, Karen Gilman, Eve Gordon, Ingrid Graudins, Lorel Greene, Jane Hamilton, Karen Hanmer, Tom Jenks, Tim Keating, Lucia and Waud Kracke, Cecile Margulies, Tom Recht, Fran Rivkin, Ann-Louise Silver, Saadya Sternberg, David Vigoda and Peter Zeldow. The writing of this manuscript was supported by an Artist Fellowship from the Illinois Arts Council. I am grateful to the Writers-Editors International Writing Awards, NAAP, the Fish Literary Awards, the James Jones Award for the Novel, the Eugene Walter Prize for the Novel, the Illinois Arts Council Poetry Awards, and the other organizations that have supported my writing with awards, honorable mentions, finalist designations, cash prizes and other forms of recognition over the years. I thank the Unicorn Café for providing me a refuge in which to write, and am grateful to Sophie Harp and Natalya Harp for their insight and inspiration, and also to Sophie for her efforts to help me arrive at the book's title. Most of all, I thank my husband, Steve Harp, for offering his support and encouragement every step of the way, and for teaching me how to value my own work in the midst of this life-I-am-incapable-of-living.

MARTHA ABELSON

NANCY BURKE is a psychoanalyst in private practice in Chicago and Evanston, Illinois. Her poetry has appeared in *After Hours, The American Poetry Journal, Permafrost,* and other literary magazines. Her recording of original songs is *American Goodbye. Undergrowth* is her first novel.

GIBSON HOUSE connects literary fiction with curious and discerning readers. We publish novels by musicians and other artists with a strong connection to music.

GibsonHousePress.com
facebook.com/GibsonHousePress
Twitter: @GibsonPress

**For an editable download of the Reading Group Guide for *Undergrowth,*
visit GibsonHousePress.com/Reading-Group-Guides**